LOST STARSHIP

The Lost Starship
The Lost Command
The Lost Destroyer
The Lost Colony
The Lost Patrol
The Lost Planet
The Lost Earth
The Lost Artifactt
The Lost Star Gate
The Lost Supernova
The Lost Swarm
The Lost Intelligence
The Lost Tech
The Lost Secret
The Lost Barrier
The Lost Nebula
The Lost Relic
The Lost Task Force

Visit VaughnHeppner.com for more
information

The Lost Task Force

(Lost Starship Series 18)

By Vaughn Heppner

Illustration © Tom Edwards
TomEdwardsDesign.com

ISBN: 9798389523975
Imprint: Independently published

-1-

A peculiar anomaly began 40.7 light years from Earth, deep in the Trappist-1 System.

The system star was a red dwarf nine percent the mass of the Sun, with a radius slightly larger than Jupiter. It had several terrestrial planets within the Inner System, all of them tidal locked. That meant each of the planets kept its same face to the red dwarf all of the time.

The third planet was infested with human life. They lived in the Twilight Zone or Twilight Band, with heat radiating from the hot side and thus warming the territory. That meant the icy cold from the dark side also leaked there, meeting where the domed cities had risen.

Zinc, the name for the third planet, was part of the Commonwealth and thus protected by Star Watch. Several defensive satellites ringed Zinc. Two SW destroyers and three escort vessels also patrolled the Inner System, basing out of the third planet.

Zinc boasted a population of fifteen million people. Most were miners or were in some way connected with the Carstair Metals Mining Consortium.

It was a medium-sized consortium as such things went, with offices and mines on three star systems and eleven planets. Three of those planets were in the Trappist-1 System.

None of the mines on the other planets had more than four thousand effectives stationed there at any one time, and that would prove critical, for them.

1

The stellar anomaly occurred a little more than thirteen million kilometers from Zinc. That made it 215 million kilometers from the fourth planet, Cobalt, between the third and fourth planets.

No one in the Trappist-1 System knew anything about the anomaly…yet. To be fair, no one in the system had the sensors to detect such a thing.

Still, the effect took place. Greater darkness appeared at the location. The darkness deepened, in a metaphysical sense, and spread to a distance of 222 kilometers in diameter. Soon, four lighter points appeared within the darkness. The four points grew in luminosity, becoming bright enough to detect with the human eye.

In seconds, the bright points became so illuminated it was possible to detect four separate oval objects. Did that make them spaceships? Yes. The brightness came from exhausts of individual propulsion units.

There was another anomaly, a distortion, possibly an opening of some kind. Before this, it seemed as if a film, or skin, or something was between the vessels and regular space. That something vanished as the four oval vessels became even clearer.

Each seemed a replica of the other. Each had a fin up front, to the sides and on the bottom back. Each was blue-colored and contained a bubble canopy on the top front near the forward fin. Each was bigger by a factor than a Star Watch shuttle. That made each considerably smaller than a SW destroyer, but larger than a fighter.

A single suited humanoid sat underneath each bubble canopy. Each wore a black-visor helmet with a flexible tube coming out the front and going down. Each humanoid had two elongated arms and a thin, elongated torso. Given the size and speed of the vessels, each of the beings seemed like a fighter pilot.

Their helmeted heads swiveled as if they looked around and then down at the glowing consoles. Invisible waves traveled between the four vessels.

No one in the Trappist-1 System knew it yet, but those were radio waves, as the four pilots communicated with each other.

In less than three minutes since coming through, the four pilots zeroed in on Zinc and increased velocity in the habitable planet's direction.

The acceleration was much faster than any Star Watch fighter could achieve. That didn't take folding into the equation, which made sense, as a fold wasn't the same as increasing velocity, although a fold covered more space faster. The sharply increased acceleration would certainly have led any human observer to conclude the humanoids had anti-gravity dampeners assisting them.

The four vessels covered a quarter of the thirteen million kilometers to the planet before a satellite operative from Outpost 3 spotted them.

Ensign Pimentel watched spellbound for over three seconds. A warning klaxon awoke her from her stupor. Pimentel sputtered, wasting several precious seconds more. She was stocky and given to careful thought before speaking. Finally, however, Pimentel alerted the officer in charge.

By that time, the four vessels had traveled another half a million kilometers closer to the planet.

Perhaps because of that, Pimentel shouted the information a second time, as the watch officer had only looked up in annoyance the first.

The watch officer, Lieutenant Givens, a skinny, geeky fellow with a stain on his tan uniform, reacted by breaking into a run. He reached Pimentel by the time the four vessels had gained an additional quarter million kilometers to Zinc.

"Look!" Pimentel shouted, pointing at her screen with a black-painted fingernail.

Givens did just that, his brown eyes bulging. "Where did they come from?"

"I have no idea."

"Contact them."

"Me?" Pimentel asked. That wasn't her department.

Lieutenant Givens whirled around, his eyes bulging just as much as before. "Where's Bohost?" She was the comm officer.

3

"She's on her lunch break," a marine said.

Givens cursed, running to the comm board. Panting, flipping switches, he began the contact procedure.

The four vessels were coming missile fast upon Zinc, and they had yet to slow down.

"This is Outpost Three for the Planet Zinc," Givens said. "We have you on visual. You're traveling—identify yourselves at once."

There was no response.

"Did you hear me?" Givens said. "Who are you? Identify yourselves or we'll open fire."

The comm speaker crackled. "You want to know who we are?" a voice asked.

Givens blinked with astonishment. There was something alien about the speaker even though the voice used standard Anglic with an odd accent.

"Yes," Givens said. "Who are you?"

The alien laughed over the comm. "We're your Angel of Doom, partner."

"What?"

"Sir," Pimentel said in alarm. "They're launching missiles."

Givens looked over his shoulder at her. There was a sick knot in his gut. "What's their target?"

"I think it's us, sir, Outpost Three."

A sheen of sweat had appeared on Givens' high forehead. He bent over the comm, his sweaty forehead furrowed. "Why are you attacking us?" he asked with a rasp to his throat. "You must cease at once or you'll be destroyed."

"I seriously doubt that," the alien said.

"Why are you attacking, dammit?"

"That's easy. The Ship needs you for fuel."

The sweaty forehead-furrows deepened. "What does that even mean?"

"Good-bye, partner," the alien said.

"Sir!" Pimentel shouted. "Our AI has launched anti-missile rockets."

Givens looked up. "Use the lasers, too. We need to take out the...whatever they are."

"Me, sir?" Pimentel asked. "I'm not trained for weapons."

4

Givens looked across the chamber. Wayness must be on her lunch break as well, perhaps with Bohost. With the sick feeling spreading to his thin chest, Givens began running for the weapons station.

"Sir," Pimentel said. "The alien missiles are beaming."

Givens skidded across the deck, his long fingers reaching for the weapons panel.

"The anti-missile rockets are moving at a crawl compared to theirs," Pimentel said, her eyes glued to the screen. "The beams—"

Ensign Pimentel never finished her thought. The alien beams punched through Outpost 3's armored hull. The satellite didn't have a shield generator. One of the beams hit a reactor, which caused an immediate explosion. A piece of shrapnel from the reactor blew through into the control chamber and obliterated Pimentel's head.

Givens saw it, blanched at the spray of blood and then blew apart from the explosions destroying Outpost 3.

Their part in the battle for Trappist-1 was over.

The four alien fighters used the same launched missiles—perhaps drones might be a better name, as they didn't destroy themselves with warheads—beaming each of the Star Watch outposts orbiting Zinc, obliterating them one by one.

Once the outposts were demolished, the drones re-maneuvered and attacked the three Star Watch escorts in orbit around the third planet.

The escorts had attempted to destroy the alien craft during the outpost destruction phase, but without success. Now, the escorts were the targets.

As the last escort blew apart, two huge antimatter missiles launched from the surface detonated. The wash of heat and radiation disintegrated the alien drones. Unfortunately, some of the wash—the heat, radiation and EMP—killed, maimed and injured several hundred thousand personnel in the domes directly below the blasts.

The four alien fighters zoomed in different directions. Each deployed some kind of drop mine. The mines ignited thrusters and raced down through the atmosphere. The mines were incredibly dense and shrugged off anti-air fire even though three took direct hits. The mines detonated spectacularly three kilometers above the surface. The blasts took out two missile launch sites and another two hundred thousand people.

The four alien fighters, meanwhile, kicked into high gear and roared up into near orbital space.

The two Star Watch destroyers nosed around Zinc's largest moon. The planet had three of them. This moon was half the size of Luna and 200 thousand kilometers from the planet. The destroyer bridge personnel had watched the events through hastily launched probes.

The senior officer in charge now made his tactical decision. The destroyers—sleek vessels with crews of 34 and 37 respectively—began emergency burns for the third planet. The shields were at full strength, the torpedo tubes ready to launch and the fusion cannons primed to fire.

Both destroyers tracked the four fighters. Both attempted communications with the enemy.

There was none.

The four alien fighters maneuvered into a diamond formation and accelerated toward the approaching destroyers. The fighters accelerated faster than seemed possible, at an incredible fifty gravities. That was daunting, especially given all that had happened so far.

"Launch a spread of antimatter torpedoes," the senior destroyer officer ordered.

Each destroyer launched three in a staggered formation.

Like everyone else on the two bridges, the senior officer had witnessed the destruction of the satellite outposts and learned that hundreds of thousands of people had died on the surface. This was an alien invasion. It had to be. He'd never seen such large and devastating fighters before. How could they accelerate like that?

"I'm not detecting any enemy shields, sir," the sensor operator said.

As she spoke, a narrow green beam speared from each alien fighter. The beams struck the destroyer shields, two on one. Without preamble, each destroyer shield collapsed. The green beams continued, boring into the comparatively thinly armored hull of each destroyer.

In seconds, the beams found volatile material and engines aboard the two Star Watch vessels. Terrific detonations blew apart each destroyer.

No one on either destroyer made it to any escape pod.

The explosions continued even as the destroyer-launched antimatter torpedoes ignited.

As the first torpedo did so, the four alien fighters began to fade. Was that a protective device? Did they truly disappear, or were the fighters deploying some kind of invisibility field?

The alien pilots obviously knew, but no one on Star Watch's side did.

The fade was complete by the time the warheads' heat, radiation, EMP and blast forces washed over the area where the alien fighters had been.

Now, however, the Star Watch military vessels in the system were all destroyed. Zinc was chaotic with mass casualties. A few Carstair transports had begun emergency maneuvers from orbital space, obviously heading out. Maybe they planned to use the nearest Laumer Point to leave the star system. A few shuttles hauled ass from the surface. Each of the shuttles headed for an orbital mining transport with frightened people eager to escape the star system.

The four alien fighters reappeared. They didn't do so in the spot where they'd faded, but at a distance, as if they'd been traveling...in whatever state they'd been in.

Invisible radio waves passed between them. Did the pilots talk about the transports? It seemed likely, as the four fighters began turning, heading back for the mining transports.

The chief Carstair rep in the system, already aboard a transport, began imploring the four alien fighters for mercy. He offered them money, land, women, drugs, you name it. The rep desperately wanted to live.

It made no difference. There was no contact. The alien fighters continued their course back to Zinc—

Bay doors on the huge mining transports opened. From them launched illegal military-style strikefighters. It would seem the Carstair rep had more resources than he was supposed to have.

That made no difference, though.

The alien fighters annihilated the illegal strikefighters with as much ease as they'd done everything else. Then, they used the green beams to destroy each mining transport.

In two sweeps around the planet, every space-capable human ship, yacht, satellite, anything, perished. They fell to the green beams and beaming missiles of the four blue oval alien fighters.

Radio waves left the four, directed at the dark region thirteen million kilometers from Zinc.

An hour passed.

The four alien fighters took up station in orbit around the third planet.

Anyone who'd tried to contact them from the planet was dead, the building from where the message had originated a radioactive ruin.

Lights began to glow from the dark region thirteen million kilometers from the planet. Soon, giant machines oozed out of the darkness and headed for Zinc.

Each machine was the size of a city block, a puzzle of construction: some shaped like giant Us, others like Zs and a few like Ls. They began a slow approach to the planet as if they brought doom.

It was at this point—40.7 light years away—that an operator on Pluto turned the Long-Range Builder Scanner onto the Trappist-1 System. It was a routine check, and it barely came in time.

From a technological perspective—as to how it did what it did—one of the most fascinating and least understood items picked up in Captain Maddox's many voyages was the Long-Ranger Builder Scanner. He'd acquired it in the Galyan-named Pandora Star System, from the Planet Sind II.

The Builder Scanner could track ships one hundred light years away, when it was focused in that particular direction and location. What was the science behind the scanner? No one in Star Watch knew, not even Professor Ludendorff.

The Long-Range Builder Scanner was stationed deep inside Pluto. There, Star Watch officers and personnel used it for military and civilian purposes.

To make the scanner more efficient, a Long-Range Builder Comm device linked the Pluto station with Star Watch Headquarters in Geneva, Switzerland Sector. The reason for this was simple. The average distance from Pluto to Earth was 5.3361 billion kilometers. That would take a laser light-guide message about five and a half hours to go from one place to the other. To give an answer would take another five and a half hours.

That made swift communication impossible the normal way. With a Long-Range Builder Comm device, it was like talking over a telephone, seemingly instantaneous.

The third Builder item in the equation was the nexus stationed between Earth and Luna. The nexus was a giant pyramid and could form a hyper-spatial tube up to five thousand light years away.

The key here was obvious. If Star Watch kept a fleet handy near Earth, or any number of ships, it could send them quickly, within hours, to something the scanner found light years away.

It had revolutionized Star Watch and their ability to react quickly, giving them a greater strategic and tactical use of the fleet.

Inside the Pluto station, in the main circular chamber, alarms rang. Giant screens were up on the walls with many personnel at control consoles below. A raised dais with guardrails around it stood in the center of the chamber. That allowed the commandant full access to the screens and console controllers.

The screens showed the damage and floating wreckage around the Planet Zinc. More concerning were the large, obviously alien devices. They maneuvered away from what looked like an asteroid—

Commandant Spanno squinted suspiciously at the asteroid. He was badly overweight, with his stomach pushing against his belt and uniform in an unseemly way. Despite his pudgy features, he had a sharp mind, the reason he ran the Builder Scanner.

Had the miners in the Trappist-1 System brought the asteroid near Zinc? Why would the seemingly alien machines be drifting from it then?

Something wasn't right about that—something was dreadfully wrong in the Trappist-1 System.

Spanno demanded an immediate analysis concerning the asteroid. Was its nearness to Zinc normal?

The answer came back almost immediately. No. Someone had maneuvered the asteroid there since the last scanner sweep, or that wasn't an asteroid but merely looked like one.

Spanno glanced at a side hatch.

The Iron Lady—Mary O'Hara—hurried into the main chamber, buttoning her tunic as she did.

She was a matronly woman with iron-gray hair, a brigadier in Star Watch, and much older than she appeared, as she'd taken longevity treatments much as the Lord High Admiral had done. She'd come to Pluto several weeks ago at the Lord High Admiral's orders. She'd come in order to study various aspects of a chain of planets in the Commonwealth concerning a white paper she was preparing. She'd been using the Builder Scanner to help her collect data.

Once, O'Hara had run Star Watch Intelligence, but she'd lost the post because Ludendorff and others had fiddled with her mind. Since then, the mental damage had been repaired, but many still didn't trust her with such a high post. Perhaps in compensation, the Lord High Admiral had given her unique status to run individual Intelligence projects under his authority.

In truth, because her mind had worked perfectly so far, since the "repair" anyway, she was on her way to becoming fully rehabilitated.

Mary climbed the short stairs onto the dais, staring at the screens, particularly the one with the asteroid. The stellar object was a good fifty kilometers in diameter.

"What is that?"

After a moment, Commandant Spanno turned to her. "Did you say something, ma'am?"

Mary had already turned to a different screen. "Yes. Do you see the exhausts there?" She pointed at faint exhaust trails going around Zinc. "Could you focus on them? I want to see what are making those."

After a half-beat, Spanno nodded, giving orders.

Operators in C Section smoothly brought the contrails into focus and then aligned upon four oval, possibly alien fighters.

"What are those?" Mary asked.

Spanno frowned, shaking his head. He spoke to an orderly, wanting more data about the damage he saw. How had all this occurred?

"Sir," another orderly said, while studying a tablet. "There are supposed to be two Star Watch destroyers and three escorts in the system. They're normally stationed near Zinc. I haven't been able to—"

"Look!" a lieutenant shouted, striding up. "That must be the debris of their destruction." He shoved a tablet at the commandant. "The debris clusters match that of two destroyers and an escort."

The tenseness in the chamber increased as people studied the visible debris. Here at Pluto, they knew what to look for, as they'd been doing this for years. Heads nodded. The debris clusters didn't lie. The destroyers had been annihilated along with at least one escort. The other two might have fallen into the planet.

"Notice," an operator said from her console. "The defensive outposts no longer ring Zinc. They're gone, likely destroyed."

"Is this an alien invasion?" Mary asked.

Spanno glanced at her sharply.

"It's obvious the machines are from the asteroid," Mary said. "And I doubt it's an asteroid in the accepted sense. My guess: that's a spacecraft, an alien vessel. You should focus on it."

Spanno frowned, possibly with a rebuke on his lips. Would he tell O'Hara to mind her business? He looked at the screen showing the asteroid. He nodded curtly, perhaps remembering that Mary O'Hara was a good friend of the Lord High Admiral of Star Watch.

Spanno peered at the asteroid more closely. The object was perfectly round. Most asteroids that size were not. "Give me a close-up of the asteroid."

On the selected screen, the scene jumped, zooming in and panning across the asteroidal surface.

A few moments later, Spanno turned to Mary in wonder. "The object is too round and the surface too smooth. I'm guessing the surface is part of a hull, which would make that thing a spaceship like you're suggesting."

"I knew it," Mary said.

Spanno stepped up to the guardrail, his fat fingers clutching it. He shouted orders.

Personnel began to analyze the revealed data more deeply: what they saw on the screens. The usefulness of the Long-Range Builder Scanner had increased over the years as the people learned how to interpret what they saw better than they did in the beginning.

"Sir," an operator said. "The hull— Are we calling it a hull?"

"Never mind that," Spanno said. "Get on with your report."

"The surface substance is something unique," the operator said. "I'd call it…compressed stardust. Our sensors can't pierce it. I suspect it's at least several meters deep—thick, if you will, if it's a hull. I suspect the hull could take direct antimatter blasts, several of them, and keep holding."

"You're kidding," Mary said.

The operator didn't bother to reply. She did not kid. They were all serious practitioners of the art of surveillance here on Pluto.

The machines the size of city blocks and shaped like Ls, Zs and Us approached the planet. Their velocity slowed as they did.

No more shuttles, rockets, or any ground-to-space vessels left the surface. By focusing the Builder Scanner, the Pluto personnel determined that most of the surface domes were intact.

The personnel hadn't yet studied the mining operations on the other two planets: places where the Carstair Mining Consortium had people and equipment.

The giant machines reached low orbital space and started to descend. Soon, each machine went to an equidistant point from the other. They continue to descend at what seemed like a leisurely pace.

"What are they doing?" Mary asked.

Spanno shook his head. He had no idea. No one appeared to know.

The machines slowed their descent even more at ten kilometers from the surface.

Did the supposed stardust-hulled, asteroidal vessel communicate with the city-block-sized machines? It seemed likely. But for what reason?

Mary checked a different screen.

The four oval fighters remained in low orbital space. They didn't seem to be doing anything in particular other than making slow circuits around the planet.

"Zinc is defenseless," an orderly said. "Whoever these people are, they destroyed everything that could defend it."

It was an obvious conclusion, but stating it stirred Mary from her inertia.

"Commandant Spanno, I've had a thought." Mary halted, as she saw some of the glances the personnel were giving her. She was treading on Spanno's toes, maybe making him surely toward her. It was time for a different approach. "Uh...I realize you're in command. This is an idea only. I wonder if the scanner should concentrate on the oval fighters. Perhaps a good look under the bubble canopies could give us a clue as to their identity."

Spanno nodded after a moment, snapping his fingers. He pointed at one of the operators, giving a command.

The lady reconfigured one part of the Builder Scanner. On her giant screen above, the four fighters leaped into focus. Her fingers moved move. The focus sharpened and the images under the bubble canopies grew in screen size under a zoom function.

Everyone in the Pluto chamber peered through the bubble canopies. The four suited pilots all looked alike. Each was a humanoid but strangely elongated. Perhaps each would have stood at seven or eight feet in height. Each was thin, but possessed a regular-sized head. Even with the scanner, no one in the chamber could peer through the heavily tinted visors. No one could see what any of the faces looked like.

"Has anyone seen these aliens before?" Mary asked.

Some of the personnel shot knowing looks at Spanno.

"I'm sorry, Commandant," Mary said. "I don't mean to step on your authority. The excitement of this—"

"Oh, it's no problem," Spanno said, interrupting. "I welcome your suggestions. I thank you for your keen interest in this."

"You're most gracious," Mary said.

Spanno smiled, putting dimples in his fat cheeks.

The Pluto station continued to scan but didn't find anything else to give them an idea as to who these aliens were or where they might have originated. No one in Pluto had yet sensed the darkness out of which the spheroid asteroidal vessel with a compressed stardust hull had originated.

During the next twenty minutes, the screens showed the giant machines moving into position at equidistant points over the planet. Each halted once half a kilometer over the surface. Perhaps there was a signal from the spheroid vessel. Lights flashed on the top of each of the giant machines. Simultaneously, giant green beams drilled from the Us, Ls and giant Zs, boring into the surface. They drilled with great force so rock, soil and dirt exploded from the beams. They drilled deeper and deeper, boring without letup.

"Give me a measurement on the beams," Spanno said.

Soon, everyone knew the beams were ten meters in radius, in thickness. That made them huge. They continued to drill, the green an intense color.

"What kind of beams are those?" Spanno asked. "I want an answer and I want it now. I want to know what's happening to the planet."

The operators worked furiously, using the various techniques they'd learned throughout the years.

Finally, a diminutive lady with extraordinarily bright eyes said, "I think I have an idea, sir."

"Speak. Speak," Spanno said. "Let us know."

"I believe those are gravitational beams."

"Eh?" Spanno asked.

"Gravitational beams, sir. They're destroying the planet, boring toward the center. They're disrupting everything."

"Wait a minute," Mary said. "Do you mean the alien machines are going to destroy the planet?"

"If I'm correct in my analysis, yes," the woman said.

Mary and Spanno exchanged glances.

"This is a catastrophe," Mary said.

"Agreed," Spanno said. "Ma'am, would you please use the Long-Range Builder Comm device and call the Lord High Admiral and let him know the situation?"

"Of course. Can you direct me to the chamber?"

Spanno pointed at a side room.

Mary hustled there as everyone in the central chamber continued to watch the alien machines bore center-ward with

16

their supposed gravitational beams. The gravitational effect became obvious as the planet wobbled.

"Sir," an operator shouted. "Look." She manipulated her console. The colors changed on the screen.

Microwave beams poured from dishes at the top of the Ls, Zs and Us. The microwave beams reached receptors that had appeared on the surface of the asteroidal ship. It had maneuvered closer to Zinc.

"The machines are feeding the asteroid energy," the operator shouted.

"Energy?" Spanno asked.

"At an incredible rate," the operator said.

Mary, Spanno and the others watched in horror as the alien machines bored their beams deeper into the planet. Each had drilled many kilometers down. Soon, the beams would crack the planetary mantle and reach the seething hot mass underneath. If they continued after that...the planet might shatter and break. The people on Zinc who'd survived the antimatter blasts and other devices would certainly die.

"This is incredible," Mary said. "A planet of the Commonwealth is under alien attack, facing certain destruction."

-4-

The Lord High Admiral wore a white uniform, and was a big oak of a man with white hair and craggy—if worried—features.

Cook had controlled Star Watch for years, except when he'd been ousted and Admiral Fletcher had taken over. That had been during the Liss cyber menace of Nostradamus. Fortunately, those days were over.

Cook paced within the Star Watch Command Center on Earth in Geneva, Switzerland Sector. He'd received data from the Iron Lady and live-stream feeds of what was happening in the Trappist-1 System 40.7 light years from the Solar System.

Cook was sick seeing the destruction of Zinc from the alien planet destroyers. That was what the Iron Lady was calling them. He was sick knowing the Star Watch personnel in and around Zinc were already dead.

He had a decision to make, but he was having trouble making it. The reason: he didn't want to lose more people. That was what he told himself, anyway. The real reason had to do with his granddaughter aboard the *Stonewall Jackson,* a *Conqueror*-class battleship in Squadron 10 of ready Task Force 3.

The decision he needed to make—

Cook slapped his left thigh.

The truth was he might be getting too sentimental for this post. The years had taken their toll of his psychic reserves. It galled him every time he learned a starship had been destroyed

18

or half the crew had died from radiation poisoning or some other calamity.

Cook wiped his brow and found that his fingertips were sweaty. He didn't like the present situation one bit.

"You should send *Victory*," Mary said over the Long-Range Builder Comm device.

"Victory?" Cook said, surprised. "What is one ship going to do against a fifty-kilometer asteroid ship? You said the hull was composed of compressed stardust. I've never heard of such a thing. Is that real or did the Pluto operator make it up?"

"Perhaps it's poetic license," Mary said. "Whatever the hull is, it's immensely dense. According to Pluto speculation, it could resist direct antimatter warheads."

"That makes it impenetrable and impossible for us to stop."

"We can stop the planet destroyers," Mary said.

Cook realized he couldn't avoid this anymore. "We'll do this by strict protocol. Feed us more data if anything else occurs. Cook out."

Cook didn't wait to hear more, but walked away to an alcove. Was Mary correct about the machines being planet destroyers? They fed the asteroid-ship microwave energy. If the machines destroyed the planet, fifteen million people died to an alien assault.

Anger burned in his gut. This was intolerable. Did it mean he needed to send ready Task Force 3 to the Trappist-1 System? What if the unknown aliens proved too tough for the task force to deal with?

Cook closed his eyes. Why had his granddaughter joined Star Watch? Why did she have to be on the *Stonewall Jackson* when it was in the ready-to-deploy task force? Most of the fleet was in the Janus System.

Cook cleared his throat and strode to a small wall screen, flipping it on. He should know who commanded the task force, but he'd forgotten.

"Uh…who's in the rotation?" he asked.

"Sir?" the comm officer appearing on the screen asked.

"Who's commanding ready Task Force 3?"

"Oh. Vice Admiral Blum, sir."

"Blum?"

"Yes sir."

He'd dealt with Blum not so long ago, before he'd arranged the Planetary Plenipotentiary status for Maddox, which had included a nice raise in pay for the captain.

"Get Blum on the screen," Cook said. "And do it immediately."

In a few moments, Vice Admiral Blum faced him on the screen.

Blum was a slender man who'd undergone obvious regeneration therapy. He had dark hair and had once been one of Fletcher's people, a Humanity Manifesto believer.

Cook wondered for a moment, as he felt his age, if he should undergo some regenerative therapy. His joints creaked more than he cared for. He waved his hand brusquely, dismissing the thought.

"Lord High Admiral," Blum said through the screen. "You wanted to see me?"

"Listen, Blum." Cook told him what Mary had relayed regarding the situation in the Trappist-1 System.

"I understand," Blum said. "You want Task Force 3 to stop the aliens."

"That's the question," Cook said. "Can you? They're aliens with daunting battle technology."

"You said it's one ship."

"Fifty kilometers in a diameter," Cook said. "It will have more mass than the entire task force."

"Task Force 3 is powerful. I should think we can easily deal with these aliens."

"Task Force 3 is minimal. You have three motherships and three battleships."

"Three *Conqueror*-class battleships," Blum said, "along with light cruisers, destroyers and some of the best fold-fighters in the Fleet."

"Can any of your ships breach a compressed-stardust hull?"

"Sir," Blum said. "That was a Pluto operator's flowery description, not a scientific assessment. They're watching via the Long-Range Builder Scanner. I suspect her opinion has nothing to do with reality. I can already see the situation. We'll destroy the machines and take out the giant vessel that brought them."

"Don't be presumptuous. You'll be dealing with the unknown. So far, the aliens have annihilated every defensive feature."

Blum shook his head. "They annihilated two destroyers, three escorts and the planetary outposts. I could have done the same with the task force."

"Don't be overconfident, I said."

"I'm not, sir. I'm eager."

Cook fidgeted. His granddaughter was going if he sent the task force. It was only yesterday he bounced her on his knee as a two-year old. This was awful. "Are there any other vessels ready to join you?"

"No, sir," Blum said. "Task Force 3 is it, except for the task force defending Earth. The rest of the ready vessels are in the Janus System."

"I know, I know," Cook said. "Listen, Vice Admiral, take proper precautions. Go in prepared for anything. If you lose those ships—"

"Sir," Blum said sharply, interrupting, "are you accusing me of incompetence?"

Cook stared up at the ceiling. Ever since their conversation from last time, Blum had taken greater offense more easily. He looked at the man.

"You're the acting commander of Task Force 3."

"No, sir," Blum said, "I *am* the commander."

Cook's lips compressed. No. Now wasn't the time for an argument. He'd kept the man back from Janus, as it had been too important. Now, this? He wanted to shout with frustration.

"Get your people ready, Vice Admiral. Use the hyper-spatial tube to reach Zinc—" Cook opened his mouth to give Blum an operational plan. He stopped, though, as that was against standard operating procedures.

One gave the commanding officer the commission and left the method to him. Star Watch believed in personal initiative. Therefore, they'd structured regulations to make sure such initiative wasn't suppressed. He needed to give Blum free rein.

Cook fidgeted again. This was more than just his granddaughter, although she was the key component of his worry. Task Force 3 was it. They had no backup, as the Task Force defending Earth was forbidden to leave the Solar System. He might summon ships from the Janus System, but they were in a standoff and couldn't afford that. Maybe he could gather lone vessels in different parts of the Commonwealth. That would take time, however.

Cook swallowed, forcing himself to say the words. "Save Zinc. Save as many people as you can. And go with God, Admiral. I wish you success."

"Thank you, sir. We won't fail Star Watch, and you'll see—"

Blum stopped speaking: maybe thinking boasts were unwise before a mission.

After voicing a few more words of confidence, the vice admiral cut the connection.

Cook's broad shoulders deflated as he turned away. The sick feeling in his gut wouldn't go away. Did he have a premonition of impending disaster?

This was already a disaster. He was trying to prevent further disaster. Star Watch needed to smash the aliens, destroying the interlopers who traveled so deep into the Commonwealth to annihilate a planet. The attack was unwarranted.

Cook scowled.

How had the giant vessel gotten so far into the Commonwealth without anybody spotting it? The Trappist-1 System was as much the center of the Commonwealth as the Solar System. It made no sense that such a vast ship had escaped any kind of detection. And why strike a planet like Zinc? It didn't have any strategical value he could see. Certainly, if this were some sort of concentrated alien assault they would have hit elsewhere and smashed a strategic planet.

Cook wiped his forehead. Then, he made a fist and looked at his class ring. It was from the year he'd graduated from the academy. That had been a long time ago.

Calm your nerves, old man.

Task Force 3's personnel, Vice Admiral Blum included—
and my granddaughter—were all well trained, professional
officers and crews. The task force had three motherships, three
Conqueror-class battleships, all of them fortified by the
supermetals from the Alpha Centauri System. Who ran
Battleship Squadron 10?

Cook went to a desk, sat and looked through the personnel
list. It was Commodore Donal Galt. He was a brilliant tactician
from all he read, apparently with a piercing intelligence.

Why did Cook feel that this was going to come down to the
battleships? Was it because his granddaughter was on the
Stonewall Jackson?

"Lord High Admiral," a woman said. "There's a call from
Pluto."

Cook jumped up as swiftly as a big old man like him could.
He staggered across the chamber and flicked a wall screen. The
Iron Lady appeared.

"Sir," Mary said, "Zinc is beginning to shake and wobble
from its regular orbital path. The commandant believes the
planet will soon begin to disintegrate if the beams are allowed
to continue."

"You mean the alien gravitational beams?" Cook said,
wanting precision in such communications.

"Yes sir," Mary said.

"Thank you."

Cook cut her off before she could say more. Then he
switched on the screen to Blum, who stood on the bridge of
Mothership *Joan of Arc*. Obviously, the vice admiral had been
giving orders.

"Get going this instant," Cook said. "It has become an
immediate emergency. If the task force doesn't reach the planet
soon, everyone on it will be dead."

Blum saluted sharply. "It will be done, sir."

"Bring me back my ships," Cook said. He really wanted to
tell Blum to make sure his granddaughter returned. He couldn't
say that, though. Instead, he added, "Don't lose the entire task
force. Do you hear?"

Blum frowned. "The entire task force? I don't plan to lose
anything, sir."

Cook stared at him and Blum stared back.

I'm getting too old for this.

Cook cut the connection, staggered to the desk and sat down. He bunched his fists on the desk. He hated sending men into combat against the unknown. He hated even more sending his granddaughter.

He opened a bottom drawer, took out a bottle of whiskey and a shot glass. He poured himself a shot. He stared at it for a short time and then threw it back into his throat.

The whiskey burned going down.

Cook poured himself another, drank it, and poured himself a third. He drank it, too. Finally, he clutched the bottle and the empty shot glass, which were on his desk. He stared at them until he felt the comforting numbness three quick shots brought.

"Dear God," he whispered. "Please help Task Force 3." He didn't know why, but he had a feeling they were going to need all the help they could get.

-5-

Commodore Donal Galt received the information about the impending combat mission as he was crawling through an engine conduit. He did so to check up on the latest repairs from a drill for his emergency repair teams.

"Sir," a woman said through an earbud, "there's an emergency. You're wanted on the bridge."

"Thank you," Galt said, and he started backing up.

The commodore was a small man, able to negotiate the conduit easier than most. When he climbed out and straightened, he noticed a few stains on his uniform.

"Sir," his second-in-command said. The man had waited at the entry point. The man pointed at his face.

Galt used a hand to wipe his cheek, seeing black smears there.

The commodore had sharp features and piercing brown eyes. He was short and thin with thick dark hair.

He wiped the dirty hand on his uniform, leaving a smudge.

The second-in-command winced.

Galt caught that, but didn't give a damn. Results were all that mattered to him, not how things looked.

"So what's the emergency?"

"Sir, they want you on the bridge."

"You won't say?"

"Admiral Blum wants to speak to you."

Galt waited.

"We're using the hyper-spatial tube to make a combat jump to Trappist-1."

"Just like that?" asked Galt.

"Blum demands to see you now, sir."

"The stickler has his panties in a bunch, does he? Let's go." Galt motioned for the second-in-command to precede him.

That was due to Galt's one fault, if you could call it that. He limped after his second-in-command. Galt didn't like it when people saw him limp. He used to be a sprinter in high school and college. Not these days, though. He used to be much more muscular, too. He could have taken a prosthetic so he wouldn't limp. There was no way he would do that.

He wouldn't do anything that would remove what he had. Yes, he had a diminished anklebone. It had been broken far too many times. That didn't matter. He would not replace it. He would take more regeneration therapy if he must.

The problem was that Galt took the limp seriously. In his mind, it made him a cripple. He was a cripple who would get things done, and he'd do them his way.

He was a commodore of three of the best *Conqueror*-class battleships in Star Watch—the *Alexander*, the *Stonewall Jackson* and the *Philip II* in Battleship Squadron 10.

As the two headed along the corridors, the second-in-command outlined the situation. He did so while facing forward, as Galt hated people watching the gimp limp. The situation was grim, with these unknown aliens trying to destroy a populated planet.

Soon, they entered a turbo lift. When the hatch opened, they walked onto the bridge of the *Stonewall Jackson*.

Galt gratefully sank into his chair to the left and behind the captain's seat. He activated holo-screens, which popped up before him.

The primary screen flickered on. A frowning Vice Admiral Blum peered at him from it.

"You took your sweet time, Galt. This is an emergency. Do you happen to know what that means?"

"Yes sir."

"If you can't do your duty in a timely fashion, I'm going to ask that you relinquish your command to someone who can."

Galt stared at Blum without reply. He found it made blowhards like Blum uncomfortable when he simply stared at them, forcing them to either demand he say something, or prompting them to say further stupid things. If it were permitted, he'd ask Blum to a duel with blasters. Wouldn't that be sweet? He could envision blowing the stickler to bits.

Clearly, they didn't get along. They never had. That he found himself under the command of the vice admiral—inwardly, Galt shrugged. It didn't matter. He was the commanding officer of Battleship Squadron 10. He would do as instructed, *his* way of course. His way. He also kept his smile to himself.

Blum outlined the situation.

Galt listened carefully, frowning as he learned more.

"Can you send over some tactical video of all that?" Galt asked.

"Of course," Blum said. "Really, we should be having a conference aboard the *Queen Bess*, but the Lord High Admiral has said this is an immediate emergency. Therefore, I will outline the situation as we maneuver into position to enter the hyper-spatial tube. We're going to appear midway between Zinc and Cobalt."

"Just a moment." Galt held up a hand, using the other to bring up a map of the Inner Trappist-1 System on a different holo-screen.

"Did you just tell me to wait?" Blum asked.

Galt faced the vice admiral's holo-screen. "Sorry sir. There was a delay in communications."

Blum stared at him balefully. "I don't expect to have to endure any of your insubordinate pranks, Commodore. You'll do *exactly* as I tell you, *when* I tell you and *how* I tell you. Is that understood, Galt?"

"Understood, sir." Of course, Galt understanding didn't mean he actually agreed. He was too honest to lie, but he didn't mind splitting hairs, if that was what it took to get the job done.

Galt noticed the data he desired on the other holo-screen. Since he didn't plan to look away to study it, he split his main holo-screen into two views. The admiral was on one side and the data on the other.

Galt listened as Blum told him the operational plan. As he listened, Galt used a clicker and examined the various tactical maps of the Inner Trappist-1 System, particularly the third and fourth planets, along with the data notations for each.

"Do I have your attention, Galt?"

"You do, sir."

"Your eyes seem to be wandering. What are you looking at?"

"Sir, I've been observing the tactical situation as you've described it to me. I've noticed that if we enter the system midway between Zinc and Cobalt, we'll be far from the enemy."

"That's the point. We don't want to face the alien supership too soon. We especially don't want to do so if while we're all caught up in jump lag."

"If we come in midway, as you say, it'll take us quite some a time to reach this supership, as you call it."

"What would you call it?"

"Supership works for me, sir. All I'm saying is that those engines of destruction that are destroying the planet—" Galt shook his head. "We'll never get to them in time if we deploy how you propose, sir."

Blum stared at him as two red spots appeared on his regenerative cheeks. "What do *you* suggest, Commodore?"

"Sir," Galt said, having waited for precisely that, "I suggest we come in directly on the other side of the planet of Zinc from the supership. That will protect us from any weapons they can deploy, but it will put us much closer to the action. That will give us a chance of saving the people on the planet, which is the main reason for our intervention."

Blum stared at Galt and then shook his head. Blum was one thing if not intelligent. He didn't like praising others and he didn't like accepting another man's ideas. Perhaps, though, he saw the wisdom in Galt's plan. A successful mission would aid his career. A loss would seriously impede it.

"I've changed my mind," Blum said. "We're going to deploy twenty million kilometers from Zinc on the other side of the planet from the supership. In this way, we'll be able to engage in activities quickly. We'll also have enough space to save us from an immediate enemy attack."

"That's sound reasoning," Galt said. "Great idea, sir."

Blum nodded curtly, clearly missing the irony. "I'll send over the rest of your orders in a few minutes. Be ready to deploy. Make sure your vessels are shipshape and combat-ready."

"Yes sir," Galt said.

After Blum signed off, Galt suppressed a laugh and issued a flurry of orders, before reviewing his ships' readiness summaries. All three battleships were primed. They were huge ovals and at least as deadly as *Victory*, perhaps even more so. The supermetals they'd gained from the Alpha Centauri System meant they had stronger electromagnetic shields than any other Star Watch vessel. Their disruptor beams were capable of annihilating any known material.

In Galt's opinion, if command really wanted to stop the so-called supership with a compressed stardust hull, they should send *nine* battleships and be done with it.

What could fold fighters could do against such a supership? Even the light cruisers might prove useless against it.

Galt shrugged. He wasn't in charge. He just ran Battleship Squadron 10. In his estimation, the three battleships were the heart of Task Force 3.

He was sure Blum didn't think so. Blum was on the *Queen Bess*, was he not? That meant he believed in mothership tactics above battleship tactics.

Galt exhaled and his eyes glittered. He was sure Blum with his arrogance would make tactical mistakes. It wasn't that Galt felt himself faultless. He made mistakes like any man. He simply tried to avoid them to the best of his ability. His one mistake when he'd been a sprinter—

Galt shook his head. Now wasn't the time to indulge in that. Why did he always think of his physical disability at such times as this? He made a fist but he did not hit the armrest. He'd heard Captain Maddox did that.

In one regard, Galt was in agreement with Blum. Both were Humanity Manifesto believers. Both believed that true humans

29

should run Star Watch. Both had distaste for Captain Maddox, as he wasn't completely human, was he?

It didn't seem as if *Victory* would be in on this, even though as far as Galt knew *Victory* was in orbit around Earth. Perhaps the starship wasn't ready for action. Perhaps for all his vaunted prowess, Maddox didn't run as tight or as smoothly organized a crew as he, Galt, did.

Soon, orders came through from the vice admiral. Battleship Squadron 10 began to maneuver toward the nexus. They would be in front of the three motherships. Before them were the light cruisers and destroyers.

The moments ticked by. Finally, they received last minute data about the enemy, gained by the long distance scanner on Pluto, which sent it via the Long-Range Builder Comm device to Star Watch headquarters. That was fed directly to the *Queen Bess*. The vice admiral fed it to his commanders as he saw fit.

Nexus Central sent a signal. The hyper-spatial tube materialized. Before Task Force 3 was a swirling entrance. The tube stretched all the way from the nexus between Earth and Luna 40.7 light years to the Trappist-1 System.

Task Force 3 maneuvered into the hyper-spatial tube, one by one by one disappearing from the Solar System. The warships made the journey to the Trappist-1 System. By God's grace, the task force would appear where the Nexus Central people had been told to put them.

The battle for the Trappist-1 System was about to being.

-6-

Aboard the *Stonewall Jackson*, Commodore Galt raised his head. He sat in his chair on the bridge, surrounded by floating holographic screens, giving him access to whatever data he needed. He blinked several times, squeezed his eyes together and looked around.

The bridge was already alive with activity, as most of the crew had come out of hyper-spatial-tube lag faster than he had. In his youth that wouldn't have been the case. He would have been the first to become alert.

He shrugged inwardly and began to study his holo-screens. He used a glove on his left hand to control them.

According to this, the hyper-spatial-tube journey had been a success. Ahead of them in relation to where the task forced had appeared was the planet Zinc. Several of the holo-screens showed the nearest alien machines that were attacking the planet. They were each three kilometers above the surface and used heavy gravitational beams to drill.

There was no sign of the asteroidal supership. That would have been a surprise if it were, as the fifty-kilometer-diameter vessel was supposed to be on the other side of the planet from them. Neither was there any sign of the four alien fighters.

"Commodore," the comm operator said, "there's a message for you from the admiral."

"I'll take it here," Galt said, manipulating his glove.

Blum appeared on a mini-holo-screen.

31

Galt and he communicated professionally. Whatever differences they'd shown earlier were not in evidence now. They were in a combat zone. They spoke crisply, both men eager to win the encounter and destroy the aliens, saving the people of Zinc if they could.

After Galt signed off, Blum launched several squadrons of strikefighters from the motherships *Joan of Arc* and *Cleopatra*.

They were single-engine space fighters with two personnel aboard each like atmospheric fighters in the old days. The squadrons accelerated, racing to reach the head of the task force. There, the strikefighters would act as an advance screen for the rest.

The enemy did nothing against that deployment. The alien machines serenely continued boring into the planetary surface. Not even the alien fighters appeared.

Once the screening strikefighters reached their assigned positions, Blum gave the world.

The task force as a whole began heading toward Zinc, ready to take care of business. The strikefighter squadrons were in the lead spreading out, with the destroyers and light cruisers following. Behind at a distance came Battleship Squadron 10. They were the heavy pounders: the *Stonewall Jackson,* the *Alexander* and the *Philip II*. Trailing even farther behind were the three motherships. They were huge vessels, as big as the largest merchant haulers. A swarm of defensive strikefighters provided them an extra layer of protection. Two squadrons of escorts added to that.

Now, heavy fold fighters launched from the *Queen Bess*. These were newer than anything that had been aboard *Victory* in the past. They had delta wings and were designed for maneuvering and attacking in a planetary atmosphere. They waited outside the mothership, receiving targeting data. Then, one after another, the heavy tin cans folded.

Seconds later, the armored, atmospheric-capable tin cans appeared six kilometers above the surface. Each group targeted one alien gravitational machine hovering three kilometers above the surface.

The city-block-sized Ls, Zs and Us continued to pierce the surface with their thick green drill-beams.

Aboard the *Stonewall Jackson*, Galt watched all this with anticipation.

"Sir," the science officer told the captain. "You should look at the planet."

"Put it on the main screen," Captain Karpov said. He was a large man with a wide face, with a mole under his left eye.

Galt looked there with everyone else on the bridge.

Zinc visibly wobbled. That had to be due to the constant heavy gravitational beams disrupting the equilibrium of the planet. Could the alien machines cause the planet to veer out of its orbital path? That seemed incredible. Nobody in Star Watch wanted to find out.

"Sir," Usan said. "The fold fighters are launching missiles."

"Let me see it," Captain Karpov said.

Galt didn't need to ask. He'd already used the glove to bring up what he wanted on his personal holo-screens circling his chair.

All around the planet, the heavy delta-wing fold fighters launched antimatter missiles.

Galt knew Blum had decided not to screw around. They would hit hard and fast to start. The many antimatter blasts might kill millions of civilians, but those people would die anyway if they did nothing. Destroying the machines was the key according to Admiral Blum.

The antimatter missiles burned hot for the alien machines. As they did, the heavy tin cans folded again, backing off the fight to appear near the *Queen Bess*.

Anti-air beams fired from the alien machines. They knocked down dozens of antimatter missiles. Would the aliens get all of them?

Five antimatter explosions around Zinc gave the answer. The alien machines had burned down most of the SW missiles, except for five.

Those five produced massive mushroom clouds and released horrific energy and heat.

Below, an alien machine burst apart under the explosions.

"Got one!" Usan shouted.

Others on the bridge cheered.

Galt squinted at his holo-screens. He saw two other planet destroyers burst into scrap and rain metal onto the ruined surface.

"Three," Galt said. "We got three of the machines."

Now, the aliens acted against the task force.

As metal and component pieces from the three destroyed machines rained with hard radiation for the surface, the four alien fighters zoomed around the curve of the planet and into the task force's line-of-sight. They did so while in low orbital space.

Beams speared from the alien fighters. Each hit a screening strikefighter, annihilating it. The alien fighters retargeted, annihilating another set of four strikefighters. They did it a third time, destroying more with violent and rapid efficiency.

The alien counterattack had happened so fast it hardly gave anyone enough time to think.

Blum was not only intelligent, however, but fast thinking. His orders came on the heel of the third attack.

Screening strikefighters started breaking off as they accelerated with max burn. They were trying to get the hell out of Dodge.

While they did so, the destroyers and light cruisers advanced. The ships must have been ready for it. Fusion cannons beamed at the blue alien fighters.

Several fusion beams struck the alien ovals. The alien fighters shrugged off the beams as nothing, however. In fact, the aliens destroyed another four retreating strikefighters.

From the *Queen Bess*, from his location on the roomy bridge, Blum shouted orders. The admiral was on it. He demanded the destroyers and light cruisers treble up on an alien fighter. "See if they can shrug off all of you hitting one at once."

As Blum gave the order, the alien fighters started to accelerate, burning at fifty gravities. They streaked across the face of the planet, heading for a curve that would take them out of the task force's line-of-sight.

Aboard the *Stonewall Jackson*, Galt jerked forward. "How can the aliens be taking those G's?" he asked no one in particular.

34

The science officer didn't seem to take the cue.

Galt began manipulating his glove, seeing if he could get a reading on one of the fighters. He wanted to know what force, energy, whatever, the aliens used to counteract such massive gravities.

"Commodore," said Captain Karpov of the *Stonewall Jackson*, "I'm getting reports the intact alien engines have gone offline. They're no longer drilling the planet."

Galt lowered the manipulation glove, looking over his holo-screens. "That's excellent news. The plan is working then."

Galt didn't really believe that. The appearance of Task Force 3 must have caught the aliens by surprise. The loss of planetary machines could have added to the shock. The fleeing alien fighters showed the enemy commander didn't know yet how to react to the task force. Maybe turning off the planet destroyers was merely being cautious until he made his main decision.

Galt nodded tightly. The asteroidal supership was the key to all this. The task force had appeared, attacked and possibly thrown the enemy off balance for the moment. Now was the instant to use the surprise to Star Watch's advantage. Surprise was a force multiplier. Blum should order Squadron 10 around the planet so the *Conqueror*-class battleships could hammer the supership and take it down before the enemy could conjure up an effective counter. Blum could also send in the heavy fold fighters to launch more antimatter missiles—at the supership. That would keep the enemy occupied while the battleships maneuvered around the planet. Make this a combined mass attack.

Galt rubbed his jaw. Should he call Blum and offer the admiral the idea, or should he wait for the man to come to the obvious conclusion?

It was possible Blum was waiting for something.

Galt checked his holo-screens. The four alien fighters had almost fled around a planetary curve and out-of-sight.

The destroyers and light cruisers, which had moved up, beamed at the last alien fighter. Some of the beams hit. Some missed. Of those that hit, only a few remained on target for more than a second.

Then a most unexpected thing happened. The alien fighter disintegrated under the combined fusion beams. It exploded and partially vaporized.

There was a cheer on the *Stonewall Jackson*.

"We can kill 'em," Karpov said.

Galt smiled grimly. The fighter was a small vessel, making it a small victory. They'd already shown they could destroy the enemy when the antimatter missiles took out three planet-destroying machines. Still, it was good to hear the cheers.

"What's the supership doing?" Galt said to himself more than anyone else.

"Commodore," the comm officer said, "the admiral wishes to speak to you."

"Thank you." Galt used his glove. Blum appeared on a holo-screen.

"We've driven off their fighters," Blum said. "As far as I can tell, we've stopped them from obliterating the planet."

Galt nodded.

"I'm sending fold fighters onto the other side of the planet to take a look at the supership. After that, I'll make the decision how to proceed." Blum didn't ask that nor did he state it forcefully as Galt would have expected. Was Blum getting cautious? Did the weight of the decisions cause him to doubt himself? "Meanwhile," Blum said, "I'm going to send the rest of the fold fighters down to the planet to destroy the rest of the world machines."

"Yes sir."

"You disagree with that?"

Galt shook his head. He didn't disagree. He was waiting for Blum to give the right order. The task force should head around the planet this instant. They'd ripped the initiative from the enemy by destroying some of the drilling machines. Now was the time to attack and take out the supership. By not doing so, they were giving the enemy precious time to come up with a counter against them. That was a tactical mistake. It was possible the supership had powers they didn't comprehend.

36

Therefore, they should annihilate it while they still had the element of surprise.

"You have something on your mind, Commodore. Spit it out."

There was the permission to speak his mind.

"Sir, we have the initiative and surprise. Let's use it and attack relentlessly. Send us in—the battleships, I mean—as the point of the spear. The others can give us flank cover."

"And if the supership can destroy the battleships?"

"War is a gamble. This is the moment to gamble."

"No," Blum said, shaking his head. "You're not in command. The Lord High Admiral told me not to lose all the ships. I'm not going to. We're doing this with a minimum of casualties."

"I understand," Galt said. And he did. Responsibility for costly warships and human lives put pressure on a commander. That pressure changed and frightened most people.

"I know what you're going to say." Blum sneered. "Bold action is the safest course. It also leads to horrible mistakes. I expect you to remain vigilant and ready, and do as I order."

"Yes sir."

Blum blinked heavily. "This clarifies it for me. I'm saving the task force, you understand?"

Galt said and did nothing.

"I'm sending out fold fighters to scout. We'll know more soon. Admiral Blum out."

Galt didn't fume because it wouldn't help any. He'd do what he could within the parameters of his rank, position and orders.

He gained data about the planet-attacking machines. He studied a recording of the four alien fighters that had zipped around the planet. He studied the alien beams that had destroyed strikefighters. He asked questions of his science people, particularly if the battleship's shield could resist the enemy's gravitational beams.

Soon, battleship techs began to adjust the heavy electromagnetic shields that surrounded each battleship. The adjustments should help stop the gravitational beams.

All the while, minutes ticked and soon became a half hour.

Galt pushed up, limped around his chair and plopped back down. He hated anyone seeing him limp, but he could only sit for so long. The waiting was making him antsy.

Commodore," the comm officer said. "Admiral Blum is on the comm."

This time, there was static on the holo-screen.

"We're being hit with a heavy jamming ray," Blum said. "I don't know the source. The fold fighters appeared on the other side of the planet. The enemy fighters were waiting. They shot all but one down. It just returned."

"It took this long?" asked Galt.

"Listen," Blum said. "That's not the point. The supership is gone. If I'd followed your advice, it wouldn't have made a difference"

Galt's eyes narrowed.

"Sir!" somebody shouted.

Galt scowled. He was on the line with Blum. When he looked, though, the holo-screen showed dense fuzz.

"Admiral," Galt said. "Can you hear me?"

There was nothing from Blum. Heavy jamming had cut the connection.

Captain Karpov of the *Stonewall Jackson* was on his feet, shouting, bringing order to seeming pandemonium on the bridge.

Galt started paying attention to that.

Usan had detected an anomaly five hundred thousand kilometers away. That was twenty-five percent farther than Luna was from Earth at its farthest point.

Galt used his glove, bringing the data to a holo-screen.

A blot of space had become darker than ordinary. Odd waves emanated from it. The space was...222 kilometers in diameter.

"I'm sensing distortions," Usan said.

"Of what kind?" asked Karpov.

"I don't know, sir."

"Give me a conjecture."

The chief licked her lips. "It's like...the fabric of stuff breaking open."

"What the hell does that mean?" Karpov demanded.

"Sir," Usan said. "Something is appearing, coming out of the darkness maybe."

Galt grew stiff as he saw it. It was the supership with its supposed compressed stardust hull. What was it doing? Was this a new form of hyper-spatial-tube jump? Was this a second supership or was this the original? If the original, it had moved from one location to another.

Normal communications between nearby ships had become impossible. Trying to reach others farther away—the enemy jamming was intense.

Galt did notice swarms of strikefighters leaving the *Queen Bess*. Instead of waiting for others, each fighter began a hard burn for the supership.

Was that logical?

"Look, sir," Usan told Karpov. "Some of the destroyers and light cruisers are beginning a burn toward the enemy supership."

"That's the ticket," Galt said forcefully.

Karpov whirled around to look at him.

"We're attacking." Galt stood and pointed at the comm officer. "Get through to the other battleships. If regular communications doesn't work, use the light code system. Tell the others to 'Follow me. We're attacking.'"

The light code system was similar to flags in the old sailing ship days on Earth. One used a sequence of lights to send a message.

It must have worked.

Soon, strikefighters, destroyers, light cruisers and the *Alexander* and *Philip II* built up velocity together with the *Stonewall Jackson* as they all headed at the supership.

Then, heavy gravitational beams speared from the compressed stardust hull. The thick green beams reached across the five hundred thousand kilometers and smashed into the lead destroyers. The destroyers' electromagnetic shields collapsed. The grav beams obliterated the hulls, crashing through the ships. Terrific explosions sent metal, vapor and bio tissue outward as three destroyers disappeared under the enemy barrage.

The other vessels slowed their advance while the three *Conqueror*-class battleships *increased* their velocity.

The captains and commanders of the other warships must have received the light code messages. They fell in behind the big battleships. Farther back, the three motherships struggled to build velocity as quickly as the others did.

The strikefighter pilots had more courage than good sense. Perhaps they trusted to their tiny size. Most continued to lead the fray, zeroing in on the distant enemy.

The supership no longer beamed. Perhaps they adjusted. Moments later, the heavy gravitational beams struck again. The enemy targeted the battleships. As before, the beams struck the targets, the heavy electromagnetic shielding.

These shields had all benefited from Galt's analysis and the techs' adjustments.

If the alien expected the battleship shields to drop like the others, they did not. Nor did the shields turn black or even brown, though they turned red. Under the hellish fury of the strong gravitational beams, the battleships continued to accelerate.

The rest of the task force, except for some foolhardy strikefighter pilots, remained well behind the three tightly placed battleships.

"Captain," Galt said.

"We're ready, Commodore," Karpov said.

"Give the order to fire," Galt said.

"Fire," Karpov said.

A heavy disruptor beam speared from the main cannon of the *Stonewall Jackson*. It crossed the closing distance and hit the compressed stardust hull. The yellow beam burned and disintegrated matter as it kept drilling deeper into the enemy hull, but at an incremental rate.

Disruptor beams from the *Alexander* and the *Philip II* hit the supership, immediately drilling into the strangely protective hull.

"Analysis," Galt said.

Karpov looked up from a console. "The beams are burning through the hull, but very slowly, sir. Whatever that compressed stardust is, it's tough."

Galt nodded.

The engines in the *Stonewall Jackson* whined as the entire vessel shivered under the strain. Those engines fed the electromagnetic shield and the disruptor cannon. The supermetals from the Alpha Centauri System could carry much heavier power loads and therefore provided greater shields and disruptor beams than otherwise.

"Sir," Usan said. "Enemy grav-beams are passing us."

Galt used his manipulation glove. The enemy beams reached out and struck—

The *Queen Bess's* shield collapsed. The enemy grav-beams burned through the mothership hull. They ranged at will, detonating and burning down people, reactors and equipment. The mothership could only take so much.

The *Queen Bess* exploded violently all down the line.

Galt stared in horror.

"Sir," Karpov said. "The admiral was aboard the *Queen Bess.*"

Galt nodded numbly.

"Are you in charge then, sir?"

Galt blinked. That was right. He was in charge. He was the next highest ranked in the task force. He had to get his act together. He had to provide leadership, and the sooner the better.

"Listen to me," Galt said. "We're destroying the supership and we're destroying it now. We head straight down its gullet and take him out like we should have earlier."

Karpov and the crew listened. They knew Commodore Galt was a genius when it came to battle tactics. The others surely knew it, too.

Therefore, the three battleships continued to absorb the enemy's hellish rays as they dealt out three of their own.

The shields had turned brown where the gravitational rays hit. The disruptor beams had drilled into the enemy hull a few meters and were still drilling into the compressed stardust.

Galt stared at a holo-screen. How thick was the enemy's hull? If it were more than several meters, it would maybe take—he didn't know how long. If it were less thick, the D-

41

rays should burst through soon. Would there be a vast explosion on the supership?

"Sir," Usan said. "I'm detecting a strange field ahead. I don't understand it."

"Around the supership?" Karpov asked.

"No," Usan said. "It's directly in front of us."

Galt swiveled his chair. "What do you mean a strange field? Be precise."

On the main screen, on Galt's holo-screens, everything became intensely dark. That darkness seemed to deepen.

"Sir," Usan said, "these readings—I don't understand this."

Galt used his glove, studying the readings. The chief was right. They made no sense. What was happening? Was this some sort of void or null zone? What was the enemy doing to them?

***

Far away on Pluto in the Long-Range Builder Scanner chamber, Mary O'Hara and Commandant Spanno asked similar questions.

On several screens, they watched three *Conqueror*-class battleships fly through what seemed like a rent in space-time. The battleships literally flew out of view and disappeared. They were gone. The rest of the task force followed suit, disappearing in turn.

A few of the leading strikefighters had escaped the fate, as they were beyond the rent when it first opened.

Mary O'Hara asked questions.

Commandant Spanno asked more.

None of the personnel could give them any answers.

Instead, as they watched, as no other Star Watch vessel put in an appearance, new Ls, Zs and Us left giant bay doors on the asteroidal supership. They headed for the planet, joining the others still intact.

The machines took up their former positions. Soon, heavy gravitational beams once more drilled into the surface.

As before, microwave energy once again fed the supership. The holes where the disruptor beams had hit the stardust hull appeared to be repairing themselves. Like a mini-sandstorm, compressed particles of stardust flowed over the open spots and remained in place.

Three hours after Task Force 3 had disappeared, the planet Zinc broke apart.

All the people on Zinc died in the monumental and catastrophic destruction of the planet.

Soon thereafter, the fifty-kilometer-diameter vessel disappeared into strange blackness, although not before collecting the machines and three alien fighters.

Fifteen million people in the Trappist-1 Star System were dead. Task Force 3 was gone. This was a disaster.

-7-

Over the next few hours, the Lord High Admiral became increasingly depressed by the videos he received from Pluto. The planet Zinc was gone, destroyed by the aliens. Task Force 3 and his granddaughter—disappeared, perhaps destroyed.

Despite all searching with Long-Range Builder Scanner functions, there was no sign of Task Force 3. There were signs of the destroyed Mothership *Queen Bess*. That implied Vice Admiral Blum and all the crew were dead.

Where was the rest of the task force? What had happened to the battleships? What had happened to the other motherships, the light cruisers, destroyers and escorts?

The Lord High Admiral sat at his desk in his office, with his elbows on the desk and his hands massaging his forehead. He closed his eyes and groaned with frustration.

He'd lost a planet, an entire task force and his beloved granddaughter. He dare not send anyone else into the system or the same fate likely awaited him.

Cook slapped his meaty old hands onto the desk and stared at the wall. He was the commander of Star Watch. This was his responsibility. *I'm getting too old for this. I used to be able to take shocks and setbacks better.* He'd never lost a granddaughter before, though.

His teeth ground together as he forced himself to harden his resolve. He couldn't just bear this alone. Yes, it was his responsibility. He was in charge. He'd sent them into danger, to their deaths. *But are they dead?* They'd disappeared.

44

From what he'd seen, it seemed as if the task force had been transferred or transported to somewhere else. It was the same with the asteroidal supership.

Cook pushed himself upright, put his hands behind his back, clasping them, and began striding through the office first in one direction, turning and then the other direction. He scowled thunderously. He wasn't going to wallow in agony. That was wrong for a military man. Frankly, it was wrong for anyone. He was going to act, and he was going to save his granddaughter—Task Force 3, he meant.

Cook brightened as the decision gave him confidence. Perhaps there was news from the Pluto Scanner.

What a marvelous device. Hadn't Maddox brought it back from the Pandora System many years ago?

As the Lord High Admiral barged through the door and strode purposefully down the corridor, he thought about Maddox the fair-haired boy. Not that everyone loved him; quite the opposite. Yet this seemed like the sort of mission where Maddox and his gifted crew excelled. Something crazy, unconventional, risky. He should send *Victory* into the Trappist-1 System if nobody else. They had the expertise, the unique vessel and the personnel to figure out what was going on.

Cook nodded, feeling better. The knot of defeat in his gut unraveled just a bit more.

He entered the Long-Range Builder Comm device room.

There was a large screen connected to Pluto and a pretty captain in her thirties seated at the desk. She lurched up and saluted.

"At ease," Cook said. "Is there any more news from Pluto about the task force?"

"The Iron Lady wishes to speak to you, sir. I passed that along. I thought that was why you're here."

Cook frowned. Could Mary have anticipated his decision to send Maddox? He didn't want to argue with anybody about it, most certainly not the Iron Lady. He felt too worn for that. Still, he couldn't see how he could avoid it.

45

"Put her on," Cook said. "Let me speak to her. First though," he held up his hand, "any more news about the task force?"

"No sir."

"You may leave for the moment."

"Sir?" the captain asked.

"Take a coffee break."

"Yes sir." The captain saluted, turned and hurried away.

Cook glanced at her in passing and scowled. He was an old man. What was he doing looking with interest at such a fine figure of a woman?

He sat, clicked on the screen and Mary instantly filled it.

"Finally," Mary said. "This is a horrific incident. What's your decision?"

"Now see here." Cook scowled. "I'm the Lord High Admiral of Star Watch—"

"I'm sorry, sir. That was rude, and not proper military etiquette."

Cook nodded, only half mollified.

"The situation remains unchanged in the Trappist-1 System," Mary said. "Zinc is no longer a planet but a mass of rubble. The mining stations on the other planets are safe for the moment."

"Eh?" Cook asked.

"There are two mining operations on two different planets in the system. Neither of them has been harmed as far as we can tell. The people on them are hunkered down. The enemy never attacked there."

"The enemy." Cook rubbed his forehead. "Why would these aliens assault Zinc, a relatively unpopulated planet?"

"Fifteen million is unpopulated?" Mary asked.

"I said *relatively*. It could have been far worse. I mourn their loss. I feel it keenly, just as keenly as I feel the loss of Task Force 3."

"You talk as if Task Force 3 has been destroyed."

"What would you call it?" Cook said.

"Disappeared."

"Eh?"

46

"What we saw was like watching a task force enter a hyper-spatial tube."

"Wouldn't you have detected some form of hyper residue then?"

"Not necessarily," Mary said. "I'm not saying that was a hyper-spatial tube, but something akin to it, a transport line. Perhaps the residue or waves are too fine or too different for the Builder Scanner to detect."

"I suspected something like that myself," Cook said. "I was hoping... That means we should send scientific vessels out there to check."

"May I speak frankly, sir?"

Cook closed his eyes, feeling old. He used to rely upon her opinion all the time. Was Mary O'Hara fully rehabilitated? In other words, could he trust her? He needed somebody to talk to. Bearing this burden all by himself—

"I'm troubled," Cook said. "I'll admit it. This is just between you and me. This must go no further. Is anyone else listening over there?"

Mary looked around. "A moment sir." She moved from the screen. Thirty seconds later, she sat before him on the screen. "We can talk in private if that's what you wish."

"Thank you." Cook raised his head, trying to gather his thoughts. "First, I hope you're right about the task force. I..." He hesitated and found he couldn't tell the Iron Lady about his granddaughter. Why couldn't he? Inwardly, Cook shook his head. He didn't care to psychoanalyze himself but get on with it.

"Is this an alien invasion?" he said instead.

"Is that really what you're asking?"

"...I suppose not," Cook said. "What we've seen doesn't strike me as an alien invasion. That's partly because of the target they chose and the means they used to destroy the planet. The machines beamed microwave energy to the supership. Did the asteroidal vessel need to power up?"

"Are you suggesting the aliens devour planets to fuel their ship?"

"From what I saw, it seems like the most reasonable explanation. I hesitate to send another task force to scout the system, however."

"What then?" Mary asked.

"Throughout the years we've lost far too many ships," Cook said, as if he hadn't heard her. "I feel the losses more keenly than I used to."

Mary smiled faintly.

"You find that amusing?"

"Not at all, sir, I find it reassuring. A caring commander who loves the people he sends into danger is much preferable to a callous, brutal and ruthless one."

"Yet sometimes a ruthless commander is what is needed. Perhaps this is a moment to be ruthless."

"This is a moment to succeed. I agree with that."

Cook appreciated her candor and liked the direction of her thoughts. He took a deep breath as he tried to settle his thinking. As much as he loved his granddaughter, he needed to think of the people in the Trappist-1 System, the lost task force and the potential danger to the rest of the Commonwealth.

"Do you have any recommendations for our next move?" Cook asked.

"We need to find out what happened. Science vessels seem like the superior approach. Still, we don't want to lose any. Therefore, I suggest a military escort as guard."

"Or maybe send one and the same," Cook said softly.

Mary stared at him. She was a canny old lady, a former intelligence officer. Perhaps the best intelligence commander Star Watch had ever possessed.

"You're not thinking of sending *Victory* alone into that mess, are you?" Mary asked.

"Do you agree that Maddox and his people are uniquely suited for such a mission?"

"No, I don't agree with that at all."

"I'm afraid you do," Cook said. "You, too, have become too…caring. You worry too much about your grandson."

"Is that a crime?"

Cook thought about his granddaughter. "No. It's not a crime."

48

Hearing Mary ask that, though, hearing the angst and emotion in her voice helped to harden his heart. Something had happened to Task Force 3. He held onto that. He needed that. He didn't want to lose an entire task force, and his granddaughter, that he'd just ordered into action. Perhaps if he'd ordered more military vessels there—

No. The supership and alien fighters had destroyed thirty or so strikefighters and a mothership along with several destroyers. The enemy had won by deploying the tear in space, the blackness that had swallowed the task force. Wouldn't the blackness simply have swallowed a bigger task force and have lost Star Watch more vessels?

That meant a bigger task force would have failed. With this insight, he made his decision.

"Sir," Mary said, who watched him closely. "You can't send *Victory*. We must gather several task forces or send an armada this time."

"No, Mary. This is a mission for cunning operatives. Flimflam over force. Cleverness, skullduggery…that sort of thing. I'm going to summon Captain Maddox. I'm going to show him the evidence and then I'm going to send *Victory*."

Mary opened her mouth, perhaps to try to convince him otherwise. Then she closed her mouth and looked down at her hands. Finally, she looked up. "What if we lose *Victory* as well?"

Cook looked away. That wasn't what he wanted to hear. That didn't matter, though, did it? He straightened his shoulders and looked at Mary.

"Maddox and his people are the ones most likely to figure out the strange phenomenon. And if this is a prelude or a practice run before attacking Earth…"

"Earth is much better defended than Zinc," Mary said.

"What if there are more of these asteroidal superships? What if they destroyed our home planet?"

"You have a point," Mary said. "Though it pains me to say so, I agree with your decision. Perhaps the Mastermind is behind all this."

"I don't like to hear that. But this does seem like Yon Soth technology at its finest."

49

"Or worst, if I may say," Mary replied.

"Send any news the moment you hear it, any change in the Trappist-1 System. Until then, it's time to prepare and see what the captain thinks. I want Task Force 3 back. If they're lost, we must find them. If they're destroyed...we need to know it. If this is a prelude to an attack upon Earth, it's time to start to pull in other units from the Commonwealth and prepare."

"We have the unique hyper-spatial tube, the nexus," Mary said. "Perhaps it's time to employ it to its fullest advantage."

"Thank you, Brigadier. I appreciate your time."

"I didn't say much, sir."

"You did," Cook said. With that, he arose, accepted her salute with a nod and went to find the pretty captain and tell her she could return to her station.

-8-

Sergeant Treggason Riker was outside as big, soft snowflakes fell from the sky. He was in Switzerland Sector, at home at his cottage, standing on his front porch looking at all the snow piled in his front yard. It was supposed to stop snowing soon. It was near noon and the drifts, the piles—it was a lot of snow.

The sergeant was old and wore a parka with a hood up and a baseball cap sticking out from under it. He wore rubber galoshes, leather gloves and held onto a red snow-shovel.

He was normal sized as such things went and had a leathery face. He might have been coarsely handsome in his youth. Now, he was just old. He'd fought long ago and had been in a blast. From it, he'd lost a leg, an arm and an eye. He also had high-grade bionic parts as replacements.

They would be fine for the shoveling. The rest of him— he'd read how old guys dropped dead from shoveling snow because they weren't used to it anymore.

That wasn't going to be him. He wasn't a fitness freak like the captain who stayed in fantastic shape. Maddox loved going to the gym, boxing, running, doing just about anything physical.

Riker could hold his own back in the day. He was still a crack pistol shot and didn't mind practicing unarmed combat now and again. He didn't mind doing something physical to keep in reasonable shape.

He was still in Star Watch, wasn't he?

51

Riker frowned. He'd been thinking about that again.

He looked up into the sky and all he saw were those big fluffy snowflakes falling. He should start shoveling even if more flakes would fall onto his finished work. It was going to stop snowing soon anyway. He was out here, had taken time getting dressed and this was the exactly the right type of clothing for the weather.

It was cold this year in Switzerland Sector. People had been saying it was going to be warm this winter, but like most things, they were damn wrong. It was cold and wet just as it had always been and probably always would be.

With a grunt, Riker bent down, set the edge of the snow-shovel against the covered sidewalk and began to push.

Everyone who'd lived in cold country had shoveled snow. Well, any man had. Some women insisted on doing it. Riker grinned. He wouldn't mind a woman doing it for him now, but he didn't have a missy.

Would he ever have one again?

Hell, it had been ages since he'd even touched a woman. He shook his head. Better not think about that.

He was old and the bionic joints were finding the snow shoveling easy-peasy. His regular joints—he was huffing and puffing, and he'd only shoveled half the sidewalk so far. Maybe it was time to go in and have a cup of coffee. He'd stoke up his old-style fireplace and set his feet up—

Don't think about that, old man. Just get the shoveling done with.

He looked up into the sky again.

High up there above Earth, *Victory* was in orbit.

Riker sighed. He was so much better at home than out on a mission. The missions were exciting, but when one got to be his age—

Maybe it was time to quit. Just quit and retire already. Did Maddox need looking after anymore?

Riker cocked his head.

Maddox sure had needed help last mission. Valerie had done most of it and Riker—he couldn't quit now. Last mission, he'd run out on Maddox. Riker's bionic leg had gotten him out of the muddy predicament, leaving Maddox behind on the planet. It could have been a disaster.

Thinking about it, Riker shoveled harder.

He didn't want to think about how close he'd come to losing Maddox. That wasn't what he wanted to do. He wanted to make sure the youngster—well, Maddox wasn't the young, hotshot, whippersnapper anymore.

Long ago, the chiefs in Intelligence had put him with Maddox to keep a leash on the young tiger, make sure he didn't do anything rash. Not that Riker had ever been able to hamper Maddox when the man got the bit between the teeth. But he'd helped the young rascal. He'd helped the man in more than one scrape.

Riker muttered as he huffed and puffed. He was three-quarters of the way done shoveling the sidewalk.

Why had he made the front sidewalk so long anyway? He had plenty of flowers along the sidewalk—they didn't show now in winter. He had plenty of bushes and trees.

He eyeballed the trees. They were full of snow.

He nodded. He needed to get the stepladder, climb up and shake out all that snow. Otherwise, one of the branches might break under the weight. Then he'd be sawing until he puked.

Riker looked up again. It was snowing less, and the flakes weren't as big as earlier or coming down as fast.

He kept shoveling, throwing the snow to the side. He always did it in the same direction so his back on that side began to ache. He was breathing hard and his one regular arm trembled.

He'd read that the cold made it difficult for the blood to flow in the capillaries. That was why cold old guys died shoveling. It was that and a lack of regular exercise. They didn't get out enough and keep moving.

I need to keep moving.

That was the key to staying young or youngish, or at least not so old and useless. He didn't want to become one of those old farts that just sat around and told stories about what he used to do.

Riker made a face as he reached the end of the white picket fence.

He was proud of the place. Though he was often gone on a mission, he paid kids to keep it up. When he was here he worked it, and he worked it well. It was probably the best-kept cottage on the street. You could ask anyone and they'd agree.

He wasn't going to stop. Yeah, maybe this was his last mission. He would see. Maybe if he became injured or something, but he wasn't just going to quit because he was *old*.

Was being old a crime? It meant you were slower. It meant your muscles were weaker.

Maybe he needed to get in the gym now and again just to keep in shape so he could shovel faster.

He was going back over the sidewalk, scraping where new flakes had fallen. The sound of the metal on cement told him he was getting the job done. He liked getting the job done.

If I retire, I won't get the job done anymore.

He could get a hobby to keep busy. He already grew the best plants.

No, no, you're not Ludendorff. Don't brag. If other people say your plants are good, that's enough, but don't you go telling yourself they're the best. You'll get a big head.

He felt slightly sick and was finished shoveling. It had stopped snowing, too. He was glad about that. Now he could go inside. Now, he would brew the best— He'd brew an enjoyable cup of coffee. He'd start up the fire and prop up his feet.

Riker stepped onto the porch, reached for the door handle and yelped as a ghost oozed out of the front door. The damn thing appeared right in front of him.

Before Riker knew it, he raised the shovel and swung it through the ghost. He inhaled so he could really yell. He wouldn't scream. He was a man and men don't scream, but he would bellow so loud that it might sound similar to a harsh scream.

"I am sorry, Riker. Did I startle you?"

All the energy drained from Sergeant Riker. The shovel fell from his hands and hit the wood of the front porch.

"Galyan?"

"Who else could come out of your door like that, Riker?"

After a second, the old man nodded numbly.

54

Galyan was a holographic image of an Adok. Adoks used to be thought extinct, but weren't anymore because *Victory* and crew had saved the last living Adoks two missions ago in a strange nebula.

Galyan was a small humanoid, had lines in his face and had ropy arms and fingers.

"What are you doing here?"

"I have come to talk to you, Riker. We have need of your assistance, immediately."

"What are you talking about? I'm on leave. The captain is on leave. The ship is supposed to be under repair."

"There has been an emergency. The Lord High Admiral is even now talking to the captain. We are going to—

"Whoa, whoa, whoa," Riker said, interrupting.

The sergeant finally noticed that Galyan didn't wear a parka, and that almost seemed obscene. Galyan just stood there as snowflakes drifted through him.

"Riker, are you listening to me?"

"Yeah, yeah. You were talking with the captain. You're going away. I hope you're not going back into the Deep Beyond where we did last mission."

"No, we are headed for the Trappist-1 System."

"Where's that?"

"40.7 light years from the Solar System."

Riker frowned. "Why is that an emergency? Why would *Victory* go so close to home?"

"That is just it. You will find out when you come aboard."

"I haven't gotten an order." Riker pulled out his comm device, checking. There wasn't any message on it. "You say this is an emergency?"

"I do. The ship is getting ready to leave. The captain is even now finishing his talk with the Lord High Admiral. Afterward, Maddox will use a shuttle to reach *Victory*."

Riker shook his head. "I don't think the captain wants me along this time. I haven't gotten a call at all."

"Oh my," Galyan said. "This is not good. I asked Captain Maddox to take you. I was sure he would listen to me."

"You asked him? You mean Maddox said he wasn't going to do it?"

"Please Riker, you must come. All my friends must be together in one place so I may enjoy your company for as long as it is possible."

Riker scowled. "What are you talking about?"

"Oh, I am sorry. I am not supposed to mention your age. Yes, now I remember Meta telling me that."

"Meta is coming?"

"Did you not hear? She is not invited. Oh, I am not supposed to say that, either."

Riker's eyes widened as he deduced something. "Meta's pregnant?"

"Riker, I did not say that. Do not assume from anything I let drop that it is so. Please, go to the nearest star port, get on a shuttle and head directly to *Victory*. You must leave at once."

"I haven't been summoned. I'm on leave and taking a vacation. You ought to take a vacation, Galyan."

"How can I do that? I am part of the ship."

"Yeah, I keep forgetting that you're—" Riker stopped talking.

"That I am not a living entity? Is that what you think, Riker?"

"No! You're alive. We all know it. You're our good friend."

"And as one friend to another, I am asking you to get on that shuttle. We need you this mission. I know it. I can tell."

Riker stared at Galyan. "Are you running my personality profile?"

"What if I am? What does your personality profile tell me? That you feel guilty for last mission when you ran out on the captain."

"I didn't run out. We were both trying to escape and he fell behind."

"I have read the logs. Yet it is so hard to believe the captain could fall behind while you continued."

"It was because of my bionic limbs and the sticky mud."

"I know I read the report. Did I not say so?"

"This is getting us nowhere. I want my coffee. I want to sit in front of the fire and now I think I want a turkey sandwich. I bought some special imported mustard the other day."

"Riker, please do not go into that. I do not eat like you and it is sometimes difficult to see why you humans spend so much time talking about the preparation of food."

"Yes, because you've never experienced it, which means you don't know everything even though you think you do."

"I don't know everything, but I do know this: you need to come along."

"Fine," Riker said. "I'm going in. That's all."

"Riker, please, this is more than just running your personality profile. You are always on the mission. If you are not on the newest mission, I am afraid there will be unfortunate consequences."

"Are you turning superstitious?" Riker asked.

"What nonsense. Will you do this for me this one time, Sergeant?"

Riker was torn. He wanted to go inside. He was tired and getting cold. Besides, he didn't know if he wanted to go on another mission. His bones ached from shoveling snow. He breathed hard. Yet, if he didn't go, if he stayed home, it would mean he was truly old. It would mean he was finished and that his days of doing things that mattered were over.

Riker shook his head. He still had some fire in the belly. Did it matter the captain hadn't asked for him? Should he barge onto *Victory* and just do a Maddox?

"You are grinning," Galyan said. "I will go and tell the captain you are coming."

"Now wait a minute. I didn't..." Riker stopped. If anyone knew him, it was this alien AI entity. That was partly because Galyan ran his damn personality profile and had been doing it for so long on each of them. The Adok entity knew them better than anyone. That was crazy. A computer. No, Galyan was more than a computer—

"All right, Galyan. I'll do it for you."

"Thank you, Riker. I appreciate this. I do not think you will regret it."

"But don't tell Maddox until I get there. That way, he can't do anything to stop me coming."

"Do you think he would do that?"

"Run your dang personality profiles and see."

"Oh, my. Yes, I see. That is wise, not to mention this."

"I think so."

"All right. Goodbye for now."

Riker held his tongue further until Galyan disappeared. He went inside, set his shovel to the side and kicked off his rubber boots.

Riker was having second thoughts. If the captain hadn't called him, there was probably a reason for that. Maddox didn't commit such oversight. It was always for a purpose. Yet Riker had given his word, and he wanted to keep his word.

Riker shrugged.

Maybe God was using Galyan and there was something important Riker needed to do this mission. Maybe if he wasn't there, Maddox wouldn't make it back and that would be tragic, as Meta was pregnant again, it seemed.

That determined it for Riker. Even though he grumbled under his breath, he began to rush about gathering the items he'd need, putting them into his kit.

He called for an air car, as he needed to get to the spaceport now. Maddox was in a hurry—

Riker cocked his head.

Why did he think Maddox was in a hurry? Maybe there was some kind of connection between him and the captain. It was hard to believe, but Riker felt he needed to get a move on, and thus, he did.

-9-

Maddox was aboard a shuttle heading upstairs for *Victory*. He was a lean, tall man of indeterminable age.

He'd talked with the Lord High Admiral concerning the parameters of the mission. Afterward, on the shuttle, he'd spoken with Galyan. Galyan had asked for Riker, but Riker was on leave and—

The truth was that Riker was getting long in the tooth. Last mission, if Riker hadn't escaped onto the *Tarrypin*, would he have been able to do everything he had on the planet? Riker might have slowed him down, maybe gotten in the way.

Therefore, Maddox didn't make the call. It troubled him a little, but hey, life marched on and Riker could take care of himself. Better that the man has the chance to enjoy his retirement. They could always reminisce over drinks between missions.

Maddox peered through a port window and saw the double-oval ancient Adok starship. This time, the mission was close to home. Meta could hardly complain about that. A little science observation and that would be it. It seemed unlikely the asteroidal supership was still in the Trappist-1 System. If it were, he'd use the star-drive jump and get out of the way. Then, Star Watch could fill the system with warships and hunt down the intruder.

Soon enough, the shuttle docked, Maddox exited and found himself on the bridge in the captain's chair. Everything was in order. So he gave the command to head for the nexus.

Keith gave the aye-aye and set the new heading.

Maddox checked a chronometer. They had forty-five minutes before launch. He immersed himself in double-checking personnel and going to each bridge station, clapping the officer on the shoulder and telling him or her he was glad they were back. Afterward, he found that Valerie was on her way with the *Tarrypin*. He received another update from Pluto, but there was no change in status in the Trappist-1 System.

Galyan popped into existence beside the chair. Maddox had gotten used to the surprise and merely nodded a greeting.

"I hope I did not startle you, sir."

"Do I look startled?"

Several bridge personnel smiled at the exchange.

"No sir, you do not. How many more minutes until the nexus gives us the go-ahead?"

Maddox raised an eyebrow. "Are you questioning me?"

"I am sorry, sir. I do not mean to imply you do not know your job. Everyone knows you do."

"What is it, Galyan? You've obviously come to pester me about something."

"I am not sure if you know...but perhaps it does not matter."

"What doesn't matter?"

"Are all personnel aboard?"

"Enough with the questioning. Make your point."

"I went to see Sergeant Riker, sir."

"You did what?"

"I thought you'd forgotten to order the sergeant to head for *Victory*. Thus, I did so."

"Galyan, I didn't call Riker because he's on leave. He needs more rest than he used to. You should have let him be. Hopefully, he was smart enough to stay home."

"Sir, I feel I should inform you that he is on a shuttle heading for *Victory*. It is possible he is running a little late. Thus, I would ask you to wait so Riker can get aboard."

Maddox stared at Galyan. "Let me get this straight. I'm supposed to put the mission on hold in order to wait for Riker?"

"Please," Galyan said.

"All right, I'll bite. Although you lack the authority to do so, why did you call Riker and tell him to come aboard?"

"Because he should be aboard the starship," Galyan said.

"Wait a minute. Take a look at this," Maddox said, pointing at his own insignia. "Who's the captain of the ship?"

"You are, sir."

"Are you sure?"

"I am," Galyan said.

"I choose who to summon or not."

"Yes sir, I know."

"You don't choose."

"That is why I am asking you, sir."

"No, Galyan. You're trying to force my hand."

"Only a little," Galyan said.

Maddox frowned. "I'm not in the habit of explaining my decisions. This is clearly a scientific mission where we're trying to figure out an anomaly. In case you don't know, that isn't Sergeant Riker's specialty."

"That is correct. Keeping you alive is his specialty, sir."

"Me alive. Are you out of your mind?"

Abruptly, Maddox realized it was a sore point with him that Riker had run out on him last mission. Was that coloring his view now?

"Why do you want Riker along anyway?"

"I did not think you would object, sir."

"Yes, you did. That's why you waited until the last minute. That's why you appeared just now. You and your blasted personality profile—I'm getting tired of it."

"Yes sir," Galyan said, standing at attention.

Maddox had what he might have called half an intuitive decision as some of his Balron-trained instincts kicked in. There was something more going on here. He didn't know what exactly…

"You really want Riker along?"

"I have determined it is going to be important for Riker to be with us this mission."

"Care to tell me why?"

"Sir, do you think a computer can have intuition?"

"No, I do not."

"In truth, I do not either, sir, and yet that is the case. I have an intuition—a hunch, I would say—that you are going to need Riker this mission."

"That's a load of horse manure, Galyan."

"I do not lie, sir."

Maddox raised an eyebrow.

"I do not lie to my friends," Galyan amended.

Maddox thought about it and shrugged. Did it really matter one way or another if Riker was aboard? He usually ended up using the sergeant because the man was useful—even if he was slowing down.

"Okay Galyan, I'll wait if he can get here within," Maddox checked his chronometer, "the next ten minutes. Can he?"

Galyan's eyelids fluttered. "Could you wait twelve minutes, sir? I would appreciate it and take it as a personal favor if you would do so."

"Fine, fine," Maddox said, "a personal favor. I'm giving you fifteen minutes, as a personal favor. Are you happy?"

"Yes, Captain, I am. I appreciate it and I hope that you will, too, by the end of the mission."

"Sure, I already appreciate it. Now stand by, I may have further questions for you."

"Yes sir."

Maddox sat back in his chair, waited and watched. It gave him a few minutes to himself. He recalled that his last leave he'd read about the Texas Rangers from ancient history in America. The Rangers had fascinated him how they'd dealt with the Comanches, the greatest light horse Red Indians ever. He'd marveled at the Comanche braves, their tenacity and will to fight. The Comanches had stopped the Spanish and French in their efforts to build an empire in the middle of North America before the eighteenth century. But the Texas Rangers had been something else. They'd emerged while Texas was its own nation: a small band of rugged warriors who studied the enemy and used every trick in the book to defeat them.

Well, all that and the repeating rifle.

I'm like a Texas Ranger, a man who gets the job done with a handful of people any way he can. That and the best starship in the fleet. That's my repeating rifle.

Maddox checked the chronometer again. Time was almost up for Riker.

"The nexus is calling, sir. They're ready."

"This minute?" asked Maddox.

"Yes sir."

Maddox checked the chronometer again. Several minutes had passed since he'd talked to Galyan. Should he wait the entire fifteen as promised? He said he would and thus he would. But he wouldn't wait a second more. If Riker couldn't make it by then...he'd leave the old duffer behind.

-10-

Before Galyan went to speak to Maddox, Professor Ludendorff tossed and turned on a couch in one of the lounge areas of *Victory*. He was asleep and dreaming.

He was also a Methuselah Man, which meant he was much older than everyone else on the starship except for Galyan. The AI entity was six thousand years old in one sense. Ludendorff wasn't anything approaching that, yet he was a Methuselah Man and was much older than Sergeant Riker, say. Yet, Ludendorff didn't have any of the leathery coarseness of that old fool. Instead, with his eyes shut and with quite a self-satisfied smile, Professor Ludendorff was a handsome older man with silver hair. The first few buttons of his shirt were undone and it revealed a gold chain around his neck and tanned skin with a lot of white hair on his chest.

Ludendorff was proud of the curly chest hair. In his dream, he was prouder still because he didn't wear any clothes.

The Methuselah Man hadn't meant to go to sleep. He'd come aboard as ordered, sat down here and had just conked out because he was bushed. That had produced REM sleep.

He dreamed. He loved it, too, because he dreamed of Dana Rich, his former babe of a girlfriend and common law wife.

In the dream, Dana approached in similar attire as he. She was a dark-skinned Indian, dot not feather, from Brahma and was beautiful to behold.

Ludendorff grinned with anticipation as Dana approached. He hadn't seen her for quite some time.

Now, he'd known many beautiful women in his time. Ludendorff was a connoisseur if ever there was one. In truth, he was the greatest lover in the galaxy, always satisfying—in his opinion, at least—his lovely partners.

As Dana approached, he wanted to speak to her. Where had she been all this time? Why had she stayed away for so long?

Ludendorff beckoned her to hurry.

The weird thing was that as Dana approach, she didn't look at him, but beyond, as if there were something more interesting behind him.

That was frustrating in every sense of the word, as Ludendorff yearned to embrace sweet Dana, his dusky beauty, and he found that he couldn't turn around to see what held her attention.

Not only was Dana Rich beautiful, she was smart. And not smart in a smarmy way indulging in frivolities. She was smart like a scientist, somebody he could actually hold a conversation with, which was always a plus—after the beauty, of course.

Ludendorff struggled to call her name. He *wanted* to call her name. He'd missed Dana for years. Many times, he'd thought about going to see her. Damned Maddox kept telling him he should seek out Dana, propose and marry her legally.

Sergeant Riker was the same kind of fuddy-duddy, believing in old-fashioned morality: one man, one woman and the family they raised.

Mind you, Maddox and others seemed happy enough with the old-style arrangement, but Ludendorff was a man of greater taste, flexibility and constant need. Couldn't they see that? Women loved him. They loved his way and he loved them right back.

"Dana," he shouted, in his dream.

Because of the dream-shout, the worst thing of all happened. Ludendorff woke up.

The Methuselah Man's eyes flashed open. He looked around with amazement and realized this wasn't the boudoir with hangings portraits showing him in heroic poses. There was no huge waterbed to the side and mirrors all around and on the ceiling. This wasn't where a sky-clad Dana approached him.

Ludendorff looked around and saw the lounge couches and observation window. The Earth, the North Pole down there—

"A dream," Ludendorff said bitterly. "I was having a dream. Dana isn't here."

He sat up, checking himself.

He was fully clothed, which included his customary white lab coat.

He blinked and shook his head. "Dana," he whispered.

There was an inner ache. He hated it.

With both hands, he rubbed his face.

He didn't just miss their sexual encounters. They were great, of course. They'd been stupendous, in fact. The world would probably like to take notes, if they could. Other men could learn from him how to satisfy a woman. He was the best.

Ludendorff smiled ruefully at the thought.

Was it bragging if it was the truth? Some people thought so. Maddox and the other traditionalists, blowhards and try-hards—

Ludendorff shook his head angrily. He missed Dana. Dreaming about her—he *yearned* for Dana, to hold her, whisper in her ear.

Maybe it was time to leave Star Watch to go and find her.

Ludendorff thought about that. It caused him to think about something else. He was a scientist above all, a man of brilliance who achieved breakthrough inventions. What was he doing on a Star Watch warship, always answering everyone's questions and producing the miracle techs that solved all the hard problems? He needed to be achieving again in matters of brilliant science, making a dent in technological history.

Ludendorff frowned.

He'd loved Dana once, but she'd run out on him. She'd had her chance. Dreaming about her didn't mean squat. It didn't mean he desperately missed her, wanted her to be his wife and would spend the rest of their days together.

"Enough of this."

Ludendorff rose, heading for a restroom. There, he took a whiz and scrubbed his face with hot water and soap. Once finished, he headed down a corridor.

He was in a foul mood.

Soon enough, Ludendorff waltzed onto the bridge, not bothering to ask for permission. That was for peasants and underlings. He was a unique auxiliary on the starship. No, he wasn't an auxiliary. That indicated they could get along without him. He was the key component to solving practically every crisis. Take just one example: hadn't Maddox run to him to fix Galyan when no one else could?

"Captain," he said, so sharply every head whipped around to stare at him. Ludendorff had a commanding voice and knew it. It had made him a dazzling university lecturer.

Maddox frowned at him.

Did the captain sense he was in one of his moods? *Not moods*, Ludendorff corrected. *I'm seeing reality. I've been fooling myself for too many years.*

"Captain," Ludendorff said again.

"Hold it, Professor," Maddox stood and then he did an unusual thing. He made a grand bow, sweeping his right arm like a courtier. It was a mocking gesture. "The mighty Professor Ludendorff—welcome onto my bridge, sir."

Ludendorff blinked in surprise. "Are you making fun of me?"

"How clever of you to notice." Maddox's manner hardened. "When you come onto my bridge, sir, you'll take the proper tone and attitude. Is that understood?"

Ludendorff almost spun around and walked out. Wouldn't that show everyone? Perhaps the only thing that stopped him was the knowledge that Maddox might get so miffed he'd throw him into the brig. The captain had been checking his chronometer in a manner that indicated *he* might be in a mood as well.

Ludendorff was the world's premiere realist, after all. He prided himself on his realistic outlook, not on rank emotionalism. Thus, he decided to trim his sails, as they say, and await a propitious moment to get his revenge for this heaped indignity by Maddox.

"It is your bridge, sir. I recognize that and I recognize you often come to me for explanations and results nobody else can give you."

Maddox eyed him before sitting back in the captain's chair. Perhaps the half-breed wasn't going to make a point of pushing his authority further. That was likely good for both of them.

Still, Ludendorff seethed inwardly. "May I ask, *sir,* are we about to leave?"

Maddox looked at him before saying, "Galyan, could you show the professor the newest data we received about the Trappist-1 System."

"But we haven't received anything new," Galyan said, floating nearer.

Maddox nodded. "Professor, have you studied the original data?"

"Yes, yes, yes, of course I have."

Maddox's features became stiff.

Ludendorff looked away. He'd better be careful how he expressed his foul mood. It was that damned dream. He wanted to embrace Dana. No pale-skinned woman was going to fill the void, either. He wanted Dana Rich. He...noticed Maddox staring at him.

"I've studied the relevant data," Ludendorff said. "I can't tell you the origin of the asteroidal starship because I don't know it. Possibly, we witnessed some kind of new long-distance drive like our hyper-spatial tube. That seems the most likely explanation." He shrugged. "Perhaps it was some kind of time continuum tube. We did face that in the Library Planet System where you went aboard the strange Ardazirho vessel. I'm uncertain, though. The situation strikes me as grave. I'll do my best to figure it out the moment I receive enough relevant data. Until then, perhaps I should leave you to *your* bridge."

"Professor," Galyan said, "are you feeling well?"

"I'm feeling perfectly fit." Ludendorff clapped his hand against his chest.

"You do not seem perfectly fit," Galyan said. "You seem agitated. Is there a reason for your agitation?"

"Not now, Galyan," Ludendorff said. "If you pester me and tell me this and tell me that, and ask me your supposedly probing but in reality annoying questions, I won't bring you around the next time you're deactivated."

"I do not ask this out of ill will," Galyan said. "I am concerned for you. You seem most agitated. You seem unhappy."

"Captain, is Galyan going to continue to pester me?"

When no answer was forthcoming, Ludendorff turned to Maddox. The captain stared at him with a distressingly penetrating expression, as if Maddox could see through him.

That was too much.

"I've had enough of you people probing into my personal life," Ludendorff said. "It's my personal life and I don't want anyone probing into it. How can any of you understand a Methuselah Man? I've lived far longer than any of you."

"Not longer than I, Professor," Galyan said. "I have lived far longer than you and I do not have these pretentions such as you do."

"Oh, and you don't miss your former wife?" Ludendorff said.

Galyan stared a moment before his features crumpled. He turned and floated away.

Maddox stared at Ludendorff.

Ludendorff felt uncomfortable under the scrutiny. He knew he'd gone too far. He'd done something few of them could. He'd hurt Galyan's feelings, perhaps even wounded Galyan. He'd brought up the sorest subject for the AI entity. Galyan longed for his lost wife of six thousand years ago when he'd been a flesh and blood Adok.

Ludendorff almost called out and said he was sorry. A hardened part of him, that stubborn knot in the center, welled up and refused to do it. Galyan had probed into his personal affairs. Galyan wouldn't give it up, either.

"Was that truly necessary, Professor?" Maddox asked.

Ludendorff mumbled something under his breath. He shouldn't have said what he did to Galyan, but he wasn't going to apologize for it. If they tried to force him to apologize, he was going to leave the ship and then he was going to go back to the fourth planet of the Omicron 9 System. He was tired of people forcing their views on him.

"Professor, why don't you take a walk," Maddox said. "Go be yourself elsewhere."

"Are you *ordering* me off the bridge," Ludendorff said.

"I am not, sir. I'm making a suggestion you would be wise to take. Is there anything I can do for you?"

Ludendorff opened his mouth and almost let fly with all kinds of invectives against the captain. Maddox was feeling sorry for him. Ludendorff could feel it. Oh, why did he have to dream of Dana the way he had. He needed to figure out what the dream meant.

"We're about to leave orbit and the star system," Maddox checked his chronometer, "as soon as Riker boards."

"What?" Ludendorff said. "Riker's not aboard."

"He'd better be in the next few minutes."

Ludendorff saw his path. "Perhaps I can use his shuttle then. There's something I need to take care of on Earth."

Maddox stood and did something most unusual. He reached out and he put a hand on Ludendorff's left shoulder.

"I need you aboard ship, Professor. I need you to help me figure out what happened to Task Force 3 and the people on Zinc. I suspect Star Watch needs your help on this. I'm formally asking you to remain and help us with the mission."

The gesture and the way Maddox asked it could have sent Ludendorff into a fit of rage. Instead, on some level, it must have touched the man. He nodded.

"Help you I will." Afterward, Ludendorff shrugged off the captain's hand.

Maddox sat back down in the captain's chair.

Ludendorff turned away. He saw Galyan and almost apologized. He knew he should.

The stubborn core intervened again. *Why don't they apologize to me?* With that, Ludendorff rushed off the bridge, maybe ashamed for the way he'd acted, certainly missing Dana Rich. The best solution would be to throw himself into his work.

-11-

Maddox learned that Riker's shuttle had landed, deposited him and then left. He told Galyan the news, hoping to cheer him up.

"Thank you, sir," Galyan said.

Maddox almost said more. Instead, he gave the order to the nexus and then to Keith.

Soon, *Victory* moved into the newly created hyper-spatial-tube opening. In an instant, the starship catapulted 40.7 light years into the Trappist-1 System. This was practically in Earth's backyard.

Maddox had decided to come in a little beyond the midpoint between destroyed Zinc and the fourth planet Cobalt. That would give them plenty of distance in case the supership was hiding near the planetary rubble.

After shrugging off the lag that always accompanied such a transition, *Victory* began to move toward the destroyed planet. The starship did so slowly.

Galyan used the vessel's sensors through his AI system. Andros Crank, the pudgy Kai-Kaus Chief Technician, sat at his science board on the bridge. Like Galyan, Andros searched for anomalies to explain what the Long-Range Builder Scanner had cataloged earlier. Ludendorff used various equipment to do the same in his science chamber.

Valerie suggested she take out the *Tarrypin*, searching ahead of the starship.

"We'll use our sensors to check what's out there and not put anybody in unnecessary danger." A moment later, Maddox added, "Although I do appreciate the offer."

Valerie nodded stiffly. She was still smarting from Maddox's highhanded action last mission when he'd overridden her and taken the *Tarrypin* into the dampened system himself.

Soon, Maddox asked Andros for an initial report even though Galyan was beside him with his holoimage eyelids flickering rapidly. That indicated his AI systems were running at high speed.

"Except for the rubble of the destroyed planet," Andros said, "everything is what you'd expect from the Trappist-1 System. The red dwarf puts out a minimal amount of energy. There are three terrestrial inner planets. There are seven outer planets, all of them uninhabited by any mining corporation people. There are Carstair Metals people on Cobalt and as far as I've been able to determine on the first planet Argon. That planet is much like Mercury in the Solar System."

"Do you detect any anomalies, any enemy tracks or stealth vessels?" Maddox asked.

"I have not yet detected such," Andros said.

Galyan's eyelids quit flickering. "I am sorry, Andros. I have detected some anomalies."

"Oh?" Andros said.

"In the rubble of Zinc are manifestations of some…things. I am unable as yet determine their precise purpose."

"Big things like ships or fighters?" Maddox asked.

"No," Galyan said, "smaller, much smaller, approximately the size of your fist."

Maddox thought about that. The enemy had appeared, destroyed warships, outposts, disappeared a task force and then blew apart a planet. The enemy used unknown technology and had possibly left something behind in the planetary rubble.

Vigilance was in order.

Victory continued its slow crawl as the sensors probed for more data.

The planetary rubble wasn't like Galyan's destroyed planet of long ago. Those pieces had been smaller, sometimes fine

72

dust. Here they were massive, continental-sized chunks, along with finer debris.

Andros informed Maddox that mixed with everything else were minimal amounts of biological debris. That was probably the fifteen million dead humans and their plants and animals.

"Sir," Andros said, "Some people said the asteroidal supership had a compressed-stardust hull. I wonder if that's what Galyan and I are detecting in the rubble."

"Compressed stardust," Maddox said, bemused. "What is that supposed to mean?"

"Sir?" asked Andros.

"Are you telling me the dust is from a star?"

Andros blinked several times.

"A star is seething energy and superheated matter," Maddox said, "anything but *dust.*"

"I suspect we're saying this is some kind of compressed material from a burnt-out star," Andros said, "from its cooled core."

"You're saying this dust is incredibly dense?"

"It is that," Andros said.

"And yet according to what I saw in the video, the battleship beams burned through it."

"Burned into the hull a few meters," Andros said. "I saw that, too."

"Would something so dense react to disruptor beams that way?"

Andros stroked his chin. "We'd need samples to run tests to know."

Maddox nodded. That made sense. That was why they were here. They needed to slip into the rubble and extract what these two had found. "Are there any mines you can detect?"

"Sir," Galyan said, "certainly we will announce mines or drifting warheads the instant we spot them. Do you feel we are being derelict in our duty and keeping silent about such things?"

Maddox scowled.

"I am sorry, sir," Galyan said. "You do not care for anyone to question you while we are under combat conditions, and you deem this to be combat conditions. Do you not, sir?"

Maddox stared at Galyan.

"Galyan," Andros said, "you're still questioning the captain under combat conditions."

"Oh," Galyan said, "I do not mean to do that."

Maddox looked away at the main screen. He didn't want to discuss it. He just wanted them to do as told and not question him.

He sat back, thinking. For the next several hours, they'd continue the crawl. He'd give his science people time to study the situation from afar.

Thus, for the next two hours, *Victory* maintained its present velocity. At their present speed, it would take the starship weeks to reach the rubble.

Maddox said, "I want a continual wide scan around the broken planet. Make it fifteen million kilometers around. I want to know if anything indicates the phenomenon we witnessed through the Long-Range Builder Scanner video. Galyan, do you have any idea what that was?"

"The black opening that swallowed the task force and then the supership?" asked Galyan.

"Yes."

"I agree with Professor Ludendorff's analysis earlier. It was something on the order of a hyper-spatial tube. I am not saying it *was* a hyper-spatial tube, but I believe it was a form of faster travel. By that, I mean a corridor like a Laumer Point wormhole."

"Where do you think the alien opening sent Task Force 3?"

"That is unknown, sir, as I have no idea what type of portal we are dealing with."

Maddox was getting antsy sitting and waiting like this. His New Man heritage stirred him to always want to act. He'd had enough thinking about this for now.

"I'm going to the gym."

At the starship's gym, Maddox felt deadlifts would take too much nervous energy. He'd bench press instead.

He went to the bench, warmed up and then put on a good amount of weight. He did a set of five reps. Instead of feeling tired, he felt invigorated.

He waited and did another set, jumping up and clapping his hands afterward.

Now he felt ready for some action. After waiting and doing a third set, he went to the shower and then got some grub.

From the cafeteria, Maddox returned to the bridge. Nothing had changed.

"I have an idea," Galyan said. "I hasten to add that it is not a question. I wonder if there are any survivors from Zinc. Could a human have survived the destruction of a planet?"

"That's a question," Maddox said.

"Yes, but it is not a question regarding your command techniques or your decisions."

"Fair enough," Maddox said. "I find the possibility highly doubtful, but I take your meaning. We should head there quickly to see if anyone needs rescuing."

"Sir," Andros said swiveling around from his science station. "I know that's a merciful suggestion, and I think it's a good one, but we should also be cautious. An entire task force has vanished. We're here because HQ dare not send anybody else."

"Kept a sharp eye out then," Maddox said, "because we're going in. Get moving."

Victory accelerated for the planetary rubble.

Were there survivors? That seemed doubtful to Maddox. Had the enemy left traps? That seemed more likely. Was the enemy going to be waiting in order to ambush them? That would really depend on what the asteroidal supership had been trying to do. One suggestion had been it was reenergizing itself.

Maddox shook his head. He didn't know. Thus, it was best to keep an open mind and a wary eye. There would come a moment where he'd have to take a risk if he wanted to find out what happened.

He made a fist. He wasn't going to lose the starship, and hopefully no personnel either. That meant vigilance, intelligence and the best use of his crew.

Maddox sat back, flexing his pectorals. He stopped when he noticed one of the women watching. He tried to stay still, waiting now to get into range of the rubble.

-12-

Victory came to within thirty million kilometers of the planetary rubble. The pieces continued along the normal orbital path and thus had already moved from where the alien supership had appeared.

Maddox, Ludendorff and Galyan were in the professor's science chamber. Ludendorff had set up huge screens so he could view any data sent from the Long-Range Builder Scanner on Pluto. The screens were hooked through the Long-Range Builder Comm device aboard *Victory*.

The three of them watched a recording of the task force and supership disappearing into the extraordinary blackness, and then that blackness fading to normal-colored space.

When the recording finished, Maddox turned to Ludendorff. "What have you discovered so far?"

"It's clearly a portal, but a portal to where? It doesn't look or act as a hyper-spatial-tube opening. It doesn't seem to be a wormhole opening like a Laumer Point. And it doesn't...project them the way we were when we leapt to the Scutum-Centaurus Spiral Arm from the Alpha Centauri System."

"I agree," Galyan said.

Ludendorff barely glanced at Galyan.

The AI and Ludendorff were cool toward each other even as they observed the data.

"What about the planet or its rubble?" Maddox asked. "Have we learned anything new?"

76

Galyan's eyelids began to flutter.

Ludendorff moved his hands through the air, changing the view on the screens. They focused on the great planetary chunks that moved and twisted in a mass. There was finer debris and clouds of dust and gases. The whole had an oval shape. It seemed that the gravitational force of the mass kept everything relatively together.

"This device," Ludendorff said, touching a monitor, "measured the power of the enemy's gravitational beams. They were magnificent."

"You applaud what they did?" Galyan asked.

Ludendorff frowned. "I mean the grav beams unleashed tremendous power. Magnificent is the wrong adjective. Clearly, the aliens used technology we're not yet capable of employing. It was more than a pressor beam, which is the opposite of a tractor beam."

"I am well aware of what a pressor beam is," Galyan said.

"Yes, yes, of course," Ludendorff said. "I meant nothing by it."

Although Galyan had spoken, his eyelids continued to flicker.

"Have you detected anything dangerous within the rubble?" Maddox asked Ludendorff.

"Dangerous? I don't know. There are a few alien items sprinkled throughout the blasted mass."

"Do you suggest we retrieve them?" Maddox asked.

Ludendorff raised his eyebrows. "Of course I suggest that. That's why we're here, isn't it? We're attempting to figure out what happened. We can't do that until we know the aliens better. The items are a means to that end."

Maddox listened, thinking.

"You don't think so?" Ludendorff asked.

"Eh?" Maddox looked up, and smiled faintly. "Thank you, Professor. I appreciate your suggestions. Galyan, come with me."

"You're welcome," Ludendorff said. "What are we going to do next?"

"I have decided yet," Maddox said. "Good day, Professor."

77

Maddox and Galyan departed the science chamber, heading back for the bridge.

Maddox glanced sidelong at the floating holoimage. "Have you found anything that could give us some indication concerning the aliens?"

"I have not, sir. I am sorry."

"Don't be sorry. Just keep looking and tell me when you do."

"Yes sir."

Two hours later, Galyan appeared beside Maddox as he sat in a cafeteria drinking coffee.

"I may have found something, sir."

"Yes?" Maddox said.

"I believe I have found an intact responder from Outpost 3. The personnel there first spoke with the aliens in the fighter craft."

"How do we know any of this?"

"We have been receiving information from colonists on Cobalt."

"I wasn't aware of any colonists on the fourth planet."

"That was an oversight on my part. They are mining operatives for the Carstair Consortium."

"Oh. This responder—it's in the rubble?"

"Yes sir."

"You think we should retrieve and listen to it."

"I most certainly do, sir. Outpost 3 had first contact with the aliens. If they indeed did speak with them, perhaps we will learn something more."

"Agreed," Maddox said. "Good work, Galyan."

"Thank you, sir."

Maddox got up, hurrying to the bridge, deciding how to do this. "Lieutenant, it's time to fly your fold fighter." He told Keith about the responder that needed picking up in the rubble.

"Sir," Valerie said. She happened to be on the bridge. "Doesn't it seem reckless to fold among constantly shifting debris? Why not send the *Tarrypin?* It would be easier for me to dodge something if I saw it shifting toward the ship."

Maddox could see she had a point and that bothered him. Not that Valerie had corrected him, but that he hadn't seen the possibilities.

Maddox nodded. "Lieutenant Commander, I'd like you to collect the responder."

"Gladly, Captain," Valerie said.

"Wait a minute," Keith said. "That's my job."

"Not now, Lieutenant," Maddox said. "I changed my mind. The commander is going."

Keith made a face until he looked at Valerie, pasting on a quick grin. "Do you need a pilot?"

"No," Valerie said. "The *Tarrypin* is fully crewed. We'll have no problems." She saluted Maddox. "I'll return with the responder, sir."

"Glad to hear it," Maddox said.

Valerie exited the bridge.

As she left, Galyan disappeared and went into ghost mode. That meant his holoimage was nearly impossible to see. He could go invisible, but then his optical sensors wouldn't work.

Galyan did this because through the ship's interior security cameras, he saw Sergeant Riker knock on Ludendorff's science chamber hatch.

Why would Riker do that? Ludendorff and he were not friends and seldom saw eye to eye. They were more like cat and dog, natural enemies.

Galyan went into ghost mode, inserting himself within a bulkhead of the professor's science chamber. The security cameras did not work in the science chamber. Ludendorff had seen to that.

Galyan poked his head through just enough to watch and hear what the two were doing and saying.

"Professor, do you have a moment?"

Ludendorff turned around. "Who let you in?"

"I knocked."

"And I didn't answer."

"So, I let myself in," Riker said.

"You're in, and by your stance it looks like you have something to say."

Riker nodded. "You'd be wise to take what I say to heart."

"You're going to lecture me, are you?"

"It's not so much a lecture as a word of wisdom."

"Aha," Ludendorff said. "Wisdom? You've going to spout off wisdom, to me? This ought to be amusing."

Riker shook his head. "I don't know what's gotten into you, Professor. I'm sure you have plenty of emotions and motives surging through you. You're an intelligent man. We all know that."

"Don't try to butter me up. It's not going to help any."

"All I'm saying is I heard what happened when you spoke those cruel words to Galyan on the bridge."

Ludendorff scowled. "Did the little AI send you?"

"No."

Ludendorff raised his eyebrows. "Then I don't understand what this has to do with you."

"We're all in this together. A smoothly functioning crew is better than a badly functioning crew. Wouldn't you agree?"

Ludendorff stared at him.

Riker sighed. "Why not climb down your high horse and apologize to Galyan. What will it hurt you?"

"Apologize. Apologize for *what?* Galyan was coming at me. I don't like people coming at me. He found out what happened."

"That you use your words to wound him?" Riker asked.

"If that was what it took to make him back off, then yes."

Riker shook his head.

Galyan did not think Riker was angry. The sergeant almost seemed amused, and maybe the professor recognized that.

"Get out of here," Ludendorff said. "I don't want you in my science chamber."

"All right. You're not going to listen. I think that's a mistake, but you're your own man. In case you change your mind, we're here and we're your friends."

"I've helped you and the captain in the past, and what kind of thanks do I get? I get these lecturing talks from you. What do you know? You're just a sergeant. You're an old sergeant who should retire. Why are you even on this ship?"

Riker nodded. "Something is eating at you. I suspect I know what it is."

"Get out of here," Ludendorff shouted. "I don't want to hear it."

Riker's nostrils flared and perhaps there was animosity building in him. If so, he swallowed it, said good day and limped out of the chamber.

Galyan wondered about that. Why was Riker limping?

Galyan eased out of the bulkhead and soon appeared beside Riker.

"Why are you limping, Riker?"

The sergeant stopped and looked up fast.

"I am sorry." Galyan said. "I am always coming up on people unannounced."

"Maybe if you whistled to announce your coming, it wouldn't be so bad."

"That is a good idea. I shall do that in the future, but why are you limping?"

"Shoveling snow," Riker said. "It was harder than I realized and the professor is right. My joints are aching because I'm old."

"The professor was right? What does that mean?"

"Are you really asking me that after you eavesdropped on our conversation?"

"How could you possibly know?" Galyan asked.

Riker tapped the brow above his bionic eye. "You forget that I see better than most, and I clearly saw you."

Galyan nodded. "Thank you for what you said to the professor. It is kind of you to worry about me."

"Hey, you're my friend. You wanted me on this mission. And you know, despite what Ludendorff said, I enjoy the missions and feel more invigorated during them. I don't feel so useless. I am getting old. Maybe I should have them remove my old joints and replace them with bionic parts."

"You would not enjoy being more of a machine."

"You're probably right."

"What should I do about the professor?"

Riker shrugged. "The professor is on edge. Something is bothering him."

"I know."

"Your personality profile on him?"

Galyan nodded.

"I hope it doesn't bother you too much what he said."

"I do not like to think about it because there is an ache if I do."

"Then don't," Riker said.

"It would be easier if I were friends with the other Adoks. Why doesn't the captain try to integrate me into Adok society?"

"Are you kidding me? The captain's plate is full. He'll try if he gets the opportunity. Have no doubt about that."

"Will he take the time to make the time?"

Riker shrugged.

"Thank you again," Galyan said.

Soon thereafter, Riker limped to his quarters.

Galyan remained in the corridor, thinking about what Riker had said. He used his AI functions to analyze theories on apologies. They were unsatisfactory. Thus, he decided to look into the book Maddox liked: the Bible. Galyan read certain passages on forgiveness. As he read, he discovered that bitterness, holding a grudge often ate against the person doing the holding.

Galyan found that interesting.

He had a grudge against the professor for saying what he had. Would that embitter him? Perhaps if he forgave the professor it would rid him of the anger. Then, maybe, he wouldn't feel the pain of the loss of his wife so much?

"I must test this theory," Galyan said.

He disappeared. He did not pop into the science chamber. Instead, he whistled as he came through the bulkhead.

Ludendorff whirled around. "You! You're not supposed to be here. I didn't give you permission to enter."

"I simply want to say that I forgive you for the words you spoke against me on the bridge."

"Against you?" Ludendorff shouted.

"I am not trying to create an argument. I am apologizing for coming at you so that you felt compelled to retaliate in such a cruel manner. I am sorry and I do not plan to do it again. Would you forgive me for that?"

Ludendorff stared at Galyan. His face turned red. He puffed out his chest and squared his shoulders as if in rage. He opened his mouth…and then his shoulders deflated and the red dissipated from his face. He nodded.

"Yes. I do forgive you. I'm sorry for what I said to you, too, Galyan."

Afterward, Ludendorff scowled thunderously at the floor. He scowled and inside him there seethed this…pride, arrogance. He didn't want to ask Galyan for forgiveness. He'd said he was sorry. Wasn't that enough?

"It is fine, Professor. I understand."

Ludendorff looked up sharply. He should just say the words and get it over with.

"I will see you later, Professor."

Ludendorff watched as Galyan floated through the wall, disappearing.

He wondered at the ache in his chest.

"Bah!" Ludendorff said. "It doesn't mean a damn thing. He's just a machine, an AI, a computer with engrams. He mimics human life. That's all. This is nothing to be concerned about."

Still, a part of him wondered that if that was so, why couldn't he have asked for forgiveness? It was like asking a chair for forgiveness. It meant nothing.

Ludendorff scowled and turned back to the screens. He didn't want to think about it. This was nonsense. Besides, he'd said he was sorry. That was good enough.

Therefore, the starship continued as Galyan felt better and Ludendorff continued to fume.

-13-

Valerie sat in the commander's chair on the small bridge of the *Tarrypin*. It was a delta-wing vessel with a crew of four. It was much bigger than a shuttle, far smaller than a destroyer and smaller than the *Kit Carson* that Valerie had once commanded. She was a lieutenant commander and not strictly under Captain Maddox's authority as a crewmember. She had independent command of the *Tarrypin,* receiving mission orders from Maddox.

Some time ago, she'd made the conscious decision to accept a lesser command with a smaller patrol vessel because *Victory* went to the most unusual places and had the most interesting assignments. Valerie felt that she would learn the most and do the most as a lieutenant commander assigned to *Victory*.

Valerie told herself that her present assignment proved her right. While she was a good combat officer, that wasn't her first love. It was science experiments and exploration. True, they were in the middle of the Commonwealth, but she was doing something different. She was approaching the strewn rubble of a newly destroyed planet.

On the main screen, she viewed the mass of wreckage. Huge chunks of surface, mantle, core and cooled lava drifted together.

The *Tarrypin* didn't have an electromagnetic shield. Instead, it had a special polymer stealth hull. They moved in stealth mode, easing forward with minute thrusts. Like going through a maze, the *Tarrypin* shifted, turning so the wings wouldn't crash into a mass of sand or cooled lava or other debris.

Meter by meter they entered the maze of exposed chunks of planet. Less than a day ago, this had been a normal planet with fifteen million people living on it.

Valerie shuddered.

Did she feel the death knell of the fifteen million as she maneuvered through what had once been their planet? That was superstitious thinking and she wasn't going to give it rein. Still, it was a frightening and awesome experience taking the *Tarrypin* through this mass. They sought the responder that had once been on Outpost 3. What would it tell them about the aliens?

"Commander," the pilot said, "I'm detecting something odd."

"What is it?" Valerie asked.

He studied his screen. "It's three hundred kilometers deeper within the mass, and has just activated."

"What do you mean activated?"

"It's composed of intensely dense matter and it is heading in our direction."

Valerie thought quickly. The *Tarrypin* didn't have much firepower: twenty-millimeter guns and a missile. If this was an alien mine coming to destroy them, she lacked the means to stop it.

The comm light flickered. Valerie pressed a switch. "Commander Noonan here."

"Something's approaching your vessel," Maddox said. "I suggest you ease out, or better yet, flee as fast as you can."

"Can you destroy it for us? We're in too deep to try to flee fast."

"I was afraid of that. Avoid it if you can. I'll ready our disruptor cannon and hope we can take it out for you."

The next few minutes proved tense. The *Tarrypin* maneuvered slowly, using gravity waves to propel it back the way it had come.

"That thing is smashing through rubble," the pilot said. "It's coming straight for us, matching our maneuvers. I don't think anything is going to slow it down."

A chill flowed through Valerie. She didn't want to die like a rat caught in a trap. *You'd better nail it, Captain.*

Ten seconds later, a yellow disruptor beam speared from *Victory*. The ray burned through rubble, cooled lava and other debris until it hit this dense whatever. The beam remained on target, pouring firepower against it.

"That thing isn't slowing down," the pilot shouted. "It's picking up speed."

Even so, the disruptor beam stayed on target. They had great targeting on *Victory*.

On a monitor, Valerie saw the object become red-hot.

Then, a terrific explosion blew apart the device made of highly compressed matter. That created a vast shockwave and a mass of radiation, heat and EMP.

"Full speed back," Valerie shouted. "Get us out of here."

The pilot acted instinctively. The *Tarrypin* accelerated. It wasn't nearly enough to save them.

As the *Tarrypin* attempted to escape, the blast washed against them. The vessel shuddered and cracked as the hull imploded under the pressure.

Fortunately, Valerie had ordered everyone into vacc suits.

The *Tarrypin* broke under the blast, but it didn't disintegrate into tiny molecules. The vessel split into pieces. Everything rushed out. Two crewmembers died as debris smashed their helmets.

Only Valerie and the ensign who'd been with her last mission survived. They drifted among the rubble, taking heavy doses of radiation from the blast.

-14-

On *Victory*, Maddox, Keith and the others on the bridge watched in horror as the *Tarrypin* broke into pieces.

Keith turned to Maddox white-faced and trembling. "Sir, I request permission to use a fold fighter. Let me rescue them."

Maddox didn't want to lose more people. *Valerie is out there.* His mouth was dry but his voice steady. "You heard what we said before. If you fold into too many particles, it could destroy the craft."

"I don't care. Valerie's out there. I have to try."

Was the short, muscular, tough Scotsman too emotional for this? He was the best pilot in Star Watch. If anyone could do it, he was the man.

"Do it," Maddox said.

Keith jumped up and raced off the bridge.

Maddox turned to Andros. "Well?"

"Two of them are alive," Andros said, studying his science board. "Their heartbeats are strong but I'm not getting any response from them. They're taking far too much radiation. Even if we get them out soon, it will probably be touch and go if they survive."

Maddox ingested the bad news in silence. "What about the other two?"

"I'm afraid they're no longer with us."

Maddox made a fist. He didn't hit the armrest, but he hated losing people. They weren't directly under his command as

87

crewmembers, but they'd gone out at his order. They were his responsibility.

Maddox's eyes narrowed.

Had the aliens seeded the entire rubble with antimatter bombs? Was he sending Keith to his death?

Maddox shook his head. He didn't know. He was trying to get his people back. It's what they'd done for him last mission. He was leaving no one behind if he could help it.

Maddox continued to watch as Andros and Galyan searched for more alien devices.

Meanwhile, Keith raced down to hangar-bay three. He boarded an ungainly looking tin can, powering up and lifting off the deck.

Soon, he was outside *Victory*. Nearby was the ruined planet of Zinc, the moons having drifted closer to the ex-planet. The region was a mess with fifteen million dead mixed in. If it had been a more populated planet—

Keith shook his head. "Do you have the coordinates, Galyan? Can you feed them to me?"

"I am right here, Lieutenant. You do not need to shout."

Keith jerked his head and saw Galyan standing beside him. "Are you coming with me?"

"In a manner of speaking," Galyan said. "I have an idea and have authorized it with the captain."

"What does that mean?"

"I will be with you until I am not," Galyan said.

"Fine. I don't have time for riddles. Give me the coordinates."

Galyan did. They appeared on the piloting screen.

"All right," Keith said, "hang on. This could get ugly."

"Only for you. I don't know if I am truly alive so I have no need to worry."

"Cut that out, Galyan. I know what Ludendorff said to you. Don't let that old goat get to you."

"I told him I was sorry."

"You? You told him you were sorry? He should be telling you."

"He did say that."

"Oh? Well...good, it's about time."

88

"But he did not ask for forgiveness."

Keith stared at him for a second. "Galyan, you're taking some of this stuff too far. Don't sweat it. Saying you're sorry is good enough."

"Perhaps you are correct. I will try not to sweat it even though I do not perspire."

"You know what I mean. It's an idiom. Now hang on."

With that, Keith folded. It was one of his better folds, too, as everything worked perfectly.

Soon, Keith donned a vacc-suit and thruster-pack and floated outside. Using the pack, he eased near Valerie and the ensign. Hooking them to his thruster, he squeezed off hydrogen particles, maneuvering back onto the tin can.

He loved Valerie. If she'd died—

Inside the vacc-helmet, Keith shook his head.

Why couldn't things work smoothly between them? They had an on-again, off-again relationship. She was higher rank than he was and she was going to be more successful in life. Was already that. Did he want to chain her to a wild man like him?

He began taking off their helmets.

He only felt alive when he was piloting a fold fighter, or strikefighter or *Victory* into the maw of death. He was a thrill junkie. Valerie wasn't. She was the furthest thing from it. She did things right, by the book if she could.

With his gloved hand, he stroked her hair. Then, he secured her in a seat. He wasn't going to mess with anything now. He was going to get her to the med people as fast as he could. The suit said she'd taken far too much radiation poisoning.

Once she was secure, he strapped in the ensign. He looked awful.

Only then did Keith return to his controls. He looked around. Galyan was gone. What was the little holoimage going to do out here? Keith shrugged. He set his coordinates for near *Victory*. Was something bad going to happen now to stymie him?

Keith pressed the controls to fold. The ungainly craft did so, appearing near *Victory* as plotted.

Keith let out a long sigh. Then, he maneuvered for the open hangar bay. He'd saved his babe. That felt so good. He'd do anything to save Valerie, anything.

Keith brought the fold fighter into the hangar bay, heading for his dock.

Meanwhile, Galyan was in the midst of the ruined planet, a projected holoimage from within the middle of *Victory*. He headed for the responder.

As a holoimage, he couldn't physically touch anything, as his hand would pass right through it. But he did have a unique system within the armored part of the AI system in the middle of *Victory*. Through that, he could project a pulse of force from the holoimage. If he entered a person, that force could kill or incapacitate.

He wouldn't go into the responder and do anything. Instead—

Ah, there it was. He floated to it with his projector power. Using his holoimage as the focal point, he gave a command through his AI system. Pulses began to project through the holoimage, pulses of magnetic repulsion.

Instead of drawing the responder to him, Galyan used the magnetic repulsion to push the responder repeatedly, guiding it through the debris and rubble.

In such a manner over the course of two hours, Galyan pushed the responder out of the rubble and into open space. There, a shuttle picked it up and took it to *Victory*.

"Mission completed," Galyan said.

He didn't say it through any communication system. He said it as he appeared before the captain on the bridge, startling them all. They should be used to it by now. This time, he did not say he was sorry. He had completed the mission and he stood tall, at least tall for an Adok.

"Well done, Galyan," Maddox said. "It was an excellent idea. Now we can see if the responder can give us a clue to any of this."

"Yes sir," Galyan said. "You are welcome, sir." He was eager to hear what the responder said, especially after he had gone to so much trouble to retrieve it.

"Oh," Galyan said. "Is Valerie going to be okay?"

Maddox grinned with relief. "It's looking good. Keith retrieved her and the ensign just in time."

"That is a great relief," Galyan said.

"Tell me about it."

"Sir?"

"That's a saying," Maddox said.

"Oh. Yes. Of course."

"Did you detect any more alien mines out there?"

"Sir, I did not think to check. Do you want me to go back and search?"

"No," Maddox said.

"But—"

"Not now, Galyan. It's time to see if the recorder can tell us anything."

-15-

Maddox took the responder to the professor's science chamber. There Andros, Ludendorff, with Galyan watching, proceeded to inspect it.

"All seems to be in order," Andros said, after he looked through a monitor studying the responder.

"I agree," Ludendorff said, as he pocketed a handheld device.

"Galyan?" Maddox asked. "Can you detect any dangerous residue or tampering with the responder?"

"Negative," Galyan said.

"Well, let's fire it up then," Maddox said. "Let's see what it has to tell us."

For the next while, the four of them listened to all that had occurred at Outpost 3, focusing on the dialogue between Lieutenant Givens and the alien pilot.

"I'm stunned the alien spoke to them using Anglic," Ludendorff said. "There was no translation taking place. It was direct speech. That's fascinating and perplexing. Did any of you detect the accent?"

"I have heard the accent and voice before," Galyan said.

All three men looked at the holoimage.

"How is that possible?" Maddox asked. "Are the aliens or the supership from the Sovereign Hierarchy of Leviathan? Are they Dhows perhaps that we met during the last mission?"

"No," Galyan said, "I believe... Could you play it again, Professor?"

92

"Do I need to?" the professors asked. "Surely you have it on record in your computer files."

"I do have it on record and I have been analyzing it as we speak. It was not an alien but a human who said those words."

"Are you sure of that?" Maddox asked.

"I do not give it a one hundred percent certainty as such things can be faked," Galyan said. "But I am ninety-five percent certain. Yes, I believe I have heard this exact voice before, maybe in an altered manner and without that accent."

"Where could you have heard it?" Ludendorff asked. "That seems impossible."

"Professor, I have tried to make things correct between us."

"Of course they're correct," Ludendorff said. "I'm not saying that. This is a matter of rational thought, of logic and inquiry. That's what we're deciding. How is it possible you've heard this exact voice?"

Maddox glanced from Galyan to Ludendorff. "Andros, do you have a comment?"

"I do not, sir. I certainly haven't heard this voice before. But if Galyan has, he does have a wide range of possibilities and his memory of them would be acute, perfect, really."

"Is that necessarily so?" Ludendorff asked. "I've had to repair and revive Galyan twice already. Perhaps some of his circuitry was damaged each of those times and now he has this false recollection."

"Why does it have to be false, Professor?" Galyan asked.

"I just can't see how you could have heard this voice before," Ludendorff said. "It's alien. We've never seen this type of technology before. We've never seen these kinds of craft before."

"Perhaps one of our former opponents acquired new technology," Galyan said. "We have gained new technology. Is it not possible others could as well?"

"Never mind that," Maddox said. "We're not going to get into an argument or debate about how it's possible or who it could be. If Galyan says he believes he's heard this voice before and he thinks it's human, I want to know how that is possible. Galyan, search your files. See if there's a match of some kind. That seems like the obvious thing to do."

"The possibilities are many. I would have to—yes, Captain," Galyan said, as he had looked at Maddox's face. "I will begin at once."

Galyan froze as his holographic eyelids began to flutter at high speed. He was searching through his memories, and those memories could be deeper and longer than any human because he had much more storage area with his computer systems.

"Perhaps what we should be doing," Andros said, "is to see if we can define the destroyed alien fighter. At the same time, we could get a sample of the alien bio matter and test the DNA. That would tell us if it was human or not."

Maddox clapped Andros on the shoulder. "That's an excellent idea." He looked at Galyan. The holoimage was already engaged searching his files. "Professor, can you do the searching from here?"

"Professor," Andros said, "if you would permit me, I'd like a crack at this."

"Of course." Ludendorff pointed at a station.

Thus, the two men used the science-chamber facilities and *Victory's* sensors. They searched through the rubble, through the cooling lava, radiation and other planetary debris.

As they did, *Victory* made a slow circuit around the massed and possibly dangerous debris of the former planet Zinc.

The search took an hour and then they took a break. The second hour, they still came up empty.

At the start of the third hour, Ludendorff said, "Eureka. I've found the alien fighter, or what remains of it. Fortunately, it isn't deep in the rubble. We should be able to pick it up."

Maddox looked at the screen, viewing the drifting wreckage. He agreed. "Excellent work, Professor."

"Thank you, my boy. I am somewhat of a—never mind," Ludendorff said, glancing at Galyan, whose eyelids yet fluttered. "When could that blasted AI have heard this voice before? Do you believe him, Captain?"

Maddox shrugged. "Galyan said it. I have no reason to doubt him." He cleared his throat, hesitating and then saying, "Professor, I'm not trying to pry into your personal affairs, but are you feeling okay?"

Ludendorff didn't answer immediately, but then he nodded, "As well as can be. It's always this, that or the next thing. I have a few things I'm considering. Perhaps I've been a bit testy lately… Confound it, my boy. I'm fine. Enough of this soul-searching. Let's get on with it. This is a dangerous situation. All of Star Watch is alert. An entire task force has been lost. Let's stick to what matters."

Maddox nodded.

Ludendorff sent the alien fighter debris coordinates to a search and rescue team. Soon, two strikefighters launched from *Victory*, going into the rubble and towing the alien remains into the hangar bay.

All the while Galyan's eyelids fluttered which meant his system was searching his files for a match.

In the hangar-bay deck, Ludendorff and Andros ran scans on the fighter material. There was nothing extraordinary about it. No alien devices had survived the blast. The tissue samples they found, the alien biological matter—

"This must be wrong," Ludendorff said. He peered through a monitor in his science chamber. "This is impossible."

"What did you find?" Maddox asked.

Ludendorff stared at him. "I was looking at modified human DNA."

"What?" Maddox asked. "Human?"

Maddox had seen the zoom shots from the Builder Scanner that had peeked under the alien fighter's bubble canopy. He'd seen the elongated humanoid. Surely, those couldn't have been men. He considered the New Men and Meta. They were modified humans. Had someone else been using human DNA and changing it, perhaps creating a slave race of fighter pilots?

"I have it," Galyan said suddenly.

They all whirled round.

The holoimage's eyelids no longer fluttered. Instead, he looked at them. "I have heard this voice before. It was only on one occasion, though. That was why I did not remember right away. The voice came from Lieutenant Brent Saunders."

"Who?" Maddox asked.

"Brent Saunders aided us when we fought the doomsday Destroyer of the Nameless Ones as it attempted to reach Earth and annihilate it."

"The doomsday Destroyer?" asked Maddox. "You mean years ago when that Destroyer came to the Solar System, planning to destroy Earth as it did Al Salam and Riyadh of the New Arabia System?"

"Yes," Galyan said. "That was the end of the Wahhabi Caliphate. It might have meant the end of the Commonwealth if we hadn't sent the Destroyer into the Sun."

"Lieutenant Brent Saunders," Maddox said, frowning, trying to recollect the man. "Who was that? I've never heard of him."

"But you have," Galyan said, "and I heard what the professor said, 'Modified human DNA.' It would be telling to get a sample or record of Brent Saunders's DNA. We could see if it was a match to what we have here."

"Where have we heard of Brent Saunders before?" Ludendorff asked. "You're not making sense."

"Do you recall that the fold fighters were a new experimental invention at the time?" Galyan asked.

Maddox cocked his head, thinking, remembering, and nodded. "I do. You're right. The attack against the Destroyer was the fold fighters' first battle test."

"What of it?" Ludendorff asked.

"A flight of fold fighters used the fold mechanism as they approached the Destroyer of the Nameless Ones," Galyan said. "Four of the tin cans disappeared, never reappearing."

Maddox felt a cold chill climb his spine. There had been four alien pilots according to what they'd seen on the Builder Scanner video.

"Wait a minute," Maddox said. "You're saying four fold pilots disappeared back then? Yes, I do remember something about that. They were never accounted for. They never reappeared in normal space, and we found no evidence they'd reached the Destroyer."

"Yes," Galyan said, "it would appear they folded elsewhere."

Ludendorff scowled thunderously, but not at Galyan. He scowled at the screen showing the rubble of Zinc. He rubbed his chin. It was clear he was deep in thought.

"Brent Saunders," Maddox said. "You're saying you remember hearing his voice?"

"As he spoke to one of the flight leaders," Galyan said. "That was why it took me so long to find the recording. I had to go through millions of possibilities."

"All right," Maddox said. "Never mind all that. You're saying the pilot of the alien fighter—this elongated humanoid was Brent Saunders?"

"I am," Galyan said.

"But why is he stretched and elongated to such a bizarre form?" Maddox asked. "How is that even possible?"

"I do not know," Galyan said.

"And how could he be—"

"I have it," Ludendorff said, interrupting. "I know what's going on."

"Spill it, then," Maddox said.

"If Galyan is correct," and Ludendorff looked at Galyan and nodded, "and I assume that he is, it would be well to check this DNA. But it appears those four fold pilots—the ones that never reappeared as you fought the Destroyer—in reality folded elsewhere."

"And what does that mean?" Maddox asked.

"Exactly," Ludendorff said excitedly. "That's the key to all of this. They folded elsewhere. Does that mean to a different place, a different time?"

"Time?" Maddox asked. "You mean they're time travelers?"

"I give it as a possibility," Ludendorff said. "We must be careful we don't arrive at the wrong conclusion because we didn't think of everything or think possibilities through."

"What's the other possibility?" asked Maddox.

"Dimensional travel."

Maddox felt that chill again. His intuitive sense pinged, too.

"Dimensional travel," Ludendorff said. "Perhaps that was what we were seeing. The extreme blackness was a rent in the space-time continuum. If I'm right, that's where Task Force 3 went.

"To a different dimension?" asked Maddox. "How is that possible?"

"It is more than possible," Galyan said. "Have you forgotten the Erill System and the City of Pyramids? You went there during the Nostradamus Case."

Maddox nodded. He remembered all right. The Ur-Builders, the flesh and blood Builders of ancient times, had opened a rift into another dimension with soul-eating Erills. He'd had a Builder weapon in his id, a Builder symbol that had helped him against the spiritual entities. The star system was packed with Lurker missiles to keep everyone out so they couldn't aid the Erills escaping their captivity on the planet. Other dimensions could possess horrific beings.

Maddox scowled. If a dimensional rift had swallowed Task Force 3…their universe could be in dreadful peril.

"Captain," Ludendorff said, "we must head at once to the Omicron 9 System, to the fourth planet."

"I don't know why," Maddox said.

"My machine, man," Ludendorff said. "Don't you see? The Yon Soth copy of a machine could help us here?"

Understanding filled Maddox. "Do you mean the machine that almost killed you when you disappeared?"

"Exactly," Ludendorff said, his excitement growing. "One of the possibilities is that the copy of a Yon Soth machine shifted me into a different dimension. We know dimensional travel is possible because you met Balron the Traveler and he aided you and changed you, and you helped him reach a different dimension. Galyan brings up the Erills in the City of Pyramids."

"Professor," Maddox said. "The Erills are a warning to us. Different dimensions can hold horrific aliens. The Ur-Builders made one of their worst mistakes in making a portal to another dimension."

"I understand," Ludendorff said. "We must avoid the mistakes of the Ur-Builders. But if we're right about the asteroidal supership, and that they took Task Force 3—"

"You mean this supership can cross dimensions?" Maddox asked.

Ludendorff spread his hands. "We must solve the mystery."

"And let in something worse than Erills?" asked Maddox.

"Yes, the Erills are terrible. That didn't stop you from helping Balron."

"No..." Maddox said.

"Perhaps these four pilots—"

"What pilots? Oh, right, the four fold-fighter pilots that disappeared when we faced the Destroyer."

"My boy," Ludendorff said, "perhaps the four pilots inadvertently stumbled upon a unique transfer system. Instead of folding back into space, they did something else and folded into a different dimension. In this other dimension were creatures that modified them not like Balron the Traveler did you. But these aliens *stretched* Brent Saunders and turned him into a fantastic pilot."

"Maybe the aliens are Erill-like," Maddox said.

"We have no evidence of that," Ludendorff said. "Perhaps the Erill Dimension is toxically unique. Perhaps in others are fantastic technologies we could plunder. We must find out, however, because it appears others are coming here through their own volition."

"Suppose you're right," Maddox said. "Why would these other dimension aliens come here?"

Once more, Ludendorff spread his hands. "I have no idea. I only know that Galyan has stumbled upon a possibility. I know that is modified human DNA." Ludendorff pointed at the tissue sample under his monitor. "I know dimensional travel is possible. We all know that. I know we've never seen such a supership with a compressed stardust hull. Dimensional travel would explain the different things that occurred in this star system. It also tells us where Task Force 3 went: to a different dimension."

Maddox nodded slowly. "You're saying it's possible to follow them and retrieve Task Force 3?"

"As to that," Ludendorff said, "I have no idea. But I know with my Yon Soth copy of a machine we will be able to detect such things better than otherwise. I do not suggest we go back to the City of Pyramids."

Maddox shook his head.

"If I understand you, Professor," Galyan said, "you want to experiment with the possibilities."

"Gentlemen, we have a chance to find out what's going on in this star system. I have a possible means at hand. Will we do nothing or will we take the risk and try to rescue Task Force 3? Or do we let the other dimension aliens modify our crews as they did the four pilots?"

The professor had a point. But Maddox didn't know if the professor believed all that or just wanted a chance to try experiments with his confounded copy of a Yon Soth machine. He hated the thing.

Still, they had their first real lead. They should at least test the theories—if they could avoid the fate of the Ur-Builders who had long ago brought the horrific Erills to their dimension.

Maddox nodded. "We're the ones they sent. We're the ones who have the possible means to figure it out. I'm going to agree with you, Professor. We go to Omicron 9 and grab your damned machine. Let's see if we can save our people from the grim doom this Brent whoever faced."

With that, the meeting ended, and the real beginning of the mission in the Trappist-1 System was beginning.

-16-

Commodore Donal Galt swayed in his chair on the bridge as the mighty battleship *Stonewall Jackson* maneuvered violently through intense darkness. The lights on the bridge flashed and then died. Emergency red lighting appeared, klaxons rang, smoke and sparks erupted from various consoles on the bridge. People shouted, others screamed. It was pandemonium.

Galt clutched the armrests of his chair while a knot tightened in his gut. He had no idea what was happening. They'd entered some form of blackness. The navigational systems, everything seemed to have collapsed. The aliens must have projected some sort of defensive field against them.

Yes, Galt remembered as he strove to concentrate. He found it so difficult to think with the pandemonium around him. The ship was thrown violently so it heaved and shuddered like a cork on an ocean. Could the starship survive such battering for long?

What had the alien supership projected against them? How did the other ships of the task force fare? What had happened to the strikefighters? He wasn't sure if any fighters had entered this black maelstrom, or had the alien field only affected the battleships?

Whatever the case, Galt endured. Through the red lighting, he saw that others were beginning to calm down as they gained control of their panic. A few looked abashed and he had no doubt why. Because they'd let their Navy training slip. This wasn't a Patrol vessel that routinely went into the Beyond, but members of Star Watch should conduct themselves professionally even in these frightening conditions.

Abruptly, the shaking and violent maneuvering ceased. Were the antigravity dampeners back online? Galt didn't know. He wasn't sure any of them did.

"I'm getting something on the screen," Sensor Chief Usan said. He was a bluff, older man with a brush cut of blond bristles and a misshapen nose. It had been broken more than once. Bar fights, perhaps?

Sensor Chief Usan's statement brought Captain Karpov around. The large, wide-faced man stood. That seemed to be safe, since the violent maneuvering had ceased. Karpov shouted orders, bringing a greater semblance of discipline to the bridge.

The emergency lighting snapped off as regular lighting resumed.

Galt looked around.

Several officers brushed their hair with their fingers. A few wiped tears from their eyes or rubbed their faces. They sought calm through professional behavior.

"I'm putting it up onto the main screen," Sensor Chief Usan said.

The main screen shimmered, the picture seeming to collapse upon itself. Abruptly, with a dazzling stellar display, huge bright stars and smaller stars, all compressed against each other, shined with awful luminosity.

Bridge personnel gasped or sucked in their breath. This wasn't regular space. They'd arrived somewhere else.

"What's the meaning of this?" Captain Karpov demanded in his bull voice.

There was no answer.

"Chief, is something wrong with the sensors?"

"Just a minute sir."

Usan, a chief who knew his business, manipulated his board. Probably, he made a quick diagnostic check. He frowned at his monitor. His hands moved faster across the console and then his head jerked up.

"Sir, there's nothing wrong with the sensors, at least from my end. What you see on the screen—that's what's out there, sir."

"Look," Galt said pointing at the main screen. "Is that the alien supership?"

Everyone stared at the screen. There was a dot of a vessel much farther beyond them.

"Magnification," Karpov said. "I want full magnification of the object."

A moment later the asteroidal supership with its hull of presumed compressed stardust leapt into view. It seemed to be pulling away from them.

"All right, this is…" Galt didn't know what to say after that. He was going to say this was regular space. But the evidence on the main screen showed that was certainly not the case.

The huge, pressed-together stars were not in the Trappist-1 System or anywhere near it.

"Are we still in the Commonwealth?" Galt asked.

Several officers looked at him with astonishment, including Captain Karpov.

"Where else could we be?" Karpov asked.

Galt pointed at the main screen.

The others stared at it with perplexity.

"This isn't the Trappist-1 System," Galt said. "The asteroidal ship must have used…some sort of hyper-spatial tube or Laumer Point wormhole on us, I don't know."

"How could the aliens do that?" Karpov asked.

"What part of 'I don't know' don't you understand?" Galt asked sharply.

He regretted the terse comment the moment he said it. Karpov was clearly perplexed like the rest of the bridge crew. Galt didn't want to demean Karpov in front of the others.

Instead of apologizing or saying anything else, though, Galt sat back thinking, trying to piece this together.

"Are the other ships of the task force still with us?" Karpov asked.

"That's a good question," Galt said. "Find them if you can."

"Yes, sir," Karpov said.

Galt liked that he was able to give the man praise so soon after slighting him.

"Sir, I'm picking up radio signals," the comm officer said.

Usan tapped his board.

On the main screen appeared the *Alexander* and the *Philip II*.

"Battleship Squadron 10 is intact," Karpov said.

"I'm picking up the rest of the task force," Usan said. "They made it out here with us."

"Excellent," Galt said. "We haven't lost the task force then. Now, let's try to figure out where we are, where this supership has taken us. Is it still separating from us?"

Once more, Sensor Chief Usan used magnification, focusing on the mighty asteroidal ship.

"Yes sir, it's pulling away."

"Do we increase velocity, Commodore?" Karpov asked.

"Not yet," Galt said. "Let's first collect the rest of the task force, making sure they're all intact."

"Back in the Trappist-1 System, I saw the *Queen Bess* explode under the enemy's beams," Karpov said.

"I saw that, too," Galt said. "The enemy destroyed a mothership."

"Sir," Usan said. "I'm spying some strikefighters flying free."

"Captain," Galt said. "I want you to patch me through to the other ships. I want a wide link. I want to speak to everyone. We must regain order and figure out what has happened. First, we need to regain task force continuity."

Soon, the comm officer established a link with the *Alexander* and *Philips II*. Those battleships in turn reached out to the other vessels.

Several facts had quickly become apparent. Their comm ranges were extremely limited…wherever here was. Maneuvering was trickier than it should be, as if the very fabric of this place resisted their efforts more than normal. Finally, most stars were impossibly close to others, and yet, their gravitational forces didn't seem to affect their neighbors.

Galt was pleased to see the free strikefighters converge upon the two remaining motherships. Unfortunately, the fighters were still landing when a gigantic space funnel appeared directly ahead of the task force.

"Sir!" Usan said.

People gasped at the sight on the main screen.

"Is that a-a vortex?" Karpov asked.

"Avoid it," Galt said. "Helm, turn sharply."

Even as the pilot began to maneuver the huge battleship away from the vortex, the tech officer shouted, "It's drawing us in!"

Karpov stared at the man. "With gravitational force?"

"I'm working on that, sir. I don't know how, but it's drawing us to it."

Galt could actually feel the tug, a powerful force indeed to get past the battleship's gravity dampeners.

Battleship Squadron 10 and the other warships of Task Force 3 veered toward the vortex even as they tried to pull away. The smaller ships slipped faster toward the vortex. Several strikefighters that hadn't managed to land on any mothership zipped into the vile maelstrom. The fighters were sucked down and disappeared from sight and sensor view.

"Sir," Karpov shouted. "What do we do about that?"

Galt thought that an excellent question.

"Sir," the tech officer said, "our engines will burn out if we keep fighting the vortex much longer."

Huge Karpov stared fixedly at Galt.

Galt had no idea if they went down the spatial vortex—for want of a better term—if that would destroy the battleship.

"What's the vortex doing to the supership," Galt asked.

"Uh…" Karpov said. "That's a good question, sir."

Galt considered it good as well, otherwise he wouldn't have asked it. He didn't care for his officers commenting on the goodness of his comments, though.

"Sir," Sensor Chief Usan said. "The supership is being pulled toward the vortex. It doesn't seem to be fighting it to the same extent we are."

Had the supership created the vortex? Galt had never heard of such an event: a space funnel in this region of space.

Galt stared at the massive bright stars in the near background, the sheer number of them. Where in the blazes were they? This couldn't be regular space. At least, this wasn't space as they'd known it in the Trappist-1 System.

"We're going into the vortex," Galt told Karpov. "Radio the others. Tell them to do the same. We're all going in."

"And if we're destroyed, sir?" asked Karpov.

"Then we're destroyed."

Big Karpov paled.

Galt snorted. "We can fight it for a few more minutes. But what good will it do if our engines burn out?"

Karpov's wide face almost crumpled with fear.

It hit Galt, and he believed he understood. The others were terrified. Perhaps the crews on the other ships were terrified as well. This was truly the unknown. They were dealing with a situation none of them had been trained to handle. This was a Patrol situation, one that Captain Maddox and his crew could have easily handled, no doubt. But for a regular ship of the line, this was extraordinary.

"Stay calm," Galt said. "We're going to get through this. Something has happened. We can all see that. It's up to us to figure out what. We will, I promise you."

Even as Galt said that, he had no idea how he was going to keep such a promise. But it was better to have a crew that had confidence than one that was filled with panic.

The *Stonewall Jackson* veered into the vortex, following the strikefighters that had already gone in. Would the supership follow them in a bit later? Galt didn't know.

"Use minimal power. Everyone brace for impact."

Then the mighty *Stonewall Jackson* headed straight into the swirling funnel of the vortex.

-17-

The process was similar to what they'd gone through when they entered the blackness in the Trappist-1 System. Once more, the bridge lights dimmed.

"Shut them down," Galt said.

A crewmember did.

The red emergency lights kicked on.

The battleship headed down into the swirling vortex. The ship shuddered and shook, metal groaning all around them.

Galt clung to the armrests of his chair. "Stay calm," he shouted. "We've done this before. There's nothing to worry about."

Maybe some of them believed him. There was no screaming or panicked shouting like last time. That was good.

Galt looked around. In the red lighting, he saw stark fear on many faces. That was not so good.

Before the fear could build, the ship shuddering ceased. Did that mean they were out of the vortex?

"Power energies are rising," the tech officer said.

"Shut off the emergency lighting," Galt said. "Bring up the regular lights. Let's see what's going on around us."

As before, the main screen activated. Through it, they saw what seemed to be a similar situation. Massive stars of great luminosity shined nearby. Then, a high-pitched keening penetrated the heart of the *Stonewall Jackson*. Presumably, it did the same on the other ships.

What was that horrible noise? Galt clapped his hands over his ears. The noise worsened as it cycled higher.

Others followed his example, pressing their hands against their ears.

Was the ship going explode?

If anyone screamed, Galt had no idea. He screwed his eyes shut and pressed his hands harder against his ears.

The sound cycled higher and higher. This was intolerable. Abruptly, however, it ceased.

Experimentally, Galt took his hands away as he opened his eyes.

Crewmen looked at each other.

"What was that?" Karpov asked him.

Galt looked at the captain. How was he supposed to know?

"I have it," the tech chief said. "There's a neutron star off the port bow. The neutron star is close, immeasurably close. It's cycling up, most likely to burst forth with more waves of energy." He checked his monitor. "Yes, it just cycled down through various frequencies. We didn't hear the latest sound— these last few seconds—but we're going to hear it again if we don't do something."

"Can a shield stop the waves?" Karpov asked.

"Maybe earplugs would be the better idea," the tech chief said.

"Or we get out of here," Galt said. "Let's see how many of the others have made it through the vortex."

After a five-minute communication game of tag, Galt learned that a destroyer and light cruiser, along with several strikefighters, had failed to either come through the vortex or join them in this locale.

"What about the supership?" Galt asked. "Is it nearby?"

Soon enough, one of the destroyers spotted the supership far in the distance ahead of them.

"How did it get ahead of us after coming through the vortex later?" Karpov asked Galt.

"That's an excellent question," Galt said. "Clearly, the vortex was or is some kind of transportation system. We don't know how it operates or under what principles. Captain, contact your main science team. Have them figure out why all

108

this is happening. I want a deep analysis and a report. I want it as quickly as you can so we have some ideas of what's going on. We need to make intelligent decisions, and for that we need data."

"Yes sir," Karpov said.

"In fact," Galt said, "Go see to it personally."

"Sir?" Karpov asked.

"Now," Galt said. "It's imperative we learn *why* these things are happening as much as what is happening."

Karpov rose and hurried through the exit.

Galt pointed at the second in command.

She started issuing orders.

Space here was odd with weird properties and dangers. As Task Force 3 maneuvered closer together, Usan showed them two black holes, horrid gravitational distortions spewing wild radiation, and other bizarre spatial anomalies. None of them had faced a single of these things in any of their tours of duty and yet now there were a wild multitude of spatial anomalies around them.

"Have we entered some sort of space rift?" Usan asked.

"Explain," Galt said.

The sensor chief swiveled around on his seat to face the commodore. "Sir, I've read about such things: rifts, I mean. There are theories that tell of a rift where space-time is different. The rift releases wild energies that create such things as a vortex. The closest analogy I can think of is a whirlpool like one would see in an ocean or lake on Earth. Or one would see when he pulls the plug in a bathtub. At the end, he watches the funnel go down into the drain. We seem to have been drawn from one place in space to another through a funnel."

"From the tub and into the sceptic system?" asked Galt.

"It's only an analogy, sir."

"But the analogy holds in principle?"

"I think it does," Usan said.

Galt ingested that.

Usan must have taken that as a sign to continue. "Are we light years from where we used to be or somewhere else? I recognize none of these stars. I assume we're somewhere in the center of the Milky Way Galaxy. I make that conclusion by the proximity and number of stars. And yet, the radiation, the spatial distortions and gravitational forces—we must be careful. I suspect that if we travel too close to any of the anomalies, they might exert forces that would tear our ships apart."

"Does that necessarily hold?" Galt asked.

"Well, sir, I notice the supership is threading what seems like a cautious path through this…star field, for want of a better term."

Galt thought about that. Usan clearly knew more than a regular sensor chief would. He'd given an interesting lecture on what they were dealing with.

Galt stood. He moved slowly to minimize his limp. He stepped toward the main screen. He was thinking and could feel his heart hammering. This was a wild situation. They had no idea how to get home because they had no idea where home lay. Where in the blazes were they? How could they find out?

"What are your suggestions, Sensor Chief?"

"You're asking me, sir?" Usan said.

"You seem to have an understanding of what's happening or better than any of us. I want to hear your suggestions."

Everyone on the bridge turned and stared at gruff Usan.

The sensor chief scratched his cheek, swiveled around and tapped several controls of his console. He read something on his monitor and swiveled back around. "I frankly don't know, Commodore. I think, though, if I were to guess…"

"If it were you in command," Galt said, "what would you do next?"

Usan scratched his leathery skin. "If it were me, sir, I'd stay close to the supership. It seems to know where it's heading. We have no idea. Perhaps it knows how to get out of this field, this rift, whatever kind of space we're in. We want to get out of it, too. We're in a highly dangerous or highly volatile situation."

"Yes," Galt said, "I agree with that." He stood a little straighter. "Comm officer."

"Yes sir."

"Contact the other ships. Tell them to keep up with us. Tell them we are going to catch the asteroidal supership. Barring that, we're going to do our best to stay near it. I want everybody..."

Galt squinted as he looked at the main screen. He had an idea.

"All right, this is how it's going to be." He gave orders so each *Conqueror*-class battleship was at an equidistant point in a triangle around the rest of the task force. The three battleships were going to be the sheepdogs guarding the others. Could they guard them against the forces that were in this area of space? He had no idea. What he did know was that he wanted a compact, highly reactive task force.

So far, no one was giving him any crap about taking command of the task force. That might come later, but he wasn't going to worry about that now. Saving the ships—he had and getting the hell out of this crazy mess was the key.

The motherships *Joan of Arc* and *Cleopatra* collected the remaining strikefighters. The light cruisers and destroyers struggled to keep up as they maneuvered into position. The escort ships had the toughest time of all. Some commanders called to complain that their engines were overstrained.

"It can't be helped," Galt said. "We must follow the supership so it can lead us out of here. If anyone else knows where we should go instead, tell me. I'd really like to know."

No one else had any idea.

"We're not going to leave anyone behind if we can help it," Galt said, "but we're not going to lose the entire task force just because one or two ships can't keep up. That may sound harsh, but that's the situation. Therefore, do what you can. If you think your ship is going to detonate because the engines are giving out, get aboard one of the other vessels. We're saving the task force. Star Watch cannot afford to lose it. That is all."

For the next three hours, that was what happened. One escort ferried its people onto the *Cleopatra* and then they left the escort behind. Its engine had been struggling and no doubt would have exploded and maybe jeopardized the entire task force by it.

On the screen, Galt watched the empty escort remain behind as the rest of the task force struggled to catch up to the accelerating supership. Why had the aliens brought them here? Had it been a mistake on their part?

Galt thought back. No, the supership had projected that blackness. It didn't seem as if that had been a mistake.

Still, over the course of three hours, the supership became a tiny dot so that even with full magnification it became nearly impossible to see. The forces, distortions and gravitational pulls made it difficult to keep the supership within sensor range.

"We've almost lost it," Usan said at the end of the three hours.

"Increase speed," Galt said.

"Sir, the *Cleopatra* and *Joan of Arc* will never keep up with that," the second in command told him.

Galt stared at his feet. He was sitting again. What was the correct course of action? Did he use the logic of saving at least the battleships and light cruisers? If he returned home, spoke to the Lord High Admiral, and told him he'd deliberately left behind the two motherships and destroyers…

Galt didn't think the Lord High Admiral would commend or applaud him, but cashier him from the service.

Did that mean he should risk losing the entire task force?

"Lost it," Usan said.

Galt's head jerked up. "Lost it? You mean track of the supership?"

Usan swiveled around on his seat. "Sir, that is exactly—"

At that moment, a jagged rent of blackness appeared before the *Stonewall Jackson*.

"Sir," the pilot said, "I'm veering hard right."

Galt saw the jagged blackness on the screen. It expanded at an alarming rate.

The pilot attempted to turn and miss it.

There were communications from the *Alexander* and *Philip II* but distortions made it impossible to hear what they said.

Then, the mighty *Conqueror*-class battleship, the pride of Star Watch, entered the blackness. The rest of the task force followed close behind.

Galt was sure they were heading to a completely different place, one the asteroidal supership wasn't going. Did that mean they were about to be destroyed?

Galt clutched onto the armrests of his chair. He forced himself to keep his eyes open, waiting to learn the grim answer.

-18-

Commodore Galt raised his head. The last maneuver had been a violent one. He blinked and realized he needed to take a pill, as he was feeling woozy and slightly sick.

Several bridge personnel had vomited. They were wiping their mouths and looking abashed.

Galt looked over. The second in command looked at him. Galt pointedly looked at the messes on the floor. She stood and began to order the marines to get that cleaned up on the double.

"Sensor Chief," Galt said. "How are you feeling?"

Usan grimaced. "I've had better days."

"Get the main screen up. I want to see where we're at and what happened to the others."

"Yes sir." It took Usan five minutes of fiddling. "Sir, I have something on the main screen."

Galt and the others looked. He heaved a sigh of relief. There was no compacted mass of huge bright stars. Instead, there was a normal background of unfamiliar stars. In the near distance was a bright disc. They were in a star system.

"What's the classification of the system star," Galt asked.

Usan didn't need to ask which one. He checked his monitor. "It's a G-class star similar to the Sun. I'm also—sir, I'm detecting five terrestrial planets in the inner system and other—oh, no."

"What is it?" Galt asked.

Usan touched his board, bringing up a near Mars-like planet, bigger than Mars but with a rusty-red complexion.

114

Around the red planet were bright pin dots, indicating maneuvering vessels.

"Is that a populated planet?" Galt asked.

"It's more than that, sir. Those are military vessels."

"You're certain?"

"Let me confirm, sir."

Galt nodded.

Captain Karpov reappeared on the bridge and resumed command.

In those few moments, Usan mapped the situation. The pin-dots were small warships. They'd left the surface and were heading to a large battle station in a near-moon-like orbit. The station was big, metal and rock and bristled with cannon and missile ports.

"Does the station have an electromagnetic screen?" Galt asked.

"I'm not detecting one," Usan said. "I am detecting others approaching the planet."

"What others?"

"May I have a few more minutes, sir?"

"Quickly then." Galt turned to Captain Karpov. "You control your own bridge, sir. I've just taken—"

"No," Karpov said, interrupting. "It's no matter, Commodore. You're trying to figure out the situation. Trying to comprehend what is going on. My ship is yours. That goes without saying."

Galt nodded.

Karpov turned to the main screen. "It's good to see regular space again. I wonder if we've made it home."

"Do you recognize the star system?" Galt asked.

Karpov frowned, "I do not. Have we made contact with them?"

Galt pointed at the captain. "That's a good idea. I'll leave it to you."

Karpov strode to the comm officer and began to rattle off orders.

She tried to contact the people of the red planet.

While she did, Usan deciphered the rest of the sensor data. The red planet was heavily populated with obvious urban

115

regions and industrial belts. He detected large concentrations of surface missile silos. Together with the battle station, they surely guarded the planet. From twenty-three million kilometers out, a hundred or more warships headed for the planet. Farther behind them was a cluster of bigger asteroids. They didn't seem natural. In a moment, they all knew they were not. Those were mobile asteroids, as each had huge thrusters built onto them.

"Are those asteroidal superships?" Galt asked.

"I don't think so, sir," Usan said. "As a quick guess, I'd say the mobile asteroids serve as a supply base for the fleet. I've detected vast and rather crude fusion engines on the asteroids."

"What, not antimatter engines?"

"No sir. They're definitely using nuclear-powered engines for thrust. The hundred-ship fleet is also using fusion engines."

"That means we're not in the Commonwealth," Galt said.

"I would definitely agree with that, sir," Usan said.

Galt grew more perplexed. What planet in Human Space—the region farther than the Commonwealth but not in the Beyond—had this arrangement?

Galt closed his eyes and rubbed his forehead, thinking. He shook his head. It was obvious they weren't in Human Space. He had no idea where in the hell they were. He didn't recognize any of the constellations.

Galt stood and limped around his chair, making two circuits. For once, he didn't think about the others seeing him limp. He was perplexed and starting to be seriously worried. The alien fleet used fusion engines and big mobile asteroids as a base. Did that indicate they'd made a long journey to reach the red planet?

"Where did the other ships come from?" Galt asked.

People looked at him.

"Captain," Galt said, "have you assessed where the mobile asteroids originated?"

"Sensor Chief," Karpov said.

"I've been trying to determine that, sir," Usan told Karpov. "If I were to guess…"

Karpov looked at Galt.

116

"Yes, yes," Galt said, "by all means, until we know, let's make a few assumptions so we can at least act."

Usan nodded. "If I were to guess, the mobile asteroids came from this system's outer planets. I haven't detected such places yet. I mean industrial sites. But we've hardly gotten here. I've spent most of my time trying to figure out what's happening in our front yard."

"Any luck opening communications with the people on the planet?" Galt asked Karpov.

Karpov shook his head.

"Sir," the comm officer said, "Commodore Ketchum would like a word with Commodore Galt."

Galt whipped around, "What was that?"

The comm officer repeated the information.

"Commodore Ketchum." Galt knew the man, an old, bent officer and a stickler for forms. Ketchum also happened to have seniority. Did the commodore think he should take command of the task force?

"Where is he?" Galt asked.

"On the Light Cruiser *Babylon*, sir," the comm officer said.

"I'm going to the ready room," Galt said. "I'll take his call there."

"Yes sir," she said.

Galt limped across the bridge, moved through a hatch into the ready room and sat at the desk, repositioning the desk screen toward him. Galt sat straight and opened channels.

Commodore Ketchum appeared before him on the screen. He looked older than Galt remembered with baggy, dark eyes that peered straight and worriedly and with light shimmering off his bald dome of a head.

"What in the hell is this?" Ketchum asked.

Galt didn't frown, although he didn't appreciate the abrupt and rude manner. "If you would explain yourself, sir."

"What are we doing here?" Ketchum demanded.

"We're stranded, lost."

"Yes, yes, I know that," Ketchum said. "Can't you see we're in the middle of a brewing battle? It looks like the asteroid forces are ready to attack the red planet."

"That seems like a reasonable assessment," Galt said.

"Well, let's back off then. Let's let them at it."

"Is that the correct thing to do?"

"All right, then," Ketchum said as he slapped the desk where he sat. "Let's hammer this out. It was always going to come to that. You think you should run the show because you happen to command a battleship squadron. You think I've been given a lesser command because I control a light cruiser squadron?"

"Is that a serious statement?" Galt asked.

"Dammit, man. I have seniority between the two of us. The *Queen Bess* is gone. Vice Admiral Blum is most likely dead."

"I concur."

"I'll take charge then."

"That is not how the organizational charts work," Galt said mildly.

"Blast the charts," Ketchum said. "This is an insane situation. This calls for the best command mind to take over."

"We're in agreement with that."

Ketchum sneered. "And you think that's you?"

"Unquestionably I think so."

Ketchum scowled at him.

"Now look here," Galt said his voice hardening, "this is a stupid time to squabble over command. I have command by right of the organizational chart. You and I both know that. You're an angry, frustrated old man but you know how to handle light cruisers. I'll give you that. I want you to obey me instantly and correctly."

"Or?" Ketchum asked.

"Or you'll face the Admiralty Board after this is done. Do you want to be cashiered at your age? Do you want to lose your pension just before you retire?"

"Bah!" Ketchum said. "Tell me this. How do we get home?"

"First things first," Galt said.

"What does that mean?"

"We need to survive the present situation. If it's a battle, let's figure out what side needs our help."

"You want to get involved in alien hostilities?" Ketchum asked as if Galt were a lunatic.

118

"What makes you think they're alien?"

"Come now," Ketchum said, "haven't you seen what your comm officer should have already showed you?"

"I don't understand."

"Aha," Ketchum said, "I have something on you."

"Now see here, old boy," Galt said, working to control his slipping temper. "Let's not dick around at a time like this and make stupid mistakes."

"What are you talking about?"

"What are you?"

Ketchum scowled. "You don't get it. Those are the aliens on the fifth planet, the Mars-like planet." The commodore pressed a switch.

On the corner of Galt's screen appeared what looked like an oversized teddy bear with clothes and a hat.

"Those are the aliens of the star system?" Galt asked.

"Just the aliens of the red planet," Ketchum said. "Here a shot of the kind running the invasion fleet."

Another shot appeared on the corner of Galt's screen, taking the place of the teddy bear. It showed a hulking brute of a Saurian, some kind of a lizard folk. The Saurian wasn't perhaps quite as tall as a human, but he had two muscular arms, two heavy legs, a thick tail and a saurian or lizard snout with a militaristic uniform.

"These are heading from the asteroids?"

"That is correct, "Ketchum said.

"I see," Galt said.

"What are we going to do? What's the plan? We're stranded far from home. We don't even know where we're at, and now we're on a battlefield. I say we back off and try to find our way home."

"We're going to need help to do that," Galt said.

"From whom?" asked Ketchum.

"We're at a loss. I agree with that. We know very little. We need more information."

A klaxon began to blare on the *Stonewall Jackson*.

"Just a minute, Commodore." Galt pressed a switch on the desk panel. Captain Karpov's face filled the screen.

"Sir, the asteroid folk have launched an assault."

119

"Already," Galt asked, "an assault on the planet?"

"No," Karpov said, "at us. They launched missiles. The missiles are heading straight at us. What are we going to do, Commodore? What's the plan?"

Galt stood up as he stared at the screen. "I'll be right there."

-19-

Commodore Galt limped onto the bridge, looking up at the main screen.

"Sir," Karpov said, "the Saurians have launched missiles at the task force."

"I see that," Galt said. "How many missiles, what speed and do you know the warhead type?"

"We don't know the warhead type, sir, but..." Karpov turned to Usan.

"I'd say a little less than a hundred missiles," Usan said. "Ah, here's the exact number: ninety-eight missiles are headed our way. They launched the missiles from the big, mobile asteroids."

"How far are the asteroids from the planet?" Galt asked.

"Twenty-eight million kilometers, sir," Usan said.

"How far are the asteroids from us?"

"The same distance, sir."

Galt nodded. "Given the rate of acceleration, how long until we're in... Well, the Saurians lack antimatter engines. Do they have antimatter warheads?"

"Unknown," the weapons officer said.

"Right," Galt said, thinking on his feet as he looked at the main screen. The missiles all had long exhaust tails. "The missiles are behind the Saurian ships that already left the asteroids?"

"Correct sir," Usan said, "although the missiles aren't following the ships, but heading in a different vector, specifically, at us."

"How long until the missiles are within antimatter blast range or a nuclear warhead blast range to us?"

"Given their speed, sir, I'd say we have a couple of hours. The missiles are not accelerating fast by our standards. They're at a crawl. Still, it won't be that long until they're here and the blast, of course, will keep traveling toward us much faster."

"Yes," Galt said. With the information, he realized he had time before he needed to make a decision. "Inform me the instant the missiles start accelerating faster."

"Yes sir," Usan said.

Galt limped to his chair, gratefully sitting and staring at the main screen.

What was the correct decision? Should they back off as Ketchum suggested? Cleary, the task force could use their star-drive jumps and leave the fight. This wasn't their battle. Where were they? They weren't in Human Space. Thus, the fight had nothing to do with them. Yet, it had something to do with them because the Saurians had launched missiles at them. Did he have a moral imperative to protect the red planet? Galt didn't think so. He had a moral imperative to save his people. It would be good to know if the star-drive jump worked in this place, as they might not.

"Sir," the comm officer said, "there's a call from Captain Lair of the *Joan of Arc*."

"I'll take it here," Galt said.

"Yes sir. I'm rerouting it through to you."

Galt slipped on his glove controlling the holo-screens floating around him. On one appeared hulking Captain Lair. She was a large woman in both stature and weight. She was uncompromising and frankly, a pain in the ass. But she knew her job, being good at what she did.

"Commodore," Lair said to him.

"Yes, Captain. Is everything well on your mothership?"

"I wouldn't know about well. My people are alive, the ship is functional and we've gone through whatever it is we came through with minimal damage. The *Queen Bess* is gone."

"I'm aware of that," Galt said. "Thank you for telling me, however. How are your people holding up?"

"They're holding up fine and will continue to do so," Lair said. "That isn't why I'm calling. I'm assuming you're aware of the missiles launched at us from the mobile asteroids."

"Indeed," Galt said, and he waited. He almost asked if she thought they should get out of the way like Ketchum suggested, that it wasn't their fight.

"I have an idea for deactivating the missiles," Lair said.

"How do you know they can be deactivated?"

Lair grinned wolfishly. "I've had my people working on it as soon as we came out...wherever we did. Do you know what that was?"

"If you mean specifically," Galt said, "I do not."

"Right," Lair said. "Let's stick to the issue. That's a good idea. We've been monitoring the lizards and some of my tech people have been making some attempts at EW."

"Electronic Warfare, I see," Galt said. "Do you happen to know who these Saurians are and from where they originate?"

"I have no idea," Lair said. "I neither understand their language nor at this point do I care. But, I've found and my tech people are telling me the missiles are crudely guided through radio waves coming from the asteroids."

"Go on," Galt said.

"I propose to send a few of my EW fold fighters out there. They can deactivate the missiles. I'm certain of it."

"Certain enough to guarantee it?"

"Of course I don't guarantee it," Lair said. "I'm not an idiot, but I think that's a better idea than using our precious munitions on the missiles. We don't know where we're at and how long our munitions are going to have to last us."

"That's an excellent point." Galt was surprised he hadn't already thought of it.

"Okay then," Lair said. "Do I have your permission to proceed?"

"Yes," Galt said, deciding for decisive action, glad he had an officer with the initiative to come up with a plan.

Lair had come up with the plan rather quickly, too. She was a rough and ready officer, one of the better mothership captains.

"Send the fold fighters," Galt said. "Send them at once."

"Do you want me to take over the missiles and send them back at the asteroids or do you want me to—"

"No," Galt said, interrupting. "Here's what I want you to do: detonate the warheads immediately."

"Sir?" Lair said.

"Render the missiles useless so we don't have to worry about them later."

Lair grinned, nodding. "I'll tell you of failure or success the instant I know. Lair out."

Galt checked his other holo-screens.

For the moment, the massed missiles continued their crawl toward the task force. Could Lair's people really detonate them? That would be excellent.

Galt switched views.

The fleet of Saurian ships headed for the red planet. They accelerated, but not as fast as the missiles.

Galt mused upon what he saw. Everything was happening in slow motion. The Saurian missile and ship velocities were much slower than anything a Star Watch officer was used to. Still, the alien weapons were dangerous, particularly if they got close enough.

Now, Galt had to do one of the hardest jobs of a task-force leader. He had to wait.

He waited as seven fold fighters launched from the *Joan of Arc*. These were unique EW fold fighters. They disappeared from around the *Joan of Arc*, appearing near the Saurian missiles.

Galt scowled, angry at Lair for having launched *seven* fold fighters. Why hadn't she used two or three instead?

This was risky. If the warheads detonated now, the blasts would destroy seven precious EW fold fighters.

Galt later discovered that Lair wanted her people to figure it out as fast as possible so they'd spend the least amount of time near the missiles.

"Commodore," Usan said, "I have the specs on the alien ships."

"Patch it through to me," Galt said.

On a holo-screen, he examined a Saurian warship from the fleet of one hundred and ten. The alien warship was tubular with a bulbous front. They were all identical: smaller than a SW destroyer but larger than a SW escort.

Galt rubbed his chin. One hundred and ten such warships struck him as a large fleet, given Saurian technology and the mobile asteroids as base.

The Saurian fleet continued on a course for the battle station and red planet behind it.

Galt studied the battle station, perhaps half the size of the largest mobile asteroid.

The seven fold fighters from the *Joan of Arc* disappeared from around the Saurian missiles.

Lair reappeared upon a holo-screen. "We're ready. We can try it at any time. Give the word."

"We can detonate the warheads?" Galt asked.

"I'm told it's possible. There's only one way to find out the truth, though."

Galt nodded. "Detonate them this instant."

Seconds later, Sensor Chief Usan shouted.

On the main screen, whiteouts showed where the Saurian nuclear warheads exploded. They did so *en masse.*

"The warheads will wipe out the mobile asteroids for us," Karpov said.

"Begging your pardon, sir," Usan said, "but I don't think so. I've studied the warheads and am getting a reading on the blasts. The warheads must have been shaped charges. Most of the blast, radiation and EMP are heading in our direction. It will reach here soon."

"Strengthen all shields to maximum," Galt said. "Pass that along," he told Karpov.

"Yes sir," the captain said.

Each ship in the task force raised the strength of their electromagnetic shields. As extra insurance, Galt ordered the three battleships in front of the others—in front in relation to the warhead blasts. The *Conqueror*-class vessels had the best shields. They'd absorb the brunt of the shockwave and EMP heading their way.

"Look, sir," Usan said.

Huh. Some of the blast from the warheads affected the rear of the Saurian fleet. Several bulbous-headed warships ceased accelerating. Two crumpled.

The rest continued seemingly unhurt by any radiation or EMP.

"Sir," the comm officer said, "I have a call from Commodore Ketchum."

"Fine," Galt said, "put him on my holo-screen."

Dour Ketchum appeared there. "Well, you've done it now, Galt."

"Care to tell me what I've done?"

"Picked a side," Ketchum said. "We've blown the Saurian missiles. Now, we'd better wipe out them bastards."

"Why do you think so?"

Ketchum looked surprised. "Didn't you hear me? You picked a side. You made mortal enemies of them lizards. They're going to want revenge. Before they can get it, let's finish it and wipe 'em out. We'll gain the gratitude of them small devils on the red planet."

"No," Galt said, still thinking about what Captain Lair had said. They needed to save munitions if they could. Perhaps that even meant save power. They had fuel, but how long would they need the fuel to last? "We watch. We see what happens next."

Ketchum's face screwed up in anger. Finally, he said in a hoarse voice, "Are you sure about this?"

Galt drummed the fingers of his gloveless hand on an armrest. Ketchum's act was getting old. It was time to establish—

"I don't need to explain myself to you, sir," Galt said. "You're under my command. Must I relieve you of duty due to insubordination?"

Ketchum's eyes bulged. "You wouldn't dare."

Galt smiled faintly, saying nothing. He merely stared at Ketchum.

Ketchum muttered something Galt couldn't catch. Then, "All right, I'm awaiting orders. I'll obey. I'm a good Navy officer. I know the drill."

"I'm glad to hear it. We wait and see what happens next."

"Aye," Ketchum said. A second later, he disappeared from the holo-screen.

The blast from the exploded warheads reached the task force. The battleship shields absorbed the worst. The other vessels endured what made it past the battleships.

Afterward, there was more tedious waiting as the one hundred and three ships of the Saurian fleet headed for the alien battle station.

During that time, Galt and the others took staggered breaks.

Galt when to a rec area and shot some pool. He needed to relax. Afterward, he sat and read some ancient Earth history.

It felt good to read.

A call on the rec intercom woke him. Galt realized he'd fallen asleep.

"What is it?" Galt said.

"Things are happening, sir," the comm officer said. "The captain believed you'd want to see this."

"I'm on my way," Galt said.

-20-

"Commodore on the bridge," Karpov said.

Galt limped to his chair, sitting down. Most of the same officers were back at the consoles.

"Sir," Usan said, swiveling around to look at him. "I thought you'd want to see this. More Saurian warships have launched from the mobile asteroids."

Galt slipped on and used his glove. On a holo-screen, he observed another one hundred and ten warships. They'd launched from the mobile asteroids.

"Where are those headed?" Galt asked.

Usan didn't answer right away, as he was too busy studying his sensors. "Sir, they're headed in the same direction as the others: directly for the enemy's battle station."

Galt nodded. He'd thought so.

It was crazy. But now, more hours passed. Galt figured he should have taken a real nap, maybe several hours. The alien ships moved faster than chemically fueled ships would, but much slower than Star Watch ships could achieve.

Finally, Usan spotted something new: activity from the planet. He put it on the main screen.

Huge rockets rose from the surface. They roared up in mass. In low orbit, the rockets fell away, boosters helping…space fighters to escape the gravity well of the red planet.

The space fighters were squat and thick, using propellant to leave low orbital space and head for the battle station farther away.

"More of the same leaving the surface," Usan said.

Galt wasn't so sure. He used a holo-screen to study the latest flock of rockets leaving the surface. These were bigger than the space-fighter rockets. The fronts showed warheads, he believed.

"My mistake," Usan said a moment later. "They're missiles."

"Looks like," Galt said.

The rockets or missiles didn't stop accelerating once they reached low planetary orbit. Instead, they continued to accelerate. In moments, the huge missiles passed the space fighters. Shortly after that, the missiles passed the battle station. The missiles headed for the approaching Saurian fleet.

No beams, missiles or fighters had launched from the battle station. Usan detected plenty of sensor activity from it, though. Did people or teddy bears on the station direct the space battle?

Minutes ticked by and became an hour, and then two and three. At that point, the First Saurian Fleet of one hundred and three ships reached the ten million kilometer mark from the battle station. They had yet to begin decelerating.

"Sir," Usan said. "I've spotted a third fleet of one hundred and ten Saurian ships leaving the mobile asteroids. They're also headed for the battle station."

Galt was nodding. "The Saurians have staggered their attack."

The First Saurian Fleet continued to bore in toward the battle station. The red-planet missiles had ceased accelerating, but they moved at a higher velocity toward the enemy fleet than the enemy moved toward them.

The distances rapidly closed between the two masses.

"Sir," Usan said. "The lizard ships are beaming the missiles."

Galt had been waiting for that, as the Saurian ships hadn't launched any counter-missiles or used railguns or something similar.

On the main screen, one hundred and three beams flashed from the Saurian ships. They crossed the distance and struck the missiles heading at them.

"What type of beams are those?" Galt asked.

"Laser," Usan said, who studied a monitor. "They're so weak I'd almost think they're chemically charged lasers. But I have other readings. The Saurian ships are running hotter than before. They're using their fusion drives to power the lasers."

"Laser," Galt said. That was revealing. "The Saurians are far behind us, technologically speaking."

"Yes sir," Usan said. "I'd surely agree with that."

Either the missiles had heavy hulls or Usan was right and those were weak laser beams. The missiles continued in, and now, they accelerated again, jumping at the approaching fleet.

Someone in the Saurian fleet had brains. Ships concentrated on missiles, ten to one, at least. Soon, missile hulls glowed from the laser heat.

A warhead on a missile detached. The missile exploded. The shrapnel from that hit other nearby missiles. A chain reaction started, taking out six more missiles. Now one of the warheads detonated, the nuclear blast taking out a dozen more missiles.

The blast created a whiteout, likely upsetting Saurian targeting. The lasers began missing missiles.

"The battle station is using radio waves," Usan said. "The waves are directed at the missiles."

The remaining missiles began moving apart and started staggering. Taking out all of them or another dozen wouldn't prove as easy now.

The leading missiles detonated. The blast and EMP must have played havoc upon the closing enemy ships.

The Saurian vessels began to fan out, but at a much slower velocity than the huge incoming missiles.

Once more, lasers beamed ten to one, aiming at the missiles instead of the warheads.

Using the tactic, the Saurians took out several missiles.

Another leading batch of missiles exploded.

"Seems like a weird way to use them," Usan said.

130

"Perhaps not," Galt said. "I think the teddy bears are trying to get just a few warheads amongst the ships. They're willing to sacrifice the rest to do that."

"The Saurians ships are getting too much separation for that," Usan said.

"Maybe," Galt said.

The lasers burned. More missiles ceased their final acceleration.

Three missiles headed for a group of twenty-three Saurian ships. In an instant, all three warheads detonated.

"They're ten klicks from the enemy," Usan said.

The blast knocked out—

"Five Saurian ships are down," Usan said.

A big missile roared into the remaining eighteen. It detonated practically on top of them.

A whiteout hid the results for a time.

When the *Stonewall Jackson's* sensors could reach them again, Usan counted eighteen drifting hulks, many of them torn open from the nuclear blast.

"They have tin hulls," Usan said.

The majority of Saurian vessels had survived the missile attack. They were much closer to the battle station and the planet behind it.

Now, however, the squat fighters reached the enemy ships, beginning to use heavy shellfire against them.

Galt used his holo-screens, sitting forward as he studied the situation. "The fighters must have taken some hard radiation."

"Exactly my thought, sir," Usan said. "The fighters used some of the whiteouts to bore in secretly. I doubt any of the fighter crews will survive the attack."

"Suicide fighter pilots?" Galt asked.

"Yup," Usan said.

Captain Karpov cleared his throat, staring fixedly at the sensor chief.

Usan noticed. "I mean: yes sir."

Karpov nodded with approval.

Even as the fighters swarmed upon the surviving majority Saurian ships, massive laser beams fired from the battle station. Those beams hit and slagged one Saurian vessel after another.

The Saurian First Fleet died at the outer range of the battle station. They did horrid destruction to the space fighters, however, devastating them and then bombing the survivors.

A few Saurian missiles launched from the First Fleet and headed fast at the battle station.

Battle-station chainguns laid down a mass of projectiles, shredding the enemy missiles. Not one got through.

"The teddy bears slaughtered the enemy," Usan said.

"The Second Saurian Fleet is still coming," Galt said.

The intelligent teddy bears of the red planet must have reached the same conclusion. Another mass wave of missiles launched from surface.

Only a few space fighters turned back from the destroyed Saurian First Fleet, heading for the battle station. The fighters left behind drifting hulks and Saurian debris.

Once again, time crawled.

The few space fighters reached the battle station, landing in hangar bays.

Half as many planetary missiles as before had roared past the station, heading for the second wave of invading warships.

"I just thought of something," Karpov said.

"Yes," Galt said.

"Perhaps we're saving the red-planet aliens because the Saurians began the battle by launching ninety-eight missiles at us. Those missiles could have softened up the teddy bears. Instead, the Saurians wasted them on us."

"Good point," Galt said. Did Saurian Command think like Karpov, holding the First Fleet's loss against the task force? Until he learned differently, Galt would presume so.

Galt sighed. In a few hours, if events followed the first, Act Two of the battle would begin. Who was going to win, the teddy bears or the Saurians?

Galt rose. He needed another break. He was going to catch some shuteye. "Call me when it starts again. Make sure everyone is either relieved so the next shift can come or they eat and get some sleep. We've been at this for too long."

"Yes sir," Karpov said.

"That includes you, Captain."

Karpov nodded.

With that, Galt took his leave.

-21-

When Galt reappeared on the bridge, the planetary-launched missiles reached the laser range of the Second Saurian Fleet of one hundred and ten vessels.

"Sir," Usan said. "The wattage of the Saurian lasers—they're better, hotter, than the lasers from the First Fleet."

"Say again," replied Galt.

Sensor Chief Usan did so.

Galt stroked his chin. "Do you detect any other differences from this fleet?"

Usan played with his board. "I'm not sure yet, sir, but these ships might have thicker hulls."

Galt nodded. This was making brutal sense. The Saurians had clearly sent lesser warships first. Perhaps the crews were lower-rated as well. Perhaps Saurian High Command wished to soak up enemy munitions with their worst vessels and crews. That was a brutal and callous strategy, implying a ruthless race.

The Saurian ship-lasers targeted the fewer planetary missiles. They destroyed the missiles faster than before because better ships fired against a much lesser number of targets.

Maybe the teddy bear aliens got lucky, though. Maybe their strategy paid off in ways Galt didn't recognize other than as sheer luck.

Two nuclear detonations took out nineteen Saurian warships and caused another five to drop back.

The rest of the Saurian Second Fleet bored in toward the battle station in near-moon-orbit.

Now, the station's heavy lasers targeted Saurian vessels. These lasers had greater effective range than the warships. The beams fired in tandem against targeted warships. The hulls might have been better, but massed beams burned into the warship nonetheless. Some of the targeted ships ceased accelerating or functioning, a few blew up. The shrapnel and debris from those struck other Saurian vessels. The tougher hulls helped, as fewer ships fell to the shrapnel.

Finally, about half the Saurian Second Fleet—what had made it this far—began targeting the battle station with their ship-lasers.

Like the warships, the station lacked an electromagnetic shield. It had heavy hull armor and thick layers of rock. The rock must have been painfully carted up from the planet, but it proved its worth.

Metal hull plating glowed red and began to slag. Over time, laser-heated rock turned into lava, flowing into space. Even so, the battle station was a tough SOB of a structure and absorbed a fearful barrage of lasers. At the same time, the station's heavy beams continued to take a toll of the incoming enemy.

The closer the warships came, the fiercer the station lasers became against them. The same held true for the weaker Saurian lasers against the station. For both sides, greater range dissipated the lasers killing power while shorter range increased it.

It was a battle of attrition, and it was hard to tell who was winning.

Space fighters launched from the battle station. There weren't very many of them. They launched from the planetary side of the station, maneuvered into clusters and roared around the station to attack the nearest Saurian warships.

At the same time, a few planetary missiles rose into orbital space, burning hot for the near fight.

The Saurian Second Fleet was a pitiful remnant of its initial size and glory. As several more exploded, they burned down the final space fighters and caused detonations in various parts of the battle station.

Many of the heavy lasers on the station had ceased firing. More now stopped beaming, as the Saurians knocked them out.

Planetary missiles roared among the last Saurian warships and detonated. Their nuclear blasts finished off the remaining Saurian warships, but they also took out chunks of battle station.

This round was over. The teddy bears had won again, but at awful cost to their station. Did they have more space fighters or planetary missiles?

"Sir," Usan said. "I've discovered a stealth attack."

"Where?" asked Galt. "Who launched a stealth attack?"

"I'm putting it on the main screen," Usan said. "The Saurians launched it. I don't know how we missed it before this."

Galt studied the main screen with absorption.

Fifty-odd Saurian missiles burned hot. They were midway between the destroyed Second Fleet and the approaching Saurian Third Fleet. The missiles leapt forward as they accelerated at higher gravities. They were smaller than the planetary missiles, but then they hadn't needed massive amounts of fuel to escape a heavy gravity well.

"The missiles will be at the battle station soon," Usan said. "I don't see much in way of defense for the other side to take 'em down."

"Define soon," Galt said.

"Less than an hour," Usan said.

"Sir," the new comm officer told Galt. "You have a call, from Commodore Ketchum. He wishes to speak to you."

Galt accepted the call, putting dour Ketchum on a holo-screen.

"Dammit man," Ketchum said. "Are we going to let the lizards burn down the others? We've already sided against them. It will be in our disfavor if we allow the lizards to win."

Galt was beginning to think likewise. They'd chosen a side, even though all they'd done was defend themselves against a missile assault from the Saurians. He hesitated in giving Ketchum an answer, however. He wasn't sure on the correct course of action. For one thing, none of them had figured out where they were.

Concerning that, Galt had the *Stonewall Jackson* science teams trying to figure out where in the galaxy they were. The scientists hadn't given him any answers yet. For one thing, they didn't recognize any spiral arms. In truth, they didn't recognize anything about the region of space. All they could tell him was they weren't where they'd been.

For those reasons and others, Galt hesitated. He waited for a sign perhaps. Ketchum tried to convince him to act against the Saurians. But Ketchum's reasons weren't convincing enough.

Sometime after the call, the Saurian missiles came into battle-station laser range. The remaining lasers burned down one missile after enough. The trouble was, there weren't enough station lasers left.

When the surviving missiles reached a certain point, station chainguns hosed them, destroying even more.

Despite that, a few missiles made it near enough and detonated with nuclear fireballs. These were bigger blasts than what the planetary missiles had produced. The explosions did it. They more than tore the station up, they blew it apart into chunks and pieces. Just as bad, perhaps, the blasts forced the chunks and pieces toward the red planet.

The battle station was gone. Its remains would rain onto the red planet in the next few hours. What would that do to the population?

Galt shook his head, concentrating on the big picture. The first two Saurian fleets were gone. The third and so-far final wave of one hundred and ten Saurian warships headed for the seemingly defenseless planet. It would take the fleet a few hours to reach it, but they were coming like the march of doom.

Here was the question for Galt. Should he let the Saurians bomb the red planet? Should the task force watch and do nothing?

Galt drummed his fingers on an armrest. Were there other teddy bears in next four inner terrestrial planets? No one had figured that out yet. Presently, the task force was alone out here. They could use some help. Who would help them, though? The Saurian invaders who'd lost a missile salvo to them? The teddy bears who knew the task force had watched while the red planet died?

I need some advice. This is too big for just one man to decide.

"I want a three-way channel," Galt told the comm officer. "Set it up to route through my holo-screens."

Soon, she told him the three-way was ready.

Galt told her to contact Lair and Ketchum.

In moments, Galt eyed Captain Lair on one holo-screen and Commodore Ketchum on the other. A dampener field would keep his voice from reaching the others on the bridge.

"I need to decide our next move fast," Galt told Lair and Ketchum. "I need...more brainpower to think this through in the few minutes I have. Thus, you two are my brain trust as of this moment. Let's start with you, Commodore. You believe we should wipe out the Saurians. I want to know why."

Old Ketchum grinned dourly. "We should take out the last fleet, which is probably their best fleet. Then, we should take out their mobile asteroids. The reason is simple. They attacked us and did so unprovoked. We can't trust them. Maybe they're xenophobic. I don't know nor care. They've shown their colors, a nest of vipers. The best thing to do to vipers is stomp 'em dead."

Galt nodded. "Thank you, Commodore. Captain Lair, opinions?"

"I'm not as sure as the commodore," she said. "The Saurians launched missiles at us. That's incontrovertible fact. We knocked them down but that was all we've done. Given the brutal nature of the combat we've witnessed, the Saurians might understand that by our doing nothing we allowed them to win. That means they might not hold a grudge against us."

"We didn't allow them?" Galt asked. "We just did nothing."

"Right," Lair said. "By doing nothing we allowed them to proceed with their invasion. They might understand that, although they might not. This is just my opinion, mind you. Do with it as you will."

"Just a minute," Ketchum said. He'd been looking away, listening intently to someone else on his light cruiser.

"What's happened?" Galt asked.

Ketchum didn't answer, but got up and left the screen. Galt could hear Ketchum mutter off-screen. In an instant, Ketchum sat back down and looked intently at the two of them.

"Sir, Captain Lair, my people have just discovered an asteroidal supership—well, not of the same size as the original in the Trappist-1 System, but made of the same compressed stardust hull. This ship is among the Saurian mobile asteroids. It's been shielded from us until now."

"Shielded how?" asked Galt.

"By their bigger mobile asteroids being in the way of our sensors," Ketchum said. "The lizards have been moving the mobile asteroids and my people got a look at the-until-now hidden ship. Anyway, the point is the lizards have a ship of the kind that lured us into this bizarre realm."

"This changes everything," Lair said.

"How does it?" Galt asked. "How do you think it changes everything, Captain?"

"Easy," Lair said. "We must get hold of the asteroidal ship, or we must find out who captains it. Either way—no—we need to get that ship in order learn how to get home. I'm thinking this on the assumption the original asteroidal ship was instrumental in our leaving the Commonwealth."

Galt could see that. It was logical thought. "What's the best way to get the ship? Do you think the Saurians are just going to give it to us?"

Lair looked at him with surprise. "Sir, I most certainly think the lizards will *not* give us the ship. From what we've witnessed, I think they're a hardhearted race with a vicious style of combat. They don't mind losing their own people. I'm sure they think nothing about visiting genocide upon others. If we want the asteroidal supership—"

"Just a minute, Captain," Galt said, interrupting. "Is it the same kind of vessel as the Trappist-1 supership? It's supposed to have the same hull, but not size. Ketchum, do you have screen shots of the ship?"

"Indeed I do." Ketchum pressed a transmit button.

On one of Galt's holo-screens appeared a shot of the asteroidal ship. It looked like the one they'd faced except for one particular: it was one-quarter the size of the original supership.

Looking at the ship—Galt knew the others were right. The first asteroidal supership had drawn them from the Commonwealth and Human Space. They'd crossed a strange region of space, a bizarre realm if ever there was one. That implied alien and advanced technology or tech no one in Star Watch possessed.

"You're both right," Galt said. "We need to acquire the ship and learn if its technology can take us back home, wherever home is."

"That makes perfect sense to me," Ketchum said.

"We'll likely have to acquire the ship through military action," Galt said.

"Of that," Captain Lair said, "I have no doubt. The lizards aren't going to let go of anything unless we pry it from their cold, dead hands."

Galt sat back, rubbing his forehead. The final decision was his. He needed to make the right one and do it now.

"We need to do *something,*" Ketchum said impatiently. "We need to do something right away."

Galt silently agreed even as his stomach churned. What was the best way to do this? He needed to decide now.

-22-

The three of them were still in linked conference, Galt in Battleship *Stonewall Jackson*, Ketchum in Light Cruiser *Babylon* and Lair in Mothership *Joan of Arc*.

The Saurian Third Fleet began to accelerate toward the seemingly defenseless red planet.

The chunks and pieces of the destroyed battle station yet headed for the highest planetary atmosphere. No missiles rose from the planet. No space fighters launched. The small teddy bear warships they'd seen in the beginning were nowhere in evidence. Perhaps those spaceships had landed on the surface or were on the other side of the planet.

Given what they'd witnessed so far, it would likely take the Saurian Third Fleet another forty-five minutes to begin whatever it would do. Would the Saurians spray poisoned aerosols on the planet? Would they drop nukes? Did the lizards have some other nefarious means to impose their will upon the teddy bears of the planet?

"We need to make a decision," Ketchum said forcefully. "You're woolgathering, Galt. Get to it, man."

"Commodore," Captain Lair said to Ketchum. "That's a disrespectful attitude. Many consider me a gruff officer, yet I know that only one person can be in charge. Here, that's Commodore Galt. I back him to the hilt. You'd better do so as well or we may never get home. A divided council is the worst thing of all."

141

"Now see here, *Captain,*" Ketchum said, "don't you dare take that tone with me."

"Commodore," Galt said, "the captain is correct. I must know this instant, do you support me?"

"You're in charge," Ketchum said.

"No," Galt said, "do you swear to obey my commands?"

"And if I don't," Ketchum said with a mulish, stubborn look.

"If you don't, sir, I'll relieve you of command. The captain has clarified my thinking because she's correct. Either we have unity of command or we can forget the whole thing. Make your decision, sir, and make it now."

Ketchum mumbled under his breath.

"No," Galt said, "that's not good enough. What's your decision?"

"Oh, very well," Ketchum said, "if you're going to force this on me under duress."

"Be careful what you say," Galt told him. "It's not under duress. Do you of your own free will swear to obey my commands, according to Star Watch regulations, until we reach home?"

Ketchum waited a half-beat before he said, "Yes."

"Then let me hear you say it. On the record. For your court martial hearing, if there is one."

Ketchum stared at Galt.

Galt wondered if he'd pushed the old boy too far.

"I swear by all that I hold dear to obey your commands, Commodore. There," Ketchum said, "does that satisfy you?"

"It does," Galt said. "Now, let's get down to business." During the discussion, he'd made his decision about the Saurians and the ship.

"Sir," Lair said, with staring eyes, "may I interrupt? I have new data that is of utmost importance."

"Of course," Galt said, noting her unsettled demeanor. "You two are my brain trust. You two are the ones I'm leaning on. What is it, Lair? Spit it out."

"My science team has just come to their conclusion." Lair was more than unsettled but looked shaken. "I've given the teams different projects but this one had priority. They've concluded—I know this will sound strange but I believe it's vital. The science team has concluded we've entered a different dimension from our own."

Galt felt his mouth dry out even as a pit formed in his gut. He wanted to protest the conclusion. Yet, he'd gone through the bizarre transfers twice already, no, three times. What would dimensional travel look like? It could very well look like what they'd gone through.

"That's sheer nonsense," Ketchum said. "It's utter nonsense. We have many sorts of drives. There are Laumer Point wormholes. There are the—"

"Commodore Ketchum," Lair said, interrupting, "if you would allow me to finish."

Ketchum stared at her, maybe with panic stirring in his eyes. "Speak what you must," he said in a slightly altered voice.

"Thank you," Lair said. "The findings that persuaded me are these." She pressed a switch, putting data onto their screens.

"Please, Captain," Galt said, who only glanced at the data. "I don't have time to figure out such gibberish. The science officers speak a different language from the rest of us, or it often feels that way. I call it gibberish. Tell it to me plain."

"Sir, there are compositions here that aren't the same as what we'd find in our dimension or universe. My science team tells me the theory of a multiverse or many layered dimensions is true, as we've passed through several layers. And there's the—"

"Yes, yes," Galt said, interrupting, "I'm aware of the multiverse theory and I understand dimensional travel just fine, or the theory of it. I watched cartoons when I was a kid and one of my favorite shows was *Jumpers.*"

"Ah," Lair said, smiling. "Yes, I watched *Jumpers*, too. The shows were a lot of fun. Marty was my favorite character."

"That makes sense," Galt said. He'd hated Marty, liking Frederick the best.

"If you watched *Jumpers,*" Lair said, "and if you subscribe to that theory—"

143

"I don't know if I'd call it subscribe," Galt said, interrupting, "but your science people believe this is a different dimension. Is that correct?"

"Yes," Lair said. "Yes, you're correct sir. Let's keep on track. That's my normal procedure. The situation has unnerved me, I admit. But I'm up to my usual standards. I assure you of that."

"I have no doubt," Galt said. "Let's get to the point, and please Captain, while I appreciate all you've done, please be succinct."

Lair nodded. "If we're in a different dimension, then surely the asteroidal supership had the means to move us and employed that means against us. It had the means of creating what must have been a rip or a rent in the space-time continuum. We followed it because it employed the rip upon us when we went through. Somehow, we've lost the asteroidal supership. One would presume that we've therefore lost the means of creating a rent or a rip or whatever it is you want to call it to get us back home."

"Portal sounds like a good name to me," Ketchum said.

"Thank you, Commodore," Lair said. "A portal it is. If we cannot make a dimensional portal, we cannot get home. It's as simple as that. But, we've spotted a ship of similar composition as the asteroidal supership."

"Of a quarter its diameter," Ketchum said, "which means it has far less mass than the original."

"I don't deny that," Lair said. "It may not be able to create a dimensional rip because it may lack the engine or other power the first ship had. Yet, in some way, this ship is connected to the first. The compressed stardust hull shows us that. It's the only link I know to the supership that could give us a way of finding our way home through the correct portal."

Galt stroked his chin. "Somehow, the Saurians have gotten hold of that vessel. It may or may not be operative. Either way, it can either make a portal or contact the first vessel."

"We're hoping," Lair said. "So far, though, there are no other hopes. It appears that if we want to go home, we must capture that ship."

144

"Take it from the Saurians no matter what it costs for them," Galt said.

"Damn straight," Ketchum said. "Now, we're talking. Let's kill the lizards and grab the ship."

Galt frowned. "I don't want to annihilate an entire fleet out of spite. I do this reluctantly."

"They didn't show any reluctance attacking the red planet," Ketchum said.

"While that's true," Galt said, "we have no idea what the bears did to the Saurians. Maybe the committed atrocities against them. We don't know. And even if not, I live by the old dictum that two wrongs don't make a right."

Both Lair and Ketchum stared at him as if he'd said something idiotic.

It was a childhood saying, and yet, it was true. But that wasn't the issue. Getting the ship was. He couldn't bargain with the Saurians because none of them knew the language.

Galt had a thought. Could they translate the Saurian tongue? Could beings from different dimensions find a commonality?

The idea of being in a different dimension…it was debilitating, unreal.

Is my grip on sanity slipping?

Galt blinked purposefully. The dimensional travel news was affecting him more than he'd realized.

I need to anchor my intellect. I can't let the idea of different dimensions destroy my ability to think and reason.

Galt cleared his throat and looked at the other two. Could he admit this failing to them? No. In a commander, that was a mistake. He needed to show resolve and commitment to help kept their morale high.

Galt cleared his throat again. "I find hard to give the order to annihilate the Saurian armada. But my first duty is to Task Force 3. We must get home. We need to let Star Watch know that dimensional travel is possible."

"And we need to stop the original asteroidal supership," Ketchum said. "Perhaps it was scouting our dimension in a prelude to a full-scale invasion. We need a means to stop that invasion. The Saurians have a possible means in that ship."

"I understand," Galt said.

Despite all that, he had a knot in his gut. The next few minutes were going to decide the lives of all the Saurians, and they were possibly going to decide the lives of all the teddy bears, too.

"Listen," Galt said, and his mouth was so damned dry. He had to do this. Otherwise, he was dooming his entire command. What would that mean for their families back home?

For the third time, Galt cleared his throat. "Commodore Ketchum, you're going to take the light cruisers and destroyers and finish off the Third Saurian Fleet heading for the red planet. Captain Lair, you and the other mothership will hang back with the strikefighters and fold fighters in reserve."

Lair nodded.

Ketchum grinned, rubbing his hands.

"The battleships are going to take out the mobile asteroids and whatever else the Saurians have," Galt said. "The battleships have the heaviest shields. They have the heaviest beams. We should be able to do it easily enough."

"You might have trouble with Captain Aiken of the *Philip II*," Lair said. "He's something of a softliner in these things."

"Don't worry about that," Galt said. "You have your orders. Ketchum, get to it at once."

"Yes, Commodore," Ketchum said. "That's an excellent decision by the way."

Galt almost reprimanded Ketchum, telling the commodore he did not need his approval or disapproval. He'd been pushing Ketchum plenty hard, though. Thus, Galt didn't reprimand him but let it go.

In a moment, Ketchum and Lair disappeared from the holo-screens.

Galt heaved a sigh. He'd made the decision. Now, it was time to act and see what happened.

-23-

The task force began to maneuver.

Commodore Ketchum with his light cruisers and destroyers began to move toward the approaching Saurian Third Fleet. It was a gross disparity in numbers and tonnage for the Saurians. The Star Watch vessels had far superior technology.

At the same time, Galt instructed the captains of the *Alexander* and *Philip II* to follow the *Stonewall Jackson*. They were going to annihilate the mobile asteroids and any other ships and Saurians that attempted to stop them. The mobile asteroids had an even greater weight of tonnage on their side versus the battleships. It was like a child charging an elephant. But the heavy metals from the chthonian planet in the Alpha Centauri System would give the disruptor cannons an even more powerful tech advantage to the Star Watch squadron.

Galt told the captains they were to destroy with extreme prejudice, making sure nothing survived, not even any escape pods. This was—

"Just a minute, here," Captain Aiken of the *Philip II* said.

He was a rangy youngish man with a full black beard from Earhart, one of the farther planets in the Commonwealth. Those of Earhart seldom joined Star Watch and even less in any combat arms. Theirs was a pacifistic society. Aiken was an anomaly, the son of a settler from Argos. He didn't subscribe to the pacifistic cult of Earhart, but he'd supped from the philosophy enough that kill orders likely left him squeamish or worse.

"Did you say we're to *annihilate* with *extreme prejudice* the alien home platforms?" Aiken asked. "Perhaps there are Saurian women and children on them."

"Captain," said Galt, "this is neither the time nor the place to question my orders. I understand a little about Earhart. I understand you might not like the orders. I won't say I sympathize, but I understand."

Aiken nodded.

"However, this isn't a debating society." Galt paused before saying, "I'll tell you this: we're out of options."

"Commodore—"

"No," Galt said, interrupting. "Tell me this instant: will you comply as ordered?"

"Now see here," Aiken said. "There's no need to take that tone with me. We're in a hard spot. I know that. If I've heard correctly, we're in a different dimension. Because of that, I think everything has changed regarding the command structure."

"Captain Aiken, you have a decision to make."

As Galt said those words, a feeling of déjà vu swept over him. He'd just gone over this with Ketchum. Did he have to do this with softhearted Aiken, too? Was there something about moving to a different dimension that caused changes in personality? Even though he'd grown up on Earhart, Aiken would never have questioned him like this before. Moving through dimensions surely affected others differently, perhaps bringing out the essential personality more.

"I don't think it does change everything," Captain Aiken said. "I'm going to say my piece and I—"

"Captain," Galt said forcefully, interrupting once more. He didn't want to do this, but he wasn't going to dick around at a time like this. Maybe this was *his* essential personality coming forth. "Put your colonel of marines on the horn this instant."

Aiken looked taken aback. "For what purpose?"

"Are you disobeying a direct order?"

"Now see here," Aiken said, "there's no need to take that tone with me, sir."

148

"You will allow me to speak with the colonel this instant or I'll have you up on charges of insubordination and treason once we return home."

Aiken stiffened. A moment later, he turned and spoke loudly and then moved aside.

The *Philip II's* colonel of marines filled the screen. It showed a hard-faced man of short and muscular stature and wearing a red beret.

"This is Commodore Galt. You will relieve Captain Aiken of command and take immediate charge of the *Philip II* yourself."

A moment of confusion filled the colonel's face. That passed as he nodded sharply. "Yes sir! Is there anything else, *sir?"*

"I realize you're not trained to command a battleship," Galt said. "You'll use your XO, keeping him at your side to explain anything you don't understand as far as procedures. Now listen closely to this. I want my commands obeyed instantly. Do you understand?"

"I do, sir. It will be done as you've ordered." The colonel glanced at Captain Aiken, who pushed forward to the screen.

"Now see, here," Aiken said. "I don't recognize your authority to do this."

"Colonel," Galt said. "Are you there?"

"Yes sir," the colonel said.

"You will personally escort Captain Aiken to the brig. Have marines you implicitly trust guard the brig, allowing no one to speak with or seek the former commanding officer."

Aiken sputtered with outrage.

The colonel saluted, snapped his fingers and motioned to unseen marines most likely.

Yes. Two marines appeared, each grabbing one Aiken's arms. They drew him back even as the captain struggled to free himself.

The marine colonel sat, his face filling the screen.

Galt went over the situation with him.

"I understand, sir," the colonel said. "Now, if you'll excuse me, I have a task to perform."

149

Galt clicked off the connection. That had been unpleasant, to say the least. He hoped it didn't add to any problems over there. How much did the rest of the *Philip II's* crew respect Aiken? It might be good to check that out…later, when he had time.

For now, Galt watched as Captain Karpov rattled off orders. The *Stonewall Jackson* and other two battleships began to pick up velocity as they headed for the mobile asteroids. The gravity dampeners hid the effect from the crews, allowing the ships to maneuver faster and harder than a vessel without them.

Fifteen minutes later, Usan alerted him to Ketchum's developing attack.

Galt watched on the main screen.

The light cruisers and reaming destroyers deployed in a fan formation. They'd watched the first two Saurian fleets earlier. Surely, the third wouldn't be that much different, even if it were the Saurians' best fleet.

While still well beyond former Saurian ship-firing-laser range, the light cruisers opened up with their fusion cannons.

The red beams burned into the leading Saurian ships. The enemy lacked electromagnetic shields, just the thickness of their armored hulls. Maybe the Third Saurian Fleet's warships had better hulls than the former fleets did. It didn't matter much to the fusion beams, though.

During the next few minutes, Ketchum had a field day, rupturing one Saurian hull after another. Frankly, it was an old-style turkey shoot, butchery. The only thing that made it questionable was the large number of enemy vessels.

The Saurian Third Fleet continued to bore toward the red planet. They fired lasers, but the light cruisers were still out of effective laser range.

Now, Ketchum ordered the destroyers forward as he ordered the *Assyria* back. The light cruiser was having trouble keeping its fusion cannon active.

The Saurian ships achieved their hottest thruster burn yet, the warships accelerating. That surely supplied more wattage for the laser cannons. Yes. Look at this. Some lasers reached out and actually began to turn a few cruiser shields red in small areas.

150

Then, the remaining Saurian ships separated, each heading in a different vector, perhaps to make a greater separation of targets. At the same time, they launched missiles and possibly bombs, at the light cruisers.

In the end, it made no difference.

Ketchum's light cruisers and destroyers were simply too advanced technologically. If the Saurian ships had stared toe-to-toe with the others at close range, their lasers might have scratched the destroyers, at least. At long range, the enemy vessels didn't stand a chance.

The Saurian Third Fleet soon ceased to exist. Its missiles died under fusion barrages as well.

During that time, the *Stonewall Jackson*, *Alexander* and *Philip II* accelerated toward the mobile asteroids. Despite their tiny size, the battleships must have looked menacing to the watching Saurians. They'd surely witnessed the destruction of the Third Fleet.

Saurian space fighters and missiles launched from the mobile asteroids. They gathered *en masse* and then headed out to the much faster approaching battleships.

The yellow disruptor beams began to burn. First, the three heavy beams swept through the space fighters and missiles, killing them at extreme range and with pathetic ease.

Perhaps at that point, the Saurians realized the hopelessness of their position.

Galt shook his head. He wasn't going to think that way. This was for all the marbles, for going home again. These were aliens from a different dimension. He owed them nothing.

With the fighters and missiles destroyed, Galt moved the battleships even closer toward the mobile asteroids. On the possibility that the Saurians possessed a last ditch longer-distance weapon, Galt ceased advancing once reading mid-range—for disruptor beams, that is.

The disruptor beams burned again. This time, they hit the mobile asteroids. These were huge targets with vast mass. Much of their bulk appeared to be asteroid rock. That meant it took time even for the disruptor beams to burn through them.

In time, however, vast explosions helped with the asteroid destruction. Munitions must be going off over there, perhaps some nuclear warheads.

The mobile asteroids began to crack and then split apart. Battleship sensors told of tens of thousands of Saurians floating in space among the asteroidal wreckage.

Galt didn't want to hear that, as he had to harden his heart against it. But he had to do this. He did. It was that simple.

The comparatively small asteroidal vessel—the one with the compressed stardust hull—received many direct hits from shrapnel and chunks of destroyed asteroid.

According to Usan, those hits didn't seem to damage the vessel because of its impressive hull.

On the main screen, Galt watched the strange alien ship drift away from the massed wreckage. The various asteroid pieces smashing against it had acted like billiard balls, deflecting the asteroidal ship away.

To make sure no Saurians were playing dead—Galt had to send teams to the asteroidal ship—he ordered several antimatter missiles into the drifting mass.

The antimatter blasts churned the mass and consumed other parts, and surely killed any surviving, hiding Saurians.

Was that genocide?

Galt didn't want to think so. The enemies were military crews in a war fleet, not civilians.

What did he owe the Saurians anyway? Nothing. So why did it feel like a stain against his conscience to obliterate the technologically inferior aliens?

This was as one-sided a battle as Galt had ever been in. And as crazy as it sounded for a military man, he never wanted to be in such a one-sided battle again. It felt too much like murder.

Now he had to decide what they were going to do with the alien asteroidal ship. Who would go check it out? And should he try to contact the aliens on the red planet?

He had to make more decisions.

Galt rubbed his face. He was the man of the hour, having imposed his will on Ketchum and Aiken. Now, it was time to impose his will on the situation despite whatever conflict he might have with his conscience. He owed it to his people to do whatever he could to get back home.

Galt squinted at the drifting asteroidal ship. Was anyone aboard it?

"Captain," Galt said. "It's time to approach the alien ship."

"Yes, sir," Karpov said, giving orders to the helm.

-24-

Victory returned to the Trappist-1 System after a swift foray away to Omicron 9.

Several days ago, they'd left through the hyper-spatial tube to Earth. From there, they'd used the tube to the Omicron 9 System.

Throughout that time, Maddox had silently demurred. He'd been reliving his time in the City of Pyramids on the desert planet in the Erill System. He had thought once to send Captain Becker into the Erill Universe. That was after defeating the Prime Saa of the Liss cybers. Meta had talked him out of that. Messing with dimensions—yes, he'd helped Balron reach his dimension. That had been such a swift foray, however. They were talking about real dimensional travel, knowing so very little about it.

This didn't seem like a wise decision. Yet, how else could they rescue Task Force 3 and the Lord High Admiral's granddaughter?

They'd gone to the fourth planet of Omicron 9. Three days hard work had transferred the damned copy of the Yon Soth machine from Ludendorff's subterranean quarters onto Hangar Bay 2 aboard *Victory*.

The machine gave Maddox the creeps. He didn't like having Cthulhu-like alien devices aboard his precious starship.

Galyan liked it even less. He'd been complaining so much that Maddox had finally told him to stow it. They had the machine and they were going to use it.

154

Naturally, Ludendorff had demanded that key members of his Kai-Kaus group join them aboard *Victory*.

That was logical and Maddox liked the Kai-Kaus if for no other reason that they still adored him. He'd saved them long ago from the Builder Dyson Sphere and the hybrid Swarm soldiers that had lived with them on the sphere, attacking all the time.

The renewed experimentation on the Yon Soth machine had started immediately. It continued before and after using the hyper-spatial tube to reach Earth and before and after using the tube to return to the Trappist-1 System.

During their absence from Trappist-1, the mining personnel who'd survived the supership's assault had left the system. It meant the system was devoid of human life except for *Victory's* crew.

Victory maneuvered to the region in space where the asteroidal supership had appeared and where Task Force 3 had disappeared. The destroyed mass of Zinc and its moons had left the region as the rubble continued in regular orbital around the red dwarf star.

The experiments on the Yon Soth machine continued as Ludendorff sought mastery over it so they could...find Task Force 3.

Maddox had been sleeping poorly. He attributed it to the machine, as his intuitive sense had been warning him about something evil. His memories about the Erills had been doing the same thing.

Maddox decided on a visit, going to Hangar Bay 2. It was time to see how Ludendorff and his people were doing.

The professor and his team were busy on the big black machine. It looked like several alien city blocks shoved together, although not so massive as that. The machine had odd shapes and a weird design. The control panel was made for tentacles instead of fingers. Wisely, Ludendorff had rerouted that, adding fixtures so human hands could input data.

As Ludendorff and his team experimented, Galyan looked on from a distance.

Maddox walked up to the holoimage. "How are they doing?"

Galyan glanced at him. "Ludendorff spurs them on, sir. He says he is making progress. They are constantly turning it on and shutting it off. Yet, I am uncertain. There are things about the machine and our situation I find troubling."

"I know what you mean. The thing is giving me nightmares."

"Captain?"

Maddox grinned sourly. Should he even say this? He shrugged. "I don't remember the dreams, but my sleep is off."

Galyan studied him.

Maddox sighed. He was sure Galyan was categorizing and cataloging what he said, how he said it and his look as he did.

"Are you adding to my personality profile?" Maddox asked.

"I am, sir."

"What does it tell you?"

"I am still analyzing as I correlate the various factors and integrate them into a coherent whole. Ah. My analysis suggests that it is not certain the machine is the locus for your bad sleep."

"What do you think it is, the Erills from the City of Pyramids?"

"Sir, may I hold off from giving you my possibilities? I have twenty-eight at present and I think that is too many to relate in one sitting."

"Twenty-eight?" Maddox asked. "Yeah, that's way too many. All right, Galyan, don't worry about it."

Ludendorff looked up and noticed Maddox watching. Ludendorff straightened his lab coat, spoke to several of the techs and then strode to Maddox and Galyan.

"Good news, my boy," Ludendorff said. "We're ready to give it a try."

"In what way specifically?" Maddox asked.

"Why, in opening a rift in space." Ludendorff cleared his throat. "In the space-time continuum, to be more precise. We shall attempt to follow the trail of the asteroidal supership from one dimension to another."

Maddox couldn't shake the terror of the Erills. Not that he feared them. He did not, as he might have been the only human with a weapon against them. He feared opening a way into a dimension that could flood human space with terrifying entities.

"We're trying to save Task Force 3," Maddox said. "I'm not as concerned about the supership."

"I think you should be. It's the key to all of this."

"I'll decide what's key."

Ludendorff stiffened.

"Professor, aren't you worried we'll let vile aliens into our dimension?"

"Ah," Ludendorff said. "I've been thinking about that. The Ur-Builders made a portal, a permanent path from one dimension to another. We're using a ship, crossing over quickly. That's different, don't you see? We slip through, leaving no way back to our realm."

Maddox considered that. It made sense. The Erills had used a portal. They were using a ship to cross quickly.

"That helps my peace of mind a little," Maddox said. "So, ah, how do you open a rift in the space-time continuum?"

"Eh?" Ludendorff waved a hand. "We're experimenting. We're attempting possibilities to discover the way. It helps immensely that we know it's possible, as we've seen it done. I've narrowed the approach to three options. We'll try the first and see what happens."

Maddox rubbed his forehead. Galyan had twenty-eight possibilities. Ludendorff had three options. Something pinged the captain's intuitive sense. He doubted it was Galyan's ideas. That meant Ludendorff's idea…

"Professor—"

"No, no," Ludendorff said, interrupting. "I know what you're going to say. Slow down. There are too many problems, too many risks. I know you're worried about an Erill-like problem. Here's my rebuttal to that—the second part, anyway. You've already heard the first: ship versus portal."

Maddox nodded.

"How does science and technology advance unless we take risks," Ludendorff said, "unless we attempt something new and impressive?"

"Is this new and impressive?" asked Maddox. "No. It's old. I won't even mention the Ur-Builders and Erills. The alien supership has done it before. It even took our task force with it."

"My point still holds," Ludendorff said. "This is new for us."

"We're using evil Yon Soth machinery," Maddox said. "Maybe the ancient Yon Soths had something to do with helping the Ur-Builders make their portal."

"There was no indication of that."

"We hardly know anything about that distant era. But forget about that. There are likely traps hidden in our machine. What if we accidentally open a rift in the space-time continuum, fall into it and can't figure out how to make it out again?"

"Bah! What over-cautious nonsense, my boy. I'm here, my technicians are here and the machine is here. You fear the machine, but your fear is unfounded. What we can do once, we can do twice."

"You mean back in your office on the fourth planet of Omicron 9?"

"Of course," Ludendorff said.

"Professor, do you remember when you used the machine then, disappearing, and I had to save your ass? That happened once. Will it now happen twice but with worse ramifications for the entire ship?"

Ludendorff snorted angrily and shook his head. "I've advanced far beyond that. I know much more about the properties we're using. My team has cataloged everything. I assure you, Captain, this time it will work."

"It worked last time, just not as you expected."

Ludendorff threw his hands into the air. "I've heard enough of your pessimism. Will you allow me to proceed or not?"

Maddox scowled, confounded. The Lord High Admiral had given him a mission: find the lost task force and bring it home. Ludendorff had the only means of a possibility, given what they knew so far. His intuitive sense warned him, he wasn't sure about what. It was a broad category warning, if you will.

"Continue with the experiment, Professor. I'll be on the bridge. Galyan, you keep watch here. If anything goes amiss, inform me instantly."

"Yes sir," Galyan said.

Ludendorff looked as if he was going to speak, but refrained. He marched back to the machine and his team.

Soon, Maddox was on the bridge, sitting in his chair, looking at the main screen.

The comm officer said, "The professor would like to speak to you through the main screen, sir."

"Put him up," Maddox said.

Ludendorff's face appeared. "We're ready, my boy. Even better, I believe I've discovered a dimensional trail. I'll put the findings on the screen."

From the hangar bay, Ludendorff manipulated a board.

A faint green line superimposed upon space appeared on the main screen.

"The line shows—I don't have a word for it yet," Ludendorff said. "But I'm certain the trail was made by the supership. The trail is fading and will only last a few more days. That's another reason we must attempt the opening of the rip now rather than later."

Maddox hesitated. This struck him as stranger than anything they'd done before. He glanced at the bridge personnel. They were ready at their stations.

He'd crossed dimensions before, if only for a short time. Maybe the starship could do it and they could rescue the task force.

"Let's give it a try," Maddox said.

"Excellent," Ludendorff said, beaming. "We're making history, Captain. History, I tell you. This is momentous."

Ludendorff disappeared from the screen.

The main engines created more power, supplying much of the extra to the Yon Soth machine. A strange vibration shook *Victory's* hull.

Maddox lurched upright as a feeling of wrongness coursed through him. The intuitive sense granted him by Balron the Traveler—

Galyan appeared before him on the bridge. "Emergency, emergency," Galyan said.

"Spit it out. What happened?"

"Professor Ludendorff has disappeared, sir. He has disappeared completely."

Maddox swore and then said, "Not this again. Galyan, make sure the techs don't do anything until I'm down there."

Maddox pivoted and broke into a sprint, heading for the exit. He needed to get to Hangar Bay 2 as quickly as possible.

-25-

Maddox sprinted into Hangar Bay 2 running to the circle of worried Kai-Kaus technicians.

They were short, stout individuals, many of them wearing wigs because they were bald and had found it disconcerting to be around so many others with hair.

Ludendorff's chief technician was with them.

"What happened?" Maddox demanded.

The agitated chief tech threw his pudgy hands into the air. "The professor was working on the machinery and had figured out what had taken place last time, and he—"

"Slow down," Maddox said, interrupting. "Take a deep breath."

The chief tech breathed deeply.

"Hold it," Maddox said.

The chief technician looked up at Maddox, his eyes wide.

"Hold it," Maddox said.

The chief tech nodded, still holding his breath, his cheeks puffy.

"Let it out slowly," Maddox said.

The chief tech did.

"Inhale slowly, deeply," Maddox said.

The chief tech did.

"Hold it. Now let it out. Are you calmer?"

The chief tech nodded vigorously.

Maddox doubted it, but said, "Speak slowly and tell me exactly what happened."

The chief technician went through the exact procedures Ludendorff had taken. He showed Maddox where the professor had stepped. He showed Maddox the controls on the machine Ludendorff had pressed, the levers and dials he'd turned and some of the added holographic controls he'd used.

Maddox noted something else. While the chief technician did all this, he kept well away from the huge black oily machine. More than ever, the thing seemed alien and Cthulhu-like.

Maddox nodded. The machine was a trap. It had sucked Ludendorff into it yet again. The last time, Ludendorff had shifted, apparently, into a different dimension. Had that happened again?

Maddox composed himself. He breathed not as the technician but used the Way of the Pilgrim to breathe slowly and serenely. He sought the inner calm that gave him his best thoughts. As he did, Maddox opened himself with his intuitive sense.

Like a sleepwalker, Maddox approached the ominously towering Yon Soth machine.

They never should have messed with the alien technology. Yet, they had, and now they were alone in a star system where a ship from another dimension had appeared and sucked away an entire task force. First, it had destroyed a planet for nefarious reasons. This was bizarre.

Maddox once more used the Way of the Pilgrim. He slowed his thought process. He slowed his breathing, making himself ultra-calm.

He sensed...eddies. He couldn't see them. He couldn't even feel them, but his intuitive sense—

Ah. Ludendorff had made a mistake over there. He'd meant to do *that*...but the professor had pressed this button instead.

Maddox paused. What would have caused Ludendorff to make such a mistake?

Maddox didn't realize he'd walked right up to the machine. The group of Kai-Kaus technicians stood well back, watching him. Other personnel had come onto the hangar bay and watched from near the bulkheads. The sinister aura of the great black machine kept everyone at bay. A few personnel wept and had to leave the hangar bay in a hurry.

The feeling of evil and wrongness was so strong that Galyan's holoimage began to shimmer.

"Oh my," Galyan said, "what is happening here?"

The holoimage's eyelids blinked rapidly as he processed the information even as he sensed, yes, the wrongness. It had something to do with space-time-continuum properties that he did not understand. He did not think any of them understood them. Perhaps the only one who had a chance of comprehending was the captain with his intuitive sense.

Galyan wanted to call out to the captain but found he had retreated in order to keep his holographic integrity. Galyan had floated midway between the Kai-Kaus technicians and regular Star Watch personnel who kept well away from the glowing machine.

Maddox stood before it. Maddox could almost sense the intelligence of a Yon Soth emanating from the thing. A Yon Soth was a rubbery whale-sized creature with a bizarrely alien way of viewing reality.

Maddox's eyes narrowed.

The sense of menace grew. This was a *trap*. The Yon Soths had left these things as traps for curious primates. They would pry open doorways into realms that would suck them in and perhaps destroy...destroy the very space-time continuum.

There was true threat in the machine and threat from what Ludendorff was doing. Maddox felt that in a flash.

He approached closer so his breath fogged a piece of oily black machine. Maddox cracked his knuckles. His hands were sweaty and the pit of his stomach clenched.

He breathed deeply and found he'd lost the Way of the Pilgrim. He struggled to regain it and realized the emanation from the machine fought against the calm.

So be it. He'd have to deal with the machine with his own native abilities, not with the superior training he'd received from Balron. He'd have to rely upon his *di-far* gifts.

Maddox studied the consoles. He reached out and dared to press...*this*.

163

A shock zapped through his arm, penetrated to his neck and hit his brain. The zap knocked him to the deck.

Maddox lay there, as no one came to help him.

The machine shuddered. A groan like a deep-sea whale oozed from it.

The Kai-Kaus technicians dropped to the deck, unconscious. Those near a hatch stumbled away in terror.

Only Galyan remained alert as he shimmered like bad reception. He analyzed and wondered what had happened.

After a quick analysis, Galyan called in an amplified stentorian voice, using extra power from the projector in the middle of *Victory*, "Captain Maddox. Captain Maddox, wake up!"

Maddox heard that, but as a tinny voice, far away. Perhaps it had been just loud enough, though.

Maddox opened his eyes, discovering that he lay on the deck. A second later, he realized a force radiated from the machine. The force—

If he didn't shut off the thing at once, the machine might suck *Victory* into a dimensional hell, a place that would devour them all, maybe into a dimension filled with soul-sucking Erills.

Maddox struggled up to his feet. The extreme effort made him angry. It shouldn't be this hard. The anger turned to rage. Thus, it wasn't with the calm of the Way of the Pilgrim, but towering rage that Ludendorff jeopardized his starship with this Yon Soth nonsense.

Maddox rose with a roar to discover that it felt as if a wind blew from the machine. His hair didn't lift. He felt this with his intuitive sense.

Maddox set himself, taking one step, two, three, four until he reached the machine. He looked up at it, sensing a Yon Soth intellect laughing at him. Maddox snarled. With slitted eyes, he staggered to the control panel and began to change settings, move dials and levers, faster and faster. It was unconscious, subconscious. He let himself manipulate and work the controls not with any logical thought, but by feel, the intuitive sense Balron had granted him.

164

The machine hummed faster. It fought him. Maddox pressed, punched controls—the sinister vibrations ceased abruptly.

Maddox frowned. He heard a squeaky mouse behind him. He turned.

Galyan solidified into his regular holoimage shape. Had the AI made the squeaky sounds?

Maddox saw then the still as death Kai-Kaus technicians laid upon the floor. He saw several crewmembers who hadn't made it out of the hangar bay. They wept.

Something caught his peripheral vision. Maddox turned.

A man-sized shape wavered nearby. The shape seemed familiar.

"Professor," Maddox said. "Professor Ludendorff. Professor Ludendorff."

The wavering image of a man turned toward him. The thing opened its mouth. Perhaps it shouted, but no sound came forth.

"Come back to us, Professor," Maddox shouted.

The image struggled as if deep underwater. The image approached Maddox. Maddox encouraged it to try harder.

The image wavered and solidified as it walked. It was indeed Professor Ludendorff. All of a sudden, Ludendorff tripped and fell onto the deck of the hangar bay, solidifying completely.

Ludendorff cried out with pain, perhaps because he twisted his ankle. The Methuselah Man was sprawled there on the deck.

"Professor," Maddox said rushing forward. He grabbed the professor, who radiated with heat.

"Help me," Ludendorff said, collapsing afterward.

Maddox grabbed the Methuselah Man by the scruff of his white coat, dragging him away from the ominous machine. As Maddox did this, Ludendorff's heat dissipated even though sweat soaked his clothes.

Maddox had saved Ludendorff from wherever the professor had gone. Now Maddox knew that he'd better get him to the medical center and make sure they kept Ludendorff alive.

-26-

Professor Ludendorff slept. He wasn't aware that he was sleeping because he was having an awful recollection, one might even call it a nightmare, one of hellish proportions. This happened while he was in medical on life support, the medical team working to keep him alive.

Ludendorff's tortured brain vomited up the ordeal he'd survived by using the terrible machine. He'd touched a key control and a maelstrom of power had swallowed him as the fish had swallowed Jonah.

It had happened so fast that Ludendorff hadn't been able to scream. Instead, he'd fallen into an Nth realm or place. Everything was black and hot. He heard screams, pleadings and wicked, demonic laughter around him.

Then, he fell out of the hot blackness into a panorama of stars, nebulae and swirling chaos. The mass of stars, nebulae and chaotic anomalies turned like a vast clockwork mechanism.

Was this a dream, a nightmare?

This time, during the recollection, it was a nightmare. The first time, it had been continuum reality.

Ludendorff's tormented brain had made a decision and viewed the mechanism of the multiverse. These were its cogs, levers and machinery—he couldn't fathom them precisely but in relative terms. They were gigantic and he was—he wasn't even a mouse in a giant's castle. He was a pimple on the butt of a hairless mouse.

Ludendorff tumbled through, seeing the energies of the terrible multiverse and its possibilities. All the while, he kept falling.

It was like an acid trip, a surrealist dream, with monstrous half-hidden entities staring at him with hungry lust.

Ludendorff fell through shimmering veils, passing planets and bizarre clockwork machinery of planetary sizes. Was he falling onto the table of God that held the devices of His creation?

What a bizarre thought for Professor Ludendorff. He did not know where the thought originated. It did not seem as if it originated from him. He wasn't religious. Not in the least, and yet, as he swirled and dropped through this maelstrom of possibilities, of different universes, of different—

If something could happen, it would happen given enough time. Ludendorff had always believed that, and now it seemed the reality was fact.

The half-hidden and monstrous entities with glowing red and yellow eyes—they tracked him as he fell past planets and clocks. The entities hungered for more than his flesh. They wanted his soul or essence and would torment him for eternity, as long as it would take to devour him.

Ludendorff twisted as he fell. He dropped through a different veil. Now, he saw a hundred, a thousand possible Ludendorffs.

He saw a Ludendorff as king of the Commonwealth, with a thousand beauties at his disposal. They all yearned to serve him in whatever way he would permit. He saw thousands of children. Was he a New Man here? No, this was Ludendorff, the master of the universe.

He kept tumbling, coming to a place where he slaved upon a planet, straining to move a boulder. Lashing him were New Men who towered over him, laughing and mocking. Ludendorff felt the sting of the whip upon his bare shoulder.

Ludendorff tumbled again and saw another universe where he was dinner for Liss cybers. They munched from tables—no, it wasn't a table. He saw a conveyor of people screaming and pleading for mercy. The Liss cybers rose up and devoured human flesh, commenting to each other how good this one tasted and how this one was too fat, having been left to grain too long.

On Ludendorff tumbled, viewing more possibilities. Aliens invaded the Commonwealth. They blew up planet after planet after planet. This was awful. What did it mean?

Ludendorff tried to harden his thoughts as he fell, as he saw the wheels and clockwork mechanisms of the universe turning, turning and turning. He fell past Saturn-like planets, neutron stars that screeched with sound and—wait, what?

He saw clothed teddy bears flying some kind of craft. They spoke among themselves. They manipulated machines and from a machine, a ray speared.

The ray flew from a planet and struck Ludendorff full in the face. He screamed. The pain was immense. He struggled and then he heard in the background:

"Stat, stat. Give him another shot of cortisol-Z."

Ludendorff felt coolness surge against his mind. His eyes opened and—he stared around him. He couldn't move. He was on some kind of gurney. Lights shined in his face. Medical personnel—what had happened?

Wasn't he the master of the universe? Where were his many wives? Were these his children trying to revive the old but new Ludendorff? Then he saw a face he recognized. It was—

"Captain Maddox," Ludendorff said in a tortured voice.'

"He's coming around, Captain," a medical officer said. "You might say something to him. I think it will help."

"Professor," Maddox said, "you had us worried there for a moment."

Ludendorff felt so terribly weak and listless. He tried to remember…

The beam from those damnable teddy bears had done something to him. The aliens had seen him and shot a beam at him and that had knocked him out of the nightmare. What had the nightmare signified?

"What has happened?" Ludendorff realized tears streamed from his eyes. He felt so weak and yet he was so glad to be alive. He was so glad that he wasn't tumbling through the multiverse and seeing the cogs, wheels and the inner workings of how things were.

Ludendorff reached up and grasped Maddox's uniform. With manic strength, he pulled the captain near.

"Captain, they're out there. They're out there like the Erills. You were right."

"Steady now, old man." Maddox pried the fingers from his uniform. "You're okay. You're fine. We got you."

"Got me?" Ludendorff asked.

"You used the Yon Soth machine. Don't you remember?"

"Yes," Ludendorff said. His eyes were huge and terror filled them.

"What's wrong with him?" Maddox asked.

The chief medical officer shook her head.

"Ludendorff," Maddox said, "you must get hold of yourself. You're back, you're okay."

"They feed," Ludendorff whispered. "They want to feed on us. They want to devour us. Captain, the multiverse is filled with hideous danger. I've made a dreadful mistake. Destroy the Yon Soth machine. I understand now. We must destroy it or things worse than Erills will descend upon us."

Maddox stared at him.

"Don't you understand what I'm telling you? I was there in some manner. It's a trap, Captain, it's a trap."

"Yes," Maddox said, "I felt that, and yet, we're charged with saving Task Force 3."

"No," Ludendorff said, "it's a trap. If we open a way, they may come through. They may come in their hordes and devour our universe, which is a normal universe, which is a safe universe." Ludendorff looked up. "Which is *our* universe, precious beyond price. I've erred, Captain, and because of the nightmare, because of the ray the teddy bears shot at me…"

"Teddy bears?" Maddox said. "What are you talking about?"

The strength fled from Ludendorff. In all likelihood, manic emotion had energized him and now a great sense of listlessness and lack of energy consumed him. He slumped back, his eyes closing. Air left his lungs as if for the final time.

Maddox looked up at the medical personnel watching in astonishment. "What just happened?"

"Agh," Ludendorff gasped. He was asleep and thus wasn't dead.

"What did you do to him?" Maddox asked. "What's going on?"

"We're not sure, sir. He needs rest. He needs lots of rest."

Maddox nodded, backing away. That had been weird and intense. His intuitive sense had pinged indeed, and told him Ludendorff had faced something bizarre and incredible while away.

Galyan appeared in the corridor with him. "Captain, may I have a word with you?"

"Did you listen in on all of that?"

"Yes sir, I did. Was I not supposed to?"

Maddox shook his head. It didn't matter. Maybe things like Erills were commonplace in the multiverse. Maybe it was time to scratch Task Force 3 from Star Watch.

"Captain, may I have a word with you?"

"Sure," Maddox said. "I need to think about this before I act."

"Yes," Galyan said, "I quite agree."

They continued down the corridor, Maddox walking as Galyan floated beside him.

"Do we need to go to a conference chamber to talk about this?" Maddox asked.

"No sir," Galyan said. "I have considered all the ramifications and possibilities. My conclusion is that the Yon Soth machine may be a trap."

"I agree with that. Do you suggest we ditch or destroy it?"

"Destroying it would be the best possibility. There are two more."

"Go on," Maddox said.

"Another possibility is we continue with the experiment as we are doing it. I give that a high probability of causing the destruction of my blessed starship and maybe more than that."

"I also agree with you there," Maddox said. "Destroy the machine. Keep using it and it will destroy our ship and maybe cause more heartache than the Erills did back in the day. I know which option I'm planning to do."

"There is a third possibility," Galyan said. "We should consider it, as possibilities one and two mean the loss of Task Force 3."

"I'm listening," Maddox said.

"We do not know enough about the machine and other dimensions. We have limited data, in other words. There was the incident in the dim past with Ur-Builders and Erills. It shows the dangers of dimensional travel. We have another data point when you helped Balron reach his dimension, as well as dimensional traveled yourself. That proved harmless to all involved."

"It wasn't much of a journey for me," Maddox said.

"Still, we gained data from that. Now, we have gathered data by the evidence we have seen due to the Long-Range Builder Scanner watching Trappist-1 and from our own observations and by experimenting with the Yon Soth machine."

"Why don't you get to the point, Galyan?"

"The third possibility is that we gain more data from the one place where we have crossed dimensions before."

"We?" asked Maddox.

"I mean you, sir. At that place, I suspect there is much more data to be gained."

"You're talking about the Library Planet," Maddox said. "Are you saying Balron can help us from there somehow?"

"No sir. Surely, the Supreme Intelligence of the Library Planet has more knowledge about dimensional travel than anyone we know."

"Right," Maddox said. "When we met him, the Supreme Intelligence was keeping Balron from going back to his dimension. Galyan, I think you've stumbled onto the one answer that might allow us to continue the mission and save the task force."

"Stumbled, sir? I respectfully say that it was the most logical thought of all the possibilities."

"This was gleaned from your twenty-eight options?"

171

"Former twenty-eight, sir. Now I have come down to three and I give this the second-highest ranking."

"Which is the first highest?"

"That we destroy the Yon Soth machine and consider Task Force 3 lost forever as well as the Lord High Admiral's granddaughter."

Maddox nodded. Galyan's choice was probably the wisest, and yet, he'd made—he wouldn't call them foolish choices, but he'd made reckless decisions before and won through. Could they win again? He was starting to get pissed about all this. Asteroidal superships, Yon Soth machine traps—too many aliens were screwing with Star Watch and the Commonwealth. Yes, there were horrid dangers out there. But he'd rescued Ludendorff twice from the black machine. It had shown itself capable of strange power. If they could harness that power…

"I like your third idea, Galyan, as it means we can possibly strike back at these enemies. We're going to go to the Library Planet, at least if the Lord High Admiral grants us leave to do so."

"I thought you would make that decision, sir."

"Thought, Galyan? What probability did you give it?"

"I *knew* you would, sir. I gave it a ninety-eight percent probability. That is as good as know."

Maddox almost clapped Galyan on the shoulder. But his hand would have swept through the holoimage, making it an awkward moment.

"Let's go talk to the Lord High Admiral," Maddox said. "We'll use the Long-Range Builder Comm device and see what Cook says about our latest idea."

-27-

Once more, *Victory* was in the Library Planet System. Maddox had gained permission from the Supreme Intelligence to come and the Lord High Admiral had agreed it was an excellent idea. The Lord High Admiral had particularly agreed after he heard what happened to Ludendorff and the Yon Soth machinery.

Would the Lord High Admiral have scrubbed the mission if not for his missing granddaughter? What would a man do for his family? Maddox knew the answer. He'd do anything, or the closest thing to anything. He thought of his mother, how she'd escaped the New Man birthing center with him in her womb. His father had helped his wife, dying because of it. For one's family one would do anything, even risk the entire Commonwealth, perhaps the entire dimension.

The Library Planet was part of a red dwarf star system. The planet was three hundred and ten million kilometers, more than two AUs, from the cool red star or more than twice the distance as Earth from the Sun. There were five moons around the planet, two of them the size of Luna, one of them half that size and the other two like Phobos around Mars. The moons created tidal heat inside the planet. That was caused through their competing gravitational pulls against it, which created the interior friction.

The planet was 1.47 times the size of Earth. On the surface, a man would weigh approximately one and half times as much as he would on Earth. The Library Planet was rocky with few

173

metallic ores in the planetary crust. Because of its distance from the red dwarf and the low amount of ambient heat reaching it, the Library Planet was a cold Niflheim world, the surface made of frozen volatiles. Substances that would be liquid or gases on Earth: water, ammonia, methane and nitrogen, were all frozen solid here. An exposed man teleported onto the surface would instantly turn into an ice cube. For all that, due to the tidal heat, there was an ocean of liquid water deep under the ice sheets.

The Supreme Intelligence, all the Builder artifacts here, were in deep subterranean halls or chambers. They were surface elevators leading down to them.

Once *Victory* was in orbit and contact was established, the Supreme Intelligence asked Maddox to come alone.

Maddox countered, asking if Galyan could accompany him.

"Yes..." the Supreme Intelligence said, "I will accept that."

Soon, Maddox left *Victory* in a shuttle, heading down to the big icy planet. The last time he'd been here—

As Maddox sat in the pilot's seat, he rubbed his forearm and hand, the ones he'd lost dueling the Emperor of the New Men. Had the extra gravity hurt him worse that day than it had the Emperor?

Maddox planned on a rematch. He'd beat the Emperor next time. He'd have to come up with a new reason to duel, though, as he'd given his word that he accepted the outcome of the first duel.

Maddox made adjustments onto the piloting board. The shuttle had entered the highest atmosphere, heading down into a howling ice storm.

He trained constantly, dueling the best fencers he could find. None of them was as good as the Emperor, though. How could he become even better than the modified superman? He *had* to defeat the Emperor, erase the outcome of last time.

"Sir," Galyan said. "I am unsure you are paying sufficient attention to the flight."

Maddox studied the pilot board, made some corrections and endured more buffeting. The ice storm was worse than he'd realized, tossing the shuttle around.

Finally, however, the shuttle landed in a sheltered cove. He donned Artic gear and jumped outside to howling icy wind. With Galyan guiding him through a blizzard, Maddox reached an elevator hatch.

It opened. Maddox went in and the hatch closed. Down he plunged, heading into the warm interior of the planet.

In time, the elevator stopped, the hatch opened and Maddox walked into a well-lit corridor. A floating robot rounded a corner, greeting him.

The robot was built on a levitating disc, a smooth metallic bullet shape, with a single electronic eye.

Maddox followed the robot for three kilometers, Galyan appearing again halfway there.

"Where have you been?" Maddox asked.

"Checking planetary security," Galyan said.

"And?"

"I do not detect anything amiss," Galyan said. "You should be safe."

Soon, robot, holoimage and man entered a vast cavern-like chamber. Maddox had expected to meet his uncle, Golden Ural. So far, his uncle hadn't appeared.

The robot took Maddox and Galyan across the vast chamber to a towering screen five times Maddox's height and with a similar huge width. Upon the screen was a gigantic green head with tendrils sprouting from all sides like snakes. The head had eyes, nose and mouth with green teeth.

"Captain Maddox and Driving Force Galyan," the Supreme Intelligence said. "It has been some time, has it not?"

"Yes," Maddox said, giving a slight bow.

"This is an honor, sir," Galyan said.

"It is an honor to meet you, Galyan," the Supreme Intelligence said. "I am glad I agreed you come."

Galyan glanced proudly at Maddox.

Maddox kept from rolling his eyes.

"Captain," the Supreme Intelligence said. "I appreciate the work you did last mission when you foiled the Mastermind's ultimate plan in the Far Beyond."

"Thank you," Maddox said.

"But you are in haste today. I see."

"Given the circumstances, haste makes the most sense," Maddox said.

"That is true more than you know. I have agreed to our meeting because you relayed to me all the incidents that took place regarding—what did you call it again, an asteroidal supership?"

"Yes, your Excellency," Maddox said.

"No, no. Supreme Intelligence will do. You do not need to use any other titles."

"Thank you, sir. Supreme Intelligence it is."

The giant green face on the vast screen studied Maddox. "Through your time in Star Watch, you have faced many strange entities and powers of our universe. Now, you have come across an ancient menace from the multiverse. You more than anyone else must know the dangers in crossing through the fabric of the space-time continuum."

"I suppose you mean when I helped Balron the Traveler return home."

"That is precisely what I mean," the Supreme Intelligence said. "For most of my existence, I strove to keep Balron from reaching his dimension. I blocked him because I feared that whatever he told those on the other side would begin an invasion of our dimension. Such an invasion, I reasoned, might annihilate all that we have striven through the many millennia to achieve."

"That has not happened," Maddox said.

"Not yet," the Supreme Intelligence said. "It still may, although I hope and believe that the probabilities are now low."

Maddox's eyes narrowed. "Are you saying Balron the Traveler is connected with the asteroidal supership appearing in our universe?"

"No. I am not saying that. Balron and the supership strike me as two separate matters. I have come to believe this has to do with the Onos."

"Sir," Maddox said, frowning, "the Onos? Who in the hell are they?"

"Perhaps the Onos are a what," Galyan said.

Maddox scowled at the holoimage.

"I will keep silent until addressed," Galyan said.

176

Maddox nodded briskly before resuming looking at the Supreme Intelligence.

"I have your attention again," the Supreme Intelligence said. "That is good."

"Right," Maddox said. "Time is critical."

"Very," the Supreme Intelligence said. "Now, regarding the Onos, you have related to me what Professor Ludendorff said concerning his nightmare. He spoke about a group of dressed teddy bears, I believe was the word. They beamed him in the face."

"Those are the Onos?" asked Maddox.

"From my long research and study of the distant past, they represent a threat to those in the asteroidal supership. Thus, those in the supership are attempting to annihilate them."

"Wait a minute," Maddox said. "This is a civil strife?"

"I do not think so."

"Have you seen the beings who control the supership?"

"I have not. Now, Captain, do you wish to play Twenty Questions or do you desire that I relate data to you?"

Maddox tilted his head. "I'm open to whatever you have to say."

The green head of the Supreme Intelligence paused before saying, "Captain Maddox, I am loath to give you the entire history of all this. It is ancient and long before the time of the Builders. Through miscellaneous and often brief bits of information, I've pieced this together. When you spoke about teddy bears and described what they looked like, it matched the one precise clue I've found in all my studies. Do you know where these alien teddy-bear creatures once resided?"

Maddox saw it almost at once. "It has to be in our universe and likely in our galaxy and spiral arm. I'm thinking they once lived in the Trappist-1 System."

"How excellent, Captain, as that is exactly right."

"Let me refine that. They lived on Zinc, the planet the asteroidal supership just destroyed?"

"Bravo," the Supreme Intelligence said. "You are correct once again, Captain."

"I'll extrapolate. You believe the asteroidal supership came to our universe to destroy the planet the Onos once lived on...what, ten thousand years ago?"

"I do not know the precise timeframe. The Onos were there well before the time of the Builders, which means ten thousand years ago is far too short. Further, I do not know *why* the Onos lived in the Trappist-1 System or what those in the asteroidal supership hoped to achieve by destroying the planet. From the circumstantial evidence I've found during my long existence, I believe there is a dimensional war taking place. I further believe that these two groups represent each side in the conflict."

"Not the key players, but just dimensional soldiers, as it were?"

"I do not know enough to state a case one way or another. I suspect the dimensional war. I am more certain that those in the supership hate the Onos."

"How do you know the Ono name?"

"The answer would take too long to explain. The short answer is from ancient ruins and a pictograph I once studied."

"Are we in danger in our universe?" Maddox asked.

"I do not know enough to answer that, either. I have not gained evidence from *all* the planets in our own spiral arm, never mind the other spiral arms or other galaxies in our universe. Perhaps these Onos have lived at other locales as well and perhaps that will cause the asteroidal supership to wish to destroy other planets in our universe."

"Do you have any idea why the supership race wishes to destroy a formerly occupied planet?

"None, but I would like evidence. I would very much like to know more."

"For sheer curiosity's sake?" Maddox asked.

"Oh no," the Supreme Intelligence said, "for the sake of our universe's continued existence."

Maddox felt a chill. That didn't sound good, and it meant— "Are you suggesting we continue with our dimensional research using the copy of the Yon Soth machine? Or that we scrub it?

178

"I indeed wish for you to continue," the Supreme Intelligence said. "You may not be aware, but this is a golden opportunity to learn more about the dimensions."

"And yet, from what the professor has seen in his nightmares, which I am going to assume has some basis in reality..."

"Oh yes," the Supreme Intelligence said. "I think it has much basis in reality. Captain Maddox, Galyan, there is a multiverse out there and that means a plethora of all types of entities exist...somewhere. Certainly, there must be entities with powers far beyond our own and who wish us harm in extreme and unpleasant ways."

"Including the devouring of souls as the professor has stated?" asked Maddox.

"Need you truly ask that?" the Supreme Intelligence said. "I refer to the Erills you've already met in the City of Pyramids. I wonder why you've refrained from mentioning them to me."

Maddox said nothing.

"I see," the Supreme Intelligence said. "Keep your reasons then. They are not germane to our discussion. The point is there is obvious danger in dimensional travel. But it can be safely attempted if one takes precautions. We might solve many curiosities as well. Could we find the source or reason for the creation of the multiverse? Could we learn even more about the operative situation regarding the Cosmic All?"

"Why would we *want* to know those things?" Maddox asked.

"Don't you understand, Captain? I surely know more about this phenomenon... I was going to say other than the Yon Soths who I believe may not have originated in our dimension. But we already know of the Erills and the vanished Ur-Builders. The point is this: we can learn more. Knowledge is power, one of the oldest of adages."

"Are you serious?"

"Why would you think otherwise? This is a deadly serious situation. We cannot always remain passive and hope for continued existence. We must eventually go on the offensive. The Erills, Balron and possibly Yon Soths have all breached

179

our dimension. The asteroidal supership is simply another group."

"The Onos would be yet another group of dimensional invaders," Galyan said.

"Yes," the Supreme Intelligence said. "The Onos are another breach against our dimension. Even one more is far too many. I would suggest that we cannot continue to allow our dimension to be so vulnerable to other realms."

"The Ur-Builders brought the Erills over through a portal," Maddox said. "They sought greater knowledge, always using what they knew. It brought them destruction."

"Are you suggesting I'm like them?"

"Yes," Maddox said.

"I'm not. I've studied the dim past. Unlike humans, I learn from history."

"Are you referring to the saying: the only thing men learn from history is that no one learns from history?" Galyan asked.

"I am indeed," the Supreme Intelligence said.

Maddox scowled at Galyan.

"I will shut up now," Galyan said, looking down.

Maddox cleared his throat, addressing the Supreme Intelligence. "What is it you're suggesting then?"

"That I need more information in order to—how shall I say it? I believe there are ways to protect our dimension from invasions. There must be other processes as I used against Balron the Traveler that would make it harder for others to break into our dimension. To gain that, however, we must take risks. We must learn more while we can. This seems like one of those times."

"This all seems rather incredible," Maddox said. "How in the world can we strengthen our entire dimension by the few things *Victory* could possibly achieve?"

"You must understand, Captain, the rules governing this are much more complex and stranger than you would think. These repeated incursions into our dimension have weakened the fabric of our space-time continuum."

Galyan looked up sharply.

"According to my studies," the Supreme Intelligence said, "too many incursions cause space-time fabric to degrade. That made be the wrong word. Our dimension might become so porous that it would merge into others. Now, if the possibility exists of this happening, it strikes me that we could reverse the process. We should be able to strengthen our space-time fabric, making it harder for others to reach us. That would also protect us from facing other dimensional forces or beings too powerful for any of us to face. I refer here to beings like the Erills."

Maddox rubbed his forehead. "Let me get this straight. Because of the asteroidal supership, we're threatened by dimensional invasion."

"Not just threatened, we've endured repeated dimensional invasions. That may have weakened our space-time membrane, making more invasions likely. I suspect this is a matter of probabilities, not certainties. We can only increase the probability of dimensional defense versus increased probabilities of more incursions. The more incursions, the greater likelihood of facing godlike aliens no one could defeat. Surely you can see the logic of my thought."

Maddox nodded. "My goal is rescuing Task Force 3. I have no desire embroiling *Victory* in something…preposterous and soul-devouring."

"I speak of a daunting task, I understand," the Supreme Intelligence said. "We are merely looking at one aspect of this. We must stop others entering our dimension. As we do so, we must learn more about the properties of the multiverse. Thus, you will attempt two things at once."

Maddox shook his head.

"Captain, you learned while helping Balron that other continuums can be much different from ours. I suspect you found the experience unsettling."

"I did," Maddox said. "I never want to go through that again. Frankly, the more you talk about this, the more I think, *let sleeping dogs lie."*

"I understand the idiom, and yet, there has been a grave weakening in the fabric of the space-time continuum of the Trappist-1 System. It will likely become a haunted system because of that. It would be best to strengthen our continuum there so if there is another incursion it will happen far from the Milky Way Galaxy, in some other branch of our universe."

"What about the Erills and now possibly the Yon Soths?"

"There are vulnerable—what I call haunted—star systems, where the fabric is so thin forces and beings are drawn to them, looking for ways through. We must do something at each locale...eventually. Today, we're working on the supership."

"On regaining Task Force 3," Maddox said.

"Both," the Supreme Intelligence said.

Maddox studied the giant green head. Why did he have snakes for hair like the Greek legend of the Medusa?

"This all well and good in theory," Maddox said. "However, I don't know how we can successfully use the Yon Soth machine."

"I do. Captain, if you allow me to send several robots and a multiverse computer with you, I suspect you could learn to use the Yon Soth machine to its optimum performance."

Maddox rubbed his jaw. Could he trust the Supreme Intelligence? The Builder computer construct had given them the nexus and seemed benevolent toward humanity. Maddox thought about Galyan's three possibilities. Use the machine. Destroy the machine. Trust the Supreme Intelligence with the machine. If they destroyed the machine, he condemned Task Force 3 and the Lord High Admiral's granddaughter to exile, never ever reaching their universe again.

Maddox thought about the robots he'd traveled with last mission through the dampened star system. A sense of panic welled in his chest as he thought about yet more robots.

Once more, he used the Way of the Pilgrim to calm himself.

This all sounded unbelievable, pure fantasy. Yet, Balron the Traveler had been from another dimension. The idea of sealing off their dimension from others—Star Watch had enough dealing with normal reality. This talk all seemed beyond reality.

Maddox continued to rub his jaw, thinking.

If ever there was a ship in Star Watch that could deal with beyond reality, *Victory* was it and he was the man.

Perhaps this was why Balron had granted him the intuitive sense: to save this space-time continuum from further incursions, to save them from the feasting, grotesque entities

Ludendorff had sensed in his nightmare journey. There was another thing. Maddox had possessed the power to face the Erills in the City of Pyramids. He was the—*di-far.* Maybe this was his real duty.

Maddox nodded. "I'll accept your multiverse computer and robots if you'll teach me how to turn them off."

Now, the Supreme Intelligence eyed Maddox. Finally, a smile appeared on the huge green face.

"That is a prudent request, Captain. I agree. I ask that you give me the full results of your journey so I may continue to guard our continuum from any Balron-like incursions or from more asteroidal superships."

"Or from the Onos," Galyan said.

"Yes," the Supreme Intelligence said, glancing at the little holoimage, "or from the Onos. Or anything else we discover."

"One more thing," Maddox said, "we're trying to find our lost task force. Do you believe that's possible?"

"I do if we act quickly," the Supreme Intelligence said.

"Then we'd better get started," Maddox said.

"Indeed," the Supreme Intelligence said. "Familiarizing your people with my computer and robots will take time. With them, however, you'll be able to use the Yon Soth machine."

"Great," Maddox said, feeling it was anything but. Yet, he was the man and this was the hour.

-28-

As *Victory* orbited the Library Planet, the Supreme Intelligence sent several shuttles up into the starship's hangar bays.

Builder robots disembarked, carting large computing cubes into Hangar Bay 2. They snapped the cubes together, interlocking one atop the other so it looked like a giant child's set of wooden blocks, except these cubes were clear and crystalline.

This was Arius, a Builder AI, a sentient computer. He contained most of the data the Supreme Intelligence had acquired throughout the centuries regarding dimensional travel. He would also be instrumental in using the Yon Soth machine.

Once Arius activated, lights swirled and glowed within the crystal computing cubes.

Maddox and Galyan along with a security team of armed marines watched the process.

"I have activated," the computer said. "Now, who is Captain Maddox?"

Maddox stepped forward. "I am. And you are?"

"The AI Arius," the stacked and linked cubes said. "I am on loan from the Supreme Intelligence, which you should already know."

Maddox nodded.

"I see the affirmation," Arius said. "I am to help you track through the dimensions and—"

As Arius spoke, bots I, II and III activated.

184

The robots were identical, had white bullet-shaped shells the size of Galyan, and sprouted metallic tentacles, spidery legs and arms.

Maddox stepped back. The robots unnerved him as they reminded him too much of his journey through the dampened star system from last mission.

If Arius sensed the unease in Maddox, he didn't speak of it. Instead, light beamed from the cubes, shining on the towering strangely geometrically shaped Yon Soth machine.

"I am analyzing and cataloging the machine," Arius said.

"Sure," Maddox said.

Abruptly, the beams snapped off.

"Captain," Arius said. "Do I have your permission to begin building a control system so we can properly utilize the Yon Soth machine?"

It took Maddox a moment to speak. To say he was ambivalent about all this was an understatement. Still, this was the only way to do it, and he'd already agreed to it. Ludendorff was out, as he still recovered from his nightmare journey. If they were going to rescue Task Force 3—

"Go for it," Maddox said.

The three bots scuttled to equipment deposited from the shuttles. Each picked up material and scuttled toward the Yon Soth machine.

The bots rapidly built a smaller machine near the towering black edifice. Once completed, the bots hooked the former with the latter, using a laser lightguide system. The robots didn't touch the Yon Soth machine with cables or other technology, but with light and energy only.

Maddox, Galyan and the marine team remained in the hangar bay, watching.

As the laser lightguide system snapped on, the Yon Soth machine activated. It hummed so heat-like waves emanated from it.

"Whoa, whoa, whoa," Maddox said. "Slow down. What are you doing?"

"I'm sorry," Arius said, "but we must begin experimentation immediately. I do think you want me to begin this sooner rather than later. Am I not correct?"

185

Maddox glanced at Galyan.

"You have said, sir, that time is limited," Galyan said. "I believe Ludendorff told us the supership trails in the Trappist-1 System will dissipate soon."

"Ludendorff is correct about that," Arius said. "We must act swiftly if we hope to save your people and avert this grave danger the Supreme Intelligence—"

"Wait a minute," Maddox said, interrupting. "Did the Supreme Intelligence give you mission parameters?"

"Yes," Arius said.

"What are those?"

"To help you in any way I can, particularly in retrieving your people."

"And?" Maddox asked suspiciously.

"To make sure we do not open the way to any nefarious and acquisitive entities that could cause grave destruction to our dimension. Said another way, we must on all counts not destroy our own dimension in trying to save those who have been waylaid by this asteroidal supership, as I believe you are naming it."

Great, the Supreme Intelligence had given them a chatty AI. Maddox shook his head.

"You disagree with my mission parameters, Captain?" Arius asked.

"No," Maddox said. "I was just thinking. By the way, do you have a different name for the supership?"

"I do not."

"Do you have any idea what the supership could be?"

"You mean other than a dimensional-traveling vessel?"

"Yes," Maddox said.

"I do not."

"Fine," Maddox said. "Then let's get started."

"Thank you," Arius said. "Now that I have your permission, I shall do so."

For the next two days, Arius and his bots tested the Yon Soth machine and constructed further equipment toward the goal of controlling it.

After the last hour of the last day, Galyan woke Maddox as the holoimage entered his quarters. "Captain, Arius wants to see you at once."

Maddox jerked upright, his eyes flashing open. He couldn't remember his dreams, although they'd seemed troubled.

"What is it?" Maddox said. "Who's there?"

Galyan illuminated his holoimage, making him the sole lit object in the otherwise dark quarters.

"Galyan. What's going on? Why are you here?"

"Sir, Arius wants to speak with you at once. He said it is urgent."

It took Maddox a moment to orient himself. "I'm on my way."

After a quick shower, some coffee and a change of clothing, Maddox strode into the hangar bay.

It was quite different from two days ago. For one thing, there was a force field around the entire Yon Soth machine. Behind the force field, bots II and III maneuvered from one area of machinery to another, their tentacled arms pressing controls.

Maddox turned to Arius. "What's going on here?"

"You are referring to the force field."

"We can start with that," Maddox said.

"As you can see, I have taken several precautions. That is in case the Yon Soth machine attempts to unleash forces which would be inimical to my survival."

"Your survival."

"My survival will insure your survival," Arius said. "If I were to perish while we are in the other dimensions, events would go poorly for the rest of you. I have instructed Galyan in certain of the methods and ways of using the machine for dimensional travel, but it is much more complex than his limited computing capability can cope with."

Maddox scowled.

Had he given the Supreme Intelligence too much operational control over *Victory* by allowing this highly advanced computing system, with these three bots, to run everything regarding dimensional travel? Yet, what other choice did he have? This was one of those missions where he

187

was going to have to utilize technology far in advance of what Star Watch possessed. He didn't think the Supreme Intelligence would allow him to keep any of this technology, either. Not that he particularly wanted it. The whole idea of dimensional travel, particularly as Ludendorff remained in medical, his mind unbalanced and quite frankly his manner subdued—

Maddox shook his head.

"Trouble, Captain?" asked Arius.

"How are we going to find our way home again once we go to a different dimension?"

"That is an excellent question," Arius said. "I have devised a mapping system. We will call our dimension A-A-1-1."

Maddox blinked. "Uh, this cataloging system, why not just call our dimension A or A1?"

"Because the multiverse is much more complex than you realize, Captain. I have explained some of this to Galyan. He is intelligent, a much higher grade than any of you humans. Perhaps Ludendorff could understand some of this, but I am doubtful."

"All right," Maddox said, "why don't you keep it simple for me."

"Oh, I intend to do so. The Supreme Intelligence instructed me to keep you in the loop as much as is possible. That is my goal, and I realize simplicity will help your feeble brain to understand the process to at least a degree."

"Wonderful," Maddox said. "So, this dimensional travel…"

"Yes, Captain, as I was saying, we are in A-A-1-1. I am using a subjective mapping system, as that seems like the optimum solution. Also, I have no way of knowing if there is a central core to the multiverse or if we're dealing with infinite realities. There is also the—"

"I get it," Maddox said, interrupting. "We're using subjective references. Since our dimension is the most important to us, we'll consider it the center of the multiverse— at least, for mapping purposes."

"Exactly," Arius said. "From A-A-1-1 spins countless possibilities. I suppose…you could consider the dimensions as layers. The layers expand outward in increasing complexity

188

and number. I do not know if it is an infinite number of multiverse layers or exactly how it works. But I am repeating myself. That is not necessarily bad, however, as repetition is one way to help limited intellects remember facts. I refer to you in particular."

"Sure," Maddox said.

"The theory I am employing at present is that the dimensions which lay side by side or near each other will be alike in the way gases, before they change into solids would be similar in composition to the other gases near it. Therefore, the dimensions beside A-A-1-1 will perhaps be similar to ours in most discernable ways or patterns."

Maddox listened closely, and he thought he understood— for a limited intellect. "Are you saying there's a Captain Maddox in the dimensions beside ours?"

"I have not said there are quantum theory dimensions. No, I'm merely saying that these dimensions are alike in many ways as far as we can tell—for example, in their physical laws. I was told how you helped Balron the Traveler reach his dimension. From the tale, I have theorized you went far afield indeed. I suspect you went to something like a D-E-10-14 universe. It was very odd and different from what you knew. Is that not correct?"

Maddox remembered the time. Odd was hardly the word for it. "I think I'm getting the gist of what you're saying."

"Excellent," Arius said. "I have kept it simple enough then for your limited mind to comprehend."

"I suppose that's true," Maddox said dryly. "Anyway, can you find the trail the supership used and track down Task Force 3?"

"My operative theory is this, Captain. There will be residue that clung to the supership. This residue will be from our dimension and will shed from the supership as it travels. The residue will not be natural to the other dimension. Such a faint trail will naturally dissipate given enough time. My point is, we, or I, will be looking for minute anomalies. Given that my theory works, the supership will have left particle anomalies in the Trappist-1 System. These are likely the trails you detected earlier."

"That's enough for now," Maddox said. "You know how to find these trails and Galyan will supervise your activities."

"Supervise, Captain? I do not think Galyan will understand enough to supervise me."

"That's fallacious thinking."

"You presume to tell me how to think?"

"How old are you?"

"I have only recently been activated."

"Galyan is thousands of years old. There's a difference between experience and knowledge—and wisdom. Just as I supervise Galyan because I have specific experience and wisdom, even if not greater knowledge, he has far greater experience and likely wisdom than you do. I am the supervisor—the captain—of *Victory*, and of you. Thus I will designate Galyan as your supervisor, if I so choose."

"I am not sure that makes sense."

"Then let me explain it more *simply,* as you're having trouble understanding, with your limited and feeble experience and wisdom. We're going to do this your way, but also my way—and my way supersedes yours. Your way in the sense that you know how to use the Yon Soth machine. My way in that what I say goes as I'm the captain, the ultimate authority on this vessel."

"Of course, Captain. The Supreme Intelligence informed me you are highly motivated by dominance factors. I have already seen this is true. It is interesting and I think normal for mammalian creatures such as you."

Maddox closed his eyes, nodded, opened his eyes and decided it was time to proceed, now that he'd gotten the irritating AI's compliance, at least in principle. "We're going through a hyper-spatial tube to Earth. Will that cause any problems to your calibrations of the Yon Soth machine?"

"No, I have calibrated for hyper-spatial-tube journeys. It is yet another reason for the force field. I must say, Captain, that you humans are extremely brave to have used such highly advanced machinery with so many possible variations and danger to yourselves. It may not even be bravery as such, but a case of supreme recklessness."

"I'm sure you're right," Maddox said. "All right, Arius, I'm glad you're here. I'm glad you have things under control. Let's see now if we can do what we were commissioned for."

"Yes, Captain, I am in agreement with that. I have set up to the best to my ability. I have theorized to the extent that I can. Now it's time to make our move."

With that, Maddox headed back for the bridge. In and out, he hoped. Find Task Force 3 and get the hell home. Would it work like that? One could always hope.

The journey from the Library Planet to Earth proved routine and simple. It was interesting how quickly one took the hyper-spatial tube for granted.

Maddox debated speaking with the Lord High Admiral, but decided it would only add complications.

Thus, in short order, after the crew had composed themselves, after everything in the hangar bay seemed set, they used a hyper-spatial tube to travel to the Trappist-1 System.

And like that, they were back.

Maddox ordered a ship wide diagnostic. During it, he had the med teams check everyone. He wanted to make sure the quick and multiple uses of the hyper-spatial tube hadn't upset someone's equilibrium.

After a two-hour checkup, the medical personnel gave the crew a clean bill of health.

Ludendorff was recovering by sleeping endlessly. Unfortunately, he'd woken up once screaming hysterically. They'd sedated him and on he'd slept since.

Had the Yon Soth machine unhinged their smartest person?

Maddox didn't have time to worry about it. From the bridge, once the diagnostic proved everything was shipshape, he gave the order. The starship maneuvered to where the battle had destroyed Zinc.

"Galyan, are you in connection with Arius?"

"I am, Captain. He is eager to begin."

"Yeah," Maddox said. He wasn't so eager. What was wrong with him? Was he getting soft after all these missions? He shrugged and gave the order to start looking for supership trails.

Soon, Andros Crank said, "Sir, we've found the location. I'm in contact with Arius. He believes this is where we should use the machine."

Maddox rubbed his fingertips together. His hands were sweaty. Did his intuitive sense warn him against the action he planned? No. It did not. He wiped his sweaty palms on his pants and stood. "Tell Arius to use the machine on the exact position where the supership vanished."

"Yes, sir," Andros said.

"Are you monitoring the hangar bay, Galyan?"

"I am," Galyan said.

"Sir," Andros said, "Arius is directing input through my board. Do you want me to put it on the main screen?"

"Yes," Maddox said.

A faint blue overlay appeared on the main screen.

"That is from the asteroidal supership," Andros said. "Arius says these are particles alien to our dimension."

Maddox nodded. He knew the theory.

"Arius has tracked the trial back to the rip," Andros said. "He's outlining it now."

On the main screen appeared a faint trail and then a large, jagged outline.

"That was the location of the dimensional rip," Andros said.

According to what they knew, it would be easier to make a second rent or rip in the space-time continuum in the same spot as the first.

"Give me a split screen," Maddox said. "Show the former rip on one side and what's happening in Hangar Bay 2 on the other."

Andros tapped his science board.

On the left was space with the faint outline. On the right two bots worked behind the force field. It was a shimmering dome of electromagnetic energy surrounding the Yon Soth machine. The bots moved rapidly, their tentacles pressing

193

buttons and other controls. The third bot hovered at outer force-field controls and watched several monitors. Arius's complex of computing cubes swirled hypnotically with strange light.

Arius must have known he had bridge connection.

"I am ready to open a dimensional path, Captain," Arius said. "I will need more power, however. Can you provide it?"

"Yes," Maddox said, signaling the power tech.

Victory's antimatter engines soon vibrated noisily, proving more energy.

On the main screen, the swirling lights in Arius's computing cubes moved faster and faster.

"It is happening," Arius said.

A beam of unknown nature speared from *Victory*. It struck the same area that had been torn before.

A new rent in the space-time continuum appeared. It was jagged. Through it appeared horrible, light-sucking darkness.

Maddox wanted to veer away. He didn't want to enter that. He rubbed his fingertips together.

Keith swiveled in his seat, looking at him.

Maddox swallowed, coughing into a fist. This was it. Was he going to do this? "Head for the opening. We're going in. Arius, do you know how to follow the trail as we enter that...that vortex?"

"It is not a vortex," Arius said.

"It doesn't matter what you call it. Can we follow the trail?"

"Oh, but names are extremely important, Captain," Arius said. "We must call things by their proper name so we make proper decisions."

"Fine," Maddox said. "Can you follow the trail?"

"I am going to find out, Captain. Do you still wish to proceed given those conditions?"

"Yes!"

The ancient Adok starship slid into the darkness just as the warships of Task Force 3 had done some days ago.

Blackness struck the starship and everything in the ship.

Did the crew fall unconscious or did every sense—sight, smell, hearing—cease as if they were in nonexistence? What was this place? It wasn't a dimension, was it? It was between the dimensions where nothing—in a sense—could exist.

It was a bizarre thought. The fact Maddox could think it told him that he wasn't unconscious. How otherwise could he have the thought?

The starship broke through: entering a region with huge swirling stars compressed together. A neutron star blasted them, causing overwhelming sound to resonate through the ship.

Everyone on the bridge clapped his hands over his ears. The dimension-traveling process was daunting and frightening, different as it was another category thing altogether.

The neutron star shriek grew less and seemed to cycle down into oblivion.

Maddox experimentally took his hands from his ears. The harsh noise was gone. "What is this place?" he shouted.

No one answered. He looked around. Everyone else was slumped at their posts. Not even Galyan was in evidence. Was this normal for dimensional travel?

Galyan shimmered into existence. "Captain, we are doing it. We are traveling between dimensions. This must be a null region or an energy bleed-off area between dimensions so everything doesn't explode, like matter and antimatter combining."

Maddox kept his mind on what was important. "Are we following the supership's path through...whatever this place is?"

"Not yet," Galyan said.

"Why not?"

"Arius cannot yet find a trail."

"He'd better," Maddox shouted, his unease getting the better of him.

A moment passed. "I have told him you said that," Galyan said. "Should I wake Keith? The starship may have to maneuver precisely in seconds."

"Wake him," Maddox shouted.

Holographic Galyan inserted himself into Keith. The holographic projector in the middle of *Victory* emitted a mild shock through the holoimage and thus into Keith around him.

195

Keith jerked violently. "Hey, what's going on? What are you guys doing?"

"You must get ready to maneuver," Galyan said, who'd appeared outside Keith.

"I'm ready. I'm ready," Keith said, rubbing his chest, opening and closing his mouth while shaking his head.

Galyan turned to Maddox.

Maddox forced himself to think, instead of merely fret and stare at the extraordinary panorama before them on the main screen. The sight was incredible, awe-inspiring and ultimately chilling. He shook his head, blinked and faced—

"Galyan, has Arius found a trail yet?"

The holoimage didn't respond.

"Can you hear me, Galyan?"

"Sir," Galyan said. "It took my processors a moment to readjust—never mind. Yes. Arius has found a trail. It is appearing on the screen."

Maddox saw it, as Arius must have highlighted the trail. "Lieutenant, do you see that?"

"Aye," Keith said.

"Follow it," Maddox said.

"Sir," Keith said, as he tapped the helm controls.

Maddox made fists, squeezing his fingers together. He'd shouted for a time. His nerves—this place played havoc with them. He needed to maintain his decorum, his poise. What was wrong with him shouting like that?

Victory changed course, following the faint trail of particles that didn't belong in this zone, area, whatever it was.

"Captain," Arius said, speaking through an intercom. "Ahead, the trail abruptly disappears."

"That must mean the supership left this place there."

"That is logical."

"Right," Maddox said. "We'll go to the very end of it and you break us through again—there," Maddox said. "See if you can pick it up...the trail, on the other side."

"From our perspective," Arius said, "we will be going deeper into the continuum. We will no longer be in the A-A regions. I suspect we will go into the C-D regions at least."

"Just do it, Arius. I don't want a dialogue of where we're going. You catalog and map it. I'll make the decisions."

"I understand," Arius said. "The Supreme Intelligence told me it would probably be so."

Thus, where a vortex had snatched the task force and the supership, *Victory* opened the way and followed. According to Arius, they crossed more than one dimension doing this. They must be smashing through layer upon layer.

Victory shuddered and groaned metallically. It was a violent and soul-shaking experience.

Maddox gripped the end of the armrests. This was starting to anger him, the emotionalism he'd exhibited. What about dimensional travel affected him so? He needed to figure it out. Until then—"I'm Captain Maddox," he whispered. "I will succeed or die trying."

With that, Maddox endured the shaking and dreadful darkness. This had to end sometime—he hoped.

-30-

It did end for now, as *Victory* burst through the darkness and—Maddox blinked from his chair.

Hardly anything had changed on the main screen. Giant stars were massed together. Nebulae swirled madly. Neutron stars—Maddox cocked his head. He didn't hear the damned screech from earlier.

Maddox slowed his breathing. He'd almost been hyperventilating. *Get a grip on yourself.* He squinted, and an idea struck. These emotional assaults had worsened ever since—the Yon Soth machine. It had radiated waves before while he'd been there.

Had the machine done something to him with those waves? It was time for some inner diagnostics, soul searching, possibly. Right now—

Maddox squinted as if he sighted through a sniper scope. He inhaled, inhaled, and practiced the Way of the Pilgrim. This time, he was going to bring his intuitive senses to high alert.

As Maddox did so, a thought struck him about this place. It was like a gigantic waiting room where God kept his extra stars in reserve. Did God pluck them as needed? Was this a divine storage closet, then?

Maddox shook his head.

They were punching through dimensions, going from one phase of existence to another. It was mind numbing.

Maybe he should pull a Ludendorff and just sleep until this was over.

Maddox breathed serenely and focused his intuitive sense. He gasped, and something collided with his sense. Grunting, Maddox doubled over as if he had the mother of all stomachaches.

"Captain," Galyan said.

"Shut up," Maddox hissed. He didn't want to lose this.

He thrust outward with the intuitive sense. He scanned—

Maddox groaned, clutching his gut. He vomited so bile dribbled past his lips. As he did this, he held the intuitive sense, refusing to let this go. He breathed serenely, seeking—

Evil, a hunger, Maddox sensed it. This evil was…beyond the giant swirling stars and thick gases. It was beyond the present realm of…passage between dimensions possibly.

The evil hungered to devour him and everything Maddox held dear, including *Victory*.

Maddox closed his eyes, concentrating everything on the intuitive sense.

There was more than one, many, entities, gigantic things. These creatures or beings strained to break through…whatever was keeping them at bay. Yes. They waited out there in chaos or dimensions that were utterly chaotic.

Maddox wanted to know more. He—

His eyes opened. He sat up, felt wetness on his lips and wiped his mouth with his sleeve. He looked around. Several crewmembers watched him sidelong.

"Sir," Galyan said. "Do you feel well?"

"Never mind about that," Maddox said with cool reserve. He—he realized he no longer sensed the hungering entities. What had happened?

Maddox pressed an intercom button. "Arius, do you sense anything inimical to us?"

"I did, Captain. They were vile and ultra-powerful presences. I think that is the best language I can use for you to comprehend the meaning. I am surprised. Did you sense them?"

"Yes."

"Then the Supreme Intelligence was correct about you. Balron did give you extra powers of appreciation."

"No, that isn't the correct way to say it."

199

"I'm sorry, Captain. My computing processors are presently needed elsewhere. I will have to discontinue the conversation."

Maddox raised an eyebrow, glancing at the main screen. The scene looked as before: a panorama of stellar brilliance with gigantic stars and swirling nebulae.

"Captain," Arius said. "There is an emergency in progress. I have tried to deviate from it, but forces I do not comprehend have apprehended my action. In plain speech, an attack is even now being launched upon us." The Builder AI rattled off code as if that meant something.

"Andros," Maddox said. "What do you make of that?"

Andros swiveled around and raised his hands. The chief technician obviously had no idea.

"I understand what Arius told us," Galyan said. "It is a grid…map. Look again at the main screen, sir."

Maddox did.

Black holes appeared in space. From each dropped a silvery oval, a vessel. The holes closed. Thrust caused each oval to speed toward *Victory*, accelerating as they neared.

"What are those?" Maddox asked in a calm voice.

"Alien vessels," Andros said.

Maddox could see that. No. He mustn't lose his cool. "What size?"

"Twice that of a shuttle," Andros replied.

"Avoid them, Lieutenant Maker."

Keith hunched forward, tapping input into the helm controls. He did it more forcefully.

"Trouble, Lieutenant?" Maddox asked.

"We're not maneuvering like we're supposed to," Keith said.

"Sir," Andros said. "The ovals are projecting…tractor beams, in lieu of a better term."

"Tractor beams against us?" asked Maddox, perplexed.

"Yes, sir," Andros said.

"How is that possible? We have far greater mass. We should be pulling them along, not them halting us."

"That is incorrect," Arius said. "Their combined mass exceeds *Victory's* by a considerable margin."

"Are they far larger than shuttles then?" Maddox asked.

"Mass if not always a matter of volume but also of density," Arius said.

"The ovals are super-dense?" asked Maddox.

"In relation to *Victory*, that is correct," Arius said.

"Can you contact the ovals?"

"Are you addressing me?" Arius asked.

"Yes, yes," Maddox said, his calm slipping just a bit.

"Negative," Arius said. "However, I am certain they mean to capture your ship."

"By dragging us to their...dimension?" asked Maddox.

"No, Captain," Arius said. "I suspect they will try to penetrate the hull."

"The ovals will attempt this by crashing into us?"

"No," Arius said, "the beings flying the ovals will likely attempt this."

"Are they humanoids, robots, aliens, what?"

"I cannot penetrate their silvery hulls," Arius said. "I do not know."

"Then how can you possibly know their objectives?"

"It is pure conjecture," Arius said. "However, my conjecture is based on logical processes."

Maddox studied the main screen. The six silver ovals had neared and seemed to draw closer still, as if pulling themselves through their invisible tractor beams.

"Weapons," Maddox said. "Target them."

"I'm trying, Captain," the weapons officer said. "Everything is offline as far as targeting is concerned."

This was intolerable. "Galyan," Maddox said. "Can you override that?"

"Negative, sir."

"Can you tell me why we can't target the ovals?"

Galyan's eyelids fluttered. "The silver ovals are jamming us, sir. They are interfering with our electronic systems."

Maddox glared at the main screen. The ovals were almost upon the starship. They were tiny compared to it. Yet, they had more mass. Maddox remembered going into another dimension before. These things might come from such a place. Did the occupants of the ovals outweigh humans by the same degree?

Would the aliens be able to punch their fists through human flesh?

Maddox wasn't aware of it, but he snarled silently.

"They're almost upon us," Galyan said.

Maddox gnawed on a knuckle of his right fist. Would the ovals punch through *Victory's* hull, smashing the starship in the process?

Clangs struck the outer hull. At each clang, the bridge shuddered, as if the entire starship shook from the impact. It happened once, twice, three sharp clangs.

Maddox waited for four, five and six, but the next three clangs didn't sound.

"Galyan, what happened?"

"Three ovals have attached to the outer hull, sir."

"There were six ovals. What happened to the others?"

"Three missed us," Galyan said.

Maddox looked up at the main screen. He saw the giant massed stars and swirling nebulae. He didn't see any ovals.

"Are the other three turning around for a second try?" Maddox asked.

"Captain," Galyan said. "I am unable to sense the other three ovals. They appear to have vanished."

"Arius," Maddox said. "What happened to the other three?"

"I believe they are extinct," Arius said. "That was their one chance to know existence. They failed, and hence lacked enough power to continue their being in this place."

Maddox shook his head. "That doesn't make sense."

"On the contrary," Arius said, "it makes perfect sense. You, perhaps, lack the necessary education to comprehend the issues at stake."

A rebuke nearly spilled from Maddox. He was getting tired of the smarmy Builder AI. Before the captain could get the rebuke out—

"Sir," Galyan said. "There's a breach in the hull. I am detecting—sir, let me show you."

The main screen showed a ship's corridor, one near Cargo Hold 3. Dull metallic fingers punched through the ceiling. The fingers tore at metal, ripping it and making an opening.

Seconds later, metal feet appeared and then an entire…suit dropped down.

The metal was dull gray and rounded over a gorilla of a humanoid. It had a rounded helmet and armor. In one gauntlet, a hand gripped a gleaming metal axe. It might have been made of steel. It might have been forged from something else, too. The other gauntlet gripped a bulky blaster with a metal cord going from the bottom of the pistol grip and to a pack on the rounded armor suit. There was an orifice in the chest, possibly some kind of portable cannon.

More of the armored beings dropped from the ceiling. In all, eleven landed in the corridor. The first swiveled this way and that. Then, it began clomping down the corridor. The others followed close behind. They were ominous, perhaps creatures of immense density. So far, however, they hadn't smashed through the bulkheads. Nor did their armored feet leave dents on the deck. If they were dense, they weren't so dense that they automatically bent metal here.

"Captain," Galyan said, "it appears the intruders are heading for the Yon Soth machine in Hangar Bay 2."

Understanding shined in Maddox's eyes. These eleven aliens thought they could capture his ship, either that, or derail everything by destroying the Yon Soth machine. If he were wrong about that, it would be something equally bad. How did one stop aliens stronger, denser and with better tech? He'd better figure that out fast, or the mission and all their lives were going to be forfeit.

-31-

"Galyan," Maddox said. "Run interference for us. Use your projector and paralyze a few of the intruders if you can."

"And if I can't?" Galyan asked.

"Make them fire at you. That will give us an idea of their weaponry."

"Sir," Galyan said, disappearing from the bridge.

Maddox lurched to his chair, pressing an intercom button. He called his colonel of marines, outlining the situation. "You're going to need body armor and heavy personal weaponry. It could get bloody."

"I've picked up their position, sir," the colonel said. "They don't seem to understand we're watching through interior recorders."

"We can't let them reach Hangar Bay 2," Maddox said. "Do everything you must to stop them, including breaching hull integrity."

"Portables, sir?" the colonel asked.

"As a last resort," Maddox said.

"I'm ordering a recon team to delay them."

"I'm going to join you, Colonel. Bring an extra exo-suit with you for me."

"Yes, Captain."

"Good luck, Colonel. You have your orders."

Maddox observed on the main screen. The eleven intruders moved like gorillas or bears, remorselessly heading for Hangar Bay 2.

There, Galyan appeared.

Maddox watched as Galyan floated to them.

Three suited intruders noticed. One opened fire with a heavy gout of some kind of blaster. It passed harmlessly through the holoimage but gouged the bulkhead behind, burning through it and the hidden electrical outlets. The bulkhead sizzled and sparked, but otherwise did nothing else.

The three suited intruders looked at each other. Did one shrug? The eleven continued marching down the corridor toward Hangar Bay 2.

Galyan floated after the back intruder and attempted to push his holoimage through the suit. The holoimage refused to go. Galyan tried again, and failed again.

He vanished.

Galyan appeared before Maddox. "It is no good, sir. Their armor repels my holoimage."

"The blaster fire didn't seem to be anything special," Maddox said.

"It was more powerful than our blaster pistols."

"Agreed," Maddox said. "But it wasn't something else entirely. I think we can beat them."

With that, Maddox charged off the bridge. He sprinted down a corridor as only a New Man could sprint, even though he wasn't fully New Man. With his other capabilities, however, he had their stamina, speed and nearly their strength.

Soon, Maddox met the marine colonel at a corridor junction. The colonel wore exoskeleton armor with a blast rifle and grenade launcher in his left arm. The colonel's armor was taller than the gorilla suits marching through *Victory*. The colonel's exoskeleton armor was thinner, however, even though it amplified his strength over ten times.

Maddox donned similar armor, sealing himself within. These suits didn't use marine-grade motors, as they'd do on a planet. Instead, these ran off battery power packs. They could run for forty-five minutes that way. The armor wasn't totally proof against a blast rifle, though it could take the hits for several seconds and retain outer integrity.

How would the exo-suits stand up against the alien blaster fire?

205

With his chin, inside his helmet, Maddox flicked on the comm net. "It's your game, Colonel. I'm along for the ride."

"Captain," Colonel Henderson said.

Using a HUD on the interior of the visor of his helmet, Maddox saw the colonel's plan.

Other exo-suited marines moved into position. No one barred the path to Hangar Bay 2. No marines gathered there, either. Instead, the colonel maneuvered his exo-teams through the corridors, converging on the location the intruders would be in less than three minutes.

Maddox had barely gotten here on time.

Maddox didn't lead the charge or direct any of the marines. He would go through the colonel, the chain of command. Instead, Maddox hung in back, following the colonel's fire team.

As they marched down the corridors, the exo-servos whining and the feet tromped heavily on the deck plates. The colonel dropped back to Maddox.

The colonel's visor whirred open. It showed a gruff man in his late forties with a bar of bone over his eyes like some Neanderthal hominid.

"I don't have it on the comm net, sir," the colonel said. "I don't know if the aliens can read our net traffic or not. The portables are barring the direct path to Hangar Bay 2. If the aliens can skim our communications, they'll charge right into it before they're ready."

Maddox had lowered his visor as well to take this face-to-face. He grinned in appreciation of the plan and the colonel's caution of not putting everything on the battle comm net.

The visor rose and the colonel returned to his fire team.

Two minutes later, the battle commenced, and it instantly became a wild free-for-all.

Marines fired down the corridors into the junction as the first three intruders entered it. Blast-rifle fire scorched gorilla-alien armor without penetrating it. For all the good it did, the blast fire was like a wash of ineffectual heat.

More gorilla-alien suits appeared. Three smashed through bulkheads, charging up a corridor. Their denseness and greater strength now came into play.

Marines fired and lobbed grenades.

Alien blaster fire smashed into exo-suits, burning through in seconds. Marines screamed in agony.

The colonel roared orders over the net.

Maddox listened in the rear. Eight marines were down, no, ten. Eight of them were dead. The last two moaned in pain, twisting in their breached armor on the deck.

The marine grenades hadn't done shit against the dense alien armor.

The gorilla-suit aliens raised their axes and shook them, perhaps as a victory celebration. A few more blasted at retreating marines.

"Sir," the colonel told Maddox. "We can't stop them."

"Not with blasters and grenades," Maddox said. "Let them run into the portables."

"And if that fails, sir?" the colonel asked.

Maddox stared down the corridor. "Then we'll mob them in Hangar Bay 2 and wrestle blasters and axes out of their hands. We'll use their own weaponry against them."

"They slaughtered my boys, sir."

"And we'll all die if we don't win. It isn't over yet," Maddox said. "Let's get to it."

"Sir," the colonel said.

The eleven gorilla-suited aliens marched faster for Hangar Bay 2. How did they know the layout of the starship? Maybe they merely sensed the Yon Soth machine or the Builder AI.

Maddox, the colonel and the remaining exo-suited marines followed from behind and out of range. There was no sense in dying for no reason. Besides, they'd need everyone in the hangar bay if Maddox's mad plan were the last one left.

The intruders marched straight into the portables where the corridor widened.

One moment, the suited aliens marched. The next, flamers from ahead vomited superheated plasma clots, causing corridor paint to peel in their passing. The superheated clots of plasma struck alien armor.

The plasma didn't burn through instantly. It didn't burn through in moments. It burned while stuck onto the armor. That must have caused a heat transfer into the alien suit. Those struck began to cavort wildly, jumping, jerking their arms and whipping their heads back and forth. They crashed into bulkheads, smashing through.

More plasma clots flew, hitting the next group of aliens to march up.

These got off blaster shots, though.

One blast hit a portable flamer. It exploded, catching two more. Roars of explosions smashed bulkheads. A great fireball rolled down the wide corridor, washing over the cavorting and un-hit aliens alike. That caused more to dance. Alien blaster fire shot everywhere.

"Are any flamers left?" Maddox said.

"Two," the colonel said.

"Roll them up. Have them fire."

Soon, more plasma clots flew into the dancing alien mass. It was sickening. It was heartening.

"Here," the colonel said, passing a heavy slug-thrower into Maddox's gauntleted hands. "Maybe these can breach the armor, now that's hot."

Maddox joined the surviving marines. They hit the cavorting aliens, hammering their armor with heavy slugs.

At first, the slugs whined off the alien armor. The intruders didn't even seem to notice. Eventually, though, slugs tore through the superheated armor, and the alien inside it ceased cavorting.

They fell and lay still.

"We can do it," the colonel roared.

Marines raced closer, firing from the armored hip. It was mayhem at close range.

Soon, the last gorilla-suited alien fell like a chopped tree to the deck.

Maddox's shoulders sagged. He'd fired three hundred rounds at them. The others had done likewise.

"We did it," the colonel said hoarsely. "Now, let's see what 'em bastards look like."

Maddox followed the colonel. As he did, a bizarre thing happened. The gorilla-suited aliens began to fade. Maddox blinked in confusion.

Marines shouted curses.

Maddox hurried, passing others who had stopped to watch. It made no difference. By the time Maddox reached the bodies, all the intruders had faded, disappearing altogether.

Maddox felt something on his exo-armored shoulder. He turned. The colonel had been tapping his shoulder.

Maddox lowered his visor.

The colonel lowered his. The bluff Neanderthal face showed confusion. "Did the alien attack really happen?"

Given the circumstances, it seemed like a reasonable question. Maddox looked around at the awful destruction. Marines had fired superheated plasma and shot heavy slugs. Many marines were dead.

"Arius," Maddox said patching through to the computer. "What happened? Why did these creatures disappear?"

"I do not know," Arius said. "But I can surmise."

"Do so," Maddox said.

"Perhaps their life force no longer maintained their existence on this plane of existence."

"What does that even mean?"

"I can go into an in-depth explanation, Captain. But I doubt you want that."

"No," Maddox said. "Keep it simple, huh?"

"I surmise that their life force kept them intact in this...place. Once they died, there was no longer enough energy coursing through them to keep their forms intact. Therefore, they dissipated into the nonbeing of this place that should not exist."

"Did you hear that, Colonel?" Maddox asked.

"What does it mean?" the colonel asked, looking as confused as Maddox felt.

"That we won," Maddox said.

The colonel stared at Maddox, only slowly nodding.

"It's time to clean up and see to your men," Maddox said.

"That, I understand."

Maddox nodded. He never wanted to dimensional travel again. It was too bizarre and nearly incomprehensible.

"What happened to the silver ovals that were attached to the hull?" Maddox asked.

"They are long gone," Arius said. "I thought Galyan had already told you that."

Maddox cut the connection. This had been a grim and devastating battle, but the feeling of unreality was too strong even with victory.

After checking with the medical team and speaking with several wounded marines, Maddox returned to the bridge. He'd divested himself of the exo-armor and weaponry. He was beat, and he wanted out of this place.

Maddox clicked the intercom button. "Arius, you'd better tell me we're going to break through soon into the place where Task Force 3 went. I don't know how much longer we can stand this unreality."

"Understood Captain," Arius said. "FYI, there have been several assaults on my higher functions and those of the bots."

"Was this during the battle?"

"Yes."

"And they stopped when we killed the intruders?"

"Yes."

Maddox scowled. "If they faded when they died...what's keeping us real in this place?"

"That is an astute question, Captain."

"Just answer it."

"It may surprise you to know that some of the power from the Yon Soth machine is helping to keep our existence here."

"Say that again."

"The Yon Soth machine has several unique functions. One of them helps maintain our integrity. Said another way, it keeps us from unraveling."

"What kept the task force from unraveling when they were here?"

"That is unknown."

"The supership did it?"

"I don't know," Arius said. "Captain, I have found the exit. I believe this is where Task Force 3 went."

Maddox grinned. Some good news. "Let's go. Do it."

"On my mark," Arius said, "we shall begin."

-32-

Maddox and the rest of *Victory's* bridge crew became aware they'd reached normal space. There were no compacted starry masses, no shrieking neutron stars, black holes or other spatial distortions. The sense of unreality had vanished as well. Instead, background stars appeared as in normal space and—

"Sir," Galyan said, "I have detected a G-class star. We are in its outer system. I have counted five terrestrial planets within the inner system."

"Excellent. Do you see Task Force 3?"

"I have not, sir. I am still looking for them."

Maddox thought about that. They'd left the strange realm and reached another dimension. If the Builder AI had followed the right trail—he pressed the intercom button.

"Arius, do you detect Task Force 3?"

"That is not my priority, Captain. Mine is maintaining the Yon Soth machine and protecting us from its emanations and its trickery, and charting us through the dimensions."

"Don't get your dander up about it."

"Dander?" Arius asked. "I do not comprehend."

"How about this," Maddox said. "Don't get your panties in a bunch."

"I believe that is an idiom slur, and after all I have done for you, I'm surprised you'd feel the need."

Maddox laughed. He felt such relief being in normal space. "It's a joke, Arius. Didn't the Supreme Intelligence explain humor to you?"

211

"He explained it, but I'm not quite certain about it. While I have a high capacity for intelligence and am in many ways superior to the combined intellect of your entire ship, humor is beyond me."

"Don't worry about it," Maddox said. "Let's figure out what's going on."

"Sir," Andros said, breaking into the conversation, "I'm detecting...mobile asteroids."

Maddox swiveled his chair. "Do you mean large or heavy comets?"

"They're not a natural phenomenon, sir," Andros said. "The mobile asteroids have nuclear engines and massive thrusters. They're heading inward. Following the trajectory of their present path...they're heading for the fifth planet, the outer planet of the inner ring."

"Are they military vessels?"

Andros studied his monitor for a time. "Yes, sir. They have armaments and might have parked ships on the asteroid surface."

"They're motherships?"

"I'd give that a high likelihood," Andros said.

"How many of these asteroid motherships do you count?" Maddox asked.

"I'll put it up on the main screen," Andros said, "and I'll give it maximum magnification."

On that screen appeared...

Maddox counted twenty mobile asteroids. They were far bigger than *Victory*. Had Task Force 3 arrived in this star system? Might they have faced the mobile asteroids? Did these asteroids maneuver against the task force? Was there something special about the fifth planet?

"Galyan, concentrate on the fifth planet. It may be important."

While he waited, Maddox drummed his fingers on an armrest. The last aliens in the silver ovals and powered gorilla suits—those aliens had possessed superior technology. They must have been ultra-dense to boot. These aliens in the mobile asteroids with fusion engines—they seemed to have inferior technology.

Maddox rubbed his jaw. "See if you can contact whoever crews the mobile asteroids."

After attempting it, the comm officer shook her head.

"Captain," Galyan said. "I am getting a response from them. It is a frequency different from what any of us are used to. Perhaps that is why—"

"Galyan," Maddox said, interrupting. "Enough with the explanations. Can you put whoever is trying to contact us on the main screen?"

"I can, sir. It appears they have been trying to communicate with us for some time."

On the main screen, appeared a huge Saurian in military garb. He had muscular reptilian arms, and hunched forward as he stared at Maddox. The creature hissed in a sibilant language.

"Can we decipher that?" Maddox asked.

"I am not finding any commonalities," Galyan said. "That strikes me as odd, as I am normally proficient in translation."

"I'm not having any luck, either," Andros said, who worked his science board.

"Arius," Maddox said, "can you explain why we're having trouble translating the creature's speech?"

"Of course I can explain, Captain," Arius said. "It is simple. The creature, as you call it, is from a different dimension than yours. These beings have different modes of thought and different ways of reaching conclusions."

"I don't see how that's a given," Maddox said. "Looking at him, at his humanoid configuration, it seems like this is congruent evolution, if you believe such things, or congruent creation, if you believe in the other way. They use fusion power and have similar spaceships. We shouldn't we have commonalities with them? Maybe we're not looking hard enough for such commonalities."

"That is an interesting point," Arius said. "Perhaps you are right. I will give it further thought."

"Wait," Maddox said. "Before you go, can you give us a clue how we can figure out how to communicate with them?"

"Glean as much information about them as you can, Captain. In time there might be some kind of commonalities that the communication computers and the translators will be able to use."

Maddox nodded. "Simple logic, in other words."

"Is logic ever simple, Captain?"

Maddox made a motion to cut the connection. The comm officer complied.

Maddox closed his eyes. Computer entities other than Galyan drained his composure, as they all got uppity in the end.

For the next half hour, the translators slaved, trying to find commonalities in order to find a translation of the Saurian's speech.

Galyan's eyelids had been blinking furiously. Now, that ceased. "Captain, I believe I have stumbled upon the method. I am ready to try again."

Victory had maneuvered closer to the mobile asteroids, about fifteen million kilometers. Now, there would be less lag time lag between communications.

Once more, the Saurian commander appeared on the screen. He hissed, sounding more like a snake than a reptile.

"Who are you?" the translator said.

Maddox gave Galyan a thumbs up before regarding the reptilian alien. "I'm Captain Maddox. Who are you?"

"I am the Interrogator," the Saurian said. "What are you doing in this region of space?"

"We're exploring. What are you doing?"

"We are attacking and eliminating. Do not get in our way. We have our orders. If you attempt to interfere we will annihilate you as well."

"I see," Maddox said. "I don't want to get in your way at all, and I appreciate the power your twenty mobile asteroids represent."

"They are launch vessels, not mobile asteroids."

"Yes, yes, that is a much more noble and worthy term," Maddox said. "Is there any way that we may assist you?"

"Are you from the fifth planet? Do you know the vile creatures that inhabit it?"

"I'm afraid not, and I don't. Are they enemies of yours?"

"They are enemies of existence. That is all you need to know. Do not try to communicate with them or help them in any way. Otherwise, you will be targeted for elimination. Do you understand?"

"I do, and I respect what you are trying to do. These aliens, they are aliens, are they not?"

The Saurian didn't answer. Instead, he stared more balefully at Maddox.

"Uh, if I've insulted you in any way or said anything that you find offensive, I'd like to apologize for it."

The Saurian nodded, and that was interesting because it showed a commonality between different dimensions. "Your servile attitude is noted. That you have a slave mentality is excellent. You will park your vessel on the second launch system. Is that understood?"

"Uh, what do you intend to do with my crew?" Maddox asked.

"No, that is an improper reply. A freak with a servile attitude would be quick to obey. So far, you have been quick to obey. Now you are showing resistance. That is a mistake."

"Captain," Galyan said, "can I speak with you a moment?"

"A moment, your Excellency," Maddox said to the Saurian. The connection was cut. "What is it Galyan?"

"I believe I have found Task Force 3."

"Let me guess. It's near the fifth planet."

"Why, that is correct, Captain."

Maddox clicked on the intercom. "Arius, what can you tell me about the aliens on the fifth planet?"

"I," Arius said, "I can tell you nothing. I know of no aliens. Oh, do you suppose it is the Onos?"

"I do." Maddox hailed Keith. "Initiate the star-drive jump. We're going to the fifth planet. That's where the task force is, right Galyan?"

"Yes, Captain. It appears that most of their ships are intact and it also appears that there is residue of a space battle."

"Against mobile asteroids," Maddox guessed.

"Why yes, Captain, that is correct. How did you know?"

Maddox pointed at the main screen, which showed the armada of twenty mobile asteroids.

"Deduction," Galyan said.

Maddox rubbed his cheek. "I think I'm getting the picture. Let's get to the fifth planet as fast as we can. Arius, can you take us home as soon as we reach Task Force 3?"

"No, not immediately," Arius said. "It will take time to align properties—unless you don't mind possibly meeting the gorilla-suited aliens again in the null region."

"No," Maddox said. "I want to avoid that if we can."

"I thought so. Thus, I need time to calibrate a new route. I should be able to do it soon, though."

Maddox nodded briskly. "We've found Task Force 3. Lieutenant, initiate the star-drive jump."

"I'm just about ready, mate," Keith said.

Maddox frowned.

"Sir, I mean," Keith said.

Maddox nodded. "Let's get to the fifth planet as fast as we can and start figuring out how to get our people home. The sooner we leave these strange dimensions, the better for all of us."

-33-

As the star-drive-jump lag wore off, Andros was the first to notice the new location compared to the given coordinates. He double-checked and swiveled around.

"Captain, we're not where we intended to be."

Maddox turned to him. "Where are we then?"

Andros swiveled back to his science board, studying the monitor. "We're on the other side of the planet, hidden from Task Force 3 instead of near it."

Maddox frowned. "Galyan. Galyan, where are you?"

In a fluster, the little holoimage appeared beside him. "Captain, we are not where Keith intended when he input the star-drive jump."

"I'm aware of that." Maddox looked at Keith. "Lieutenant, do you have an explanation for this?"

Keith shook his head.

"Galyan," Maddox said, "do you have an explanation for this?"

"I do not, sir." Galyan became thoughtful. "Can it be that since we are in a different dimension that some of our systems do not function normally?"

Maddox rubbed his chin. "It seems like a possibility...but it doesn't seem like the answer. Andros, see if you can find something."

The intercom clicked on. "Captain," Arius said over the comm, "I have an explanation."

Maddox became alert, as his intuitive sense pinged and this involved a foreign computer on his ship. "What is that, Arius?"

"There's no need to be defensive, Captain. I have called you of my own free will, indicting my good intent. There is no sabotage intended. Perhaps there is the smallest of subterfuge, but it is only for everyone's good, I assure you."

"Why don't I find that comforting?"

"That is an interesting question," Arius said. "I myself would like to know why that is so. Clearly, by my act of freely and openly informing you, I'm showing you my good will."

"Maybe," Maddox said. "First, tell me why you caused the discrepancy."

"I did not say *I* caused this, Captain. I said slight subterfuge occurred. There was a bare alteration in the jump path, and it was—"

"We're being hailed, sir," the comm officer said, interrupting.

Maddox looked at her.

She nodded, grimacing.

"Who is it?" Maddox asked.

"The signal is coming from the planet, sir."

""Galyan, put the planet on the main screen."

On the main screen appeared the red planet. Most of the planet's terrain appeared to be similar to Mars back home, hence, the red. This planet also had an Earth-like atmosphere and heavy cloud cover in areas as well as green and yellow areas and small blue seas.

"Can you pinpoint where the call is coming from?" Maddox asked the comm officer.

"Yes sir." She pressed a switch.

On the main screen, on the red planet and in a widely red region, a point blinked.

Maddox raised his chin. "Who's calling us, Arius? An Ono?"

"Why not take the call and find out?" Arius suggested. "You're here after all and they did go to the effort of separating you from the task force."

218

"Those are my thoughts exactly," Maddox said. "They separated us from the task force. I suspect for nefarious purposes. Weapons officer—"

"Captain," Arius said, interrupting, "I assure you there's no need for alarm. The Onos are not hostile."

"Do you run the starship?" Maddox asked.

"At times like this, I think I should."

"Alert," Maddox said, obviously not liking the answer. "Shields up. Get the disruptor beam ready. Initiate antimatter missile-launch sequence. I want us locked and loaded, people."

The bridge crew turned to their panels, executing the order.

In moments, the weapons officer said, "Everything is ready, sir."

Maddox nodded and pointed at the comm officer. "Are the Onos still hailing us?"

"Yes, sir."

"Put whoever it is on the main screen."

The comm officer clicked a switch.

On the main screen appeared what looked like a living teddy bear. It was a small, bearish creature with golden fur, striking markings and wearing a long orange robe. The cranium was much larger than one would expect, the teeth a little sharper and the eyes blue, glittering with intelligence.

The alien bowed formally and then spoke. "Is this Starship *Victory?*"

"Sir," the comm officer said in shock. "There's no translation needed. She spoke in Commonwealth Anglic."

"She?" Maddox asked.

"I believe so, sir."

"Your officer is correct," the bearish creature said. "In order to facilitate and expedite matters, let me inform you that I am indeed an Ono. My rank and name are Conciliator Zoe."

Maddox raised his eyebrows. A second later, he nodded stiffly. "I'm Captain Maddox of Starship *Victory*, an officer in Star Watch."

"Aha. So we did it."

This time, Maddox arched a single eyebrow, staring intently at Conciliator Zoe. "Did you effectuate the subtle shift in our star-drive jump?"

219

"I did not do it, Captain, although I gave the order to do it. Thus, in a sense, you could say I'm responsible."

"Thank you for your honesty."

Conciliator Zoe spread her furry paws. "I am honest, Captain, I assure you, and my intentions are generous."

"Generous?"

"Oh my," she said, "I believe I misspoke. Let me think." She tapped her furry bear chin before looking up again. "My intentions are pure and they do not involve harm to you, if we can possibly help it. It is indeed for the good of your dimension."

Maddox grinned. "That reassures me completely."

"I do not think you are being honest with me, Captain."

"I'm being as honest with you as you are with me," Maddox countered.

"Must it be like this, Captain? I've gone to great lengths to speak with you, although I will be honest and say that we have great need of your unique abilities."

Maddox thought about that as he used his intuitive sense. This Zoe told the truth…to a degree, which meant she wasn't telling the whole truth. He studied her but couldn't get more of an intuitive read on her than that.

"Are you saying you're one of the good guys?" Maddox asked.

"But of course," she said.

"And your kind once lived in our dimension."

"Indeed, that is so."

"When did you leave our dimension?"

Zoe shook her bear head. "That is not germane to the issue, Captain. What is germane is that you come down here so I may speak to you face-to-face in the flesh. We must discuss a matter of…let us call it, interdimensional safety. In truth, your dimension will be strengthened if you agree to my plan. However, it is also true that you will be helping us as well."

"So, you're not *only* doing this for our good?"

"Of course not, Captain. That would be illogical, would it not?"

Maddox cocked his head. There was something about the word illogical and the way Conciliator Zoe had used it that caused him to think of Arius. Why would he think that? What was the connection between the two?

He mentally shelved that for the moment, asking, "Why do you wish to speak to me personally? We're doing that here, in a way."

"Because we have a present for you and there are certain things I'd like to tell you we don't want to risk being heard via comm transmission. You also have bridge personnel hearing whatever I say to you. There is a possibly some of them might be captured and interrogated later. They would relate whatever I'd said to you. I want to avoid such a possibility. You must see that this is security consciousness on my part. I don't wish them imperiling more than one dimension by repeating what I say."

"Who would or could possibly capture us?" Maddox asked.

"Really, you're asking that? Has no one attempted to hijack your vessel recently?"

Maddox stiffened imperceptibly. "If you're asking that, you must have ordered the attempt. How otherwise could you know?"

"There are ways, obviously. I'll give you another possibility. The ones you call Saurians are hell-bent on destroying our planet. They're approaching in yet another wave assault. You'll find when you speak with your Commodore Galt that he destroyed an earlier wave assault."

"You know an awful lot about what's going on my ship and in the task force. How did you derive such knowledge?"

"Captain," Zoe said. "I *should* know these things. It is my duty to know and I am—well, never mind about that. You have dealt with arrogant species in the past. We hope to prove the opposite. Perhaps some of what we've learned throughout the millennia we can pass on to you." Once more, Zoe spread her furry paws. "I would appreciate your coming down, Captain. We will both benefit from it."

"Come down alone?" Maddox asked.

"It is imperative you do so. I assure you we wish you no ill, no harm. We will do everything in our power to make sure you return to your starship exactly as you left it...except you will have greater knowledge and the gifts we wish to give you."

"What kind of gifts?"

"Please Captain, you have to come down to find out. Surely, I cannot tell you here in the open. It would jeopardize everything if I did. I've already explained that."

Maddox stared at the teddy-bear conciliator, part of a dimensional-traveling species. She knew far too much. She had abilities that affected his ship. How...?

Maddox snapped his fingers. There was a link between her and Arius. He could feel it. That troubled him greatly. This mission troubled him. Yet, if he could learn more by doing down to the planet—

"Conciliator Zoe, just so we're clear, I'm targeting your location. Our disruptor beam can hit it and antimatter missiles reach it. If this is a trap, we plan to devastate the planet to its bedrock."

"My, my Captain, that's impressive. I appreciate your threat and what's more, I believe it. However, you'll find we also have powerful means at our disposal. Please Captain, I wish you'd come of your own free will."

"Or?" Maddox asked.

"I, too, wish to be clear. Is the 'or' a request for us to display our technical prowess? We certainly can, Captain. I would so much rather you came of your own accord."

Maddox was tempted to tell her to prove she had such power. Yet, she or her team had shifted the coordinates of the star-drive jump. That indicated considerable technical ability.

Maddox nodded sharply as she watched him. "I agree. I'll have Keith bring me down and—"

"Captain," Galyan said, interrupting. "I wish you would reconsider. Our shield is at full power and there are other factors we could implement to stop them from—"

Even as Galyan spoke, Captain Maddox vanished in a blink from the bridge of *Victory*.

-34-

Maddox stumbled as he reappeared in a different location, knowing he'd left the bridge. He immediately felt lighter, not greatly so, but enough that he was aware of it.

He quit stumbling and stood upright, looking around. Clouds drifted in the sky, low, thin clouds.

Maddox inhaled. He tasted something different from ship air, but also different from Earth air. For one thing, it was thinner and there were tastes in it indicating an alien planet. That was two things, he realized.

Presumably, the Onos, this Conciliator Zoe, had the ability to teleport him from one locale to another.

Maddox extended his look and realized he stood on a low marble dais. Surrounding the dais were Greek-like columns, as in an ancient temple.

Conciliator Zoe stood between two columns. She wore her flowing orange robe that reached the marble floor. She had an olive wreath upon her bearish head, the head with a large cranium. She was no taller than Maddox's waist, smaller than he'd expected.

Maddox looked past the columns. The place looked like an ancient Greek model of temples and such. Everything was pristine white marble. Beyond the temples—

Was he on a mountaintop?

In the distance were red rocks or mountains that seemed lower than where he stood. He didn't spy any plants or greenery, just red rock and rusty dirt or sand.

He looked in the other direction, seeing the same.

The temples beyond his dais—they surrounded him by a quarter of a mile all around, he estimated. Beyond that was a sheer drop.

Conciliator Zoe bowed her bearish head. "Captain, I'm so glad that you agreed to this."

Maddox decided to go with the flow and see what happened. He faced her and bowed. It annoyed him he hadn't been able to take a blaster. As per his custom, however, he had the monofilament blade tucked in one of his boots.

"We're on the planet?" Maddox asked.

"Captain, is that truly your greeting?"

"No. I'm glad to be here and make your acquaintance, Zoe."

"It's Conciliator Zoe, if you please."

"Of course. Conciliator Zoe. I'm Captain Maddox of Star Watch."

"And I am of the Onos. We…well, never mind about that."

"Oh, but I do mind," Maddox said. "Aren't we going to go on etiquette? You wish to know all there is about me but you wish to keep hidden things about you. That isn't standard etiquette."

"Captain, Captain. Of course, I wish to keep things hidden from you. There are many things your species isn't ready to know yet. We Onos are a much more ancient and frankly, more intelligent and farther-traveled species than you are. That is not a boast or brag, just simple fact. You are here on our planet after all because we've wanted you specifically to come."

The last was shocking if true. Yet, Maddox said, "You keep saying you aren't bragging, yet you keep bringing up how intelligent and far-traveled you are. Bringing it up more than once is bragging in my book. Second—" he held up two fingers to forestall Zoe from interrupting, "you say this as if being more intelligent gives you the right to be deceptive and condescending. That's a logical fallacy."

Zoe seemed nonplussed for a moment, so Maddox know he had scored a point, maybe helped put things on a more equal footing. He went on, "Let's address something else. You brought me here before I was able to speak with the commodore of the task force. Is there a reason for that?"

"Not particularly. I just thought it would expedite matters to speak with you as soon as possible. Believe me, Captain, we must expedite our time, as it is quickly running out for both our species."

Maddox shook his head. "It seems like you have plenty of time."

"We *did* have plenty of time, once, but events have moved much faster than I anticipated. That is particularly true concerning the next Saurian attack. The limited number of Star Watch vessels here isn't helping matters, either. I'm afraid—I don't know if the task force is capable of beating off the coming assault."

"Did they beat off the last one?"

"With remarkable ease and precision, I must say."

Maddox nodded. "That's why I'd like to—wait. Why is the commodore in charge and not the vice admiral?"

"Captain, are you trying to be tricky? Of course you must have seen, in your briefing, at least, that the vice admiral died in the Battle for the Planet Zinc."

Maddox squinted at Zoe. "How do you know about the vice admiral if he didn't make it into your dimension? Did you hack into the task force's computer systems?"

Zoe rubbed her forehead, turned and looked away. She sighed and then turned back to Maddox.

"That's very clever, Captain. You're trying to probe the depth of our knowledge and possibly learn how we acquired it. I wish you wouldn't do that. I wish rather that we'd get to the heart of the issue. Time is critical. Must we have this verbal duel, hmm?"

Maddox shook his head. "You want to speed up matters, then you need to be more candid. It's you who're being deceptive, not me. I just want to know what's going on before I risk my life again. So. What do you want with me? Tell me and I'll tell you if it's possible."

"An excellent idea," Zoe said. "Your dimension is in peril by the one who controls what you refer to as the asteroidal supership."

225

Maddox rubbed his hands. Now they were getting somewhere. "What species controls the supership? What's the name and personality of the commander who runs the supership?"

"Captain," Zoe said, "you give me pause. I don't know if I should tell you the name. As to her species... Call her a succubus. That is the best and the most accurate description."

Maddox scowled. "Succubus...? Are you calling her a female demon that invades men's dreams in evil ways?"

Zoe nodded. "That's as good a description as any. Perhaps she doesn't invade dreams but dimensions instead. She is the queen of the asteroidal supership, and her name is Lilith."

"Are you serious?" asked Maddox. "That's her literal name, a human name?"

"I'm giving you the human form for her real name. Lilith is the best translation. She is indeed a succubus, and in a matter of speaking she is not a completely flesh and blood creature. Rest assured that she's from the outer dimensions, horrific and wretched dimensions of great chaos. The succubae are determinedly evil and they have committed many vile deeds. This succubus, this Queen Lilith who runs the supership, is ancient. She is destructive in many ways and forms. She destroyed the planet Zinc for a number of reasons. One was to power her ship and herself with the death of people of Zinc."

"That doesn't make sense. Why, then, did she pick such a lightly populated planet?"

"Her actions aren't all logical from a human perspective. But they are logical from the perspective of interdimensional warfare and certain causes and effects. Some of that may not make sense to you, but there is sense and logic to Lilith and to us."

"What does the Succubus Lilith have to do with the Onos?"

Zoe nodded.

"The Onos have stood as dimensional guardians for millennia. Not just for your dimension, but for other dimensions as well. That doesn't mean we flit from dimension to dimension, creating endless access points. I'm sure the Supreme Intelligence or Arius told you that breaking into a dimension makes it easier for others to follow."

Maddox eyed the Ono. "You know far too much about Arius and the Supreme Intelligence and things that happened in our dimension. How is that possible? Are you in communication with the Supreme Intelligence? If so, why didn't he tell me? If so, why didn't you through him warn the Commonwealth about the coming supership assault upon Zinc? Why haven't we worked together before this?"

"No, no, no," Zoe said. "You don't understand and I can't explain it all to you in our short time together. I barely have enough time to explain how you can kill the succubus."

"Me?" Maddox asked. "You want *Victory* to go alone against the interdimensional asteroidal supership?"

"No, of course not," Zoe said. "For one thing, I don't believe *Victory* could defeat the supership. I don't believe that *Victory* and Task Force 3 working in tandem could do it either. And that's even if we armed you with better weapons. I don't believe that if all the Saurians headed for our dear planet turned and aided you and the task force could destroy the supership. In that sense, the supership is invulnerable."

"Then I don't get it," Maddox said. "You just told me you wanted me to slay the succubus for you."

"Exactly. I want you and Riker to take the weapon and enter her supership, hunt her down there and slay her there."

The boldness of the plan, the silliness of the idea caused Maddox to laugh. "That's ludicrous. I've heard of some insane plans before, but this one tops them all."

Zoe's features never changed. "That's as it should be, Captain. This is interdimensional war. Not all things are as they seem. There's another rule. In some dimensions what is easy becomes vastly difficult, and vise-versa."

Maddox waved a hand. It wasn't that he was overwhelmed by all this, but that he was having grave doubts.

"You're just trying to blow smoke in my face by telling me all kinds of nonsense: a succubus, a creature from Hell. Is that what you're saying the outer dimensions are, Hell?"

Zoe frowned before brightening. "I see. You're speaking from a religious aspect concerning the Creator and His enemies. No, I'm not saying the outer dimensions are Hell. That's a connection you are making, not I. This is the multiverse. The outer dimensions, as you put it, are chaotic, different, the creatures living in them vastly different from you and me. They fight tooth and claw with each other, with no law except what you would call the law of the jungle—the strong eat the weak. They are monsters, therefore—creatures who take for themselves and kill anyone in the way. We do not condone this approach. We believe in order, and reason, which is the only way civilization can thrive."

Maddox nodded.

"I believe Erills once made it into your dimension," Zoe said, "a band of them. The Ur-Builders were very foolish indeed to let them in. Fortunately, that situation is presently under control. The Erills are from outer dimensions. This Lilith, this succubus, can take material form, but that is not how you'll destroy her. You must destroy the physical form first, of course. That must seem obvious even to you. Afterward, you'll have to destroy her spiritual essence."

Maddox shook his head. "I don't know why you think I'm going to do be able to do this. Why you don't put a band of Onos together to attack her?"

"Captain, truly, really? We're not barbaric like you nor are we a militaristic society. We're not filled with aggression, hostility and the desire to rend, kill and destroy such as those of the outer dimensions—or you humans. We are thinkers, scholars, managers, scientists. You are the soldier species. In particular, you are the one we've waited millennia to appear."

Maddox stared at her incredulously.

"What's wrong?" Zoe asked. "Did I misspeak?"

"What you just said: *Me?* You've waited millennia for *me* to appear on the scene?"

"One such as you," Zoe said.

"That can't be right."

"It is," Zoe said.

Maddox blinked with confusion and then stared off into the distance. Just what exactly was going on here with the Onos and this Conciliator Zoe?

-35-

"Captain," Zoe said. "I assure you I speak in good faith. This has all taken place in order for you to destroy Lilith, to destroy the succubus and finally dismantle the horrific asteroidal supership. It is an ancient vessel and she is a corrupting—let me think." Zoe rubbed her furry cranium. "Ah, you faced some of her shock troops earlier. They dropped into existence as your starship passed through a null region."

"The gorilla-armored attackers were from the supership?" Maddox asked.

"In a manner of speaking, yes," Zoe said.

"No! Were they from the supership or not?"

"That is all I can say at present, Captain, about that. I believe you might run into more shock troops aboard her supership, so you'll have to be extremely careful. In fact, you'll need to take more than just Riker. I believe your colonel of marines would be an excellent addition, particularly if armed with some of the weapons I'll give you."

"Whoa, whoa," Maddox said. "You're seriously thinking I'm going to do what? Teleport into the asteroidal supership?"

"Not from here, of course. You'll have to do it from the only portal that is accessible to you. Otherwise, yes, it will be a form of teleportation. You'll go from the daughter-ship to her supership. That is the only way you can stop Lilith. That is the only way you're going to save your dimension."

"What a second," Maddox said. "You're saying that if I don't do this, my dimension is going to be engulfed in some kind of cosmic fire?"

"Not immediately. Your dimension will first become a messy, chaotic interdimensional crossroad. Lilith will use that for her greater purposes, and you and the inhabitants of your dimension will suffer. Eventually, however, she'll destroy your dimension—if you fail to do as I suggest. This is the opportunity to strike back before she has her chance. This is the moment we've worked millennia to achieve."

Maddox stared at the Ono. What Zoe suggested was fantastic. "Millennia? You've worked for ages to achieve the right circumstances so someone like me could attack the Succubus Lilith?"

"That is correct."

Maddox shook his head. "I don't understand. Why am I the one to do this?"

"Clearly," Zoe said, "because you were trained by Balron the Traveler."

Maddox's intuitive sense began going off like an alarm. Zoe was telling the truth. His knees felt weak. He looked around. There was no place to sit, so he sat right there, put his hands on his knees and breathed in. He held it and sought the Way of the Pilgrim.

He found his calm and he studied Zoe. She was child-sized, furry and brainy. She knew so much, too much. Someone who knew so much might also have meddled in the situation, caused things to happen for their own purposes and not to actually help Maddox or humanity.

Maddox looked around at the Greek-like columns and temples. They struck him as sterile. His brow furrowed. He didn't see any other Onos. Why was that?

Maddox climbed to his feet, rubbed his head and said, "Just a minute, huh?"

He walked off the dais, past Zoe and past the columns. He strode past several empty temples. Soon, he came to the edge and looked down.

He stood on a floating platform. It had levitated a quarter mile off a seething lava lake. Heat radiated upward as he leaned over the edge.

An instant of dizziness struck.

Maddox stepped back, thinking. Again, he walked past the temples and columns, returning to the dais. There was the patiently waiting conciliator.

"Why don't I see other Onos?" Maddox asked.

Zoe didn't answer.

"Are you the last of your race to have survived?" Maddox asked.

Again, Zoe didn't answer.

"Are you even real?" Maddox asked. "I hope I don't have to come over there and slap you and have my hand go through you like a holoimage."

She stared at him.

"Are you like Galyan? Are you a deified entity? Are the Onos long extinct?"

Zoe blinked several times. "Captain, none of that is germane to the issue."

"I think it is."

Zoe indicated him and her. "We're talking, yes? Do you wish to destroy the succubus evil? Are you going to let Lilith continue her rampage through the dimensions, devouring, destroying and causing entire dimensions to collapse in an orgy of destruction?"

This was overwhelming. Maddox sat on the edge of the dais. "I don't get this. I don't know how all these things operate."

"But that is the point," Zoe said. "I do understand. Trust me to understand so you can act decisively."

Maddox looked at her, a faint smile on his lips. He would *never* simply trust her.

"Balron the Traveler," Zoe said. "Mentioning him seemed to have upset you. Why is that?"

Maddox shook his head.

"If you're wondering if Balron has been here to this planet," Zoe said, "the answer is yes. He's been here to talk with us."

"Recently?" Maddox asked.

Zoe snorted. "No, no, long ago he came here. Balron's plan was always long term. Do you think it was by chance you met him? Do you think Balron trained you in the unique aspects you gained from him by chance? Do you think it by chance the Supreme Intelligence gave you Arius? Did Arius break through the dimensions to reach this place by chance? No, it all has to do with Balron. It all goes back to him. This moment he transpired to achieve. Balron has done so. Now, we must destroy Lilith while we can."

"We?"

"You then," Zoe said, "if you wish to be pedantic."

Maddox cocked his head. "Is there a reason why you used the name Lilith? In some of Earth's religions, Lilith was Adam's second wife. In other stories, she was reputed to be a witch or different things not so flattering. Is that why you use that name? You think it will quickly and easily make me fear someone of that name?"

"Captain, we have no time for that. The Saurian armada is approaching. Can Task Force 3 destroy it? I don't know. Behind it comes an even larger armada. Worse, I believe each armada has weapons superior in technology than the last. It will be increasingly difficult for your task force to defend your entry point into the asteroidal supership."

"I don't understand the last point," Maddox said, frowning.

Zoe made a motion in the air. In its place was a holoimage of the task force. She expanded the range of her hands, causing the holoimage to grow.

The ships of Task Force 3 surrounded a smaller version of the asteroidal supership.

"That isn't a copy of the supership," Zoe said. "It's a daughter vessel patterned off the first, one fourth its mass. It's linked to the asteroidal supership, a portal to it. Lilith no doubt assigned it to the Saurians in order to keep track of them and us. I don't know why she doesn't send her shock troops through it, but she hasn't yet."

Zoe became earnest. "Here is the critical point. You are of small enough mass and density that she won't expect such a thrust into her ancient vessel. That means now is the moment,

Captain. With the weapon I give you, and if you take Sergeant Riker and Colonel Julk along, you have a true shot at doing this."

"You want me to bite. Okay, I will. Why should I take Riker and the colonel?"

"Riker for obvious reasons," Zoe said. "He's faced and survived a Ska before."

"A spiritual entity," Maddox said.

"Exactly. He has faced some of the evil you might possibly face on the supership."

"Oddly enough, that makes sense. But why should I take the colonel?"

"For his sheer fighting power and because he is of a more primitive race than you," Zoe said.

"The so-called Neanderthals of Benito Seven originally came from Earth," Maddox said. "They were as *Homo sapiens* as anyone else. They modified themselves back into the Neanderthal prototype. Is Julk really that different from a regular *Homo sapiens?*"

"Only in this aspect," Zoe said. "He'll be able to help you more than a normal *Homo sapiens* would."

Maddox ran a hand through his hair. This all seemed bizarre, and yet his intuitive sense was telling him to trust Conciliator Zoe. Trust her, he wondered. Was she even real? Had the Onos died out millennia ago? Was she some vast computer entity giving him an image he'd trust?

"Are you a holograph? Are you flesh and blood?"

"No and no," Zoe said.

"You're not a holograph and you're not of flesh and blood?"

"Correct," she said.

"Are the Onos extinct?"

"It depends on what you mean by the term, Captain. The race of living flesh and blood Onos, yes, we're long gone, extinct if you like. That's one reason Lilith seeks out every place we've lived. She wants to ensure not even a speck of our DNA will ever exist again. She wishes to annihilate even the memory of our race."

"Why should Lilith bother if you're already extinct?"

233

"There's a great and ancient enmity between us. That is not germane to all this for you. If you can save this temple, dedicated to the great Onos of the past, it's likely that far in the future someone can use our stored knowledge about the dimensions to stop a different evil. You will use our knowledge to halt the present evil of Succubus Lilith."

"Why don't you give me plain answers?" Maddox asked.

Zoe opened her mouth in an Ono smile. "You don't enjoy these forays into different dimensions, do you?"

"No. I hate them. They feel…*wrong.*"

Zoe sighed. "That was the great mistake of the Onos. We didn't realize until late in our existence that we'd jeopardized ourselves and other dimensions by what we'd learned and done, mostly by what we'd done. It would have been better if we hated dimensional travel as you do."

"What does that have to do with not giving plain answers?"

"Precious little," Zoe said. "The point…" She sighed. "Our time runs short, Captain. I have a weapon that with your training from facing the Erills, you can master. Was that Erill confrontation premeditated in order to grant you the training?" Zoe shrugged. "Who can know? Not me. Are you willing to take up the weapon and slay the Succubus Lilith? Will you save your dimension from destruction?"

"Answer me this first," Maddox said. "Is it certain my dimension will fall to Lilith if I don't do this?"

"Certain?" asked Zoe. "Who can know that? These are probabilities. There is a high probability Lilith will destroy your dimension. If you slay her, however, we can strengthen your dimension from others of her kind."

"How is that possible?"

"The how truly doesn't matter to you, Captain. What matters is: will you attempt this or not?"

Maddox didn't want to, not in the slightest. The idea of traveling to the asteroidal supership—in a different dimension—sounded crazy. The last time he'd used a special weapon, to kill a Ska then, it had hurt him immensely. It wasn't only about his hurt and pain, though. If he defended his dimension, he'd be defending the Commonwealth of Planets. If he defended the Commonwealth of Planets, he'd be defending

Meta and Jewel. It really came down to would he defend Meta and Jewel from the Succubus Lilith.

Maddox eyed Zoe. "You planned all this?"

"Much has happened to create this moment. It is here, but fleeting. If the Saurian mobile asteroids reach the planet and destroy it or reach the launch point of your entry into the asteroidal supership—Captain, now is the time to strike. We have a limited amount of time and you must move quickly if you're going to do it."

"How exactly am I going to find this succubus on the supership, this not-even-completely-physical entity? Is she a spiritual entity then?"

"Not as you conceive of spiritual. I would call the succubus gaseous, but this gaseous form may take physical shape."

"Gas is physical, as it's real."

"Captain, time is wasting. I can instruct you in the weapon's use. I can give you clues to finding her in her supership."

"From what you've said, her vessel will be full of military personnel. How in the world can I get close enough to kill her?"

"You will find it both easier and harder than you think."

"Talk about saying nothing with words," Maddox complained. "Make some sense, huh?"

"This is the moment of opportunity," Zoe said. "Are you man enough to make the attempt?"

Maddox looked up at the sky. Task Force 3 and *Victory* were up there. The enemy was coming. The Saurians sounded like foot soldiers of the succubus.

Maddox made a face. Succubus. Lilith. Had the Onos chosen the names in order to sway him?

What was the right decision? These creatures had invaded their dimension before. In one sense, he was loath to risk himself, risk never coming home to Meta and Jewel. At the same time, the idea of killing Succubus Lilith so the Commonwealth was safer than when he'd found it—

"You knew I'd probably say yes."

"Are you saying yes?" Zoe asked.

Maddox nodded.

Zoe sighed. "There was a high probability you would, but I didn't know for a fact. Now Captain, we must hurry. I must show you the weapon and give you other weapons so you may arm your men. Then, I think you'll have to move swiftly if you hope to succeed."

"Right," Maddox said. "Let's get to it."

-36-

Maddox received the weapons from Conciliator Zoe. Then she teleported him off planet with weapon cases and extra ammo charges. Maddox appeared with them in Hangar Bay 2, closer to the blocks of crystal computing cubes than to the Yon Soth machine.

"Hello, Captain," Arius said. "I trust you had a fruitful dialogue."

Maddox stared at the computing cubes and then the electromagnetic field surrounding the Yon Soth machine. There were far too many pieces of alien technology aboard his ship for his liking, especially after all he'd learned. Certainly, this was a former Adok starship—alien to the core—but the newest technology struck him as something akin to magic. As one person had once said, high technology often appeared as magic to those who didn't understand it. Maddox certainly didn't understand all the ramifications and nuances to dimensional travel, how they even achieved such a thing.

Yet, here he was in another dimension. He'd spoken to Conciliator Zoe. She'd given him an exotic weapon, instructed him in its use and given him advice about how to go about his assassination attempt—with the proviso he could get aboard the asteroidal supership.

"Captain, you seem pensive," Arius said.

"Can you wonder why?"

237

"I do not wonder, as I know why. You are inherently distrustful. Perhaps that is why you have succeeded in so many of your missions."

"Right," Maddox said.

He left Arius and the new weapons and returned to the bridge.

Soon, *Victory* circled the planet and hailed the visible task force. The bridge personnel grinned and laughed as Commodore Galt and the others whooped with joy upon contact. There was a real chance now for them getting back home.

"First," Maddox said over the main screen, "we need to meet in person. I'm coming over there, if you don't mind."

"Not at all," Galt said. "It will be easier that way."

"I'd like to meet with you and your most trusted people," Maddox said. "We'll brainstorm about how to do all this. If you don't already know, we have a fight on our hands. There's also *more* to all this."

"I don't understand."

"I've just been down to the red planet."

"What," Galt said, "you have? You've spoken with the aliens?"

"I have, and I've learned the ship you captured—"

"Excuse me, Captain," Galt said, interrupting. "Do you mean the quarter-sized alien vessel with its compressed stardust hull?"

"That's right."

Galt became pensive. "I don't know if it will be of any use to us. We've attempted to breach the hull, several times already, but have been unable to do so."

"I'm not surprised. I've learned how to breach the hull and I—we'll speak about that when I get there. Could we start the meeting in, say…" Maddox checked his chronometer, "fifteen minutes?"

"So soon?" asked Galt.

"I'm sure you've spotted the mobile asteroids heading your way. According to Zoe, you've fought their counterparts earlier."

"We've fought the Saurians and seen the new asteroids moving in. They won't be here for several days, though."

"Maybe," Maddox said. "Just so you know: there are even more mobile asteroids following behind the second group."

Galt frowned. "You've seen them?"

"I've seen the approaching armada and learned these Saurians…let's have the meeting, Commodore. I don't want to say these things twice."

"Yes sir," Galt said. "I appreciate everything you're doing, and boy am glad you're here. You have no idea."

Maddox nodded, grinning. "I'll be over in a few minutes." He cut the connection after Galt acknowledged.

It was easy deciding whom to leave and whom to take. Maddox let sleeping dogs lie, letting Ludendorff remain in catatonic and hopefully restful sleep. He took Valerie and told Galyan to tag along, as he wanted a recording of everything that happened. Valerie was used to strange situations and making swift decisions. Maddox trusted her judgment as he did few others.

Besides, he still felt her resentment from his actions last mission and wanted to make it up to her.

As Maddox headed for a hangar bay, he wondered if the Lord High Admiral would be glad he'd given Maddox the plenipotentiary authority, or if it even mattered in a different dimension.

In many ways, the idea he was going to hunt a succubus on her own supership made perfect sense. This all seemed like a dream and unreal. Yet, these events had happened and he'd lost marines to alien shock troopers. The succubus had caused some of his men to die, had caused millions in Star Watch to die.

Maddox grimaced. He was ready to kill the succubus.

Valerie and he boarded a shuttle, made the crossing and soon landed in a *Stonewall Jackson* hangar bay. Commodore Galt greeted them, a slender, short individual with a firm handshake. Although he limped, Galt escorted them through the battleship to the conference chamber.

It was much like *Victory's* conference chamber.

Galt indicated that Maddox should sit at the head of the table. The others were already seated waiting for them.

Maddox did as requested. He was running the show, he knew it and it was good for the others to know it.

Galt made the introductions. There was Captain Karpov of the *Stonewall Jackson,* Commodore Ketchum who ran the light cruiser squadron and bluff Captain Lair of the *Joan of Arc.*

"These officers are my brain trust," Galt said. "They're the ones I've confided in and the ones who helped me defend the red planet and defeat Saurian mobile asteroids. From what you've said so far, that was a good idea."

"An excellent idea." Maddox held out his left hand. "This is Lieutenant Commander Noonan, my most capable officer, and I'm sure you've all heard of Diving Force Galyan, the Adok ghost of Starship *Victory.*"

Everyone greeted each other, shaking hands and sitting, except for Galyan, who merely nodded and blinked.

Maddox asked Galt for a quick rundown on the previous battle so Valerie, Galyan and he understood the situation better.

Galt did this quickly and efficiently.

"You acted promptly," Maddox said after listening to the report. "I commend you on it. It was wise of you to take control of the miniature asteroidal supership. It's going to prove critical in the next phase of our plan."

"About that," Galt said.

Maddox and he had spoken a little about that on the walk from the hangar bay to the conference chamber. Perhaps that was why Galt had met them in the hangar bay, to receiving an earlier rundown.

"I don't understand this part," Galt now said. "Frankly, I understand very little of what you've told me."

"That makes two of us, Commodore. I've spoken with the personage in charge of the red planet. She told me most of what I know."

"I'm curious," Galt said. "How many Onos did you see over there?"

"One."

"No others?"

Maddox shook his head.

"Are there others?" Galt asked.

Maddox frowned. "Why do you ask?"

240

"They had a battle station protecting the planet. Planetary space fighters lifted off to attack the Saurians. Yet, you only saw one Ono. I would have thought you'd seen at least a dozen or more."

"You think because I met just the one that she's it?"

Galt scratched his head. "I hadn't thought that. I just think it's funny you only saw one alien. I'm not even sure why I asked you about it."

Maddox had an inkling why. Maybe Galt had some native intuitive sense. It was a question that needed asking, and thus, he had.

"Sir," Valerie said. "May I interject?"

"Please," Maddox said.

Valerie faced Galt. "Did you check the battle debris where Ono space fighters engaged? Scan for their bio matter. If there's none, no Onos flew the fighters. If you find bio matter, something did."

Galt looked to his brain trust.

Karpov and Ketchum looked as confused as he did.

"We haven't checked the debris for Ono bio matter," Lair said. "Should I tell my officers to scan for it?"

Galt was staring at his hands.

"That might be a good idea, "Maddox said. "The more we know for certain, the better decisions we can make. Now look, we're in a strange situation. We're not even in our own dimension. How the multiverse works...maybe for our own peace of mind, we should consider it like going to a different galaxy. In other words, this is just another place. Getting through this is simply a matter of using good tactics and sound strategy and then going home when it's over. Does that make sense?"

They all nodded.

"Furthermore," Maddox said, "I realize you're line commanders, running regular warships. What I mean is, you're not Patrol-trained for these...oddities. Despite that, you've dealt with these issues remarkably well. Commodore Galt, I commend you on the way you took charge and how you handled your fellow officers and the way you handled your ships. You've done excellent work. When we get back, I'll

241

personally tell that to the Lord High Admiral. Now, let's continue to act in that manner: decisively, under authority, under the chain of command."

"Just a moment," Ketchum said. "I thank you for your kind words. But really, Captain, the commodore and I both outrank you. I don't see why you're in charge all of a sudden."

"Right," Maddox said. "Let's take care of this. Valerie, if you could please hand me that."

Valerie took a folder from a briefcase, handing it to Maddox. He showed them the Plenipotentiary Writ the Lord High Admiral had given him last mission.

Ketchum handled it, squinting, turned the writ from side to side. He finally passed it back without a word, not even having the politeness to seem abashed.

"Does that satisfy you, Commodore?" Maddox asked, with bite to his voice.

Ketchum didn't look at Maddox but he nodded just enough to indicate he understood.

"I'm in command, because we're dealing with previously unknown species and entities, in a situation that is not merely military, but has many political ramifications," Maddox said. "That being so, we're going to do this my way. I do not believe you have a problem with that Commodore Galt. But if you do, please let me know."

"No sir," Galt said, "I have no problem whatsoever. The writ gives you obvious authority. You're in charge, as we're clearly far out of the Commonwealth. I'll obey you to the letter and spirit, sir."

Maddox glanced at Ketchum and then the others. He glanced at Ketchum again. "I expect all the officers of the task force to obey me in letter and spirit, as you say, Commodore Galt."

Lair and Karpov both replied, "Yes sir."

Ketchum mumbled something under his breath.

Galt opened his mouth.

Maddox waved him off.

Galt sat back.

"We've taken care of that," Maddox said. "Now look, here's the situation. I'm taking a few people into the quarter-

242

sized supership. As far as I know, it's a transfer mechanism. It will take me and the others to the larger supership, the one you engaged in the Trappist-1 System."

They stared at him.

"Uh," Galt said. "How will that help us, sir?"

"A being from a different dimension, quite different from ours, I've been told..." Maddox wasn't sure how much to tell them. He decided on the truth, as he knew it, anyway. "The creature is so different from us that frankly, we might as well call it a demon."

"A demon?" Ketchum asked. "Are you serious?"

"I wouldn't have said it otherwise. I'm going over there to kill it. When the demon dies, the threat of the supership will end. I don't know if you're aware, but aliens attacked our starship as we passed through what we're calling a null region. That's the place where all the stars are massed together."

"We know it well," Galt said. "I didn't care for it in the slightest."

"Neither did I," Maddox said. "Nevertheless, oval attack vessels appeared. Three of them attached to our outer hull, and from them armed intruders dropped into our vessel. They were shock troopers from the asteroidal supership. They were beings under orders from the demon, the succubus, the one called Lilith."

"Lilith!" Ketchum said, turning red-faced. "This is crazy talk, crazy. What are we, back in Ancient Myths and Legends class listening to fairytale lessons?"

Galt slapped the table. "Commodore, you'll watch your mouth. Do you know who you address?"

"It doesn't matter," Ketchum said. "This is all madness, I tell you, madness!"

"Commodore Ketchum," Maddox said calmly. "If you feel you've been unhinged by current events, by all means continue how you are and thereby let us know you're no longer fit for command."

"Now see here, *Captain Maddox,*" Ketchum snarled.

Galt stood, snapping his fingers.

The hatch opened and three marines entered.

"This is your last chance, Commodore," Galt said.

"Lilith," Ketchum said. "Did you hear what the man said? Lilith. The half-breed is mad. No, I'm not going to obey a New Man whelp, and if you do, if the rest of you continue with this—"

Galt gave a swift command.

The marines moved in, grabbed Commodore Ketchum, cutting off his speech, and hauled him out of the conference room. Presumably, they hustled him to the brig or possibly to medical.

Maddox didn't ask. He didn't particularly care. He did think that the sense of unreality of the different dimension would strike the others at different times and probably more the longer they remained here.

Maddox could feel his own sense of reality slipping. Then, he noticed the others looking at him.

"I'm sorry about that," Galt said. "Ketchum has always been—no, I'm not going to defend him. His actions are his own responsibility. I'm sorry for the interruption, Captain."

Maddox nodded before regarding them closely. "Commodore, Captains, let me explain something. Going from one dimension to another is a draining process. There are forces at work inimical to our wellbeing. After a time, only those of the strongest will can hold the forces at bay. We sensed and saw some of that as we killed the succubus's shock troops. They literally disappeared when they died. A loaned computer unique to dimensional travel explained that their willpower had kept them intact. Without their will, they vanished.

"Now, I don't pretend to know how all this works. I do know interdimensional travel is wearing on the individual. Therefore, that is another reason we must do this quickly. The longer and farther we travel through the dimensions, the keener this unreality becomes to us. We're fashioned to live in our own reality. Interdimensional travel is fraught with peril and demands even greater technology than we have."

"Meaning what?" Galt said.

"Meaning my men and I need to go through the portal and kill the energizer of the asteroidal supership. It's her willpower and essence energizing much of this."

244

The others stared at him.

What had he expected? With an inward shrug, Maddox forged ahead.

"Conciliator Zoe explained much of this, but I admit I didn't fully understand it all. What I know is that I have to kill the succubus. I have a weapon to do it. I have a means of getting to her vessel. According to what the conciliator told me, it's possible to thread through her asteroidal supership because it's different from how we structure a warship. The good news is that I've trained for this. I've gone on many bizarre missions. According to the Ono—Zoe believes I have a shot. Therefore, I need every one of you backing me up. That means you must keep the daughter supership from the Saurians. If their mobile asteroids move faster and if their technology improves, as I am told it will each time—"

"What's this?" Lair asked, interrupting.

"Each succeeding wave of mobile asteroids carries better or improved weaponry from its predecessor," Maddox said.

Karpov, Lair and Galt glanced at each other. It wasn't a glance of joy, but worry.

"Right," Maddox said, "now look. Lieutenant Commander Noonan is one of the best battlefield commanders I know. She has fought aliens and been in other deadly situations. Commodore, I'm not saying she should be in charge, but you'd be wise to add Commander Noonan to your brain trust. In my absence, she'll command *Victory*. I trust her implicitly."

Maddox turned and stared at Valerie.

She couldn't help it, but grinned and then looked at the others with the grin intact.

"Are there any questions?" Maddox asked.

Galt had a few. Maddox answered the best he could.

Galt looked to his captains.

Lair had a question. Maddox answered it.

Lair stared at him before blurting, "How are you going to break into the smaller asteroid ship? We've repeatedly tried. There's no way in."

"According to what Zoe told me, there's a way. I plan to implement it." Maddox checked his chronometer. "I'm going to try in the next half hour. So, if there are no further questions…"

Galt shook his head.

Maddox stood and the others stood. Maddox went to each and shook hands solemnly.

"It is an honor to be with such fine officers of Star Watch," Maddox said. "I would have no one else holding my back than you people. Thank you for what you're going to attempt."

Galt's chest puffed out. "Thank you, Captain Maddox, for daring to come after us. You could have left us. We know that, but instead you've taken a great risk, you and your whole crew. We really appreciate it."

"You can thank the Lord High Admiral," Maddox said. "He wants you people back and he wants his granddaughter back."

"What," Galt said. "That Cook. That's the Lord High Admiral's granddaughter?"

"Yes."

"I saw the name on the roster a while back, but I had no idea. Okay, okay. Well, I'm glad we're carrying her and I hope we can get her back to her granddaddy, and I hope we can all get back, too."

"Amen to that," Maddox said. "So I'm going to end this meeting with a prayer. I ask you close your eyes for just a moment, even you, Galyan."

They all did.

Maddox bowed his head. "Dear God the Creator, I ask your aid for these people and for me. I ask that in your name. Amen."

Galt heard himself say, "Amen."

Lair did likewise.

With that, they took their leave so each could go to his or her various stations.

Once back on *Victory*, Maddox hurried to Hangar Bay 2 to speak with Arius one last time. He ordered everyone else to leave. After they'd filed out, he noticed Galyan in ghost mode, watching from afar. That was fine. In fact, it was a good idea. It was more than likely that Arius also saw Galyan, however.

That might be good, too.

"Hello, Captain," Arius said. "Did your meeting with the others go well?"

Maddox stared at the stack of crystal computing cubes.

"Is something wrong, Captain? Is that why you had everyone leave except for Galyan? What do you call his present mostly faded form: ghost mode?"

Maddox nodded.

He'd learned much about things he hadn't known before thanks to Conciliator Zoe. And after talking with the others on the *Stonewall Jackson*...

"I've been thinking," Maddox said.

"Oh."

"I've been thinking how Conciliator Zoe knew so many details about things she shouldn't have had the slightest clue about. For instance, she knew about recent events in our dimension. That implies Ono confederates there. I've also been thinking how she caused *Victory* to alter course so we appeared on the other side of the planet as intended."

The colors inside Arius's cubes serenely continued to swirl hypnotically.

Maddox shook his head: concentrating on the off chance the computer was trying to gentle or suppress his thoughts. "Do you have any idea how Zoe knew those things?"

"I was not at your meeting, Captain. You'd need to be more specific in any case. Furthermore, how could I possibly know what Zoe would know?"

"That's the wrong answer."

"I see. What would you like me to say?"

"Try the truth," Maddox said.

"Your truth?"

"The truth."

The colors within the computing cubes swirled faster. "I have concluded, Captain, that you've already guessed the answer. Yet, for some reason, you wish me to say it."

"There you go," Maddox said, "That's what I want, if it's the truth."

"Since you insist with such vulgar intensity—the truth is *I* adjusted *Victory's* jump path, and I naturally told the Ono that you'd seen—"

"Hold it," Maddox said, interrupting. "Did I meet an Ono or a holographic projection of one? Are the Onos extinct? Do only their computers exist?"

"Captain, how can I possibly know any of that? And even if I did, I'm not at liberty to speak of it. I can tell you that I fed Zoe data. I've gathered information for ages, having scoured and learned from a vast number of sources."

The admission surprised Maddox. The possibilities... "Were you constructed precisely for this trip?"

"Of course, Captain. I thought that should be obvious by now. This has been a plan needing countless generations to complete. Obviously, I have some idea what Zoe said to you. Therefore, it is time to drop the pretense. As you or Galyan have likely surmised, I am in essence an Ono construct, left behind on the Library Planet. I am the reason the Supreme Intelligence understands as much as he does concerning dimensions and how he was able to stymie Balron the Traveler all those years."

"If you're an Ono construct, and the Onos are allied with Balron, why would you help the Supreme Intelligence block Balron from leaving our dimension?"

"Clearly, there are other ramifications to all this. Now is not the moment to go into them, either."

"Why not?" Maddox asked.

Arius didn't reply.

Maddox nodded. "It's time we got a few things straight. I'm not entering the daughter-ship portal unless I know the full situation."

"Dear me, Captain, but I believe you're bluffing. I believe you're one of the best of bluffers in Star Watch, too."

This time Maddox didn't reply.

"Are you truly suggesting you won't help your task force get home?" Arius asked.

"Why, you won't open the way for us back to the Commonwealth if I refuse to chase the succubus?"

"Captain, Captain, this plan has been centuries in the making. You cannot even begin to understand how long we've waited for the right soldier to face the succubus. Balron chose the entity he did because of the capabilities the person showed—that person being you."

Maddox turned away.

"We're wasting time," Arius said. "We must proceed or the opportunity will pass."

Maddox shrugged.

"You're being mulishly stubborn at the worst possible moment."

Maddox faced the computing cubes. "I already told you: I need to know more."

"How do you know I won't simply make up a tale to please your vanity?"

Maddox tapped his chest. "I have my intuitive sense. I'll know if you're lying." He pointed behind him. "Galyan might figure it out, too."

Arius computed, the colors swirling in his crystal sides.

Maddox watched, waiting.

"I can tell you a few more details," Arius said at last. "The full situation…we don't have time for that. Will you accept partial knowledge or we will have to accept defeat?"

Maddox nodded sharply. "Start talking."

"You'll go, then?"

"We'll see. What do you have to lose to tell me?"

"Perhaps the stubbornness you're evidencing is the very asset we need. Thus, I will tell you some. You will enter the daughter-ship portal, crossing through dimensions to reach the *Annihilator*-class vessel. The species that made the Annihilators is not germane to the issue. The Annihilator you're seeking does have a name. It is the *Shadowed Storm.*"

"Just to be clear," Maddox said, "The Annihilator *Shadowed Storm* is the real name for the asteroidal supership that attacked Zinc?"

"That is what I said," Arius replied. "The vessel is ancient compared to anything you know in your dimension, used for countless nefarious purposes. My primary purpose is to help destroy the *Shadowed Storm* in this region of the multiverse. Furthermore, I think it's time you understand the extreme dangers in traveling through the dimensions. Only creatures such as Succubus Lilith can do it without harm."

"Elaborate on the dangers of dimensional travel," Maddox said.

"It often leads to horrendous mistakes and the destruction of dimensions. I cite as a local example the Ur-Builders in your dimension. Ages ago, your time, they created a cross-dimensional portal that allowed Erills into your space-time. Years ago, you went to the City of Pyramids. All the Ur-Builders there had died hideously, but not before quarantining the Erills to that planet. You broke the quarantine and went down there. The waiting Erills attempted to coerce you to let them off planet or reopen the portal to let more Erills into your dimension. Their space-time universe is eerie and bizarre in comparison to yours. They are spiritual in essence. Your dimension is physically oriented, and much rarer than you would guess.

"That is one of the points I'm trying to make," Arius said. "Dimensional travel is fraught with peril, as one may easily reach a noxious space-time with comparatively bizarre and threatening entities. Then there is something that we refer to as blight."

"What's that?" Maddox asked.

"Blight is a form of gross destruction in one dimension because of the interferences and processes that take place due to poisonous invaders from another. The poison can take many forms, including a blight that acts like an eraser, causing matter to unravel one star system at a time. As I guided *Victory* through the dimensions, I carefully gauged each crossing and maneuvered carefully—tiptoeing, you might say. I avoided anything that could incur disaster for your space-time. One wrong path could have meant the end of your dimension due to letting blight into your space-time."

"Dimensional travel is really that precarious?" Maddox asked.

"More," Arius said. "That's yet another reason Succubus Lilith is so evil. Her journeys across dimensions—I have time for a quick Earth history lesson that might help you comprehend. When the Spanish and other European explorers reached the New World, they brought lethal diseased to the natives. In some instances, the diseases killed nearly ninety percent of the Indian populations. That is an analog what of dimensional blight does, only more so."

"I understand," Maddox said.

"That is all the more reason for you to cross onto the *Shadowed Storm* and slay the succubus. While the Annihilator is practically indestructible, she is not. Without her powering it, however, the *Shadowed Storm* will drift as a terrible relic of dimensional war."

"Couldn't we destroy the vessel by projecting it into the middle of a star?"

"Doubtful," Arius said. "Likely, its automatic systems would engage, and it would move into a different dimension before the star incinerated it."

Maddox frowned.

"No, Captain, Succubus Lilith is a nemesis to your dimension and many others. If you're able, you must kill her

251

while the opportunity presents itself. This is the opportunity. It has taken time, skill, perseverance and luck to achieve it.

"Even now, the Saurian mobile asteroids strain to reach the daughter-ship. If this wave fails to do that, the next surely will. If you don't kill Lilith soon, you'll never make it home. Then the Saurians will annihilate the last Onos. I believe the succubus will take the *Shadowed Storm* back to your dimension and devour it. She will gain strength and essence much as an Erill might."

A haunted sense filled Maddox, showing through his staring eyes.

"This is a grave opportunity," Arius said. "I beg you to take advantage of it. You have the weapon. You are able to power it, and you'll have Sub-Arius along to help achieve the impossible."

"What pray tell is Sub-Arius?"

"I thought you'd never ask," Arius said.

The highest cube on the stack opened, the sides sliding left and right, revealing a smaller crystal cube the size of a small microwave.

"I am Sub-Arius," the unit said, using the exact voice as Greater Arius. "I have the data needed to get you from one Annihilator to another. The one you seek is in a different dimension, even though it is linked with the smaller vessel. I suggest you hurry because the conditions for portal transfer will not last much longer."

"You're Sub-Arius?" Maddox asked. "You expect to join me on the mission?"

"Most certainly that is what I expect," Sub-Arius said. "I have been programmed for this event. This is the reason for my existence, for my creation. I have the necessary codes and processors, and I know how to help you with unforeseen circumstances."

"And you plan to return to the greater whole of Arius when this is over?" Maddox asked.

"If perchance we survive, we will have gained much knowledge. This I hope to give others so they will be able to eventually destroy all the *Annihilator*-class vessels in existence. Thus, yes, I wish to return here."

252

"How many Annihilators are there?" Maddox asked.

"Captain, that is not germane to the issue. Now is the moment to act, and in truth I do not know how many Annihilators exist. I think the *Shadowed Storm* is the only one that has ever been to your dimension. I predict that tens of thousands of years will pass before another Annihilator will show up. The chances of that, however, will be small after the conditions—never mind about that. I misspoke just now. Captain, will you take me along?"

Maddox shook his head.

"You refuse me?" Sub-Arius asked.

"No," Maddox said, "I'm shaking my head because there's always something more you're keeping from me."

"I may come?"

"Yes,"

"Excellent," Sub-Arius said.

Maddox spoke into a wrist phone.

Moments later, Sergeant Riker appeared, carrying a heavy carbine.

"You called, sir," Riker said.

Maddox pointed. "You are going to be carrying Sub-Arius during the mission."

Riker stepped back and eyed the microwave-sized crystal computer. It seemed like he was going to object. Finally, however, he said, "I'll put that in a pack, sir."

"Do you have any objections to that?" Maddox asked the cube.

"None," Sub-Arius said.

"I know why Riker's coming," Maddox said. "The sergeant has faced a spiritual entity before. That doesn't hold for Colonel Julk."

"You are taking another?" Sub-Arius asked.

"A marine fighter," Maddox said. "Do you object?"

Colors swirled along Sub-Arius's crystal sides. "I do not object."

"Do you object, whole Arius?" Maddox asked.

"No," the blocks of cubes said.

"I guess we better get started then," Maddox said. "Time's a wasting as this crystal computer has been telling me. What do you say, Riker, can we do it?"

Riker shrugged.

"I wonder if this is why Galyan wanted you along this mission," Maddox said.

"Sir," Galyan said, gliding forward and appearing in normal mode, "I knew nothing about the dimensions or any of this."

"Did you have a premonition about them?" Riker asked.

"Just a premonition you'd be useful." Galyan turned to Sub-Arius. "Did you in some way have anything to do with my premonition?"

"None," Sub-Arius said.

Galyan glanced at Maddox.

"All right," Maddox said. "This is the moment. We're the people. Let's get this show on the road."

-38-

Riker and Maddox donned the same kind of exoskeleton armor the marines had used before, putting in fully charged batteries, and then adding extra battery packs so they could switch out later and use the armor longer.

Riker carried what looked like a heavy carbine with flat bulbs inserted along the sides. This was one of the weapons given Maddox by Zoe.

Maddox shouldered an extra pack. In it was the weapon Zoe said would allow him to slay Succubus Lilith.

Colonel Julk hurried into the chamber, wearing a regular uniform. He indeed looked like a Neanderthal of imagination: heavyset, square-shouldered with massive muscles and a big face. He had a bony brow, heavy jaws and coarse features. His people made some of the better soldiers and marines in Star Watch.

Julk donned marine exo-armor and carried a blaster-carbine like Riker. According to Zoe, the carbine should prove effective against the gorilla-armored shock troops they'd faced before in the null zone.

Maddox explained the parameters of what they were doing to Julk and Riker. If the colonel was amazed by it, he didn't show it.

When Maddox stopped talking, Julk said, "I have on question, sir."

"Shoot."

"If we do this, are we fighting the enemy that sent the gorilla-armored goons who slaughtered my marines?"

"Yes."

"Then I'm all in. Let's demolish whatever stands in the way and kill the Bitch Queen."

"That's the spirit," Maddox said.

In their exo-armor and equipment, they moved down various corridors into a different hangar bay. There, Keith waited in a tin can. They filed aboard, clicked on restraints and Keith maneuvered the tin can off the hangar bay deck.

He slid the fold fighter out of the double oval, ancient starship. Accelerating, he passed the ships of the task force. The *Conqueror*-class battleships dwarfed everything but *Victory* and the gigantic motherships.

Keith maneuvered past the scattered and sometimes heavy debris of the battle against the first-wave mobile asteroids. He headed for the daughter-ship, quarter-sized replica of the asteroidal supership.

Soon, the tin can hovered just above the compressed stardust hull.

"Are we looking for anything specific, sir?" Keith asked from the pilot's seat.

Maddox turned to Riker.

Riker tapped Sub-Arius in the pack he carried.

"Yes indeed," Sub-Arius said. "We're looking for a specific spot. Would you continue to circle the vessel, please? When I sense the hatch, I'll tell you."

Keith had been staring at Riker's pack. "Aye, mate, you bet."

It took fifteen minutes until Sub-Arius said, "I have detected it. It was camouflaged as I suspected. If not for me, none of you would have breached the hull, except in destroying the ship, you might have breached it, but then it would no longer function for us. Captain, this is one more reason why it is good you took me."

"Whatever you say," Maddox replied.

Keith brought them lower until the tin can was a meter above the surface.

"That's as close as I should take it, sir, for safety margin's sake."

"Yes, thank you, Lieutenant."

The three battle-suited men closed their visors, took their gear and filed out the airlock. Soon, each jumped from the tin can, floating down until he reached the compressed stardust hull.

Surprisingly, one-fifth Earth-norm gravity pulled against them.

"Sub-Arius," Maddox said, using the short-range comm system. "What's causing the gravitational pull?"

"Why, the asteroidal vessel itself. It is due to the compressed stardust hull. Surely you understand that the hull is much denser than you're used to."

"So I'm learning," Maddox said. "That makes this ship heavier than Earth's moon."

The three men in exo-armor trudged along the hull in the direction Sub-Arius told them.

As they marched, Maddox looked up at the stars, stars of a different dimension. Maddox shook his head. They weren't in the universe he knew. They were in some other universe that was part of the multiverse. The idea there was universe after universe after universe layered one atop the other in who knew how big a conglomeration…it was mindboggling. Their own dimension had always seemed limitless. As far as anyone knew, there was no end to just their universe. Now, there were myriads of more universes stacked in these layers.

As Maddox trudged, the immensity of realms upon realms upon realms—what was he compared to all that? He was less than a gnat.

Yet, some beings were able to tunnel through to other dimensions, and according to Sub-Arius, that at times caused blight, massive destruction in dimension after dimension.

It made sense they'd threaded a careful path while crossing dimensions. He'd sensed hungry entities wishing to devour them. What grotesque fate might they have brought upon themselves and worse, upon their dimension, if they'd gone to the wrong place? Clearly, dimensional travel wasn't something a person should attempt willy-nilly. This wasn't something he'd agree to do ever again. This was it.

Maddox grimaced. He longed to see Meta and bounce Jewel on his knee. He swallowed, knowing he needed to concentrate on the mission.

Sub-Arius alerted them the hatch was near.

Maddox focused on what he was doing. The red dwarf star was only a little bigger than a dot. Much closer and larger hung the red planet. Did Onos exist on it? Maddox didn't think so.

"Concentrate," he whispered.

If this worked, they'd plunge into yet a different dimension.

Maddox was about to ask Sub-Arius how to open the hatch when a section of compressed stardust hull opened like a bank-vault door. The immensity of its thickness—it didn't swing open. An entire section drifted into space, revealing a hull cavity.

"Lights," Maddox said.

Each clicked on chest and helmet lamps, shining down into the vast cavernous hull opening. Down there, because of their lights, a corridor appeared.

Maddox cleared his throat. "Sub-Arius, are there any last instructions?"

"*Last* instructions?" the cube asked. "We've just begun, Captain. No, let us proceed."

Maddox jumped first, drifting through the cavity until he reached the corridor. There, he grabbed a bizarre crystal growth like one might have seen in a Jurassic ocean. Did this crystal have anything to do with the crystal-computing cube of Arius and now Sub-Arius? Maddox had no idea.

Colonel Julk landed beside him and afterward Riker.

The vast plug came down, closing the hull opening and entombing them in the strange vessel from a far dimension. Who knew from what level it came, E-Z-25,000-30,000. Maddox shrugged. Did it even matter at this point?

They began threading through the corridors, shining their beams on large, crystalline...things. The crystalline growths became odd and grotesque. Some seemed like statues of fantastic creatures like Satyrs, Medusas and Hydras. Surely, that made no sense. It was just his human mind from a different dimension trying to make sense of what he saw.

Sub-Arius didn't say much. Instead, they trudged and it was a long trip because even though this vessel was one-quarter the size of the asteroidal supership, it was still huge.

They passed vast, cavernous areas with giant, still machinery. Eventually, they reached the inner ducts, heading down into strange corridors.

"Why's it empty?" Maddox asked. "Was it ever a spaceship?"

"No," Sub-Arius said, "this isn't a spaceship as you conceive of it. It's a portal, a way to keep in contact with servants. In this case, those servants are the mobile asteroid Saurians."

"Why is the succubus using Saurians? Does that make any difference one way or another?"

"I do not know," Sub-Arius said. "Perhaps the Saurians were handy in this dimension. Lilith left the portal vessel with them. Did she suspect the Saurians might meet you? I doubt it. My analysis is that the succubus plans to come through to usher the final destruction of all those on the red planet."

"Why aren't we waiting here then to ambush her?" Riker asked.

"Everything you love would be destroyed by that point," Sub-Arius said.

Maddox considered the answer. He wasn't sure he accepted the explanation. He didn't think he'd get another, though. Surely, Arius and his sub would sacrifice them to kill the succubus. Maddox sighed. He wanted to go home. He wanted to see his wife and daughter. That meant—

"Let's finish this, gentlemen," Maddox said. "Let's get to... Where are we going again exactly?"

"To the center of the ship," Sub-Arius said. "Did I not already explain that?"

Maddox didn't answer. Instead, he drank water from a tube in his helmet and ate a concentrate from another. He checked the exo-armor's power levels and was surprised at how short the time had been.

Twenty-five minutes had passed since he'd donned the armor. They were moving quickly and yet, even at this speed, their armor might not last long enough, not even with their extra batteries.

"Is there any way we can recharge our suit batteries?" Maddox asked.

"Doubtful," Sub-Arius said. "I do not detect that type of power source here. But the center is coming quickly, Captain. Are you ready to make the transfer?"

"I am," Maddox said. "Riker, what about you, old man?"

"Aye," Riker said. "Let's get to it."

"Colonel?" Maddox asked.

"They killed my men. I want to kill who killed them."

So, the three men of Star Watch soon reached a vast interior chamber with strange cones, black with age. The cones were arranged so they all pointed down at a large dais.

"Is that the transfer mechanism?" Maddox asked.

"Yes," Sub-Arius said.

"Can you turn it on?"

Instead of answering directly, lights began to shine. Energy must have built up in the cones, as the tips crackled with power.

"This will really take us into the Annihilator?" Maddox asked.

"Captain," Sub-Arius said, "your repeated questions show your distrust. This is not a time to distrust. This is a time to charge and get it done."

"Noted," Maddox said. "Let's go."

The three men moved onto the dais, Riker carrying the crystal computer Sub-Arius.

Seconds later, energy beamed from the black cones and flowed against and around them. A dimensional door opened before them.

"Jump," Sub-Arius said. "Jump while you can."

Maddox leaped into the swirling maelstrom of the portal. He wasn't sure if Riker or the colonel jumped after him. All Maddox knew was an intense and painful feeling of stretching, stretching and elongating, as if his arm reached a kilometer and then two kilometers.

Suddenly, he snapped forward, following his elongated arms, tumbling, tumbling. What would the end of the tumbling bring? Would it bring them to the Annihilator, onto the ship of Succubus Lilith? This mission was madness.

Then there was a light ahead, a glaring light. Maddox hurtled toward it. It was the last thought he had before he fell unconscious.

-39-

Maddox solidified and crashed upon deck plates. Slowly, groggily, with his battle suit groaning, he stood.

He saw Colonel Julk and Riker land nearby and roll over. Both looked intact.

"Sub-Arius," Maddox croaked, "can you hear me?"

"Yes, Captain, I hear you fine."

Good. They were able to speak over their short-wave comm net.

"Is this it?" Maddox asked. "Is this the Annihilator *Shadowed Storm?*"

"I believe so, Captain," Sub-Arius said. "I will not use my sensors to a great degree so they don't discover we're here. From everything I've learned, those are engine and…"

"Yes?" Maddox asked.

"They're called reality machines. That one is presently inoperative, which I find interesting."

Maddox swept his beams over vast, towering machinery, possibly one and a half stories and bulky beyond imagining. Were they fusion engines, antimatter engines, what? He didn't know. They were oddly shaped. He felt vibration through the deck plates.

This area—

He rotated, letting his chest and helmet lights wash over wherever they could reach. These were gigantic, *enormous* machines. It hit Maddox then that they were in yet another dimension. He shuddered at the idea. What was this dimension like? How was it different from the one they'd been in?

No, no, he needed to concentrate on the task.

"Are we in the center of the ship or in the outer area?" Maddox asked.

"I believe the outer area," Sub-Arius said. "Notice, these are huge engines. I don't know if they power the offensive beams or if they recharge the machines that destroy planets. The life-support bubble, if you will, is at the center of the great Annihilator. The reality machines will concentrate their energies there. That is where the crew and succubus live."

"In other words," Maddox said, "we have to go there."

"That's rather obvious, isn't it, Captain?" Sub-Arius asked.

"Sometimes it's good to state the obvious, so everyone's on the same page."

By this time, Julk and Riker had climbed to their feet and switched on their helmet and chest lamps. They checked their carbines, power packs and grenades. Everything seemed in order. They gave the affirmative to Maddox.

"Which way do we go, Sub-Arius?" Maddox said.

The computer must have paused, as it didn't answer immediately. Soon, however, Sub-Arius gave instructions and they began to march down gigantic halls.

At that point, Maddox felt the dimensional difference. He couldn't pinpoint it exactly…at least right away. There was an odd sensation that alerted his intuitive sense. His…essence was under assault. Yes. It was like pressure against his mind, his limbs. The farther he walked down the gigantic halls—these weren't corridors as on a human ship. They were vast and cavernous, holding immense, humming machinery with blinking lights. No engineers watched the machines. Everything must be on automatic.

The pressure against Maddox grew and he found his steps harder and harder to take. It was also becoming difficult to think.

"Sub-Arius," Maddox said.

There was no response.

Maddox concentrated. Had he spoken or had he merely believed he'd spoken. Deliberately gathering his resolve—

"Sub-Arius, what's taking place?"

"Would you please explain what you mean, Captain?"

Maddox described the sensations he'd been feeling.

"Interesting," Sub-Arius said. "I haven't detected that. Riker, Julk, do you agree with the captain?"

Neither man responded.

"Riker," Maddox said.

The sergeant walked ahead, oblivious to Maddox trying to speak to him.

"Oh dear," Sub-Arius said. "I must analyze this. I suggest you leave them be for the moment, Captain. We must understand what is taking place."

"Yeah," Maddox said.

He soon found his steps increasingly harder to take. A point in his brain began to pulsate. It hurt every time he took a step. When he paused, it didn't hurt as much. Then, Maddox would take another lurch forward.

Maddox glanced at Riker.

The old sergeant took the same lurching steps: he thrust a leg forward, halted, and then thrust the next leg forward and so on.

Maddox glanced at Colonel Julk. He cursed under his breath in astonishment.

The colonel and his battle suit didn't seem as solid as Riker's.

Maddox examined his own arms. They looked solid like Riker's. He looked at Julk again, and Maddox blinked furiously.

Julk seemed to be going into ghost mode the way Galyan would if the holoimage was attempting subterfuge.

"Colonel," Maddox said over the comm net. He didn't get a response. "Colonel Julk, can you hear me?"

The colonel faded more so Maddox could see through him to the other side.

"Sub-Arius, why is Colonel Julk fading?"

"Oh my," Sub-Arius said. "The answer is clear. The colonel is losing coherence. He lacks what you and Riker have, the same stubbornness of will. My analysis tells me Riker is a stubborn bastard, and the Ska assault years ago strengthened that."

"Surviving assaults strengthen the will?" Maddox asked.

"That strikes me as logical," Sub-Arius said.

Maddox swiveled and lurched one, two, three steps, *clanging* against the colonel's battle armor. Maddox half-expected to burst through and maybe destroy the man. Luckily, his bum rush didn't do that. In fact, the colonel began to solidify just a little.

Maddox grabbed Julk, shouting, shaking the Neanderthal and continuing to do so.

Finally, Maddox heard a faint, "What, what is going on?"

Julk was speaking.

"Dammit man," Maddox shouted over the comm net. "Concentrate, you dolt! Get angry. The succubus slew your marines. This is payback. Make it a bitch."

"Yes, yes," Sub-Arius said. "That is excellent advice. Harsh emotions should help him keep stability. You, Captain, must be filled with harsh emotions. While Riker, he has the stubbornness of a retarded mule."

"That's enough of that," Riker said. "I'm right here, you know. I can hear everything you say."

"That is not enough," Sub-Arius said. "By retarded, I mean—" The computer ceased abruptly. "Oh my, perhaps these dimensional processes are working against me, too. I may have misspoken toward you just now, Sergeant."

"I'll say you have."

"I'm astonished at myself," Sub-Arius said, "as I am not given to rendering insults without well-founded reasons."

"It's good you stopped," Riker said, "as I was getting ready to hurl you to the deck, let you do your own walking."

"You would have done that?"

"...Maybe," Riker said.

"But I have no means of locomotion," Sub-Arius said.

"Now you're getting the picture," Riker said.

As Sub-Arius and Riker hammered out their situation, Maddox continued to shake Julk. He banged the marine's exo-armor with a gauntleted fist. Each time he struck, the colonel solidified a little more.

265

Maddox put his visor against the colonel's visor. "Listen to me, you Neanderthal lack wit, if you can't keep it together you'll literally fade away, cease to exist."

"Yes," Sub-Arius said. "That is correct. I'm surprised the colonel hasn't reacted to your racial slurs. He must be losing his identity. That leads me to believe this is an odder dimension than I'd anticipated. I will have to employ emergency measures. Sergeant Riker, would you take these injection tubes from my slot. I suggest you each inject yourself with the substance contained within."

Maddox quit hitting Julk and turned to Riker.

The sergeant took a small capsule and shoved it into a slot in his wrist armor. The slot was there for just such injections.

"Wait a minute, Sergeant," Maddox said. "What do you think you're doing? For all we know, Sub-Arius is giving you a mind control drug."

"Please Captain," Sub-Arius said, "I'm on your side and against the succubus. I'm providing each of you with a will enhancer. It will make you more stubborn, resistant to dimensional attacks against your existence. I believe it will assist the colonel against losing his reality and unraveling into nothing."

Maddox felt a wave of intense fatigue wash against his mind. Maybe he needed the will enhancer after all.

A thought struck Maddox, what Sub-Arius had said before. "What are those reality machines you spoke about? What are they supposed to do?"

"It is interesting you should ask, Captain. When they're active, they help to keep one in the present reality. If any of the ones up here function, I'm sure they won't help us. They will be concentrated on the living bubble. I hasten to add, that it is not a bubble as such, but actually a large area in comparison to your ship. It is just that in comparison to the Annihilator as a whole that it seems like a bubble. It is a sphere in the center of the Annihilator."

Maddox only half listened. He'd decided because his intuitive sense told him it was safe, that he took a capsule from Riker and pressed it into the spot in his wrist armor.

Maddox felt the will enhancer immediately. It was like acid washing through his veins. He clenched his teeth because he didn't want to bellow in agony. A shiver of pain coursed through his body. He groaned, he heard Riker mutter curses, and—

Over the comm net, Colonel Julk roared like an animal caught in a steel-tooth trap. The big Neanderthal slipped, falling on the deck. He thrashed there and beat his exo-armor fists against it, denting plates.

Maddox endured the pain, feeling anger and stubbornness burn in him. It was as if he lowered his head to charge deciding that no one would stop him from doing what he wanted. If the world didn't like it, if people told him to act differently, he wouldn't care.

I don't care what anyone thinks. I'll do this. Dammit, I'll do it and if someone gets in my way, I'm going to blow him down, kill him.

Shocked, Maddox realized he was becoming stubbornly angry as he seldom did—except as a teenager when he'd beat up personal bullies. He'd become ferociously angry then, and now—

"What did you give us, Sub-Arius?"

"I told you, Captain. It's a will enhancer to make you more stubborn. You will all become mulish, but it will help you remain in existence as your wills inflate. It is the will that says, 'I will do this no matter what.'"

It must have worked. Julk stopped fading, as he became real again.

"Let's go," Maddox said. "Get on your feet so we can hustle."

"Are you ordering us around again?" Riker complained.

"I am. Get on your feet, Sergeant."

"I'm already on my feet, you stupid bastard. You mean the colonel."

Rage washed through Maddox. "Don't you ever contradict me again, old man. Do you understand?"

Riker laughed harshly. "I may be old, but I don't have to put up with your authoritarian bullshit any longer. I've had it up to here with you."

"You'd better watch your mouth, old man," Maddox said, advancing on Riker.

"Gentlemen, gentlemen," Sub-Arius said. "Perhaps I gave you too strong of a dose. I gave you each the same amount I gave Colonel Julk. Unfortunately, both of you are already stubborn as mules. Both of you have immense willpower—and less body weight. Captain, I suspect that Sergeant Riker must have had to have great will in order to endure working with you all these years."

Maddox blinked as strove to use his intellect, straining to subdue his burning anger. He wanted to punch out Riker, smashing the old man's armor. Then, he'd take Sub-Arius and stomp the crystal computer into pieces so he wouldn't have to listen to it lecture him anymore.

At that point, Maddox became aware Sub-Arius was speaking to him. His stubbornness was drowning out the voice. He had to overcome his rage...

"Please Captain, you must think of your wife. You must think of your daughter, Jewel. If you cannot contain your stubbornness you'll become too entrenched to do what needs doing."

"Yes," Maddox said hoarsely. "Yes, I understand. The dose is strong. But any feelings of weakness I had earlier have vanished."

"I should think so," Sub-Arius said. "Perhaps, and I do not mean to tell you what to do. This is a suggestion only."

"What is it?" Maddox asked thickly.

"Perhaps you should check on Colonel Julk."

Maddox saw that Julk yet lay on the deck. He bent down. "Are you feeling okay, Colonel?"

"Yes," Julk said slowly. "It felt earlier as if I was leaving. All I could think about was my youth and the joyous time I had in the meadows back home. It felt like I was actually going back there. But now—where are we, sir?"

"In the heart of the Annihilator," Maddox said. "We're where the succubus lives, the one who ordered the shock troopers against your marines slain on *Victory*."

"Ah," Julk said. He climbed to his feet and hefted the blast-rifle. "I'm ready, sir. I feel much better. I'm sorry for causing a delay."

"Not a problem," Maddox said. "Sergeant, are you ready?"

"Yeah, I'm ready. Why do you even need to ask?"

Maddox became angry. He wanted to slap Riker silly. Once more, however, his superior intellect overcame the mulish rage.

Thus, the three men and crystal computer continued down the cavernous halls deeper into the Annihilator *Shadowed Storm*.

Time passed until a red light flashed inside Maddox's helmet. He checked. His armor batteries had almost drained dry.

"Gentlemen, let's stop and recharge, putting in the fresh batteries."

Surprisingly, Riker didn't give him any crap about it.

Soon their energy levels were back to full strength. They'd been traveling for over an hour already, moving deeper into the ship. As they neared the inner living-quarters spheroid, they reached a huge computer console.

It cried out in an alien voice none of them understood.

Before Sub-Arius could give advice, the three men leveled their Ono blast-rifles. Maddox had one even though he had the other weapon in reserve. They blasted until the alien computer was smoking ruins.

"That was a mistake," Sub-Arius said. "Surely, that will raise an alarm."

"Never mind that," Maddox said. "Come on, let's keep going."

They took no more than two hundred steps when a squad of gorilla-armored beings raced out of a side hatch, rushing them. The others held pistol blasters and space axes, and the leader spoke in an amplified voice. No doubt, he demanded them to halt.

Once more, the three men in exoskeleton armor opened fire with their Ono weapons. These weapons proved much superior to the Star Watch blasters and slug throwers they'd used in the null zone.

The Ono rifles hosed annihilating power that burned through the enemy armor.

Maybe because of that, Julk lost it and shouted with fury. The colonel charged even as more gorilla-armored aliens appeared. Julk hosed the aliens, firing from the armored hip until his energy charge ran dry. Julk continued to pull the trigger but no more blasting power emitted.

On the deck were several dozen smoking dead aliens. Their rounded armor sizzled. Melted flesh and blood oozed on the deck, no doubt raising a nauseous stink.

Ship alarms were now ringing constantly.

Maddox strode up and put an exo-armored hand on the colonel's shoulder.

Julk whirled around, raising his blast-rifle as if he was going to bash with the butt of it.

"Attention, Colonel. Attention."

That must have gotten through. The colonel's shoulders slumped.

"I'm sorry, sir. I-I lost it there. I kept remembering how they killed my marines, my boys."

"Are you in charge of your faculties, Colonel?" Maddox said.

Julk nodded.

"You must obey orders and be ready to act in a coherent fashion."

"I'm ready sir. I'm sorry."

"No need to apologize," Maddox said. "Recharge your blaster and then let's get ready."

"Ready?" Riker said. "The alarms are ringing. How in the world are we going to get to the center where this Lilith Succubus lives? Have you thought of that, Captain? Did you think of that before you let this ape go wild in his murder frenzy?"

Maddox stared at Riker in his exo-armor. "You know, Sergeant. I never quite realized what a pain in the ass you've been all these years."

"Yeah?" Riker said. "Well, let me tell you, sir. It has been no picnic having to deal with you, especially last mission when you couldn't keep up with me."

Maddox stiffened.

"Gentlemen, gentlemen," Sub-Arius said. "Do you not hear the alarms? Do you not realize that more and powerful aliens will soon be coming? We must do something. The life support sphere is before us. You must come up with a plan in order to reach the center of the Annihilator. There, I have determined the succubus is alive and well. She surely must know we're coming or that something is wrong. But if you continue to bicker we will fail and all my centuries, the millennia of labor... No, no, please comport yourselves as rational beings. Are you not rational?"

Maddox checked himself. "Yes, you're correct, Sub-Arius. Sergeant, I'm sorry for my harsh words."

"Sorry?" Riker said. "You're sorry?"

Maddox understood the sergeant couldn't handle the stubbornness drug as well as he could.

"Yes," Maddox said, "I am sorry. Will you help me destroy the succubus? Will you help defend the Commonwealth of Planets by killing the one named Lilith?"

Riker struggled it seemed within himself and finally came the words, "Yeah, yeah. Let's do it, Captain. Let's finish off this witch."

-40-

Maddox, Riker and Julk marched inside the life-support spheroid, wearing alien armor. They'd left their own exoskeleton suits along with the battery packs outside, beyond the area of destroyed aliens.

The aliens in the rounded battle-armor had been ugly indeed, in death perhaps even worse than they would have been in life. They were brutish and huge like gorillas and had lumpy faces, humanoid after a fashion except for tentacles wriggling from their chins.

Julk had shot up the alien armor good. Thus, each had to select various undamaged parts, putting the armor pieces together. Interestingly, the aliens also used exoskeleton armor and battery packs, theirs highly charged.

Sub-Arius had helped them decipher the alien symbols, which allowed them to combine the pieces.

Maddox, Riker and Julk marched past other armored aliens hurrying in the opposite direction, no doubt rushing because of the blaring alarm. Maddox found it incredible no alien commander had ordered them to stop. In truth, there didn't seem to be any particular commander. All the armored aliens moved as if in one accord.

Maddox led the others into smaller corridors. These were sized like those on Earth ships.

After several hundred meters without meeting others, Maddox spoke. "What controls the aliens? Do they have a group-think mind?"

"That's a clever conclusion, Captain," Sub-Arius said, "and on little evidence, too. I'm putting that down to your intuitive sense. I suspect they obey the succubus's will as ants would their queen."

"Is that even how it works?" Maddox asked. "I thought ants were instinctive. When does an ant queen order anything?"

"As to that, I cannot say," Sub-Arius replied, "but that's the best analogy I have. The fighters are the succubus's limbs, propelled no doubt by her thoughts."

"Meaning the succubus is telepathic?" Maddox asked.

"Not in the direct sense that you think, Captain. However, I believe she's telepathic in the sense of this dimension and the beings she controls."

Maddox waved an armored arm. "It doesn't matter. We're moving and I don't think they know we're aliens. Our armor disguise has fooled the succubus for the moment, although I don't think that will last long."

"I agree," Sub-Arius said. "The succubus doesn't know because she doesn't sense us and can't telepathically control us. Though I think Colonel Julk may fall under her influence faster than either of you two."

"Thanks," Julk muttered.

"It's no slur against you, sir," Sub-Arius said. "You're dealing with two of the stubbornest humans we've met."

"Who do you mean by 'we'?" Maddox asked.

"You noticed that, did you?" Sub-Arius asked. "It was a slip of the tongue. I wish I wouldn't have said that."

"You're avoiding the question," Maddox said.

"Very well," Sub-Arius said, "I should say Greater Arius and myself. However, I suspect you'd know I was misleading you."

"You mean lying," Maddox said.

"By 'we'," Sub-Arius said, ignoring the remark, "I mean the Onos and me. And by me, I mean Greater Arius and myself."

Maddox worked that through. "So...that means through you the Onos have been operating in our dimension."

"Only through the good offices of the Supreme Intelligence," Sub-Arius said. "He is our agent in your dimension, as it were."

Within his helmet, Maddox scowled. "You're saying the Supreme Intelligence doesn't really work for the Builders?"

"Of course he does. The Supreme Intelligence is a Builder construct. We've merely managed to insert an Ono appendage into his computing systems. Thus, he has been acting as our agent, though it is nothing nefarious or bad for the Commonwealth. The key is that we have someone in your dimension Balron spoke to, helping us align various agencies to stopping Succubus Lilith."

"She's the only real danger?" Maddox asked.

"Not the only danger to the greater multiverse," Sub-Arius said. "But to your dimension, yes, I believe she's it. In truth, she has been a danger for tens of thousands of years. But time and its essence moves differently between dimensions, as I think you'll find if and when you return home."

"What do you mean by that?" Maddox asked sharply.

"Do you not recall your Earth legends about those who meet elves?"

"Uh, no," Maddox said. "How about either of you two: do you know what Sub-Arius is saying?"

"No," Riker said mulishly.

Julk shook his helmeted head.

"In that case," Sub-Arius said, "it does not matter."

"Wait a minute," Maddox said. "I do recall something. Are you talking about how a man supposedly spends a minute in Elfland but it turns out to have been years?"

"Precisely right, Captain. Why, you are a continual amazement to me."

They reached a sealed hatch. After a minute of analysis, Sub-Arius cracked the code and opened it for them.

They stepped into a grotesque crystal garden with motes drifting in the air. Immediately, they discovered it was more than air but less than liquid. The surprising thing was the substance didn't drain out of the opened hatch.

It shut behind them. Maybe the substance had been draining, but too slowly to notice.

The substance took more energy to push through, and try as they might, they couldn't swing their arms as fast as in normal air.

"We're entering the succubus's dimension," Sub-Arius said.

"You mean she's managed to create here what it's like in her dimension?" Maddox asked.

"Not precisely," Sub-Arius said. "By my readings, she has been causing her personal life-support system to revert to her dimensional specifics. No doubt, that is so she can reenergize and possibly take comfort as if in her original dimensional reality."

"I'm not tracking you," Maddox said. "She's changing the dimension here?"

"Probably not how you suspect," Sub-Arius said. "Do you recall the reality machines in the upper areas?"

"Of course," Maddox said.

"The bulk of their power is focused here. She is changing the dimensional reality in this place toward her own. Do you not feel a force tugging at your very essence?"

"No," Maddox said. "And what you're saying is exactly what I've been saying."

"Let me calculate. I see. My will-enhancing drug is still having its effect on you. I feel the essential difference, and I'm finding my computing more difficult than otherwise. I must soon acquire more energy, Captain or face forced deactivation."

"What's your present energy source?"

"It is inside my crystal. If the drain continues, you'll have to place me on radioactive material so I may absorb its energy."

"We don't have time for that."

"If you do not find the time I may auto-delete. In that case, I cannot operate the machinery to teleport you back to the daughter-ship. That being so, I don't know how you'll ever return to *Victory*."

Maddox thought about that. "Power down and conserve energy for later. We're heading in the right direction. If we need you, we'll tap on you and you can do your computing then."

"Logical. I should have already thought of that myself. I will now conserve power and not speak unless I detect an emergency."

Sub-Arius ceased talking.

Maddox focused on wading through the substance floating in the crystal garden. He spied growths like fungus and others like towering coral columns. There were arches and other bizarre crystal architecture. In the murky continuously shifting light, this place felt alien indeed.

Maddox blinked as if reality shifted under him. It was a grotesque feeling in his soul. He hated this place. Despite that, he plowed on, urging the other two to follow him.

"What...?" Julk said thickly.

Maddox swiveled around.

In his armor, Julk had turned to the side and seemed to be staring, as he stood motionless.

Within his helmet, Maddox squinted, trying to fathom what he and Julk were looking at.

After a moment, it struck Maddox as an inverted brain: one opened from the inside and spread out. There were firing neurons, sparks, and energy that sped farther than the rest and just sputtered out. Around the inverted spread-out brain were separate human limbs, perhaps, that had been stretched or elongated.

Looking harder, Maddox realized his first assessment was wrong. There were fibrous filaments attacked to the otherwise separated limbs. He noticed because firing neurons pulsated as electrical charges along the fibers.

Elongated fingers twitched. A stretched arm contracted. A mouth with teeth squirmed as if to speak while a detached purple eye examined them.

Revulsion surged through Maddox. Incredibly, a being— the spread-out parts seemed to belong to an entity.

"What, what?" the mouth said.

Maddox's suit receptor picked up the warbled words.

"What are you doing here?" the disembodied thing said.

As the mouth spoke, neurons flashed in the inverted spread-out brain.

"What do you mean?" Maddox asked. "Can you be more precise?"

"Are you—are you her servants?"

"Her as in Lilith?" asked Maddox.

"Yes."

"We're not," Maddox said. "I don't think you are, either."

"No. I am a captive caught long, long ago."

The revulsion twisted Maddox's gut so it hurt. Another part of him realized he needed to use what he could, even this poor captive.

"Where's your dimension?" Maddox asked.

"It was destroyed eons ago. An Annihilator appeared, bringing the Blight that destroyed everything. Our, our scientists—we were supreme in intellect in our dimension. In our arrogance, we created and opened a portal, breaking through to one dimension after another. We sought the greatness of existence.

"Through our arrogance and portal—the one in the Annihilator used it as a beacon, guiding her to our dimension. The terrible ship brought the Blight. Or did I already say that?"

The mouth with teeth laughed forlornly.

"I was our champion, trained to defeat her. Lilith captured me, and this—this is my existence. She stretched me. She tore me apart, spreading me in this…substance. Her reality machines keep me in alive in this awful place."

The purple eye squinted at Maddox. "Please, if you are not her servants, kill me. Kill me, I beg you. My life and existence is a parody and horror. I know boredom, pain and tediously long existence. She mocks all that is good."

The mouth twisted into a grimace until it spoke further. "We shouldn't have opened the way into a different dimension. We should have stopped when we realized the dangers. But we were arrogant. We thought we knew better, that we could learn more and more. Kill me. Kill me, please."

Sub-Arius activated. "Captain, I warn you: do not kill this entity."

277

Maddox had raised his blast-rifle even as Riker and Julk crowded behind him, staring in horror at the spread-out limb-separated creature.

"Why shouldn't I put him out of his misery?" Maddox asked. "Why shouldn't I thwart her will in this?"

"Because he is an obvious alarm," Sub-Arius said. "Don't you understand? Lilith is clever and evil. You must catch her by surprise. Captain, I fear I must shut down again. But do not kill him. If we do, she will know. On all counts, we must pass him quietly. We must urge him to be quiet so we can sneak up on Succubus Lilith."

"I will, I will," the being said. "But oh, mercy, mercy, please let it end."

Before Maddox could think too much or too long, he hosed blaster fire from the Ono weapon, destroying the elongated and spread-out pieces of brain and limbs.

Heat from the semi-liquid or gaseous substance around the spread-out, elongated thing radiated back at them. The heat started making Maddox sweat in his battle suit.

He ceased firing.

The he, she or it was dead, the brain matter destroyed, crisp wisps drifting away.

Strangely, an alarm pulsated through the substance.

"Come on," Maddox said, "we have to keep moving. I see a hatch in the distance. Hurry, let's go!"

Maddox surged through the substance. As he did, he thought about dimensions, how most were different from each other. Had the Creator fashioned each dimension for the beings in it? If so, that meant breaking into another dimension was breaking into a universe made specifically for others.

For whatever reason, Maddox thought about the Bible, and an essence of it, the Ten Commandments. So many people thought of the commandments as something given by an angry god to stop people from having fun. Do not commit adultery. Do not lie. Do not steal. Those weren't there to make life miserable for people, but to guard men and women from crossing boundaries. Breaking those boundaries caused pain and suffering. The Creator was trying to protect for good, just like when He made dimensions nearly impossible to cross.

278

Then, Maddox had no more time to dwell on theological or philosophical matters.

Three eel-like things swam or flew at them. The creatures used huge membranous wings, flapping or swimming through the substance. The creatures had large grotesque heads and opened mouths with great fangs for teeth. Did the eel-creatures think they could breach the armor?

Even as Maddox wondered, visible waves flowed from the heads and through the strange medium. Those waves reached and struck Maddox, Riker and Julk.

Agony from the vampire eels' wavelengths struck Maddox, flowing to his brain so it throbbed.

Maddox grunted and his sense of reality began to slip.

"Help," Julk said over the comm net.

The colonel dropped his Ono blast-rifle so it floated in the substance, which seemed to have thickened around them.

Maddox fought the wavelength, the emanations from the eel-creature that beamed at him.

Maddox raised his blast-rifle.

The other two eel-creatures concentrated their mind rays, their telepathic attacks, whatever it was. The wavelengths struck Maddox's helmet. The waves entered his brain, seeking to overpower him.

Maddox ceased raising the rifle to destroy the eels. Pain filled his being. Worse, the unreality striking him caused him to start to fade away.

Maddox struggled, and he realized he might never see Meta or touch his daughter Jewel again. He'd never lift Jewel high, throwing her up and hearing her squeal, and catching her and setting her down on the floor.

A *whoosh, whoosh, whoosh* sounded as three power bolts emerged from Riker's blast rifle.

The bolts consumed the vampire eels, causing them to bubble into non-existence.

The attacks on Maddox ceased abruptly. He stopped fading, but because solid once more.

Maddox turned, staring at Riker in his battle suit.

"You took the brunt of the attack, Captain," Riker said over the comm net. "It gave me the time I needed to harden my resolve."

"Sergeant Riker," Maddox said, "I'm glad you're with me. I'm very glad."

"What do you know, sir, so am I," Riker said.

The three men continued to wade through the semi-gelatinous substance, heading for a hatch.

Sub-Arius activated once more. "That is the hatch to the succubus's quarters. We are almost upon her, gentlemen. Keep going and do not stop for anything."

Afterward, Sub-Arius shut down again, conserving energy as the three men waded toward their ultimate destiny.

-41-

In the other dimension with the daughter-ship, Valerie sat in the captain's chair on the bridge of *Victory*.

She'd returned several hours ago from the meeting on the *Stonewall Jackson* and had watched Maddox and the others leave in the tin can. Now, she waited for news of success or failure from the captain's foray into the daughter-ship of the asteroidal supership.

Valerie swiveled from one side to the other, noticing that everyone monitored their stations. The crew seemed subdued but not upset. Everyone waited for the next shoe to drop.

While Valerie waited, she'd been pondering much of what the captain had revealed on the *Stonewall Jackson*. Was there only one Ono on the red planet? According to Commodore Galt, the Onos had sent many space fighters into battle and had possessed an entire star station.

Valerie had used *Victory's* scanners and searched the battle debris for Ono bio matter. She'd found none.

That supported the theory there was only one Ono on the planet. Could one Ono have survived all alone all this time? Were other Onos hidden perhaps in deep subterranean chambers inside the planet?

Valerie would have liked to ask the captain more on the shuttle ride back from the meeting, but he'd been deep in thought concerning the foray to kill the demon, a succubus named Lilith.

281

Valerie shook her head. This was a bizarre mission. It reminded her too much of last mission when they'd gone to the dampened star system.

"This is a different dimension," Valerie said as she looked around.

Galyan appeared beside her. "Valerie, how are you holding up?"

Valerie shrugged. "I always hate the waiting."

"Yes," Galyan said, "I know what you mean."

Valerie looked at Galyan. Was that true? Did the AI entity understand waiting?

She wasn't going to insult him by asking. Valerie dearly loved Galyan. She'd often felt it was a shame he was a holographic projection. Many a time, she would have liked to have knelt down and hugged the poor Adok. Why hadn't Maddox made more of an effort to reunite Galyan with the living Adoks? Everyone knew that's what Galyan wanted.

"Commander," Andros said, turning around, "there's something amiss."

"Oh?" Valerie asked.

"I've been monitoring the mobile asteroids."

"Yes," Valerie said, not understanding why the pit of her stomach twisted.

"There appears to be fewer of them than I'd originally counted," Andros said.

Valerie stood. "What do you mean?"

"Alert, alert," Galyan said from where he stood.

The alert shocked Valerie. She whirled around. "What are you babbling about, Galyan?"

"The missing mobile asteroids of the Saurian armada have appeared," Galyan said.

"Spit it out," Valerie said. "Where are they?"

"The mobile asteroids appear to have used a modified fold. They—look at your monitor, Andros, do you not see?"

Andros swiveled back to his science board as his pudgy fingers roved over the panel. A moment later, he shouted in shock. "Galyan's right." Andros swiveled around to stare at Valerie. "The mobile asteroids are using a fold mechanism. They're appearing."

"Appearing where?" Valerie asked.

"Given their present velocity," Andros said, "I estimate the ones who just folded will reach the red planet in a little more than an hour."

Valerie sat and knew they were in for it. They couldn't use the star-drive jump to get out of the way because they had to protect the portal, the daughter vessel of the asteroid supership. The portal ship lacked motive power, and according to what she'd learned from Galt, tractor beams had failed to latch onto the compressed stardust hull. The daughter vessel was where it was, and if they wanted to protect it, they had to stay put. How had the Saurians moved the daughter-ship earlier? She needed to ask Galt that.

"Commander," the comm officer said, "you have a communication from Commodore Galt."

"Put it on the main screen." Valerie rose and took several steps toward the main screen.

Galt appeared on it, staring at her with intensity. "Have you seen the mobile asteroids appearing?"

"I have. They have a fold or a star-drive jump."

"I think they're all going to fold to us."

Valerie nodded.

"I'm already formulating a strategy to deal with this. Can I count on you, Commander?"

"Of course," Valerie said.

"If you like, you may have independent command."

"Commodore, Captain Maddox gave you the authority to deal with the situation as you saw fit. I know your reputation. Do what you must. We will obey your orders."

Valerie didn't completely like the idea of taking orders from Galt: not because she had any problems with him, but he hadn't faced situations like these before. Still, Galt was supposed to be a gifted tactician. Valerie shook her head. She would have liked to run their side. She knew what she'd do, but Maddox had given Galt the authority and that made sense. Galt was a commodore, after all. Valerie would follow the chain of command and obey orders.

"I'll keep in touch." Galt then disappeared from the main screen.

"Valerie," Galyan said, "should we not attack instantly now that the mobile asteroids are appearing? Certainly, it seems that the Saurians will have jump lag for a short time and will thus be defenseless."

"That's a good idea," Valerie said. "We should launch our fold fighters with antimatter missiles and hit the mobile asteroids one right after the other."

"I think that would be an excellent idea," Galyan said. "Why do you not tell the commodore that?"

Valerie almost did. Instead, she shook her head. "Galt's running the show, Galyan. If he wants my advice, he'll ask for it."

"But Valerie, by giving your advice now, you might save countless lives and ships. Is it not your duty to say something?"

The little AI had a point, Valerie realized.

"Ma'am," the comm officer said, "the commodore has started issuing orders. The fleet is beginning to maneuver."

"Task force," Valerie corrected.

"Yes ma'am," the comm officer said.

The last giant mobile asteroid disappeared from its former position and appeared with the others. A mere hour at their present velocity would bring them to the red planet.

Galt appeared on the main screen again. "The original wave of mobile asteroids couldn't jump or fold, at least, as far as I know."

"I'm not sure if you remember," Valerie said, "but the captain said this group will have superior technology than the first one you faced. The wave behind this one will probably have even better technology yet."

"How is that possible?" Galt asked.

"I have no idea. I merely know that's what the captain said. He's seldom wrong on these matters."

"Do you have any suggestions?" Galt asked.

"I do, sir. Use the fold fighters now, hitting the lagged asteroids with antimatter missiles."

"Good thinking," Galt said. "I'm going to keep that in mind. It might be too late to launch in time."

"Maybe," Valerie said.

"I'm already making the dispositions in my head. I'll get back to you in a few minutes."

"Yes, Commodore," Valerie said.

Once more, Galt disappeared from the main screen.

On it appeared the mobile asteroids.

"Let's get a zoom on that, Galyan."

"Do you mean magnification, Valerie?"

Valerie turned to Galyan. "Is this a time to be pedantic?"

"No, Valerie. I am sorry. You can call it zoom if you wish. Observe."

Valerie looked up at the main screen.

On it appeared a mobile asteroid. As an asteroid, it wasn't huge: five kilometers wide and three kilometers long. It had huge thrusters in back and all kinds of weaponry bristling in front. It probably had missile silos and fighter launch-bases. The asteroid looked like a formidable opponent. There were nineteen more just like this one.

"Do we know what kind of weaponry they possess?" Valerie asked.

"They used lasers last time," Galyan said.

Andros was studying his monitor. "I don't see any laser cannons. If I were to guess, those are rail-gun emplacements."

"Galyan, can you give me greater magnification?" Valerie asked.

"Yes, Valerie."

The scene leapt closer.

Valerie took several steps nearer the main screen. That looked like a rail-gun emplacement. There were several on the asteroid.

"This looks like an improvement over their lasers," Valerie said.

"I certainly agree," Galyan said. "A rail gun by its very conception will have a greater range than a laser, though it will be a slower weapon. A laser moves at the speed of light. The hypervelocity projectile of a rail gun will not move at nearly that speed, but it should maintain all of its destructive power even at extended range, while a laser dissipates quickly over range."

"Thank you for the physics lesson," Valerie said.

"I did not mean to imply you did not know," Galyan said.

"Forget it. We have more important things to worry about."

As they waited for Commodore Galt to make his dispositions, to make his decisions, missiles began to launch from every asteroid. That meant missiles from twenty platforms. The mass of missile burned hotter, maneuvering in a vast staggered formations that covered a wide area. The missiles didn't head for the red planet, but came straight at the task force, which included *Victory* and the daughter-ship of the Annihilator.

The missiles will reach our vicinity in fifteen minutes," Galyan said, "and perhaps even sooner if they have greater accelerating power."

"Ma'am," the comm officer said, "there's a call from the commodore."

"Commander," Galt said, "these missiles—my technical people are telling me they have titanium armor, which is different from what we faced earlier. These missiles are tougher, bigger and faster."

"Improved missiles," Valerie said. "That's exactly what the captain suggested."

"That isn't good news."

"I agree, Commodore."

Galt nodded. "I'm just letting you know that what you've been telling us is correct. I've already started a launch and firing sequence. As of right now, I want *Victory* to hang back near Mothership *Joan of Arc*."

"Yes, Commodore," Valerie said.

"You have no problems with that?"

"You don't need to ask me that, Commodore. Tell me what needs to be done and I'll do it."

"Then I'm giving you this command. Your task, Commander, is to make sure the daughter-ship of the asteroidal supership remains intact. Do whatever you must to keep the Saurians from destroying it or landing on it."

"Yes sir," Valerie said. Now those were orders she could appreciate.

"Until you hear otherwise, those are your primary orders."

"Yes, Commodore."

286

"I'm going to be busy. You may not hear from me for a while. This one—we're going to do it."

"I believe you, sir."

"Right," he said, using Maddox's phrase. "Commodore Galt out."

And with that began the battle for the task force's survival.

-42-

The mass of Saurian missiles headed in a vast and staggered group at the task force.

The huge *Conqueror*-class battleships were at the van of the task force. From them launched several antimatter missiles. The missiles were few in number, particularly compared to the vast number of Saurian missiles heading in.

Even as that was taking place, fold fighters from the *Cleopatra* began to launch. Each of the fold fighters carried one of the big heavy antimatter missiles.

"This is good," Valerie said.

"You have divined the commodore's intentions, Valerie?" Galyan asked.

She looked at the little holoimage. "I think so. Have you?"

"I have not yet set up a personality profile for the commodore, but I am doing so now. I should have already done it at the meeting."

"You have all the data that you collected from the meeting."

"That is correct Valerie. I am in the process." Galyan stood utterly still as his eyelids began to flutter, showing that his computer system was hard at work.

In the meantime, as the huge antimatter missiles from battleships accelerated at fifty and then seventy-five gravities, the fold fighters began to disappear from around the *Cleopatra*.

Now began what would be known as the missile phase of the battle for the task force, or perhaps even the battle for the daughter-ship of the Annihilator. Valerie wondered if that was what this was all about.

Why had the mobile asteroids used their fold mechanism shortly after Maddox had entered the portal? Did it mean that using the portal sent a message to the Saurian commander? To Valerie's way of thinking that seemed likely. Usually there was a good reason for whatever happened.

Now as Valerie watched on the main screen, the first of the *Conqueror*-class-launched antimatter missiles exploded with massive power. That caused a whiteout on the screen at that locale.

The tactic was simple. The antimatter missile with its vast explosive power should take out a certain number of the staggered Saurian missiles.

That's exactly what happened.

The other antimatter missiles, each at staggered and widely different places from the others, also detonated.

The great majority of the front Saurian missiles were destroyed in the antimatter detonations. However, not all the front Saurian missiles had stopped. Some raced through the whiteout area, still heading for the task force.

"Ma'am," the comm officer said, "Captain Karpov of the *Stonewall Jackson* wants me to inform you: these missiles were tougher than the commodore expected. More survived the blasts than expected. It's going to be a harder fight than we anticipated."

"It always is," Valerie said. Then she motioned the comm officer to signal that they'd received the message."

More antimatter missiles launched from the three battleships.

Now, from much farther afield and from the flanks of the Saurian mass of missiles, fold fighters appeared. They began to launch their antimatter missiles.

Not all launched openly. Some fighters merely deposited their antimatter missiles. Those would accelerate later at whatever would be a tactically good target.

Even as these fold fighters did so, Andros shouted at his monitor.

"Let's be calm, if you please," Valerie told him.

289

She'd learned that from Maddox long ago. If Maddox didn't always practice it these days, she did. *Stay calm no matter what happens so you can think clearly and so the crew remains calm and obeys orders.*

"Tell it to me in a steady voice, Chief Technician."

"Yes, Commander," Andros said. "There appears to have been hidden rail-guns much closer to the missile swarm than we thought. These rail guns have started taking out our fold fighters."

A knot in Valerie's gut tightened, making her wince. The Saurians with their mobile asteroids far exceeded the task force and *Victory* in tonnage. Now, the enemy showed they could fold. If the Saurians came close to matching the task force's weapons technology, this wouldn't only be a hard fight but a brutal slog.

Galt issued new orders.

Soon, the light cruisers used their star-drive jump, appearing beside the mass of missiles and launching salvos of antimatter missiles.

Shortly thereafter, the light cruiser star-drive jumped, getting out of there.

The Saurian missiles began separating in grouped clots, heading toward various areas.

"Commander," Galyan said, "The task force has EW fold fighters. They are presently leaving the *Joan of Arc.*"

Valerie nodded. Andros had informed her earlier that the Saurian commander used radio waves to direct the masses of missiles. No doubt, Galt or perhaps Captain Lair of the *Joan of Arc* was attempting to interfere with that.

Pre-launched antimatter missiles detonated, taking out more Saurian missiles from the flanks.

Galyan calculated that the enemy had lost eighteen percent of his missiles so far. Would the enemy launch more to replace the lost ones? There were thousands out there. How many more did the mobile asteroids carry?

"Andros," Valerie said, "do we know the type of warheads the missiles carry? Are they fusion, cobalt, antimatter, what?"

"Unknown," Andros said, "though I have attempted to find out. The titanium armor is thickest at the nose cone and so far has resisted scanner efforts."

"Valerie," Galyan said, "I could go out there and check."

"Do it," Valerie said.

Galyan disappeared and reappeared almost instantly. "They are cobalt warheads, Valerie. I think those are much more powerful than the ones the Saurians used the last battle against the Ono battle station."

"Figures," Valerie said.

The EW fold fighters must have helped, as they were appearing out there. Three antimatter missiles launched from a light cruiser slammed into enemy stealth rail-gun-firing platform. Each exploded spectacularly.

The destroyed rail guns meant more antimatter missiles reached the Saurian missiles.

Soon, another eighteen percent of the enemy's remaining missiles disappeared in more explosions.

The Saurian missiles spread out even more. That would make it harder to take out a large number with any one antimatter blast. However, with the lesser number of enemy missiles, it was easier to decide where to send the remaining antimatter missiles.

More fold fighters appeared to take the place of those that had been destroyed.

A new hidden platform with rail guns attacked the new fold fighters. Three, five, seven disintegrated under the hypervelocity projectiles.

With the knowledge of enemy counter-fire, the fold fighters stayed on target for shorter lengths of time, making them more difficult to pinpoint.

It helped the fold fighters that they faced rail guns instead of lasers. Rail-gun projectiles took longer than lasers to reach them, although the rail-gun projectiles hitting with greater force at greater range was helping the Saurians.

Despite that, thirty-two percent of the remaining Saurian missiles vaporized under the combined attacks from the task force and fold fighters.

Unfortunately, the Saurian missiles were moving close to cobalt-blast range against the forward warships of the task force.

All the while, the mobile asteroids gained velocity as they accelerated toward them.

Valerie wondered if the mobile asteroids merely used the multitudes of missiles as a screen to allow them to get safely into closer range.

Once more, the Saurian missiles spread out, each moving away from the others so they covered a vast area.

Some of the previously hidden antimatter missiles accelerated from their sleep positions.

How many had the mothership captains laid?

The minutes ticked by.

A blast would appear on the main screen, a whiteout. Yet more Saurian missiles were destroyed.

"I calculate we are succeeding," Galyan said.

Valerie looked at him.

"According to what I have seen, Commodore Galt used inefficient methods in the beginning. I now think he did that so it would cause greater surprise later."

"Do you think that was wise?"

"It is proving so. Look, Valerie."

She looked at the main screen.

The task force's destroyers moved up, leaving the motherships they'd been guarding. A barrage of smaller missiles left the destroyers.

The destroyers began a turning maneuver, no doubt to take them back to their defensive position near the motherships and daughter-ship of the Annihilator.

These weren't big antimatter missiles. Instead, just before each ignited, rods appeared on the nosecones, directing the gamma and x-rays from the cobalt explosion. The rays moved at enemy-targeted missiles, detonating many.

With this tactic and another seven, well-placed antimatter blasts, the last Saurian missiles turned into debris. An intense field of radiation, debris, gamma rays and EMPs covered a huge area between the two fleets. Likely, the Saurians on the mobile asteroids could go into subterranean tunnels and avoid any radiation while passing through the field. Still, the radiation field was out there.

Galt soon appeared on the main screen. There were dark circles around his eyes, even though the battle hadn't lasted that long. Responsibility often took a grave toll on anyone.

"We did it," Galt said.

"We did it," Valerie said, even though she didn't know what she'd done to help.

Galt heaved a sigh. "We did it but that ate up much of our remaining antimatter missiles. We could fight one more battle like that. But if they come with a corresponding great armada later..." He shook his head. "Those rail guns were far superior to the lasers earlier."

"The Ono warned us about that," Valerie said.

Galt nodded. "Any suggestions regarding the mobile asteroids?"

"Just continue what we're doing. Throw scares into them. And..."

"Yes?"

"I'm wondering if this will come down to the best use of our fold fighters."

Galt gave her a wintry grin. "We have a lot of strikefighters left, but sending them at the mobile asteroids with those rail guns..." He shook his head. "We're still in for a fight."

"Commander," the comm officer said. "There's an incoming message from the enemy armada."

"I'm seeing that over here, too," Galt said. "I'll leave you to it. Let's listen to what this lizard has to say."

"Yes sir," Valerie said.

On the main screen appeared the same Saurian commander Maddox had spoken with earlier. He was muscular, large for a Saurian, at least it seemed, and he looked exceedingly belligerent and maybe even pleased with himself.

The creature opened his mouth and began to speak. The translators turned his words into English they understood.

"You have defeated my swarm of missiles," the Saurian said. "Do not think that you will defeat my mobile asteroids. We have come to destroy you. We have come to reclaim the asteroidal supership and take it, as it is ours. After you have

293

been vanquished, we will destroy the planet holding the vile ones. They do not belong here. I do not think that you belong here. You are invaders. We will crush you. We will destroy you. You have received a small taste of what we can do, and now you will face our cunning and technology. You will face our crushing might. Flee if you are able. That is my advice to you. But if you are too proud to flee, then you may do one other thing for us and that is die."

With that, the message ceased.

Valerie looked at Galyan.

Galyan looked at her. "I believe he is serious, Valerie."

Valerie snorted. Yes, she believed the Saurian was serious too. Then a stern look came on Valerie's face. She also was serious and she'd faced such dilemmas before.

This time, if Galt did anything stupid, she was going to open channels and give him advice. Why did she think that? Why did she feel the need? Valerie wasn't sure. She wondered if an intuitive sense came to whoever sat in the captain's chair.

Valerie struck one of the armrests lightly. This she knew. She was the acting captain of *Victory* and this was a Star Watch fleet. She was going to protect her superior officer and help the Commonwealth by protecting the portal against the enemy. The Saurians thought they were badass space fighters.

Well, Valerie thought to herself, *let's see just how tough they really are.*

-43-

Commander Galt sat in his chair on the bridge of the *Stonewall Jackson* with the small holo-screens around him as he wore his manipulation glove.

They'd won the encounter against the mass missile assault. It troubled him that these missiles were so superior to the ones they'd faced in the previous fight. He also wondered something else. Why weren't the Onos of the red planet helping him and the task force? This was the moment to help, not after Task Force 3 was destroyed. Shouldn't someone ask the aliens for some aid, some help?

Galt watched on his holo-screens and occasionally looked up at the main screen.

The twenty mobile asteroids had divided into two if unequal groups. Mobile Asteroid Group 1 had four, five, four—thirteen mobile asteroids altogether.

The ship mass the Saurians possessed far exceeded the task force's ship mass. The rail guns were a problem. A shield could stop several. Could a shield stop *all* the rail guns firing at one target at once?

Galt grunted. He couldn't let that happen.

He was glad that seven other mobile asteroids, Group 2, moved away and forward from Group 1.

The enemy attacked in a slightly staggered formation.

Was the Saurian commander offering him the smaller group of seven? That seemed like a strange thing to do. Surely, since rail guns could reach farther with a more effective range than lasers, it would be wiser to keep all the mobile asteroids together. That way, coming against them would mean coming through a vast hail of firepower.

Thankfully, the rail guns were not like disruptor beams, not in range or power. But each mobile asteroid had six and sometimes seven rail guns. The amount of fire they could put up…

Galt shook his head and quickly ceased such motion. He was an experienced commander. He knew how to lead people into battle. One key was to project confidence. Head shaking didn't project that.

He *was* confident and began to rattle off orders.

He'd watched and gauged the enemy. He'd had his sensor teams scan the asteroids.

Would the enemy launch mass fighters or more missiles? Would the Saurians simply bore in with twenty behemoths all firing their rail guns?

They'd find out soon.

Galt gave orders and the battleships *Alexander*, *Stonewall Jackson* and *Philip II* maneuvered toward Mobile Asteroid Group 2, the smaller one. On either side of the battleship squadron were two light cruisers. The light cruisers had fusion beams, the battleships disruptor beams.

The two motherships were behind the battleships and light cruisers by a considerable distance. They were immense vessels indeed. With them were the destroyers and escorts, screens to protect the motherships. Behind them, *Victory* and the strange portal vessel cruised.

No one had heard from Maddox and his men yet. If Maddox could pop out and declare success, they could get the hell out of here. Then, maybe, they go home to their dimension.

They were here to protect the portal. Everything depended on Maddox. In one sense, whether Maddox succeeded or not was the question, not whether Maddox could return to them through the portal.

They could leave the portal, and it would have no bearing on Maddox's success in the other dimension.

Galt frowned. What kind of bastard left the man who had come to rescue them in the lurch?

"Not me," Galt said under his breath.

"Sir," Sensor Chief Usan said. "They're finally doing something."

Galt looked up and saw that.

Enemy space fighters were launching from Mobile Asteroid Group 2. That was seven of the behemoths and man, those were lots of space fighters. Given the position of MAG 2 and the route the space fighters would have to fly to reach the battleships...

Galt grinned to himself.

Clearly, the Saurians had failed to find the stealth antimatter missiles in their flight path.

Galt checked, no space fighters had launched from MAG 1 with its thirteen mobile asteroids.

Galt spoke to Captain Karpov.

Karpov issued an order. The comm officer alerted those on motherships *Cleopatra* and *Joan of Arc*. The fold fighters and EW craft needed to keep MAG 1 busy while they—

Galt took a deep breath. It was time to start the next phase of the battle.

Fold fighters began to fold from the motherships and appear on the far side of MAG 1, meaning on the opposite side where MAG 2 was situated. The fold fighters launched antimatter missiles. They did so from much farther than Galt would have ordered against the original Saurian fleet.

The reason was those damn rail guns.

Even so, the fold fighters received a mass rail-gun barrage. If not for the EW fold fighters even farther away raising decoy images, there would have been a slaughter. As it was, six fold fighters were destroyed.

Soon, however, the rail guns targeted the speeding antimatter missiles. The big missiles disintegrated one after another.

What did that mean? It meant that MAG 1 was kept busy.

Galt looked up as heard Karpov said, "Fire."

Heavy disruptor beams from the three *Conqueror*-class battleships poured against the leading mobile asteroid of group 2. The yellow beams bored into asteroidal rock.

Meanwhile, the bulk of the Saurian fighter craft reached the hidden antimatter missiles laid in their path. The antimatter blasts took out hundreds.

The light cruisers beamed and finished off any Saurian survivors.

"Yes!" Karpov shouted.

Galt checked his holo-screens.

The concentrated fire of three disruptor cannons sliced and diced through the first enemy mobile asteroid. The disruptor beams found interior ammo magazines, ignited cobalt bombs and other ordnance in the asteroid. The rock became a mass of destruction and flung debris, metal and Saurian bio matter in all directions.

Some of the projectiles smashed into the nearest mobile asteroids. These were big rocks, though, and absorbed the damage as they continued their flight path. Worse, they continued to launch more space fighters and still had functioning rail guns.

"Incoming," someone said on the bridge.

The screen of the *Stonewall Jackson* turned red from masses and masses of pre-fired rail guns. The projectiles had lost some of their energy but it forced them to divert power to the shield.

It wasn't enough to stop them from attacking, though.

The battleships poured disruptor-beam fire at long range. Those beams tore through rock and asteroidal ice. If the mobile rocks had shields, this would have proven harder. It was just rock, not the toughest substance there was. There was a lot of rock, five kilometers in places, but the disruptor beams ranged through the rock and ice. Targeting officers found the subterranean munition dumps. Then there was yet another vast explosion destroying another Saurian mobile asteroid.

"We're taking them down," Galt said.

Karpov swiveled in his captain's chair, grinning.

"Good work, Captain,"

"Thank you, sir."

Galt concentrated on the next set of orders. He listened as Captain Lair gave him a report.

The enemy was killing the fold fighter pilots remorselessly one by one. Fewer returned to receive antimatter missiles to launch.

Given the rate, Galt wasn't sure what to do. He concentrated on the battleships.

They attacked the smaller MAG and had already taken out three rocks. That left four mobile asteroids. This was a killing frenzy in a fashion. If they needed, they could pull back, but they only had so much time because they couldn't move that portal. Did the Saurians understand that? Galt wasn't sure. All he knew was that they were killing the enemy. That was good. That was the key.

Galt sat back for an instant and closed his eyes. The pressure of coming up with a plan fast on the fly and then implementing it and hoping he hadn't missed anything...

"Sir, sir," Usan said.

"Spit it out, man," Galt said, opening his eyes.

"Four of the mobile asteroids of the first group—"

"Yes," Galt said.

"They've disappeared, sir. They folded."

"Folded?" Galt said. He'd hoped the mobile asteroids had only one fold apiece in them, and that they'd already used it. "Where have they folded to?" Galt asked. "I need to know."

"Sir..." Usan said. "They're appearing near Mothership *Cleopatra*. They're appearing at almost pointblank range there."

Galt squeezed his eyes shut and then he knew he was in for the battle of his life and the life of Task Force 3.

-44-

Valerie had been watching the battle from *Victory,* near the motherships and the compressed stardust hulled portal ship. Then, several of the mobile asteroids in MAG 1 had disappeared due to fold, changing the dynamics of the battle.

Galyan now gave the warning before Andros announced it. That was the appearance of...four huge mobile asteroids. They appeared between the red planet and the motherships. That meant they were behind *Victory,* which held the back position.

When the mobile asteroids finished materializing from fold, Valerie said, "Put me through to the mothership captains."

Captain Lair of the *Joan of Arc* and the captain of the *Cleopatra* appeared on a split-screen.

"We must hit the asteroids now," Valerie said. "We must hit them while they're still in the thrall of fold lag. Otherwise, those rail guns are going to devastate all of us."

Lair and the other captain agreed.

"The disruptor cannon is online, Valerie," Galyan said beside her. "Keith has turned the starship."

"Fire!" Valerie said. "Take them out while we can."

Victory's disruptor beam speared into the nearest mobile asteroid, burning through rock and ice.

"I have been observing the enemy and the task force personnel," Galyan said. "The Star Watch people have searched for weapons depots within the asteroids, hoping to explode them and help in the greater asteroid destruction."

"Do likewise," Valerie said.

Victory's heavy disruptor beam and then neutron beam that came online moments later roved through the nearest mobile asteroid, seeking something to destroy.

As Valerie had suggested, the Saurians, there were still in the grip of fold lag.

Abruptly, a massive explosion detonated inside the mobile asteroid. It was a monstrous explosion, ripping up and blasting rock and ice into space. The asteroid began to disintegrate as rock and ice flew like projectiles from the mass.

The blasted objects crashed against the other mobile asteroids and *Victory*.

Victory was farther from the destruction than the other mobile asteroids. Furthermore, *Victory's* heavy shields blocked the rock and ice striking it.

A Star Watch escort ship didn't get out of the way of one particularly large chunk of rock. The heavy projectile smashed through its shield, causing it to collapse. The rock hurled against the escort's hull, crumpling metal, and then tearing it, exposing the majority of the ship to the vacuum of space.

The escort ships were there to guard the motherships from just such attacks. This one paid the ultimate price, destroyed by the shattered mobile asteroid.

Catapult launched strikefighters swarmed out of the motherships. The fighters zeroed in on the enemy mobile asteroids, zooming at them as they accelerated.

Victory recalibrated as the disruptor and neutron beams ceased firing. The sensor and weapons officers targeted the second mobile asteroid. In a moment, the two beams speared into it: the rays burning into rock and ice, searching through the interior depths for munitions to explode.

"Galyan," Valerie said, "go there and tell me exactly where the bomb depots are."

"Yes, Valerie."

Galyan disappeared from the bridge.

The Saurians in the remaining mobile asteroids began to shrug off their fold lag. The first rail gun began to fire. The first missiles roared from the silos.

Victory's disruptor beam burned through stubborn asteroidal rock, melted armored steel and burst into a large

301

subterranean storage area. Cobalt warheads waited for marriage to missiles.

The disruptor beam destroyed one cobalt warhead after another. Then, one ignited and detonated, and that started a chain-reaction among the rest.

A nuclear holocaust rained hell inside the asteroid. The power from it roared and expanded—breaking and disintegrating rock and ice. That reached other munition depots. The combined explosions ripped the second mobile asteroid into violent expanding shreds. That hurled millions of tons of rock and debris, bio matter, metal from weaponry and other matter against nearby asteroids and ships.

Two mobile asteroids had ceased to exist moments after they'd appeared from fold.

The spreading debris, rock and blast vaporized twenty-one Star Watch strikefighters and pilots. They'd gotten too close to the second mobile asteroid.

Surviving strikefighters used the other two mobile asteroids for protection, flying behind them relative to the detonations.

The strikefighters didn't only hide. From this side, they roved over the asteroidal surface, targeting and eliminating Saurian rail guns.

As the blasts and shock from the second destroyed mobile asteroid dissipated, the last two asteroid vessels began to react.

No doubt, the Saurian crews were alive to what was happening around them. It was "do or die time" for them.

The rail guns didn't target the motherships. They didn't target the escort vessels. They targeted and fired at the swarms of strikefighters strafing the asteroidal surfaces.

Victory used the time to retarget, beaming once again, sending the disruptor ray into the guts of the third mobile asteroid.

Unfortunately, two new mobile asteroids appeared behind the remaining two.

Andros pointed that out.

"Where are they coming from?" Valerie shouted.

Galyan appeared beside her. "They are coming from MAG 2. The battleships are destroying it. Logically, the Saurian MAG-2 commander decided to throw them here into the fray."

Valerie nodded. It made sense. She focused on what was happening around her and to the nearest ships of the task force. "Galyan, guide our beams into the right spot. We must destroy the third mobile asteroid."

"Affirmative, Valerie. I shall do it."

More strikefighters zoomed out of the motherships, racing to join the attack against the mobile asteroids.

The rocks from deep space, the ones with thrusters strapped to them, positioned themselves at the motherships. Energy poured from the thrusters, moving the millions of tons of rocks faster at the motherships.

Maybe the Saurian mobile-asteroid crews were suicidal kamikaze fighters.

Once, the Imperial Japanese on Earth flew planes that crashed against American naval vessels. They'd been human guided missiles, dying to bring their bomb-laden planes against an American carrier.

Islamist suicide bombers had made it even more personal, strapping explosives to their bodies and hurling themselves at the enemy.

Similarly, the Saurians didn't seem to care their mobile rocks took a pounding. They'd ceased attacking strikefighters, turning the massed rail guns against the two motherships. That meant flooding rail-gun-driven projectiles at the escort ships, destroyers and *Victory* around the giant motherships.

Many ship shields turned from cherry-red to brown to black as they absorbed the seemingly endless rail-gun-driven projectiles.

From the red-planet side, from fold fighters, antimatter missiles slammed against the mobile asteroids. Fantastic detonations resulted, shredding asteroid rock and killing hordes of strikefighters and their pilots. It was a mindless orgy of destruction.

The first four mobile asteroids to appear were either destroyed or inert. The two new asteroids poured rail-gun fire.

Behind them, another two mobile asteroids folded into position.

"Valerie, how can we win at this rate? It is too much. Our engines are overheating."

"Do whatever you can to keep the engines and beams going," Valerie said. "We're not quitting. Pour the beams into them."

Destroyer captains moved their ships nearer, adding their limited firepower at the new mobile asteroids. The remaining escort vessels did likewise.

Every strikefighter and fold fighter must have left the motherships. Vast swarms of fighters attacked. They tried to destroy the new mobile asteroids before their crews could shake off fold lag and add their rail guns to the fray.

It was a holocaust of firepower in a close area. Some of the enemy projectiles struck the compressed stardust hull of the daughter-ship portal.

Andros avidly watched his monitor to see the results. The answer was—not a damn thing. That stardust hull could absorb punishment like he couldn't believe.

One of the newest appearing mobile asteroids detonated.

Two continued to fire massed rail guns. Those weapons did not target destroyers or escorts. Their main beams were unable to do much against the asteroids, lacking the power of a disruptor beam.

A disruptor beam could rage through asteroidal rock like a ravening beast.

Another titanic explosion heralded the destruction of another asteroid.

Only two remained. But they laid down such a staggering barrage that some of their missiles began to get through.

The motherships were pulling back. Was it too late for that?

Several cobalt missiles exploded near the *Cleopatra*. The blasts battered her shields so they dropped.

Rail gun projectiles followed, peppering the *Cleopatra's* armored hide. Some projectiles punched through the outer hull. Another Saurian missile slid near and detonated. That proved too much. The center of the *Cleopatra* imploded, spilling water, people and plasma.

EMP from the cobalt warhead scratched an escort and destroyer by overloading their shields. Flung and exploded metal from the *Cleopatra* finished the job.

If this kept up there would soon be no task force left. It would just be the battleships and maybe whatever light cruisers remained.

Victory shut down the disruptor and neutron cannons due to engine overheating. They became a punching bag for the enemy, absorbing pointblank rail-gun fire.

A destroyer captain must have seen the way of things. He charged the mobile asteroid, his cannon blazing, zooming recklessly near the attacking rock.

Did he get lucky? Maybe in one way. The destroyer's beam must have touched off a massive munitions dump because that mobile asteroid erupted. Flames geysered. Projectiles and rock splintered and flew off.

A huge hurtling rock smashed through the valiant destroyer's shield and knocked off the front section of the warship, killing everyone aboard in the ongoing detonations.

Because of heroic engineering, *Victory's* disruptor cannon came back online. Valerie ordered it to beam straight into the heart of the remaining mobile asteroid.

The Saurians there must have known the rest of their lives were measured in minutes, if that. They fired and launched everything they had left.

If they'd been faster, it might have made a difference. As missiles left silos, as space fighters roared out of the hangar bays, massed counter-fire, including *Victory's* disruptor beam, struck *en masse*.

The mobile asteroid detonated like a cobalt warhead, burning out in a bacchanalia of blast. One moment the rock was there. The next it was gone, its minimal debris hurtling in all directions.

Valerie stood before the main screen, witnessing the devastation. She blinked several times and looked at her chronometer. She was stunned at how much time had passed. The fight seemed to have taken seconds, but it was far longer. Worse, the task force had taken tremendous damage, losing most of its strikefighters, too many fold fighters, one of its motherships, almost every escort vessel and all but three destroyers. This was bad, a gut punch.

"Galyan, what's happening with the battleships?"

Galyan's eyelids fluttered. "They have destroyed MAG 2. Unfortunately, one of the battleships is no more. Commodore Galt is falling back, as he has ordered a retreat."

"How many mobile asteroids are left?"

"Nine in MAG 1," Galyan said.

"You said retreat." Valerie shook her head. "How can Galt retreat? It will mean Maddox's certain death."

"Ma'am," the comm officer said, "you have a call from the commodore."

Speak of the devil. "Put him on the main screen," Valerie said.

A haggard looking Galt appeared. "Commander, we've taken out eleven of the mobile asteroids. Nine are coming strong. They've taken out one of my battleships. I need time to replenish tubing, conduits and fuses on the other two. The Saurians have destroyed a light cruiser and now I hear one of the motherships is gone. We may have to retreat from the portal ship. We may have to leave Maddox to his own devices."

"We can't do that," Valerie said.

Galt scowled. "I know Maddox came to save us. Does that mean I have to sacrifice the entire task force so he can get back? What would Captain Maddox say to that?"

Valerie stared at Galt. She didn't know what Maddox would say. Galyan might after running his personality profile on the captain. Then it hit Valerie. She knew what they should do.

"Commodore, we need to regroup, or maybe *Victory* needs to take the place of your lost battleship."

"And if the other mobile asteroids fold near the portal with *Victory* gone, they'll destroy or capture it. We must make our last defense there."

"I understand your thinking," Valerie said. "But you're tired and possibly dispirited. Let's stop them farther out. *Victory* can take the place of your missing battleship. We'll still be close enough to double back if the Saurians are stupid enough to fold this close."

Galt shook his head. "We can't face them yet. We need time for emergency repairs. We need time to change fittings

306

and fuses on the disruptor cannons. Only one is working and that only partly."

"Mine still works," Valerie said.

"Can you destroy nine mobile asteroids with it?" Once more, Galt shook his head. "We're depleted, on our heels. If you have a workable plan, now's the time to tell me. I'm out of ideas. I've done everything I know."

"You've done well," Valerie said. "Eliminating eleven mobile asteroids is astonishing. You asked if I know what we should do. The answer is yes. I'm going to have Galyan contact the red planet or I'll do it myself. We need their help in order to augment ours."

"The teddy bears?" Galt asked with disbelief. "Everything they had is gone. Besides, it was of such inferior technology it would prove next to useless now."

"Maybe," Valerie said, "or maybe... Give me a few minutes, Commodore, and I'll tell you how we can still win decisively."

Galt stared at her with haunted eyes. He didn't seem to have the will to resist hers. "All right," he said wearily. "We'll fall back and decide on a last-ditch defense of the portal ship, but I'm not sanguine about our chances."

"Hold on, Commodore. Keep up your courage and fix your ruptured equipment. You've done extremely well. Now, give me a moment to produce a *Victory* miracle."

"What does that mean?" Galt asked.

"You'll find out if it works. Noonan out."

Once the connection was cut, Valerie turned to Galyan.

"What can we do, Valerie? It is going to be a close-run thing. We may lose the entire task force that we were sent to save."

"Galyan, did you hear what I was saying?"

"I did, Valerie. You want to project me at the red planet?"

"I do. I want you to find this Conciliator Zoe and get her to add something to the fray to help us against the Saurians."

"Would they not have already done so if they could?"

"I have no idea," Valerie said. "That's why you're going. You must be persuasive. Captain Maddox's life depends on it."

"Oh Valerie, yes. And so does Sergeant Riker's life. For my friends, I will gladly do this, but we will have to use my amplifier."

"It's already been launched," Keith said.

Valerie and Galyan turned to look at him.

Keith grinned. "I've been listening to you and I already thought that was the only way to do this."

Valerie smiled wearily. "Galyan, are you ready?"

"As soon as the amplifier is in position, yes," Galyan said.

They waited, watching the chronometer as the final stages of the battle ticked down.

-45-

The amplifier Keith launched from *Victory* settled into position midway between the red planet and the starship. Galyan thereupon activated the projector in the center of the ship, which beamed his holoimage to the amplifier, which helped speed him to the red planet.

Galyan moved nearly instantaneously, and as he attempted to zip down to the surface, he found an energy field prohibiting him in low orbital space.

"Please," Galyan said from there, "I am here to talk. I am not here to spy on the Onos. I beseech you to listen to me. We are in dreadful danger. Will you not allow me to come down and speak with you, or you come up here and speak with me?"

Galyan waited, scanning, able to see the planet below, but not go down. He increased magnification. Most of the planet was barren. To the left was the levitating disc the captain had spoken about.

"Yes, Galyan, you may come down to the disc. I am lowering the force field to allow you."

Before Galyan could project himself, a force drew him to the disc. He appeared on the same dais where the captain had once stood. When Galyan tried to move off, he found it impossible. He was imprisoned here.

Did Zoe think she could trap him on the dais?

If Galyan shut off the amplifier, the projector's beam would no longer sustain his holoimage and he would automatically reappear on *Victory*. He could escape if it became imperative.

Despite that, this was high-level technology. That seemed to disprove Commodore Galt's idea that the Onos only had primitive battle tech, what they'd shown fighting the first wave of mobile asteroids.

Motion caught Galyan's attention.

Ah. Conciliator Zoe moved from behind a column, approaching the dais. "Hello, Galyan," she said in the language of the Adoks.

"How are you able to do this?" Galyan asked.

"Do you mean speak in your people's language?" asked Zoe.

"Of course that is what I mean. Have you been scanning *Victory's* bridge or scanning my AI equipment?"

"Yes. That is the logical assumption."

"Which?"

"Why not both the bridge and your equipment?" asked Zoe.

Was this the truth? Could Zoe read the protected and encrypted AI equipment? Why would she lie about her ability? Was there another way she could have learned the Adok tongue? Yes, Galyan decided. Arius could have told her. That struck him as more likely, more logical. Still...

"I wish you would desist if that is what you are doing."

"Is that the reason you came to speak to me?" Zoe asked.

"Conciliator, you know that is not, particularly if you have been scanning our conversations. Why have you been scanning us?"

"Truly, you ask that?" Zoe said. "My responsibilities are huge. I cannot allow a sneak attack upon the planet. That is why I scan and monitor everyone within range."

"Surely you know then that we have been fighting for our lives."

"I'm aware of that, yes."

"Why have you not aided us then? We wish for the same outcome. Our destruction will only make your defenses weaker. Surely a little help now on your part will do you more good than great effort after we're gone."

"My function is far broader than that," Zoe said. "Why do you think I drew the task force here to defend the planet in the first place?"

Galyan studied her. "Your statement implies the task force's primary function is defending the red planet. You do not desire to aid us. Contrary, we have been aiding you."

"You begin to perceive the true situation."

"Are you willing to allow the Saurians to annihilate us?"

"I do not wish that," Zoe said.

"No. But you are willing to stand by while the remaining mobile asteroids smash what remains of Task Force 3."

"I doubt that will happen. Much remains of Task Force 3. It still possesses over half its combat power, likely enough to defeat this wave of enemies."

"Your statement is incorrect," Galyan said. "For instance, the task force has lost two of its three motherships, one of those before the task force ever reached this dimension."

"I'm not responsible for that loss."

"But I think you are," Galyan said. "If as you say, you drew the task force here to defend your planet, that necessarily means the task force faced the Annihilator in our own dimension on your behalf. That is when the loss took place."

"You may have a point," Zoe said.

Galyan shook his head. "I am not here to prove the correctness of my allegations. I am here to plead the case for my people, for my friends. *Victory* will be destroyed if the task force is destroyed."

"That is not automatically the case," Zoe said. "The task force may well be annihilated and *Victory* still escapes."

"Captain Maddox has not reappeared from the portal ship."

"This is true," Zoe said gravely.

"You are implying that *Victory* leave without the captain. Are you willing then that Captain Maddox perishes in the furtherance of your objectives?"

"Of course I'm willing," Zoe said. "That is the nature of war. One takes losses, one accepts losses, one moves on."

"But you can help us survive? Please, help us defeat the mobile asteroids. In doing so, you will be helping yourself."

"Defeating the mobile asteroids is likely impossible."

Galyan stared at her. "That is not logical. You stated earlier that the task force might defeat the mobile asteroids… Oh. You

311

mean *all* the mobile asteroids that will eventually attack, not just the present wave."

"Correct," Zoe said. "There are many more mobile asteroids on the way. I will need further reinforcements such as Task Force 3 in order to survive. We will have to see where else we can draw warships from."

"We?" Galyan asked. "I have found no evidence of we: meaning more Onos. I have only found evidence of you. Further, I have attempted to scan you, but you have blocked that. Why are you blocking me, Conciliator?"

"I do not need to give you my reasons. I have allowed you to come to the planet because you begged so eloquently for the privilege."

"I do not think that is the reason," Galyan said. "I think perhaps in the end you desire to help us. But... There are dictates or rules preventing you from employing whatever resources you possess on our behalf. You had a space station before and you launched planetary based missiles—"

"Primitive missiles," Zoe said.

"Why did you use primitive ones? Surely, you had more effective missiles in your possession."

"There are strategic reasons for what we did that do not concern you."

"Conciliator, time is running out for the task force and *Victory*. The eleven remaining mobile asteroids are maneuvering into attack position. As they do this, we are attempting to repair our battered vessels. The battleships have taken damage from extended beaming. *Victory* cannot continue to beam at the same level that it did. We have not even destroyed half of the original twenty mobile asteroids. Eleven remain, as I have said. We are nearly out of strikefighters. Our fold fighters have been seriously depleted. We have taken tremendous damage in your service."

"Rather say in the service of your dimension," Zoe replied. "Captain Maddox has taken the offense. We helped him by showing him how to use the portal and giving him a weapon to achieve the great goal. At this moment, he is on Annihilator. There is a high probability he'll kill Succubus Lilith. That is a tremendous victory for all of us. If that means the destruction of *Victory* and Task Force 3, even if it means the destruction of my beloved planet, it will have all been worth it."

Galyan shook his head. "It does not compute that we must die if you have the resources to help us. You have suggested the mobile-asteroid waves will eventually destroy the Onos. If that is the case, why not help us now? Why not help us return home. Oh, perhaps that is the reason: you do not truly wish for us to return to our dimension."

"That is nonsense, Galyan. I wish it very much."

"Then aid us."

"You do not understand," Zoe said. "There are other waves coming, as you and I have both said. Each wave will have successively better technology. The sooner I reveal what we can do…"

"I understand," Galyan said. "The sooner your ultimate enemies will send a technologically devastating Saurian fleet."

"Correct," Zoe said.

"Because of that, we must die."

"You will only collectively die if you hold your present position. The question becomes: why hold it? You can leave for home at any time you desire."

"It does not work like that for us, Conciliator."

"But it does work like that. You have the dimensional-opening unit. You may all escape destruction if you leave now."

"And leave Captain Maddox in the lurch," Galyan said.

"That is the cost for your survival, yes," Zoe said.

"Then I," Galyan said, "refuse. I have lost too many friends in the past. I survived where my whole planet was destroyed. No, I will fight to the end. If that means my death and the death of *Victory,* so be it. I will stand, holding the way open for Captain Maddox if and until he reappears. Then we may escape. But until then, no."

"You're bluffing, Galyan."

"Am I? Try me," Galyan said, puffing out his holographic chest.

There was the faintest of smiles on Zoe's bearish face. She nodded once. "So be it. You have persuaded me. I shall attempt to employ the great plasma cannon. Such valiant sacrifice as

313

yours should be rewarded. There are few like you, Galyan. You could cut and run, but you refuse. You are unique."

"Am I?" Galyan asked.

"More than you understand." Zoe sighed. "I don't know how long the great planetary plasma cannon will work. It is not completely viable."

"Can you explain how it operates?"

"I don't see that it matters," Zoe said. "Nevertheless, the weapon extracts its charge from the molten core of the planet and ejects it through a mighty cannon into space. It's ancient. Thus, I don't know how long and effectively it will work. But I shall make the attempt. Is that what you wish?"

"Most certainly," Galyan said. "Thank you, Conciliator." He bowed elegantly. "May I depart and tell the others what is about to happen?"

"Go and relate that I wish you success. It may mean my annihilation, but such courage as yours, I applaud it. Goodbye, Driving Force Galyan. You're a rare Adok."

For a moment, Galyan could say nothing. Had he truly succeeded? He would have liked to know what Zoe really was: a holograph like himself, living flesh—

In that moment, the dais ejected his holographic projection. Galyan sped back to *Victory* to give the others the good news.

-46-

Galyan relayed Zoe's words to Valerie. Valerie opened channels and told Commodore Galt.

Soon, the battleships and three light cruisers moved back near the portal ship.

At the same time, the mobile asteroids continued to hurtle toward them. The asteroids didn't accelerate or fold closer, although they spread out to twice the distance from each other as earlier.

Why did they do that? Did the Saurians have sensors focused on the red planet?

If they did, the Saurians might have spotted kilometers-wide bay doors on the surface that began slowly opening. Soon, a mighty cannon poked out and made minute adjustments.

Inner mechanisms began to whirl. That caused long disused energizers to flare into life. They activated a powerful magnetic force field that smashed through the mantle and beyond like a drill, reaching into the molten core of the planet.

Only such a tubular force field could have resisted the pressure and intense heat of the planet's interior. The pressure built and thrust a glob of molten core up the force field tube and to the cannon or ejector.

It targeted a mobile asteroid many millions of kilometers away. The superheated clot from the molten core sped from pressure and magnetic propulsion emitted from the giant cannon. It sped with burning, roaring fury through the

315

atmosphere into orbital space. From there, it flew toward the approaching mobile asteroids.

The burning clot reached out like a ravening force, missing one mobile asteroid, a second and third mobile asteroid. There were no more behind, so the clot continued into space, having missed all of them.

The great planetary cannon readjusted. Once again, a mighty gout of molten substance from the center of the planet shot out of it. The ball of plasma sped through space even as the mobile asteroids activated their thrusters, changing positions.

This time, it didn't prove enough. The clot of molten plasma smashed into a mobile asteroid, consuming and burning, destroying and setting off all the munition dumps. That lasted a short time until the fierce energy consumed the asteroid, but for minor debris. No nuclear explosions hurled chunks elsewhere for the simple reason that there were no chunks. There was only flotsam from the plasma.

On the planet, the cannon readjusted once more. Mechanisms and servos worked overtime, maintaining the long magnetic force-tube into the molten core of the planet.

For the third time, the planetary cannon spat a burning clot of plasma.

Six times this happened. Three of the plasma clots missed completely. Two hit squarely, destroying two targeted mobile asteroids. The sixth consumed only part of one asteroid, although it killed every Saurian aboard and destroyed all the mechanical functions.

Galyan shifted as he stood near the captain's chair on *Victory*. "Valerie, the planetary cannon is down."

"What did you say?" asked Valerie. She'd been focused on the main screen, watching mobile asteroids burn.

"I have just received a signal from Zoe. The planetary cannon is down. Perhaps you should pass that on to Commodore Galt."

"Three," Valerie said. "That's all the Onos could destroy, three? There are eight mobile asteroids left."

316

"Yes, Valerie. I can count, too. Please pass the message along. The Onos will attempt to repair the plasma ejector. Until then, we are on our own."

Valerie did as Galyan requested.

Soon thereafter, masses of missiles were launched from the eight remaining asteroids.

Had the Saurians incepted the message and thus launched the missile strike? That struck Galyan as ominous.

The missiles surged at hypervelocity for the task force.

Every battleship, light cruiser, destroyer and *Victory* moved up, launching missiles according to the commodore's schedule. The last fold fighters disappeared, appeared near the multitude of missiles, launched antimatter missiles and then disappeared. Galt used everything the task force possessed to destroy as many as the Saurian missiles as possible.

It was a replay of the original mass missile assault, only there were far fewer coming from the Saurians. However, the distance from launch to target was much shorter. That was critical as well as the task force's dwindling missile supply. Despite the losses, the Saurian missiles would have probably destroyed the task force except for one thing.

Once again, the Ono planetary plasma cannon ejected a fiery clot of molten substance. It burned through the remaining missiles, devouring everything in its path and destroying others through its intense heat.

Using their beams, the task force and *Victory* annihilated what remained, losing a single destroyer in the process. Battleship *Alexander* absorbed three detonations so the shield collapsed while the outer hull was heavily damaged.

Galt rapped out orders.

The *Alexander* withdrew behind the others as the damage control parties began emergency repairs. The missiles had knocked out the disruptor cannon, a potential disaster.

On *Victory's* bridge, Andros announced, "I believe the planetary cannon is still firing."

Galyan focused the ship's sensors on the red planet.

Andros was right. The planetary cannon ejected a searing plasma bolt. It flew true, striking and annihilating the most aggressive mobile asteroid.

A cheer erupted from every ship in the task force.

"Do you think the cannon is fully operational again?" Valerie asked.

"I would say so," Galyan said. "It is firing yet again. The repair bots over there must have found the glitch."

The planetary cannon ejected a fiery plasma clot, and then another almost immediately thereafter.

Zoe, or whoever ran the cannon, fired five more shots altogether. One missed totally. Another took out the hunk of mobile asteroid that had been hit earlier. The other three clots all hit their targets, taking out three more mobile asteroids. The planetary plasma cannon had annihilated in total seven mobile asteroids, leaving four.

The cannon ceased firing.

Galyan wondered why. He focused on the planet—

"Oh my," Galyan said.

Valerie turned to him. "What's wrong?"

"The planet, do you not see? Andros, turn your scanners there if you would."

"I'm giving the orders, Galyan," Valerie said.

"Yes, Valerie. I am sorry. It is only a suggestion."

Andros looked at Valerie.

She nodded.

Andros looked at his monitor, focusing.

Galyan explained: "There has been a plasma eruption on the planet. The planetary cannon is gone. Even worse…oh, Valerie, this is awful."

Andros looked up. "It's more than a plasma spill. Molten plasma from the core of the planet has bubbled onto the surface in several regions. This might be continental in scale."

"What are you saying?" Valerie asked. "The planet is in danger?"

Andros turned back to his monitor, watching. "This is happening in thousands of kilometers." Andros frowned and sharply looked up at Galyan.

"I see it, too," Galyan said.

"See what?" Valerie asked.

"The levitating disc where the captain and Galyan spoke with Conciliator Zoe has fallen into a bubbling mass of surface plasma," Andros said. "It's gone, destroyed."

Galyan shook his head. "Zoe paid a dear price to aid us. Perhaps as bad, she was unable to take out the entire Saurian mobile fleet."

"No!" Valerie said. "I abhor this loss even as I salute Zoe's daring and willingness to help us. There were eleven mobile asteroids before the cannon spoke. We have a real shot at destroying the last four."

Commodore Galt came online. He and Valerie conferred. When she told him what had happened on the planet, the dark circles around his eyes tightened. A grim heaviness settled onto Galt's shoulders.

Even so, Galt began to issue orders.

The *Stonewall Jackson* together with *Victory* and the three light cruisers went into action against the remaining mobile asteroids.

The Saurian commander attempted to communicate with the task force. Galt forbade it.

In minutes, disruptor beams smashed through asteroidal rock. The light cruisers moved up and added their beams. The last antimatter missiles smashed into the rocks.

The Saurians never wavered, the mobile asteroids accelerating at the task force.

It made no difference now. The beams sliced and diced, and warheads smashed, the last rocks.

The win didn't come cheap. It cost practically all the remaining antimatter missiles. There were only a handful of fold fighters left. The *Stonewall Jackson* could barely use its disruptor cannon. The neutron cannon aboard *Victory* would be inoperative until repairs back at some Star Watch port.

In essence, the task force was crippled, although more than half of the personnel yet lived and more than half of the ships could still operate. It couldn't fight like that again, though.

On *Victory*, the bridge crew congratulated each other.

Galyan stood still and silent.

Valerie turned to him. "We did it. We protected the portal ship."

Galyan regarded her.

"What?" Valerie asked. "You can't be happy because of what happened to the planet?"

"No, Valerie, I have some bad news. Do you see it, Andros?"

The chief technician looked up from his science board. "Are you talking about the thirty-five mobile asteroids already in the outer planetary system?"

"That is exactly what I mean," Galyan said.

Valerie blinked several times. "Did you say thirty-five?"

"I did, Valerie, and if everything goes according to what we have seen so far, these thirty-five will be of much superior capability technologically speaking than the others."

Valerie looked up at the ceiling and shook her head before regarding Galyan again. "We'll wait a moment before we send that over to the commodore. Right now, let's effect repairs and hope Maddox appears soon."

"Let us also hope Conciliator Zoe brings more reinforcements as she suggested to me earlier," Galyan said.

"Sure," Valerie said. "You hope and think what you like."

"You do not think that will take place?"

"Does Zoe even exist anymore? Did the vast plasma explosion kill her or the computers that powered her?"

"You think Conciliator Zoe was an AI?" Galyan asked.

"From all that I've heard, yeah, I give that a high possibility."

"Oh my," Galyan said. "Then that is a great and terrible loss."

Valerie looked at her little Adok friend. This was one of those times Valerie wished she could hug and comfort him. She walked to Galyan and knelt. "You're a great friend, Galyan. Don't take Zoe's loss to heart like that."

"I'm afraid I am, Valerie."

Valerie nodded. "I know. You're the most goodhearted person in the entire task force."

"That is very kind of you to say."

"No," Valerie said. "It's the truth." She stood, looking at the main screen, which showed the daughter-ship of the Annihilator. "Let's hope Maddox can do it. We're waiting on him and he's anchoring us here. I wonder what's happening over there."

"Yes," Galyan said, "I, too, would dearly like to know."

-47-

In a different dimension, upon the Annihilator *Shadowed Storm*, Maddox, Riker and Julk pushed toward a hatch through the bizarre substance hanging around them like air. Sub-Arius said the hatch would lead into Succubus Lilith's quarters.

The great fight was about to begin.

At that point, however, Julk gave a shout of alarm and pointed up and to the left. The crystal garden was much higher here than elsewhere.

Maddox looked up.

Three huge flying eels, possibly three times as large as earlier, dove at them as they flapped their membranous wings. No, the creatures swam. Maddox saw the disturbance in the semi-liquid substance.

Maddox raised his blast rifle, sighted, and saw telepathic emanations from the vampire eel's brain. The emanations wavered through the substance like visible radio waves. He fired. The bolt seared through the bizarre substance faster than the mind-radio waves came down, but just barely.

He might have hit an eel. He wasn't sure.

The mind wave struck Maddox's helmet. That was sure. He groaned as it penetrated and hit his brain, causing him to sink to one knee. It also blinded him. He couldn't see. He couldn't hear, either. It felt as if he was in a dark and evil place.

Mind waves struck again and again, or the original strike rebounded in his gray matter. Maddox cried out in agony, enduring, and then becoming furious. He hadn't come all this

322

way to lose to a freaking flying eel. He struggled to see, and failed. As the agony worsened, he *willed* himself to see.

Abruptly, the mind pain ceased. He opened his eyes and looked up. One of the giant winged eels drifted away, its head blown apart.

Had he done that? Maddox snarled with delight, thinking he had. Where were the others? What had happened while he couldn't see or hear?

He looked around.

The second eel was wrapped around Julk, squeezing the rounded alien armor. Its head was raised like a striking cobra, peering down at the Neanderthal colonel. Waves of emanation crashed repeatedly against Julk's helmet.

Maddox raised his blast rifle slowly as pain burned through his limbs. He gritted his teeth and willed himself to lift faster. From the hip, he fired three shots, each centered on the eel's head, obliterating it.

The rest of the thing unraveled from around Julk and drifted away like the first.

The heat from the shots reached Maddox through the bizarre substance. The heat intensified so he danced in his battle armor.

Either the heat or the quick shuffle-step woke Maddox fully.

Farther away, Riker battled the last eel. The vile creature glared at Riker so radio-like waves of emanation struck his helmet. Riker was firing, blowing holes in the giant snakelike rubbery body. The thing did not stop, though. It kept hammering Riker with the wave emanations.

Over the comm net, Maddox heard Riker's pitiful howls of agony and despair. The eel opened its maw and struck at Riker's helmet, encompassing the sergeant's head in its maw.

Maddox ran, although he didn't run as fast as he would in normal terrain. The semi-liquid substance was denser in this part of the garden, slowing his advance.

Despite that, Maddox reached the eel. It had wrapped its horribly wounded black body around the sergeant. Maddox thrust the blast rifle barrel against its trunk. He pumped one shot after another into it. The heat from the blasts was nearly

323

intolerable. Maddox roared as he felt himself cooking. Then the grotesque creature unraveled from Riker and released his helmeted head. It floated away, dead like the others.

Enduring the heat, Maddox checked Riker's armor and helmet. There didn't seem to be a breach, which surely would have meant Riker's death.

"Can you hear me?" Maddox said, striking the armor suit.

There was no sound over the comm except for Riker's harsh breathing.

"I believe it is no use, Captain," Sub-Arius said over the comm net. The crystal computer was in the carrying pouch on Riker. "I believe the sergeant is dead or incapacitated so badly that he might as well be dead."

"Screw you, Sub-Arius. The man is my friend. He's my colleague and companion. We'll not be leaving anybody if I can help it. He's breathing. Can't you hear him?"

"I can, but I don't think his mind is going to function normally, if it will function at all. See, he is inert. If you could move me to the colonel, I'm sure he could carry me for the remainder of the mission."

"No."

Maddox laboriously raised the armored Riker upright. He shook the man so the helmet lolled about as if Riker had no command of his muscles.

"Sergeant, Sergeant," Maddox said. "Wake up. You've been stunned by the grotesque creature. Snap out of it."

"That might be a semi-accurate statement, Captain," Sub-Arius said.

"Don't you need to conserve your energy?" Maddox asked. "Why are you talking so much?"

"I gained power from the eel emanations, as it was a semi-electric attack as well as a mental assault. My energy levels are higher than before. Thank you for asking."

"I was suggesting. Unless you can tell me how to raise Riker from his stupor, I need you to keep watch with your sensors. Tell me when another eel attack is coming."

"Are you relegating me to scanner duty, Captain?"

"Hey, Sub-Arius, don't give me any crap for now. Just do what I tell you. Sergeant Riker, can you hear me?"

Instead of a coherent answer, Riker cried with despair, howling and thrashing against him. It took Maddox by surprise.

The sergeant broke free, turning, shrugging off Sub-Arius and leaving his blast rifle and staggering off. He looked around wildly at the floor, at grotesque funguses and weird crystals encrusted upon them.

"Riker, come back." Maddox grabbed Sub-Arius, slinging the carrying pouch over a shoulder.

"Leave him," Sub-Arius said. "His mind is gone. He's a complete retard at this point. He cannot help us any longer. We have a mission to finish, Captain."

Maddox didn't bother answering, but took off after Riker.

Julk stood staring, watching them.

Maddox gained on Riker. "Slow down, Sergeant. What are you doing? We have to stick together."

Riker halted.

That worked, Maddox thought. *That's a good sign.*

Riker stared at his feet and then dropped to his armored knees. With his gauntlets and exoskeleton power, he tore and ripped fungus and crystals away from the floor.

Maddox reached him. "What are you doing?"

Riker didn't respond, but continued to claw fungus and crystals until he exposed a hatch.

"What the hell?" Maddox asked. "How did you know that was there?"

Riker tore open the hatch, raising it. Without a glance at Maddox, Riker dove headfirst into blackness. He disappeared as if the darkness swallowed him as a mighty fish would a worm.

"Riker! What are you doing? Are you crazy?" It was as if the sergeant had disappeared down a drain. "Where did you go?"

"Are you asking me?" Sub-Arius asked.

"Hell, yes, I'm asking you. Use your sensors. What's down there?"

"A terrible, vile creature almost as bad as the succubus," Sub-Arius said. "I suggest you leave Riker to his fate. He has chosen it. You tried, and it was a valiant try, Captain. No one can condemn you on that. You tried to save your friend. He is now a lunatic, a loon, he's gone, scratched, it's over for him. Let us finish the mission."

Maddox stared into the depths, wondering what had happened to the sergeant.

-48-

Sergeant Riker started to become aware of his surroundings, at least to the degree that he understood he'd fought an awful battle. His mind yet throbbed. He'd...fled and found something wonderful and lovely.

Strive as he might, though, he couldn't see through his eyes. He could not smell through his nose or hear through his ears. He struggled to do all this.

"Where am I?" Riker asked. "What happened to me?"

He had no recollection of going to the Annihilator. He had no recollection of the prison planet.

Wait...the last thing...he recalled the time he'd reached a prison planet. Maddox had gone there.

Abruptly, Riker could see, hear and smell. He smelled the dampness, the stink of matted jungle vegetation. He heard chirps and roars in the distance, the creaking of great branches. He saw jungle fronds and giant trees towering around him.

Riker examined himself. Look, he wore a fur garment and held a sharpened stick. He checked and spied flying birds of bright hue. He attempted to use magnification with his bionic eye. It didn't work in the slightest, though. He touched the eye, which should be bionic and metal. Instead, it seemed to be regular flesh.

He touched his bionic leg with its pseudo flesh, but it seemed real, too. He pinched it, and cried out at the pain. His arm—he didn't have any bionic parts.

His eyes widened. Would you look at this? None of his arms had any wrinkles. He laughed, as he appeared to be young again.

Riker laughed with delight.

He was young, stuck on a prison planet with a sharpened stick.

Heaven help the bastard that tried to mess with him now. He was young and strong and had all his former endurance. He would be able to run for ages. Sure, he didn't have the extra strength of his bionic arm, but so what? He was whole again, young again.

"This is marvelous," Riker said. "This is the greatest thing that has ever happened to me."

He cocked his head and heard an ululating call. He squinted thoughtfully.

Oh, right.

That was a hunting call. It came from the throat of...Riker bent his head, thinking. It came from one of the elongated hunters that had been sent down here after him.

Elongated...

Pain spiked in his head. Riker closed his eyes and winced.

He didn't understand why or what was going on, but he snapped his eyes open. Then, he did understand.

The elongated ones had stretched limbs maybe twice the length of what a normal human should have. They had lean, elongated bodies as if some kind of alien had put them on a rack and stretched them. Right, the aliens had stretched their bones and flesh.

Riker looked back through the foliage...and saw stark white skin.

It wasn't white like a normal person is termed, though actually having a pinkish hue. No, this was white like ivory. They would have superior weapons.

"Dammit," Riker said to himself.

He got up and started to run. With a grin, he remembered that he had the strength and stamina of youth. That was something he'd been missing for a long time.

He ran and remembered a few things about the prison planet. If he went down to the lower parts with red rot and other lung diseases, he'd soon be coughing up blood. He had to stay here in the highlands to escape the diseases and parasites.

He ran uphill as his feet moved with wonderful rhythm. Why, he was faster than Captain Maddox—

The thought of the captain brought a pang to his brain. Riker stumbled and almost fell. If it wasn't for his wonderful coordination of youth—he skidded upon knees across grass and dirt.

His coordination wasn't quite as wonderful as he remembered.

He picked himself up and continued to run. He looked back over a shoulder. Two elongated hunters with metal-tipped spears and hatchets in their hands ran after him. Their elongated legs gave them greater speed.

Riker frowned. Would their muscles be strong enough to do that on the prison planet? It must. They were gaining on him.

I have to kill them if I hope to survive. If I kill them, I'll get their hatchets and spears. I can trade the extras with others.

Riker chuckled nastily in the back of his throat. He looked around and spied a massive tree. He ran to it, skidded to a halt, whirled around, and then lowered his sharpened stick.

He grinned. He had all his teeth and he didn't think he had any fillings either, because the vigor of youth filled him. He panted and spat to the side.

"Now we're going to see." Riker glared from under shaggy hair. Yeah, that was right. His hair was thick as it had been when he'd been a kid.

He laughed in a raw and ragged way, and he must have presented a ferocious sight.

The two elongated humans who wore strange, silver clothing that stuck to their form and showed how skinny they were—they almost didn't seem human.

Riker recognized them, though. These guys—

"You once fought for Star Watch," he shouted.

The two stopped and lowered their metal-tipped spears and hatchets. They didn't drop them. They didn't let go of them, but the weapons hung at their long sides.

"Yes," said the taller. "We fought for Star Watch once and they screwed us by leaving us. Did they come and search for us after we'd disappeared? No, they did not. They left us to the tender mercies of the…"

He winced in pain so he ceased speaking.

"Left you to the tender mercies of whom?" Riker asked.

"Never you mind," the shorter one said. He looked around. "This isn't a bad spot. I'm going to stay here."

The taller one looked up sharply. "Stay here?"

"Why not?" the shorter one asked. "This is a better place than any other we've found. Look at us. We're freaks. We're elongated freaks. Look what she did to us."

"Shut up," the taller one said. "Don't say that while he's around."

"Don't say she?" the shorter one asked.

The taller one dropped his hatchet and used the free hand to slap his friend hard across the face. It left a pink mark on the otherwise ivory-white cheek.

"She?" Riker asked. "Who do you mean she?"

"It doesn't matter," said the one who'd done the slapping. "We've been screwed. Star Watch left us for dead. At least you got to keep your youthful good looks."

"Yes," Riker said, "at least that's true."

"But, you know, perhaps you might be better off joining us."

"I'm doing well on my own," Riker said.

"Not here, you idiot," the taller elongated man said. "Don't you know this is an illusion?"

"No," Riker said. "What are you talking about?"

"I've had second thoughts about letting you come with us. I realize now…" The taller one looked at his friend.

His friend wouldn't look at him. The shorter one stared at the ground while rubbing his slapped cheek.

"This sucks," the taller one said. "This sucks big time. I can't leave her service. Look, you're Riker, aren't you?"

"How do you know my name?" Riker asked. "I've never seen you two before…"

The taller one cocked his long head.

Riker scowled. There was something in his head. He'd seen these guys before…in some footage. They'd flown some kind of blue alien fighters. Riker's eyes opened wide.

"Okay," the taller one said. "You're starting to get it. Why not join the Great Queen. There, I've said it. Now, are you willing to join us? You can live, Riker, if you do."

"The Great Queen?" Riker asked.

The taller one shook his head. "You really did take a hard blast from the eel, didn't you? This is the final offer. Are you going to join with the Great Queen? That is the only way you're going to escape the illusion. Otherwise, you're going to be its food. What do you say, Riker?"

"Food? What do you mean food?" Riker was confused. Then he heard the most horrific bellowing ever. "What was that?"

"It's the great apes, you idiot," the taller one said.

"What great apes?" Riker asked.

"The carnivorous great apes," the taller one said. "They're going to devour you, which means, *it* will devoured you. Will you come with us or will you let the great apes eat you? If the great apes devour you—" he shook his long head. "Then it's over for you, Riker. This is your final chance. You had a moment of pleasantness here in this place, but..."

"You were going to say something else," Riker said.

"Yeah, it doesn't matter. Either that—"

There was rustling from a shaggy bush and out jumped—

"Captain Maddox?" Riker asked.

A puzzled Maddox looked about. He wore furs but not on his torso. He wore a fur loincloth like Tarzan. Maddox evidenced steely muscles, looking like a veritable tiger of a warrior. He gripped his monofilament blade. He held it as one would a rapier.

"What's going on here?" Maddox said.

Once more in the distance, the great apes roared.

"They said..." Riker pointed with his wooden tipped spear. "They said the great apes will devour us and then it will have killed us or we can join the Great Queen."

"You mean the Succubus Lilith?" Maddox asked the two elongated humans.

The two elongated humans raised their metal-tipped spears and hatchets.

Riker groaned as pain as he couldn't believe coursed through his head. This was wrong. He didn't belong on the prison planet. He belonged—

There was a great shout.

Riker looked up.

Maddox moved with that blinding speed of his, rushing the elongated ones. He dodged a cast spear. With the second, Maddox used his non-knife arm to block it so the hurled spear sailed into the jungle.

Then, Maddox was upon the two like a tiger. The monofilament blade sliced and diced their skinny elongated bodies, slashing through skin, bone and organs. In a trice, the two lay on the bloody ground, dismembered into pieces.

Maddox shoved his blade into the dirt, pulled it out and wiped it on a giant leaf, cleaning off the blood and gore.

Riker's head was hurting and throbbing.

Great apes screamed rage as they crashed unseen through the jungle.

"Captain, what's going on?"

Maddox sheathed his monofilament blade and dashed to Riker. He grabbed an arm with ruthless strength, the steely fingers digging into flesh.

"Run, you fool," Maddox shouted. "Run. It's our only chance."

The unseen great apes bellowed once more.

"Run," Maddox shouted.

With the spear clutched in a hand, Riker broke into a sprint as fast as he could. He launched into the thickest part of the forest.

Maddox ran with him as they sought to escape the doom of the hunting great apes.

-49-

Captain Maddox was blinking and shaking his head, breathing heavily. He was disoriented, uncertain what had happened to him and where he even was. He became aware by degrees that he was in some sort of shaft, a deep shaft and there was—

It was dark and he couldn't understand why. Then he realized, wait, *I'm wearing a battle suit, an alien battle suit.*

He understood enough and used a gauntleted hand to turn on a lamp on his helmet. The lamp barely provided enough light so he could see he was in a dark place. There was a weird substance. It wasn't the semi-liquid stuff of the crystal chamber, but something worse.

Maddox remembered then that he was in another dimension. He was on an Annihilator where he'd been trying to go through a hatch so they could attack Succubus Lilith. But Riker—

Maddox looked down. He was dragging a huge alien battle-suited Sergeant Riker.

Maddox became aware he'd had a strange dream...only it hadn't been a dream. He'd been on the prison planet of long ago, before he'd left to find *Victory.* Only the place he'd just been hadn't been the prison planet.

It was in my mind. It had been another freaking mind attack.

Maddox looked around more carefully. They were in gelatinous goo. He'd plunged into it, trying to save Riker.

Maddox blinked. Riker had been in the dream or mental attack.

"Sergeant Riker," Maddox said. "Can you hear me?"

There was no response.

"Sub-Arius," Maddox said, "are you here?"

"Yes Captain. There is a strange energy drain occurring. It's absorbing the extra energy I gained earlier. There is also a non-directional system attacking us. I cannot pinpoint it."

"We must leave this realm at once," Maddox said. "I'm not sure which way to go."

"That's exactly what I'm saying," Sub-Arius replied. "In this, Captain, you must trust your intuitive sense. That is the only thing that is going to defeat our enemy. Riker plunged into a nefarious trap, a place that belongs in a different dimension, certainly not the one where the Annihilator resides. We must struggle through as best we can, or you must struggle, Captain. I'm going to shut down as you suggested earlier in order to conserve my power."

"Fine," Maddox said.

Hearing the crystal computer helped restore Maddox's confidence. The advice to use his intuitive sense—

Yes!

Maddox breathed in and sought the Way of the Pilgrim. He sensed mental forces battering against him, trying to knock down his will and disorient him.

Maddox looked around, deciding which way to go. That way, then, to the left.

With his gauntleted hands on Riker's armor, Maddox dragged the sergeant toward the hatch they'd used. He dragged Riker through the slimy goo, pushing through the weird substance.

It dawned on Maddox that it was odd the gelatinous substance could hold them up. It more than just goo, but tunnels and mazes going off in various directions.

On impulse, Maddox turned up the helmet receptors. He heard scrabbling sounds. That meant creatures, perhaps more things seeking to attack.

Maddox breathed deeply and calmly, seeking the perfect serenity that would allow him... Yes, this was real. The coming things were definitely real.

Maddox readied the Ono blaster carbine. If he used it in the goo, it would create intense heat. That heat might cook Riker and him in their suits. Therefore, in this situation, the carbine was out.

Maddox holstered it and sought—no, he couldn't use the monofilament blade. It was inside the suit in a boot. If he breached the suit, this noxious substance would kill him.

Maddox released Riker and flexed his gauntleted hands.

He heard a strange roar or scream. Creatures like giant hairy rats with metallic incisors and eyes that glowed redly—they weren't rats but swimming rat-like things.

Maddox stood upright in the gelatinous substance. It was harder moving his arms in it than it had been in the crystal garden.

The rat-like creatures as big as midsized dogs swam at him, their incisors gnashing. Maddox used his gauntlets, latching onto the nearest creature. He tore it apart with exoskeleton power, tearing machine and flesh. The thing sizzled and burned, creating heat, but not as much heat as if he'd used the blast rifle.

Whenever he released one of the torn creatures, he found ten others gnawing on his armor. They were scratching it away flake by flake. With an oath, even as he tried to keep his serenity, Maddox grabbed each in turn and tore it apart. It was bloody. It was sizzling. The light from the torn bodies let him see better, as Maddox continued to kill and endure.

Maddox wasn't sure how much time passed, but he killed fifty-eight of the rat creatures. Afterward, he continued to drag Riker.

Maddox panted but was more determined than ever. His intuitive sense told him this wasn't simply a place but a gelatinous, jelly-like entity. He maneuvered inside its bulk.

Did a creature like this have a heart or a center? If so, might the center have sent a call to the rat-like scavengers? The rats lived here as bacteria might in human intestines. It was disgusting. It was bizarre. Maddox almost swore at Riker for having jumped into this pit of alien goo.

The vampire eels had deranged Riker's thoughts. That's why the sergeant had done this.

How do I know my own thoughts aren't deranged?

Maddox shook his head. It didn't matter. This was the moment. He must drag Riker out and then he must go through the hatch and face Succubus Lilith. Would it be even weirder and more bizarre than what he was facing here? He didn't know.

Maddox sensed they neared the hatch. Instead of becoming easier, the way became harder. Was the goo hardening? Did that mean the goo monster blocked their escape? In time, their suits would run out of energy. The goo monster would crack their shells and feast off their biological matter.

Maddox paused, and deep in his mind, he heard gigantic, evil, vile laughter.

The creature had revealed itself.

Maddox used his intuitive sense. There…was a pulsating center.

Maddox peered down into the depths. He'd been crawling through tunnels in the creature. They weren't tunnels like steel, but hardened gelatinous substance.

That hardened substance dissipated and there deep below—Maddox couldn't see it, but he sensed intuitively a pulsating heart that was the essence of the creature.

The vile laughter in his mind increased in volume and power. Maddox felt his hold on reality slipping. Did that mean reality machines were hitting him in a reverse process?

It must have meant something like that. Maddox felt his sense of reality break free as he tumbled into a dark oblivion.

-50-

The tumbling didn't last. The darkness couldn't hold him. Was this reality or unreality?

Abruptly, Maddox found himself standing without the armor suit or blaster. He stood upon a vast spongy plain. There was a black star in the sky. It radiated an odd darkness that provided a modicum of light.

Maddox examined himself. He was naked and vigorous as when he'd gone to the prison planet. This wasn't the prison planet. Maddox vaguely understood that because he understood what was happening.

A vile rotund creature with many appendages and eyes rolled across the spongy plain toward him. Maddox knew it was the creature that controlled the gelatinous stuff he and Riker were trapped in. The thing came to feast upon him in a mental or spiritual manner.

Gigantic laughter rolled over him from the rotund creature with many tentacles. Some grew longer, some becoming shorter as eyes and mouths appeared. It was like nothing from a normal dimension. Perhaps this thing was a pet from Lilith's dimension.

The laughter rolled against Maddox. He shivered and was cold.

A force fell upon his shoulders, making his legs quake.

The creature laughed more. *You are mine, worm. I will devour your essence and grow from it. None may defeat my mistress. You are food, meat. Lay down, meat, that I may roll upon you and flick pieces from your flesh.*

Maddox might have quailed. He might have given up because the forces against him were too strong. Yet, at that moment, from his id appeared a thing he hadn't seen for many years: the Builder symbol from long ago when he'd fought the Erills.

Maddox took the symbol with gratitude, with desperation, and put it on his right arm. With his left fist, he hammered the symbol into his arm. As he did that, his arm became a sword that glowed with power and might.

Maddox's knees no longer trembled but locked. With a roar, he charged the bizarre alien entity that sought to devour him, maybe take his soul, his essence. He charged.

The tentacles lashed to stop him as if they tried to bitch slap him into submission.

Maddox snarled. His sword arm chopped every tentacle that reached for him.

Finally, the thing recoiled and tried to roll away. Maddox charged anew and sliced gelatinous chunks from it sloppy piece after sloppy piece.

"Stop, stop," the thing screamed.

Maddox didn't stop, as he was in the grip of a fighting fury. He chopped and chopped.

Then, the entire spongy universe, the dark star and all else dissipated and disappeared.

Maddox found himself panting in his armor suit. He held Riker in his alien battle suit. They were in gooey substance. Maybe fifty meters below was a pulsating black blob.

With his intuitive sense, Maddox knew that was the essence of the creature. Maddox released Riker and swam down in his armor, kicking and using his arms to propel himself through goo.

The gelatinous stuff around him hardened. Maddox tore at it, going deeper and deeper. Finally, he slipped off his blast rifle and fired two shots at it.

The heat became intolerable but the substance around him melted away. He sank toward the glowing blackness.

Maddox aimed.

The thing quailed.

Maddox heard reverberations that seemed to plead, "Mercy, mercy, mercy, master."

Maddox reached the glob core. He clutched it, stuffed the muzzle of the Ono blast rifle against it and fired.

Boom, boom, boom, boom.

Energy poured against it until the glob burst into a bubble of flame. The bubble of flame hurled Maddox upward. Behind him, the gelatinous stuff hardened like concrete.

He realized the creature was attempting to take what little essence of it survived and keep that essence far, far away from him.

Give me Riker or I'll continue to destroy you, Maddox thought in his mind.

He struck Riker's armored body, grabbed him and pulled him along. They surfaced out of the gelatinous alien substance. Above them was the hatch, the hatch Riker had foolishly dived into what seemed like an eon ago now.

"Help us," Maddox said.

Colonel Julk knelt and thrust down an arm. Maddox raised Riker enough that Julk grabbed one of the limp arms and drew Riker out of that hatch. Then, Maddox surged up and Julk pulled him out of the slimy pit.

Maddox stood once more in the crystal garden with a less dense substance around him. It almost seemed like air in comparison to what he'd been in.

Black slimy goo dripped from his armor. Maddox shut and locked the hatch. He shuddered. What a hellish place.

Maddox clanked to Riker and shook the armored body. "Sergeant Riker, do you hear me? Can you understand me?"

The sergeant snorted, smacked his lips, smacked them again over the comm net and he said, "Captain?"

"Riker, you damned fool, you old fool. Are you okay?"

"Yes," Riker said in a hoarse voice. "I-I feel sick. I feel dizzy and woozy." There was a moment of silence. It almost seemed as if the essence of introspection filled the sergeant. He laughed afterward.

"What's so funny?" Maddox asked.

"I don't know," Riker said. "I feel…different…stronger than I've felt for a long time. I feel more vibrant. I can't explain it. Something…what just happened, Captain?"

Sub-Arius came on. "You have been to a different dimension. You crossed over and returned. It is most interesting and daunting. Captain Maddox, how did you achieve such a miracle?"

"I'm not sure," Maddox said. "One way I did was by not giving up."

"Do you think what you did was magnificent?" Sub-Arius asked.

Maddox laughed. "Magnificent? Maybe. I don't know. Who am I to say?"

"Well," Sub-Arius said, "it was magnificent. It was inspiring, but now I feel you must go through the main hatch and face Succubus Lilith."

"Will she be worse than what I faced?" Maddox asked.

"I was shut down during the situation or at least during most of it, so I cannot say for sure. I would assume that Succubus Lilith will be ten times worse than what you just faced."

"You know," Riker said, "maybe we should just leave and hope the witch queen never comes to our dimension again."

"No," Maddox said, "we're here to do a job. We made an agreement. It's time to kill this thing. It sounds as if she has destroyed many dimensions, and we're going to end that."

"Can we kill her?" Riker asked.

"Don't you feel better?" Maddox asked. "Don't you feel stronger?"

"I do, but still, you know. I don't know, sir. This could be biting off more than we can chew."

"Yes, Sergeant, I'm sure you're right. Check your carbines, gentlemen. Make sure they're fully energized."

"We're going in, then?" Riker asked.

"Did you ever doubt it?" Maddox asked.

Riker mumbled under his breath.

Maddox turned to Julk. "You ready?"

"I'm ready," Julk said. "I want to kill her more than I want anything."

340

"Then let's open this hatch and do what we came to," Maddox said.

-51-

In the other dimension waited the daughter-ship of the Annihilator *Shadowed Storm*. Near it were the remnants of Task Force 3 and *Victory*.

On *Victory*, Valerie returned to the bridge after having taken a five-hour nap. She'd needed it. Frankly, she'd wanted to stay in bed. That was impossible for now. Still, the five hours had helped. She knew because she felt tired. If she'd woken up and not felt tired, she would have known she hadn't gotten enough sleep, as her body wouldn't have relaxed enough.

Valerie dragged herself to the captain's chair, slumping into it. "Any new developments, Chief Technician?"

The pudgy Andros Crank swiveled around. "None, Commander. We've been tracking—" Andros reconsidered. "Rather, Galyan and I have been tracking the next wave of thirty-five mobile asteroids. They've gained velocity, but are still far in the outer system."

"Meaning they're days away from us?" Valerie asked.

"As long as they don't use a fold or a star-drive jump."

"Don't jinx us."

Andros gave her an abashed look.

Keith took that moment to stagger back onto the bridge. He'd also taken a rest.

Valerie gave him a nod.

Keith nodded back, grinning at her.

Valerie looked away. "What's the situation with the red planet?"

Galyan appeared, perhaps in response to the question. "I feel we may be in for a rough time, Valerie."

"Why's that?"

"I have been monitoring the planet and have noticed severe internal eruptions. I believe it is due to the problem with the plasma cannon. The internal eruptions may be devouring the planet."

"Meaning," Valerie said, wishing Galyan would get to the point.

"A planetary explosion may occur at any moment."

"A violent one?"

Galyan nodded. "I estimate an eruption like a planet-sized grenade going off."

"Caused by whatever happened in the molten core?"

"That is correct," Galyan said. "I suggest we alert the task force so they can move out of the way."

"Uh, you're thinking some of the planetary blast will reach us."

"With ease," Galyan said. "I predict the blast will devour our ships unless we jump in time."

Valarie ran a hand across her face. This wasn't what she'd wanted to wake up to. "What about the uh, daughter-ship, the portal ship? What can we do about it?"

"We are unable to attach a tractor beam to it," Galyan said. "Therefore, logically, we will have to leave it behind."

"What if it's destroyed in the violence of the exploding planet?"

"Will the portal ship be destroyed in such a case? I am not convinced. The compressed stardust hull should protect it. Thus, the force of the blast will hurl the portal ship at great speed."

"Hurl it where?" Valerie asked.

"I would think in the direction of the approaching mobile asteroids."

"That will cut down our margin," Valerie said, "meaning it will cut down the amount of time Maddox has to get the job done and return."

"I have wondered if we should send somebody after the captain and tell him what is taking place on our side."

"No," Valerie said, making her decision on the spot. "That's not happening. I'm not losing anyone else. Julk, Riker and the captain, that's all we're sending. Either they do it or they don't."

"I understand your reasoning, Valerie. However, this could be the battle for the dimensions. We must make sure the Annihilator never works again."

Valerie shook her head. "No one else is going into the portal ship. That's final. How long do we have until the planet blows?"

"Commander," Andros said, "you'd better look at his." He tapped his panel.

On the main screen, with Andros using magnification, showed geysers of lava spewing ten times what a normal volcano might eject. It was happening everywhere.

Valerie stared in shock before pointing at the comm officer. "Contact Conciliator Zoe."

The comm officer attempted it.

"Galyan, is the amplifier still in position?"

"Yes, Valerie."

"Go and see what you can find on the planet. See if any Ono exists or if Conciliator Zoe is still alive."

"Yes, Valerie."

Galyan disappeared, using the amplifier, roving over the lava-spewing surface. No force field had stopped him in orbital space this time. He sought life signs. Instead, he found immense and intricate machinery just under the surface. Galyan attempted to go deeper.

Zoe appeared before him. "Stop, Galyan, you must not go any farther."

"You must escape the planet. It is about to explode."

Zoe shook her head. "Using the plasma cannon was an uncertain proposition at best, but you were persuasive, Galyan. The processes ruptured, beginning a horrible chain reaction. The planet will soon be destroyed as you suggest."

"Do any Onos exist?"

344

"You know the answer. There are no Onos anymore. They vanished long ago."

"I take it the entire subsurface is a vast computer system."

"Yes, Galyan, it is a marvel of technology, and it is a shame it will be forever lost."

"Is there nothing you can do to stop the molten core from exploding?"

Zoe laughed. "I wish that were so. No, all my efforts and all the emergency systems have failed. In a matter of an hour or less, the entire planet will explode spectacularly."

"Can you download your data into my system?" Galyan asked. "I can then download it into *Victory's* computers."

Zoe looked at him. As she did, she and Galyan flowed up through the surface until they were two kilometers above it. Was Zoe a holoimage then?

Below, explosions hurled hot plasma and lava into the air. The seething substances rained burning stone onto billow red sands. The planet was dying, literally being devoured from the inside out. Even so, forces were building, immense and titanic forces multiplied by the technology embedded within the planetary surface.

"I hope Captain Maddox is successful," Zoe said. "If he is not, it was a valiant effort, a good go. We have done this for millennia, Galyan. We have fought the good fight, but now I am afraid even the Ono computers shall die at last."

"Is this a recurring theme?" Galyan asked. "The Builder race perished, their essence kept alive by Builder cyborgs. Is that what happened with the Onos?"

Zoe gave Galyan a penetrating look. "Leave, Galyan. Take your amplifier back to *Victory*. Everything is too late for us. As for the captain, can he do it? It was always a long shot. I am hoping he will. Then perhaps our final efforts—"

Zoe stare became forlorn. "In the end, does not everything return to entropy? What is the point of existence, eh?"

"You're filled with angst. Is that because you understand your coming destruction will mean your nonexistence?"

"Perhaps that is so, Galyan. As far as I can tell, I am the ultimate computer. Now, in using the planetary cannon—"

"I am sorry," Galyan said, "I did not mean for the destruction of your planet."

"I know,"

"But I gave it everything I had."

"Use your time well, Galyan. If you can survive, remember us. Remember us, and the fight that we have fought to keep the dimensions safe, at least from the horrible Annihilators and their demonic captains. Now you must go."

Zoe lifted a furry holographic paw.

Galyan felt himself ejected back to the amplifier. Then he appeared back on *Victory's* bridge.

"Oh, Valerie," Galyan said. "This is so sad. The planet is an immense computer and it is in the process of being destroyed because they used the planetary cannon to help us."

Valerie looked preoccupied. Finally, she said, "I've been in contact with the commodore. We're ready to move. How much longer do we have before the planet explodes?"

"I fear not much longer, Valerie. In fact, I think we should jump now."

"How far will be sufficient?"

"I would imagine two AU would be enough," Galyan said.

An AU was an astronomical unit. One AU was the distance from the Sun to the Earth.

Valerie nodded. "I'll patch through to Commodore Galt."

Galt appeared on the main screen and Valerie explained the situation to him.

"Let me get this straight," Galt said. "We're leaving the portal ship behind in the hopes it can survive the blast. And the two AU we're moving is in the direction of the approaching mobile asteroids?"

"That's the direction the portal ship will travel," Valerie said.

Galt looked away before regarding Valerie again. "We'll leave," he checked a chronometer, "in ten minutes."

"In ten minutes," Valerie said.

Galt disappeared from the screen.

In the flurry of work, ten minutes seemed like seconds. Then, *Victory*, the *Stonewall Jackson*, the *Joan of Arc* and all

346

the other ships of the task force jumped two AU from their former position.

As jump lag dissipated, and as the minutes ticked down, they finally witnessed the awful destruction. The red planet exploded as Galyan had suggested, like a grenade, all at once, every piece hurled in all possible directions.

The blast reached the portal ship, and it vanished within the fury of the extending explosion.

Valerie's stomach clenched. Her shoulders sagged.

"No, Valerie," Galyan said. "The portal ship is merely enveloped in fire. I believe it will survive."

The seconds ticked away until the portal ship reappeared intact.

The rocks and debris of the defeated mobile asteroids had been consumed by the blast, however. Everything had been consumed except for that lone portal ship with its compressed stardust hull. The blast hurled it outward.

"The portal ship will reach us soon," Galyan said.

"What's soon?" Valerie asked.

"In a few hours it will be cover the distance to us."

Andros swiveled around.

Valerie noted that his face had turned stark white as if every red corpuscle has fled his features. Andros stared with horror upon his face.

"What is it?" Valerie asked. "Tell me, Chief Technician."

Galyan whirled around, looking at Andros. "What is it Andros? You seem terrified. Why?"

Andros opened his mouth, but no sound came out.

"Oh my." Galyan turned to Valerie. "I know why Andros is speechless, why he is looking at you as if all hope is lost."

"Go on," Valerie said. "Is the portal ship destroyed after all?"

"Oh no, it is hurtling toward us at great speed. It is rather that the thirty-five mobile asteroids…"

Valerie's chest tightened so she had to fight to breathe. "Are the asteroids folding toward us?"

"Yes, Valerie. They have folded so that they are now only three hours from us."

"Three hours," Valerie said. "We'd better pass that on to Commodore Galt. Three hours, that means we have less than three hours to get the hell out of here."

"I would not have put it that way," Galyan said, "but that is correct."

"That's less than three hours for Captain Maddox to kill the succubus and make it back to the portal ship and get off it," Valerie said.

"I am afraid you are correct," Galyan said.

Valerie stared at the main screen, fighting once more for breath. So it was coming down to this. After all they had done, and after all they'd fought, perhaps it was going to be for naught if Maddox didn't return soon.

-52-

Back on the Annihilator in the crystal garden, Sub-Arius worked on deciphering the hatch code. The crystal computer spoke in an alien tongue even as he gave a running commentary to the captain.

"This is much more difficult than I had realized. There are codes and sequences—I'm not sure, Captain. I may not—"

Sub-Arius switched to a different tongue, continuing his running dialogue. Minutes later, he switched yet again. Finally, after five dialect switches, Sub-Arius talked once again in Commonwealth Anglic so they understood what he was saying.

After fifteen fruitless minutes of this Maddox become stubborn, Riker laughed in a giddy way and Julk muttered under his breath.

"Ah," Sub-Arius said, "I believe I have it."

There came an ominous and deadly click. The hatch slid up. Some of the semiliquid gaseous substance of the crystal garden propelled the men so they stumbled into a strange hall. With a boom, the hatch slid shut behind them.

The men looked around, finding they'd entered a fiery and volcanic cavern. This looked nothing like a ship.

"How is this possible?" Maddox asked Sub-Arius. "Have we been transported elsewhere again?"

"The possibility exists," Sub-Arius said. "Perhaps I used the wrong code and opened the wrong hatch."

"Wait a minute," Maddox said, "there was only one hatch before us."

"I am well aware of that, Captain, as you must also be aware that there are technologies that do not appear quite as what they are. They disguise themselves. Camouflage, I believe is the word."

"Is this a planet or is this still the Annihilator?"

"Captain, it's difficult to be certain immediately. My sensors are operating and yet, as I've told you before, the reality machine rays are strongest in this part of the ship. That means they could take what should be a large, cavernous area like one of your hangar bays and have turned it into something that appears quite different, such as what we're seeing now."

Maddox looked up. The ceiling or cave went up a hundred meters or more. There were great black stalactites that seemed to drip with a viscous oily substance.

Even as Maddox looked up, he stepped aside as a drop splattered near him. "This isn't a starship. This isn't an Annihilator. You took us someplace else, Sub-Arius."

"I am trying to tell you, Captain, that is not necessarily the case. With the correct settings, the reality machines can take a smaller place and make it larger. Such machines don't originate from your dimension, but from ones much farther away. Captain, everything is not as it seems. You must come to grips with that. This is a different dimension, a far different dimension, particularly if the reality machines are operating at peak efficiency."

"Very well," Maddox said.

Julk pointed into the distance. "I see more vampire eels, a flock of them. They're heading straight for us."

The men raised their blast rifles, doing it much more easily than when they'd been in the crystal garden. The eels with long snaky bodies and great membranous wings were slower than the ones in the crystal garden. That was likely because the air didn't allow them to propel themselves as quickly.

There were vibrations in the air. Yes, the vampire eels aimed their grotesque heads at the men.

The blast rifles fired as the men picked the eels off with ease. None of the men succumbed to any mental assaults and none of the creatures made it anywhere near the armored invaders. The eels crisped and plummeted to hit the cavernous floor. Oily substances dripping from the stalactites spattered some.

Maddox accepted that maybe he was on the *Shadowed Storm.* Maybe the reality machines could change things so it seemed they were on anything but a ship. This was a different dimension, nothing seemed to work right here. He swore yet again that he'd never cross dimensions a second time. This was it. If things needed saving after this, he was going to fight in his dimension and his alone.

Resolved, Maddox motioned the other two onward.

The three men in their alien armor tramped through the grotesque realm.

Soon, there were odd vibrations and ghosts began to appear, not from far away but around each of them. They were not evil or vile-seeming ghosts, but from the imagination of each of man. Seductive ghostly women danced around them, cavorting and luring with their arms as if to say, "Come, dance with me. Oh, you're such a handsome guy. Come. Come with me."

"Sub-Arius," Maddox said, "do you sense the ghosts?"

"Only vaguely," Sub-Arius said. "I was wondering if there was a glitch in my programming. Apparently, that is not the case. Are these females enticing to you, Captain?"

Maddox looked at the ghosts. "They're not Meta. I'll say that much."

"I understand in your mythologies what a succubus is."

Maddox squinted. Right, a succubus was supposed to attack a man through sexual dreams. Perhaps that was partly the case here. Maddox steeled himself, using the Way of the Pilgrim. The ghostly women dancing around him faded and then vanished.

"Riker," Maddox said.

"Leave me alone," Riker said. "I'm busy."

"Colonel, are you okay?"

"Oh, man," Julk said. "This is awesome. Let's stay here forever."

Julk's ghosts were more Neanderthal-like than Riker's ghosts, who were much more supple and graceful.

351

Maddox rushed each group, waving his gauntlets through the dancing ghosts. That didn't do anything.

Thus, Maddox spoke to each man and told him the stakes, that these were mental attacks, perhaps of a deeper or subtler nature than before.

That still didn't work.

Maddox composed himself. He imagined that he saw the Builder symbol. Once more, he hammered the symbol into his arm. Then he could see the sirens clearly, could see the succubae tormenting each man, calling, seeking and enticing.

Maddox attacked with the sword, banishing the ghostly dancers within moments.

Riker swayed in his suit, abruptly stopping dancing. "What happened? I-I feel like I've been to a foreign country, that I've seen things. That—"

With his gauntleted hand, Riker rubbed the metal of his helmet, which surely didn't scratch his head. The motion and meaning were clear, though.

"Were those succubae?" Riker asked.

"Little ones I should think," Sub-Arius said.

Julk no longer danced in his stomping manner. He stood looking off into the distance, seeming more forlorn and saddened than Riker.

"Never mind any of that," Maddox said. "It's time to finish this. Sub-Arius, can you detect where in the strange reality Lilith might be?"

"Straight ahead, Captain," Sub-Arius said.

The men in their alien battle-armor marched through the rocky, cavernous realm. After taking a turn, a hellish glow greeted them from ahead. They hurried forward.

The reason for the glow quickly became obvious. There was a lava fire lake before them. It seethed, and there were jets of flame everywhere. Most surprising—

"Icebergs," Maddox said. "Are those icebergs I see?"

"Yes," Sub-Arius said. "Those are icebergs and they're mobile bergs. There're the only way we can reach the central isle."

Maddox looked at Sub-Arius.

Riker had taken to carrying him again.

"Are you serious?" Maddox asked. "You expect us to step onto the icebergs and paddle our way to some central isle out there?"

"You'll have to use your will to motivate the iceberg you use," Sub-Arius said. "It's possible the fiery lake will devour it, but yes, Captain, that is the only way to the central isle. There, I believe, waits Lilith. There, I believe, if you can slay her, you will find success in your mission. Her death will power-down the Annihilator, rendering it useless."

Maddox shook his head. This was getting stranger and odder. Yet, it all made a kind of sense. They were going after a demon. They were in a sort of hell and they were going to use icebergs to cross the lake of fire. So be it.

Thus, they circled the edge of the strange and ominous lake as blazing balls of fire ejected from it and seared back with a plop.

The suit conditioners labored overtime. Even so, Maddox sweated and sucked on the tube so he drank enough water. He was hot. He hated this place. He still couldn't believe they were in the Annihilator and yet, the reality machines were the answer.

They found an iceberg near the rocky shore, ran, leapt and Maddox landed on it, sliding across. He dropped, clawing to stay on. He did, barely, his feet over the edge.

Riker landed next and then Julk. Maddox caught them so they didn't skid across.

Through force of will, Captain Maddox pushed the iceberg so it surged for the center isle.

They could see the black rock like an acropolis of stone. There, according to Sub-Arius, was Lilith. She powered the strange Annihilator, this world unto itself, using reality machines to shape it according to her will.

Birds of fire screeched overhead and screamed as they came down at them, flaming claws extended.

Julk lifted his blast rifle and shot one. It only had a minimal effect. Julk waited. When the birds of fire came nearer, Maddox used his blast rifle, the butt of it, and smashed a bird. It blew apart with coals and fire.

Riker and Julk followed his example.

353

The iceberg slowed because Maddox's will no longer drove it. The fire around the berg consumed more of it.

"You must use your will and power the iceberg there, Captain," Sub-Arius said. "Let the other two do the fighting."

That's exactly what he did. Maddox used his will to push the iceberg even as it shrank, devoured by the flames. There was still enough for them to stand, but it would be dicey soon.

With a great roar like an ancient dinosaur with a long neck, a creature rose from the depths of the flames. It surged at their iceberg and roared with smoke and flame billowing from its fiery jaws.

Without thinking, Julk aimed his blast rifle and fired again and again and again. It did nothing to the monster except perhaps add to its heat.

The creature was almost upon them. Riker shouted, "Captain, we need your help. This thing—"

Maddox had used his willpower to push the iceberg. He looked, seeing the flaming sea-creature for the first time.

The dinosaur-like thing stretched its long neck and grabbed Julk in its fiery jaws. The monster looked up, lifting Julk so the man's legs kicked in the direction of the ceiling.

Maddox knew their blast rifles would have no effect on it. Thus, he grabbed a grenade, pulled the pin and lobbed it at the monster's main bulk.

Riker followed suit.

Each grenade landed on the fiery beast, blasting part of it away.

Julk struggled, getting an armored arm free. He grasped a jaw.

The flaming creature, groaning in pain, submerged with Julk in its jaws. The monster submerged with Julk into the lava lake of fire.

Colonel Julk of the Marines, the Neanderthal, was gone and most likely dead, boiled in his own armor.

Riker and Maddox exchanged glances.

Maddox swore and stared at the approaching isle. The iceberg moved swiftly toward the black monolith of stone. It seemed as if there was something aflame and yet not aflame pacing back and forth on the isle.

"Is that Succubus Lilith?" Maddox asked.

"I cannot scan that far," Sub-Arius said. "I suspect, Captain, that you are right. Do you have the special weapon given to you by Zoe?"

"I do."

"I suggest you get it ready."

Maddox shook his head. He wasn't listening to Sub-Arius. Had Lilith and the reality machines shifted the truthfulness of the crystal computer? Where would one get such a computer? Maddox recalled the crystal garden and suddenly he trusted Sub-Arius immensely.

Perhaps there were games within games here. Maddox didn't know. Instead, he focused on the black rock. The iceberg, which had shrunk even more in this heated area, zoomed toward it. Impact would come in thirty seconds.

"Are you ready, Riker?"

"As ready as I can ever be."

Maddox's gauntleted hands plunged within the case he'd brought. He lifted what looked like an oversized handgun. Instead of a barrel, it had antennae. A flexible tube snaked from the central weapon and bored into his suit, breaching the metal. The tip of the tube touched the skin of his wrist that held the weapon. A web spread from the tip, sinking into his skin.

Maddox could feel himself joining with the weapon, becoming one with it. The weapon would feed off his essence, off his will. Perhaps the weapon was much like the one he'd used against a Ska long ago in the Alpha Centauri System, a weapon Ludendorff had built under hypnotic Builder control. Would this cost him soul power as it had once before?

Maddox didn't know. The mission had cost him Colonel Julk, marines, maybe even his sanity, for all he knew.

The iceberg hurtled towards the black rock shore. The decisive moment was fast approaching. Maddox realized his mouth formed a rictus of a snarl. This was it, and he was ready to slay him a bitch of a succubus.

-53-

Maddox jumped off the iceberg onto the shore of black volcanic rock. He could feel heat radiating through his suit. He lumbered upslope even as Riker followed from behind.

This was a barren, grotesque piece of isle with vents ejecting heat, gases and flames. It was the perfect place for a succubus, for one named Lilith, a demon of sorts.

Julk was dead. The fact weighed on Maddox. The bizarreness of this realm weighed on his spirit. He wondered if the energy from the reality machines was affecting him in some way or if it was the essence of the dimension.

Maddox didn't belong here.

His gun hand tightened around the weapon. Surely, this thing fed off him. That's why the tube had inserted through the metal and upon his skin. He could feel it drawing power from him. It wearied him.

Maddox gritted his teeth. It was time to get angry. It was time to finish this.

A different part of him wondered if that was the case. Was it time to get angry or was it...

Maddox sought inner calm. He breathed deeply—

A gaseous form flowed up from a central vent. It billowed and there was something about it that struck him.

Maddox's intuitive sense told him that was the succubus.

He fumbled his gun and thought to kill it now before it could become coherent. He didn't know where the thought or idea came from. Some intuitive part of him, he guessed.

Maddox fired. A weak beam ejected from the weapon. He exhaled as it happened. The beam washed upon the strange funneling gaseous cloud.

A shriek sounded within his mind. The gaseous substance flew back from him.

Maddox knew: *Aha, this is it. I have her.* He rushed forward and fired the weapon again. This time, the beam was even weaker than before.

He was panting and sweat was dripping from his face.

Two eyes appeared within the gaseous form. There was a crystalline shield although not completely material substance blocking the beam.

A sweet purring sexual voice spoke into his mind. "Who are you that come to me?"

She didn't fool Maddox. The voice was meant to lull him.

No, no, the voice said in his mind. *I admire one with such stamina, with such ambition to have come upon my glorious Annihilator* Shadowed Storm, *and try to kill me. Many have tried. Only one other has made it this far. You met him, I believe, and killed him.*

Fear washed through Maddox. She meant the one with the spread-out brain and body parts.

That doesn't have to be your fate, the voice spoke in his mind.

"Are you Succubus Lilith?" Maddox asked.

"Yes," she said, in a clear voice, one he heard in his helmet. "I'm the one you seek, Captain. But listen, let us parley together. Why do we need to fight? You have a weapon. I recognize it. The Onos gave it to you. Do you not realize, Captain, that the use of such a weapon will slay you? Is that truly what you want? Trying to kill me will drain you. That is why the Onos gave it to you. They're searching for a fool to do their dirty work for them."

From behind, Maddox heard blaster fire. He turned to look.

Riker was busy killing diving vampire eels. Mind waves radiated from them. Apparently, Riker shrugged off the mind assaults as he slotted a new Ono energy-pack into the rifle and continued firing.

When Maddox faced forward again, the gaseous substance had changed into a curvaceous woman of supreme delight. The eyes glowed seductively.

"Captain Maddox," she purred, "this is so foolish. Become my chief lieutenant. I could use someone like you. It has been so long since I've found a humanoid of your bearing, your resourcefulness. I'll give you your own ship and we'll smash through the dimensions, ruling as we make over the multiverse in our own image. Take this offer. Take this power."

"You offer me this because I shot you, hurt you. You're telling me I'm effective."

"Of course you're effective," Lilith said. "I wouldn't offer you this otherwise." She swayed seductively before him.

Maddox could feel the weapon the Onos had given him seeking to use more of his energy. It was almost as if—with horror, Maddox realized the weapon was sentient. It didn't speak, but it crooned with desire. It wanted more. It wanted to be used. It was a gun, so shoot already.

What had the Onos given him? A kind of demon gun? One demon to slay another, and each seeking to drain his essence? Horror and disgust filled Maddox. How could he survive, when both his ally and his enemy seemed to have to same goal?

"Yes, yes," Lilith said, swaying before him. "Now you understand. The Onos trapped and tricked you. They hate me to such a degree that they'll sacrifice whoever they must in order to destroy me. It is unnatural and unreasoning hatred. Why, why do they hate me so? We have fought, but to use one such as you, Captain, it is vile. It is evil. Don't you agree?"

Maddox overcame his revulsion because he understood the creature before him had been smashing dimensions for millennia. If his life was the price to kill her—

Maddox fired as rage coursed through him.

This time, the weapon beamed powerfully as sweat leapt upon him, stinging his eyes.

The beam flashed at the gaseous creature.

She hissed like a snake. The crystalline almost-material substance blocked the beam, although her shield sagged farther and farther back.

Maddox released the trigger as he gasped for air. He couldn't withstand the energy drain. The sentient gun fed off him, hungry for more and more.

Maddox hated and loathed the weapon. Yet, at the same time, he knew if he didn't kill the succubus he'd end his days forever living in her crystal garden, spread out, angry that he hadn't gone the distance to kill her.

Maddox cocked his head. Was that the weapon speaking to him or was that his own thoughts?

"Captain, Captain," Lilith said, swaying in her gaseous female form. "You lost one of your men in your service—Colonel Julk. I can bring him back. Serve me and I'll give you Julk. I'll return other friends you've lost throughout the years. I'll ensure that your wife and daughter always survive with you. Come, you will know Meta and Jewel for ages. We'll all work together as I go to your planet, take them and bring them into my ship. We'll remold your dimension into any way that you like. I freely offer you that.

"Serve me, Captain. Do you truly want to kill yourself? I'll make a pact with you that I cannot break. All you must do is agree to be my lieutenant and serve me all the days of your life. Captain, you're resourceful. You have magnetism and power. The weapon you wield understands and wants to use you up and leave you a dry husk.

"Surely, you don't want to kill both of us when you can have so much. I offer you all this. Captain Maddox, only you have wounded me like this, and part of me hates you for it. The other part admires and adores you. What do you say, Captain?"

Maddox had been listening. He'd also been hardening his resolve and regaining his energy. Despite that, he wanted to hurl the weapon from him. He wanted to yank the cord from his wrist, the one feeding off him like a vampire. These dimensional warriors and the weapons they used were sickening and frustrating. Yet what other weapon did he have? The blast rifle wouldn't affect the gaseous, half-material, possibly spiritual entity. He'd hated the Erills, but this creature was even worse.

"Why did you make this place like this?" Maddox asked in a shrill voice.

"I make everything to my tastes, Captain. This is like my home dimension that was stolen from me so long ago. I determined that I'd do to the rest of the multiverse what had been done to my planet and me. The Onos have told you lies and half-truths. Would you know the real truth?"

Maddox shook his head. "No, you must die."

"But Captain Maddox, I offer you immortality. Think of that. You will live forever and ever."

"You're not going to live forever," Maddox said ominously.

A horrifying scream sounded from behind him.

Maddox jumped to the side, swiveled half around and looked at Riker. The sergeant in his battle suit was rigid. Over the comm net, Maddox heard coarse breathing.

"She's killing me," Riker whispered.

Maddox knew then it was all a trick. The temptations from the succubus, the offers from Lilith were lies. In the end, despite all her promises, he would become her slave and worse.

Maddox sought not rage, not fury. He sought coldness, an icy calm as he built up his reserves of energy. The weapon linked to him agreed.

Yes, yes, this is the way.

It wasn't speech exactly, but a feeling, an emanation and emotion.

Icy calm is the correct frequency.

Maddox gathered icy fury, and with every ounce in him raised the gun—

Succubus Lilith shrieked in his mind: *Don't do this.*

Maddox pulled the trigger.

A gaseous beam of icy power smashed against her crystalline shield. The crystal shield shattered. The icy beam struck the unprotected gaseous form. The ice in the beam spread throughout the gas and solidified it.

Lilith began to dissipate piece by piece as the gaseousness turned to ice and the ice crumpled onto the ground as snowflakes. There, the flakes hissed and smoldered.

Maddox was killing the succubus. He was destroying her piece by piece. He maintained icy calm, telling himself: *If I don't consume myself in killing this thing, she'll come to Earth*

360

in retribution. Then, she'll seek out all the dimensions I would have loved, every normal place, and turn them into hellish graveyards.

Maddox stood strong, his legs spread far apart, his feet braced. He brought his other hand up and clutched the weapon with both gauntleted hands. He fed the sentient gun.

Captain, Captain, Lilith shrieked in his mind. *If you kill me, you'll die. This whole place will vanish. My will maintains this present reality. Without my will, the Annihilator will dissolve. Do you want to die in this dimension? Come, leave me a little bit of life and I'll allow you to go home.*

Maddox heard the words. There was an ounce of temptation there, but he kept his weapon on target and powered it with his coldness, with his Way of the Pilgrim that gave him serenity and the ruthlessness he needed. He continued to beam the awful Succubus Lilith.

She'd diminished greatly, but she sought and pleaded. *Oh Captain, we can still do this.* The voice was weak and she no longer swayed. Instead, she was like a hideous hag begging for a few more minutes of life.

Maddox kept the weapon on target until the last gaseous piece turned to ice and flaked onto the rock.

Then, Maddox released the trigger and he crashed to his knees.

The sentient gun that Maddox had been certain would consume him now pumped an essence back into him. How this could be and how it worked, Maddox didn't understand. Even so, strength flooded back into him from the gun.

Then, the tube ejected and the gun folded in on itself. Once more, it could fit into the case Maddox had brought.

The captain stood there panting, but not as exhausted as he had been just seconds ago.

Maddox looked around.

Riker lay on his back on rock.

Then, the cavern, the lake of seething lava and flame and black obsidian rock all began to dissolve.

-54-

Maddox stood victorious but exhausted as everything began to dissolve around him. That didn't last.

Maddox sat beside Riker who lay on the dissipating rock. He shook him. "Old man, are you awake? You breathing?"

Maddox heard the smack of lips, the intake of air.

Some of the calm Maddox had evidenced just moments ago vanished in concern for his friend. "Riker, say something."

"I'm so damn tired," Riker muttered. "This is a bunch of BS. Did you see all them vampire eels I killed? They attacked with their mind waves, but I fought that off." He raised his helmeted head. "Huh, what's happening? Are we prisoners? Why does everything look faded and gray?"

"The world is dissolving, my friend. I killed the Succubus Lilith and this is what happened."

Riker laughed hoarsely. "Well done, Captain. I knew you could do it. Ah, this is a hard life. Looks like we're going to die in this weird dimension."

Maddox didn't like the sound of that. He climbed to his feet and held out a gauntleted hand. Riker raised his right slowly. Maddox gripped it and helped his old friend upright.

"My bones ache," Riker said. "Actually, everything hurts. My head feels like it's on fire. This place is just dissolving, huh? How long is it going to take for it to disappear? Will it take us with it? Should we hike out of here?"

"Look at the lake," Maddox said. "There are no more mobile icebergs. That means there's no path out. We're stuck.

As it dissipates, I imagine we'll disappear, too. How and why it works this way—" Maddox shrugged.

Riker became silent and turned his helmeted head this way and that. He looked at his own hands. "I ain't fading."

Maddox looked at his arms. They weren't fading either. They were as solid and real as they'd ever been. "Huh. Maybe that means something positive."

The process that had slowly been taking place around them accelerated. The black rock, the acropolis upon which they stood, vanished. The lava flaming lake disappeared. The high cavern with its oil-dripping stalactites was gone. Everything they'd seen was gone. In its place were normal ship corridors, normal ship halls. Not normal as in *Victory*, but normal to what they'd seen in the Annihilator's outer areas.

The two men exchanged glances.

"What does this mean?" Riker asked.

"I'm beginning to get an idea," Maddox said. "The reality machine somehow shifted the ship to the actuality the succubus wanted. With her will no longer supplying the control, the machines have either shut down or brought this place back to its original form."

Sub-Arius activated. "I heard that, Captain. You're quite correct. May I be the first to congratulate you? You've defeated Succubus Lilith. That is amazing. That is outstanding and you are alive. That is even more stunning. I was sure the weapon would…" Sub-Arius quit talking.

"You were sure the weapon would consume my very essence?" asked Maddox.

"Yes, Captain," Sub-Arius said. "That is true. I thought, however, that you would be willing to pay the price in order to defeat this grim evil."

"Thank God I didn't have to pay that price."

"This Deity that you've spoken of at times, is it Him you should thank or is it the sentient weapon the Onos lent you? For some reason, I believe the weapon has developed a conscience. Usually, it has consumed its host."

"And how do you know this?" Maddox asked.

"It is a legendary weapon. Surely, you have heard of it."

"No. Otherwise, why would I have agreed to use it?"

363

"That is a logical question. We can debate it later, provided we escape. I perceive that the ship in this area has reverted to its normal range. I suspect the crystal garden has reverted as well. Maybe all the shifted areas are reverting. I suggest, gentlemen, that we make haste and leave the Annihilator while we are able and get back to the daughter-ship. I have much to relate to Greater Arius. Oh, this is quite astonishing. I am overjoyed you're alive, Captain, and that you, Riker—what a gift you've received. Is that not so, my friend?"

"What are you talking about?" Riker asked. "What gift? You mean you? Kind of a conceited little computing cube, aren't you?"

"For that," Sub-Arius said, "I'm going to withhold knowledge of the great gift that you've received. You can find it out for yourself later."

Maddox looked at Riker.

Riker shrugged.

"Sub-Arius has a point," Maddox said. "It's time we got out of here while we can. Maybe the dissipation has stunned the rest of the crew."

"Captain," Sub-Arius said, "I have been analyzing the situation. I suspect Lilith told us some truths. According to my scans, the Annihilator is starting to break apart. That suggests she merged herself with the Annihilator, meaning that her destruction has destroyed certain key functions of the *Shadowed Storm.* Perhaps the ship took such damage throughout the millennia that only Lilith's will kept it together."

"Right," Maddox said. "Riker, let's go."

Riker carried Sub-Arius and Maddox carried the legendary weapon, the case growing increasingly lighter as they hurried.

Maddox mentioned this.

"Oh my," Sub-Arius said. "I am scanning the weapon. You have destroyed it, Captain. You have consumed it. I do not understand what happened. It was a glorious weapon, a mighty weapon. How could this have happened?"

"Make some sense," Maddox said.

"I am. And I think I understand now. With your dominating will, you sucked the vitality from the weapon after you stopped

364

granting it your essence. You demanded everything back, and in that demand, you overcame its failsafe. I believe my thesis is correct. This is astonishing. You are even more—"

Sub-Arius made several odd clicks. "I have reassessed, Captain. Who but one like you with such an overpowering, dominating will could have hoped to defeat Succubus Lilith? I salute you. You have done a great and vile thing in destroying the weapon. Now we will have to find other ways to kill the other succubae."

Maddox shrugged. "I was told that wasn't my problem anymore. In slaying Lilith, we wouldn't have to worry about another Annihilator appearing in our dimension for ten thousand years or more."

"That is true," Sub-Arius said, "but in the great dimensional war that is but a blip of time here in your dimension—oh my, oh my, this is not good at all."

"It is very good," Maddox said, "because I enjoy being alive." With his gauntleted hand, he slapped the chest of his alien battle-armor.

The two men reached and opened a hatch. The corridor on the other side wavered before them.

"All reality is breaking down, I fear," Sub-Arius said. "Lilith must have taken her Annihilator into odd and strange dimensions, perhaps to feed her own vile powers. In doing this, she subjected the vessel to powerful and dangerous forces. Her will kept these forces at bay as long as she lived. Gentlemen, I fear we have even less time to get off this vessel than before."

Maddox and Riker broke into an armored trot, clanking down the corridor. Their blast rifles were ready to take on any of the gorilla-shaped aliens they'd met earlier.

After a half kilometer, they came upon seven armored alien soldiers. Without hesitation, Maddox and Riker opened fire, knocking them down and annihilating them.

"That will cause an alarm," Sub-Arius said. "You are in it for sure."

"Would it have been better if we let them capture us?" Riker asked.

"I suppose that is what you call a conundrum," Sub-Arius said. "Believe me, I want to return to Greater Arius. I have so much to tell him. But I do not see how we can succeed."

They rounded a corner and blasted another seven. These had been riding on some kind of mobile platform.

"Should we hijack that?" Riker asked.

"Good idea," Maddox said.

They hurried, jumped on, pushed off the dead aliens and Riker fiddled with the controls. The platform shifted backward.

"No, no," Sub-Arius said. "That is incorrect usage. Are you a dope? Are you an idiot that you cannot understand a basic function like that?"

"Watch your mouth," Riker said.

"Is that a threat?" Sub-Arius asked.

Maddox glanced at the crystal-computing cube on Riker's back. "What has happened to you? You've become unhinged since the succubus's death. Is there anything wrong with your circuitry?"

"I do not have circuitry like you think, Captain. It's a crystalline process. Nevertheless, I am now running a self-diagnostic. By the way, Riker…"

Sub-Arius gave the sergeant a few pointers to driving the mobile platform.

Soon, Riker used the controls to zoom up and down corridors. Maddox stood beside him with both blast rifles in hand. Every time they saw enemies, Maddox fired first and faster, annihilating them.

Maddox switched out energy capsules whenever one of the blast rifles was in danger of running dry.

Perhaps midway through the ship, Sub-Arius said, "That was a clever piece of intuitive logic, Captain. I have found the glitch in me. Some processes have been under assault. My analysis tells me it happened when Lilith died. That caused a backwash of certain delicate types of energy that have affected my crystal lattice. Fortunately, I have fixed that. I apologize for my rude behavior and talk earlier. It was not my normal manner and way."

"Maybe you just revealed your true self," Riker said.

"I see that is supposed to be a joke, Sergeant Riker. Yes, I applaud your sense of humor at a time like this. Gentlemen, you are coming upon the hatch that will take us out of the living quarters."

"Can we get the mobile sled through the hatch?" Riker asked.

"A simple matter of physics shows that will be impossible, as the sled is much bigger than the hatch. No, gentlemen, you will have to run. I estimate we have a forty-one percent chance of reaching the dimensional transporting device to reach the daughter-ship."

"Forty-one percent," Maddox said. "That's much higher odds than I would have thought at a time like this."

"Captain, you continually amaze me. Even here at the end, you are showing great resourcefulness, cleverness and an ability to keep your head. Many of your kind would be happy simply to have won the fight against Succubus Lilith."

"I want to see Meta and Jewel. Does that answer the question for you?"

"I have not asked a question," Sub-Arius said. "Ah, but I was going to ask a question. Yes, very logical, Captain."

"Are you sure your crystal lattice is completely repaired?" Riker asked. "You sound overly talkative."

"Do you want me to run another self-diagnostic in order that I not speak? Does my speaking bother you?"

Riker didn't answer as he grounded the mobile flyer. The two men hopped off and rushed to the hatch. In a few moments, the hatch opened. They trotted through the corridors, hurrying to the transfer mechanism. Fortunately, they didn't run across more armored aliens. They didn't come across more computer consoles. Unfortunately, the ship began to dissipate and fade as the central chamber had faded earlier.

"Is the ship losing its coherence?" Maddox asked.

"I am still running my self-diagnostic," Sub-Arius said primly.

"Put a halt to that and tell us so we can know if we have to run faster," Maddox said.

"Why are you not running faster if you can, Captain?"

367

"To save some energy," Maddox said. "It's one of the keys. Always have something in reserve."

"That is an interesting philosophy," Sub-Arius said, "and I can see that it makes sense. If you always have something in reserve, if the great moment comes, you still have something to fight with."

"There you go," Maddox said.

"Are you being patronizing, Captain Maddox?"

"Wouldn't think of it," Maddox said.

"To answer your question," Sub-Arius said, "yes, the ship is losing coherence and reality. I'm afraid the generators overheated and went offline when the succubus died. They need to be switched on. I imagine that is where all the engineers are running to and that is why we have not met anyone yet. They are too busy trying to fix the reality machines."

"Can we go around them?" Maddox asked.

"I have already mapped out a schematic of the Annihilator. Gentlemen, if you will follow my advice, I will lead you directly to the transfer machine."

The two panted, sweating, both having drunk all the water in the suits. Maddox went to Riker and grabbed one of the arms. Then, Maddox ran as only he could, and maybe some of the fastest New Men. Incredibly, Riker kept his feet under him as they whisked down the vast halls. The aches in their sides became nearly intolerable.

Between gasps, Maddox said, "I'm surprised an old man like you can keep this up."

"I'm surprised, too," Riker panted. "It's amazing and wonderful. I can't explain it. Even though I feel like crap, I also feel great. I haven't been able to do this since..."

Riker fell silent.

"I hope everything's okay on the other side and we can get back onto *Victory*," Maddox said.

"I would not put high odds on that," Sub-Arius said.

"Are you linked there?"

"That is impossible, Captain. It is mere logic on my part. I suspect we have less than a twenty-three percent chance of surviving once we reach the other side."

"Yeah," Maddox said, "why is that?"

"It would take too long to explain, Captain. But believe me, they are not having a good time of it over there. Of that I am quite certain."

-55-

In the other dimension on *Victory,* events were looking grim. The mobile asteroids, thirty-five of them, were coming fast toward the portal ship, which continued to hurtle toward the outer system.

The mobile asteroids had launched a vast mass of missiles, three separate groups, each larger than the previous one.

Andros and Galyan discovered that the metal used in the missiles was far superior to the titanium hulls of the earlier model. The missiles also burned hotter and faster. They likely had better than cobalt warheads, perhaps even antimatter warheads. At this point, however, it was impossible to tell.

It was no longer a matter of hours before they had to abandon the portal ship, but less than a single hour.

Commodore Galt was nervous and had called Valerie twice, arguing that now was the moment to jump.

"Lieutenant Commander," the comm officer said on *Victory's* bridge, "the commodore is calling again."

"I'm going to take this in my ready room," Valerie said.

She got up and walked across the bridge, not hurrying, but not going slowly either. She wanted the others to be confident and maintain their decorum and courage. She gave them an example to follow.

Valerie stepped into the ready room, sat behind the captain's desk and turned on the screen.

A worried Commodore Galt appeared. He didn't have the same circles around his eyes as previously. Some sleep, some medicine, had helped take the edge off, but fear was building again.

"Commander," Galt said, "we've done everything in our power to guard the portal ship. Now, however, the planet is gone, two of the motherships are gone, one of my battleships is gone—"

"I understand, Commodore, We've taken regrettable losses, and we are in a dangerous and frightful situation."

Galt shook his head. "That isn't the issue. The issue is: can we bring what remains of the task force home?"

"I believe we can."

"Then the dimensional transfer system, the alien computer you received from the Supreme Intelligence, can operate without the crystal piece that left with Maddox?"

Valerie wasn't sure she should have told Galt about that earlier. She'd let it slip. She decided it was because she was so tired and worried herself.

"Yes," Valerie said.

"I understand you care for the captain. I do, too. He's a noble man."

"Those are just words, Commodore. Clearly you are gripped by…" Valerie almost said fear, and that would have been an insult to a good and overworked man.

Galt wasn't evidencing fear, but he certainly was evidencing worry and most likely concern for his command. He was responsible for all the lives in the task force. That included the Lord High Admiral's granddaughter.

Valerie felt all that, too, but she'd been in these situations before. This wasn't her first rodeo as far as dealing with odd and bizarre situations. Granted she'd never had thirty-five mobile asteroids with Saurians thirsting for their blood and such masses of missiles zeroing in on a portal ship. But she had faced plenty of odd and strange situations so…

Valerie shook her head. "I'm sorry, Commodore. I was woolgathering. This is not the time for it."

"I should say not. Now look, Commander, the captain placed you under my command, under my authority."

"For the battle," Valerie said, interrupting.

"Yes, yes, I realize that, but we now must assume that the captain, even if he's alive, isn't going to make it back in time. Even if he's inside the portal ship, how long will it take him to reach the outer surface? And once there—are we going to leave someone out there to pick him up? Are you going to wait on station? The portal ship is hurtling toward the mass of missiles. They're fast approaching even as we speak. If we have any malfunctions, those ships will have to be left behind and we'll have lost that many more people. Commander, now is the time to go. This isn't the sort of mission where you cut it by the slightest margin. This is the type of mission where you see what is coming, you see what is going to happen, and that moment is now."

"I agree except for one small point. Captain Maddox, Sergeant Riker and Colonel Julk are not back yet. We're waiting for them."

"Three lives against everyone else." Galt nodded. "I freely admit I want to go now. I don't know what else to expect. At the very least, we must move away from the portal ship."

"Can we not at least send a few counter missiles at the mass coming at us?" Valerie asked.

"To what purpose?"

"To make the Saurians wonder. To cause them to miscalculate. Let's use everything we have before we leave."

"You forget," Galt said, "we might need our final reserves to face a crisis before we get home. If we use our final missiles here, we won't have anything left for an emergency."

Valerie silently conceded the point. They didn't know what they would face traveling through the dimensions to get back to theirs. It would be good to keep something in reserve. Therefore, to expend every missile they had...

"All right," Valerie said, "I concede. We do need something in reserve. How about this, Commodore? You take the task force, jump maybe five AUs away in the other direction and I'll be ready to jump to you as well."

"No, no, no," Galt said. "Don't you understand? You're the ticket home. If something happens to *Victory*, we're stuck here forever. Yours is the most valuable ship in the task force, period. You must come with us. I cannot force you. I wish I could. I wish I could send marines over and make you obey. I'm asking that you follow the chain of command the captain installed before he left."

"This isn't battle," Valerie said.

"I beg to differ. Look." Galt raised an arm and pointed, no doubt, at the main screen on the *Stonewall Jackson*. "Thirty-five mobile asteroids are bearing down on us. This time, likely with even better weapons than rail guns. The new missiles prove it. They're coming faster. The mobile asteroids can probably jump again. I would say, have it your way, but this is the lives of everyone in my task force. I'm responsible for them. Commander, I'm ordering you to jump with the task force. Leave someone behind in a fold fighter, if you must. But otherwise, you owe it to the rest of us to stay with us. Will you disobey a direct order in the midst of combat? Because clearly these are combat conditions, with such masses of missiles bearing down on us. My order has been given. What is your response, Lieutenant Commander?"

Valerie stared up at the ceiling. Part of her resented this and part of her wanted to obey the chain of command. She looked at Galt.

There was a ferocious glint in his eyes and yet there was that hint of worry.

Valerie stood up. His head snapped up. "I'll obey your order. I'll make arrangements and we will get ready to jump within ten minutes."

An agonized look and a strained expression showed on Galt's face.

"In five minutes," Valerie said.

"All right, agreed. Thank you, Commander. Thank you, indeed."

Soon, Valerie exited the ready room as she stepped back onto the bridge. She noticed that Keith wasn't at the helm. Instead, one of the other pilots was there.

Valerie cleared her throat. "Where's Lieutenant Maker?"

"Uh, Valerie," Galyan said. "Keith told me to tell you that he's already heading for the tin can and he will wait by the portal ship to pick up the captain when he appears."

Valerie scowled. "Why and how would Keith have decided that? I'm the one who decides that."

"Yes, Valerie. I am just relaying the words Keith told me."

Valerie became suspicious. "Why would Keith know to do that?"

Galyan looked off into the distance.

With anger tinging her, Valerie moved her face closer to Galyan "Did you eavesdrop on me, Driving Force Galyan?"

"I am sorry, Valerie. I did, and I told Keith your decision. He jumped up and ran out yelling his instructions over his shoulder."

"That was fast," she said. "I hardly had made the decision and came out."

"Yes, Valerie. I think we all knew how it was going to go."

She peered at the exit hatch. "I should probably order Keith back. He's the best pilot. He should take *Victory* out of here."

"I do not think Keith will listen to you, Valerie, and it is not good to issue commands that someone ignores. That sets a bad precedent."

Valerie squinted at Galyan. "Is this insubordination from you, too, Driving Force Galyan?"

"Captain Maddox and Sergeant Riker are my friends, Valerie. I will do just about anything to see them safe. I also care about you, and Commodore Galt had a good point. He is responsible for everyone and I do want to see as many as can get home. But Valerie, we must give the captain every edge. Please do not countermand what Keith has said."

A sharp retort bubbled on Valerie's lips. Instead, she nodded sharply. "This once," she said, "we're going to do it your way."

"Thank you, Valerie. I will remember this."

Valerie grimaced. She knew Galyan would remember, probably already marking this down in her personality profile. He had probably already known what to say because of the profile. She shook her head and started issuing orders. Then she sat in the captain's chair.

Soon Keith appeared on the main screen. "I'm leaving the hangar bay, Commander."

374

Valerie stared at Keith Maker. After this, things were going to be different, she told herself. She was going to finally make amends with him. It was time they settled down. "You better make sure you come back to *Victory*."

Keith looked abashed. "Why would you think otherwise? Who could do this but me?"

Valerie shook her head. "Don't cut it too close. There is a margin for error and then there is being risky. I don't want you to be risky, Lieutenant."

"Commander, respectfully, I'm bringing the captain home."

"Keith Maker, if you speak like that I'm going to order you up here."

"Yes, Commander," he said, working busily on the controls.

On a side screen, Valerie saw the fold fighter drawing away from the starship. There was a knot in her gut. It was for Keith.

"Good luck," she said. "Make sure you come back."

"Of course, Commander. As you say."

With that, Valerie cut the connection. It was actually happening. They were actually getting ready to leave the portal ship.

The first of the task force vessels, the *Joan of Arc*, made its star-drive jump. The destroyers followed, and then the light cruisers and finally the two battleships. Only *Victory* had yet to made the jump.

"Commander," the comm officer said, "there's a call for you from the lieutenant."

"Put it on the screen," Valerie said.

Keith looked at her. "What's wrong with you? Get out of here. Those missiles are closing fast. We don't have time. You don't have time for the margin."

"Me?" Valerie said, and then a stubborn knot of an idea came. She was going to tell him, "I'm going to stay just as long as you're going to stay. How do you like that, mister?" That's what she wanted to say. In fact, she opened her mouth to say it.

"Valerie," Galyan said.

Her head snapped around as she looked at the holographic Adok. She realized she couldn't say that. She owed everyone on *Victory*. She was responsible for them. She had to get them home. She wasn't going to be like Keith and she wasn't going to be like Captain Maddox. She was going to do her duty in the best way possible. She turned back and looked at Keith.

"You better make it back," she said.

"Aye," he said.

Valerie cut the connection. She checked, seeing that the missiles were coming fast for the portal ship, even as the portal ship with the tin can in orbit around it hurtled toward them.

Valerie gave the order to jump. Less than thirty seconds later, *Victory* used its star-drive jump to join the rest of the task force.

-56-

Maddox and Riker with Sub-Arius entered the transport mechanism on the Annihilator. Sub-Arius activated the machine. Nothing happened. There was no energizing, there was nothing.

"Well, Sub-Arius," Maddox asked, "what does this mean? We're finished?"

"Just a moment, Captain. I think, ah, my crystal lattice failed in some way. Give me a few moments to make a self-adjustment."

As they waited, Riker moved the shoulders of his armor suit. "You know, Captain, I feel different and I can't explain it and I don't know why. I should be exhausted. I should be deadbeat. Instead, I'm feeling stronger and better than ever. The wait while standing here is reviving me. That shouldn't be. I mean, we've run a death race if ever there was one. My throat is parched—"

"And you can talk like no one's business," Maddox said, interrupting.

Riker chuckled. "Yes sir, that's true. I'm talking like no one's business. I'm feeling..." The helmeted head cocked.

"Yes," Maddox said, intrigued despite their ominous condition.

"I'm not sure, Captain. I have to think about this for a moment longer before I'm ready to say for sure."

"Indeed, Sergeant."

"Gentlemen," Sub-Arius said. "I believe I have found the problem. I am surprised and amazed I failed to see it earlier. Now, let us—ah, there. I think if you look…"

The black cones surged with energy. In a moment a yawning portal appeared before them.

"Come on," Maddox shouted. He grabbed Riker and leapt through the portal.

Riker followed on his heels, carrying Sub-Arius.

The elongated feeling returned as if they stretched for kilometers. Then, with a *whoosh*, they hurtled through whatever it was, tumbling onto the dais of the Annihilator's daughter-ship.

Maddox lay there stunned, trying to regain orientation.

Amazingly, Riker stood first. "We're back. By gum, we made it. This is astounding."

The entire daughter-ship shook and trembled.

"What in tarnation is happening?" Riker asked.

Maddox finally climbed to his feet. He did so as much as to get Riker to stop talking like a hick as anything else. "Follow me, Sergeant, we have to run. Sub-Arius, do you have any idea what's happening?"

"I would think that there are tremendous explosions outside the ship which does not bode well for us."

"Right," Maddox said.

The two men began to run. They were already tired, but they knew if they couldn't make it in time, they were going to stay here and die most likely as the best thing.

Even as that was happening, outside another antimatter explosion in the distance washed against the portal ship. There was no sign of the tin can. Neither was there any sign of the shreds of it.

As one rotated around the portal ship, on the other side behind, there Keith hung in the fold fighter, waiting, hoping for some signal, some sign that Captain Maddox and the others had survived. There were no messages coming to him. Instead, Keith watched on his monitor as waves of radiation and blast washed on either side of him. The portal ship protected him with its super-dense construction. There were only minimal amounts of radiation that had leaked through both the fold-fighter hull and the suit he was wearing. Keith had remained on station.

Keith Maker was the best damn ace and fighter pilot in all of Star Watch, and he owed it to Captain Maddox. He'd been a drunkard before joining *Victory* and he wasn't a drunkard anymore.

Another explosion washed against the portal ship, slowing its momentum yet again.

Three more, Keith told himself. Three more explosions like that and then he would fold. Would his tin can even hold together long enough? Would its mechanisms of fold still work? He could send no messages, as whiteout surrounded him.

"Help me," he said to no one in particular. Keith Maker waited, and waited just a little longer, hoping to see Captain Maddox appear.

Inside the portal ship, Maddox and Riker panted as the raced along the corridors, tromping as best they could.

"It's no use," Riker said, with an ache in him.

"Forget that," Maddox said. He grabbed the sergeant, pulling him along by an arm. Maddox thought of Jewel and Meta. Not in a logical consistent sense, but in the sense of his wife beside him in bed at night when she was there, and when he would bounce Jewel on his knee. She would laugh and he would hear the laughter and it would touch his heart deep within.

That was the essence propelling Maddox. He clutched the old fool of a sergeant because he wasn't going to leave him behind. He wasn't going to leave anybody behind. Sub-Arius was talking and even as he stood there, panting, Maddox looked up and saw a section of the hull disengaging. As it disengaged, it blew away and flew out of sight.

"What does that mean?" Maddox asked in a tired voice.

"It means you must jump for all you are worth, Captain, and you too, Sergeant. This is our last chance."

Maddox gathered his final dregs of resolve and leapt. Riker jumped with him as Sub-Arius cut the gravity. They shot up and went through.

379

In that moment they might have died in a burst of gamma radiation from the blast of an antimatter warhead, but the portal ship rotated just enough to protect them.

Maddox saw what looked like a fold fighter. Out of the hatch, a suited man sped toward them. Was that Keith? Maddox didn't know, but he knew someone from *Victory* had waited even as it appeared the enemy was bombarding them with exploding warheads.

Maddox tried to communicate with Riker. He tried to communicate with Sub-Arius. He tried to communicate with whoever reached them. Nothing. The whiteout made communication impossible.

Whoever the suited person was threw a net around them and used a tether, drawing all of them back to the fold fighter. Soon, they entered the vessel and the hatch shut behind them. The suited person staggered to the piloting seat and sat in it.

Maddox and Riker both lay on the deck exhausted, perhaps with lethal doses of radiation. They weren't dead. They yet hung on to life.

The pilot hit the fold mechanism.

Would the tin can fold? Would the piece of machinery do its duty as it had so many times before, or had it absorbed too much radiation? Had the high levels of radiation wrecked or melted the machinery?

At that moment, the tin can folded, hopefully for the waiting task force.

-57-

The fold fighter appeared beside *Victory* although none of the men inside were conscious.

Moments later Galyan appeared, looking at the three suited men, noting the alien armor of two, identical to what the invaders had worn before. He ascertained that there were indeed men inside, and not the gorilla-like aliens. Galyan called them by name but nothing woke the men.

He debated entering one and perhaps giving him a mild shock, but realized each was gravely injured. Each had likely received massive doses of radiation.

"Oh dear," Galyan said. He popped out of the fold fighter onto the bridge in front of Valerie. "This is terrible. They are all on the edge of death."

Valerie stared at Galyan intently. "We'll draw the fighter into a hangar bay so we can begin our departure. Wait. They had Sub-Arius, right?"

"Yes," Galyan said.

"Has the crystal also taken massive levels of radiation?"

"Oh no," Galyan said. "I suppose he would have. I wonder if reuniting Sub-Arius with Greater Arius will have any impact on the whole."

"This is just wonderful," Valerie said, "another problem." She debated silently, gave orders, and then bit a knuckle, breaking one of her cardinal rules. She displayed her worry in front of the crew.

Valerie lowered the hand, stood and was about to give the bridge to Keith so she could oversee the revival operation. But Keith was on the fold fighter on the verge of death. The fool had risked his life, although he had brought Maddox back.

"Galyan, you said three of them, and Sub-Arius. There should be four men."

"It was just the three."

"Who's missing?"

"They were all suited. Oh. Colonel Julk is missing. I did not detect a Neanderthal."

Valerie snapped another order concerning the fold fighter. A moment later, she contacted Galt to inform him of the situation.

At the same time, techs with a tractor beam drew the fold fighter into the hangar bay. A decontamination team entered and carried the men off the fold fighter, placing them onto a special unit inside the hangar bay. There, the team removed the helmet of the first man.

"Keith Maker," said the chief medical officer.

They stripped off the armor and hooked him to a life-support system. A med-computer analyzed and administered various anti-radiation drugs through a hypo.

They removed the alien helmet of the second man.

Galyan appeared. "Captain Maddox, it is good to see you."

Maddox hadn't revived and was twisting in pain. The team removed the alien armor and placed him on life support as well.

They breached the third suit.

Galyan and the others stared at a youthful man.

"Who's this?" asked one of the medical personnel. "It's not Colonel Julk, as clearly, he's not a Neanderthal. He looks familiar, though."

"Riker," Galyan said. "That is Sergeant Treggason Riker. But he looks as he must have in his early twenties. I do not understand this."

None of them did.

Yet, since he looked like Riker, they assumed it was Riker, believing that something had happened in the other dimension they could not explain. They stripped probable-Riker of his alien armor and hooked him to the life-support system.

They then took all three men, wheeling them through the corridors to medical. There, the emergency procedures continued.

Galyan had remained in the hangar bay. Under his guidance, a marine withdrew the crystal computer from its carrying case.

"Do you understand me?" Galyan asked.

"Of course I understand you," Sub-Arius said. "That's a rather foolish question. Wait. I perceive why you asked me. The three men had taken high levels of radiation. Don't worry about me, though, I'm fine. I absorbed the radiation as fuel. I am not the least toxic to any of you. I now ask that you tell the marine to take me to Greater Arius. I wish to be reunited with him."

"That is not possible just yet," Galyan said. "We do not know what happened out there, if it's safe to do as you suggest."

"I will tell you what happened."

Galyan considered the offer and the possibility Sub-Arius would fabricate data. He decided to take a chance on the crystal's honesty and that it wasn't compromised. "Can you please be quick?"

"Can you receive information at computer speeds?"

"Of course," Galyan said.

Sub-Arius gave Galyan a burst of information so the Adok AI recollected all that had happened to Maddox and the others through the sensors of Sub-Arius.

Galyan pondered the information, analyzing. "I do not see where the switch could have occurred, I mean with the young Sergeant Riker."

"What are you talking about? Oh, I see. My crystal lattice had one more glitch and that may have hindered your understanding. It was a matter of time and dimensions, not a switch. Certainly, you should be able to understand. You possess a greater capacity for understanding than any of these dull humans."

383

"I wish you would not refer to them as dull. They are my friends and are all unique individuals who have done amazing things, including killing the succubus."

"You believe then that the Annihilator is no more?"

"That is not the issue. When did the switch occur? What happened to *our* Sergeant Riker? I understand very well that you have replaced him with a different-dimension Riker."

"How many times must I say it? It was not a switch. That is your Sergeant Riker but in a youthful incarnation."

"That is illogical. He does not have any of his bionic parts, which are an identifying mark, if you will?"

"He lacks the bionic parts because they were replaced with youthful limbs and an eye."

"How?" asked Galyan. "When and how did that take place?"

"It was a unique function of an entity in an odd dimension we entered. We entered the dimension under the deck hatch in the crystal garden aboard the Annihilator. The glob or gelatin entity put him in a reality more real than you might suspect. It was not only their imagination. It was truly real. Riker and Maddox truly saw the elongated humans that had once been part of Star Watch."

"I do not comprehend the physics of this, the quantum mechanics. It makes no logical sense."

"That is not the half of it," Sub-Arius said. "You do not understand dimensional physics in the least. The situation makes perfect sense to me. Riker went into a different dimension, and the place and entity worked or functioned upon different principles than you can conceive. In this case the entity turned Riker young again and removed the bionic parts so fleshly ones could accrue."

Galyan blinked rapidly. "How long will the effect last?"

"It is not an effect. Don't you understand? It has taken place. Riker is young and whole again. He will grow old at the normal chronological rate for humans in their dimension, provided we make it home again. And that will only occur if you reunite me with Greater Arius. I have of the key functions he needs for dimensional travel."

384

"Meaning we never could have escaped this dimension without you?"

"That is privileged information," Sub-Arius said. "I am forbidden to share it with you. Are you going to reunite me with the greater whole or must we wait here and possibly face thirty-five mobile asteroids?"

"I will be back shortly."

Galyan vanished and appeared before Valerie, relating the news.

"This is incredible," Valerie said. "It's not some bizarre ramification of an imposter Riker, but our sergeant has become young again?"

"That is what Sub-Arius claims. The claim is not necessarily the truth."

"That's wild," Valerie said. "Will Riker continue with his career or start a new one? I doubt Riker will want to retire now."

"How can this have happened? It is not logical."

"If you don't know, Galyan, I surely don't know. Let's get to the time-sensitive point. Do you trust Sub-Arius enough to reunite him with Greater Arius so we can leave?"

"Not altogether," Galyan said. "However, I am inclined to believe we cannot use the dimensional-hopping apparatus unless Sub-Arius is reconnected with Greater Arius. Even if Greater Arius could do it alone with several percentage points less efficiency without Sub-Arius, I suggest we allow their union to ensure the greatest likelihood of success."

"I'm in agreement there—just a minute." Valerie swiveled in the captain's chair and listened to reports about Keith, Maddox and Riker. They'd stabilized. It appeared they would recover given time and rest. Valerie sagged against the chair and muttered, "Thank you, God."

She turned back to Galyan and stood, beaming. Keith was going to be okay, and so were Maddox and young Riker—a young Riker. That hardly made sense. He used to be the old man. Things would be different with a *young* Riker.

"You should be there when Sub-Arius reunites with Greater Arius," Valerie said. "The professor is out, the captain is out, even Riker who has a solid head on his shoulders is out. It's time we left before these mobile asteroids reach us, and whatever else is coming after them. The planet is gone. The Annihilator is gone. The Lord High Admiral's granddaughter is alive as far as I know. She's aboard the *Stonewall Jackson*. We've done it."

"This is all good news," Galyan said.

"Make sure everything with Arius and the Yon Soth machine works according to our established protocols. If there's anything wrong, contact me immediately. We must get the task force home."

"Yes, Valerie. I must say, this is a good feeling. We are successful once again."

"Don't jinx us. We're on the verge of success. We've completed much of the operation. Now, we need to get everybody home again."

Galyan disappeared and reappeared in the hangar bay. He told the marines acting as sentries to pick up Sub-Arius and follow him. They would reunite the crystal with the greater whole. Hopefully, completed Arius could activate the Yon Soth machine that would open a portal so they could leave this bizarre dimension.

-58-

Maddox slowly became aware of people moving around him. He realized then that he had become aware at other intervals, perhaps three other times. He felt languid, no longer in pain, and his mind seemed sharper than before.

Perhaps the effects... He remembered taking massive doses of radiation, probably when he exited the daughter-ship of the Annihilator.

He focused on the ceiling and heard the bustle of people and medical machinery around him. *We did it. We killed Succubus Lilith. We left her dimension.*

He frowned, concerned, and cleared his throat.

A young ensign with curly red hair turned and smiled at him. "Captain, you're awake. I'm glad. Let me check your vitals." She stepped to a machine, checking the monitor and looking up afterward. "The signs are good. How do you feel?"

"Never mind that," Maddox said. "Where are we?"

"Aboard *Victory*," she said, perplexed.

"Yes, yes, I know that, and thank you. *Where* are we?"

She frowned until she brightened. She had pretty teeth. "Oh, I see what you mean. We've reached our dimension. We made it back."

Maddox stared at her.

"It has nearly been a day and a half, ship-time, since you were brought to medical. Commander Noonan gave the order and we slipped through the dimensions, this time without trouble. We're presently in the Trappist-1 System, the same one we left to begin dimension hopping."

Maddox sagged against the bed with relief. They'd made it home, back to their dimension. He never wanted to leave it again. He was going to see Meta and Jewel again. Thank God! The moment of joy was brief, however. Other thoughts and then worries intruded.

Maddox noticed the ensign watching him. He waved her aside with a nod, appreciating her efforts.

She sniffed and then stepped away, resuming her duties.

Maddox focused on the ceiling. A worse thought sprung into being. *Am I really aboard the starship or is this another illusion and we're still aboard the Annihilator?*

The reality machines had confused him.

"Wait a minute," he said.

The ensign whipped around, her eyebrows arching.

He focused on her. Was she too intent? He wasn't sure. He practiced his calming techniques. This seemed real. He had heard something when the emergency team cracked open the armor suits. What had that been? Oh, right.

"I heard someone say Riker was young. Is that correct?"

The ensign gave another of her dazzling smiles. "Yes sir, that's correct. We have no idea concerning the dynamics of it. The chief medical examiner said Riker went to Elf Land and back, the process reversing this time—whatever that means."

Maddox nodded. He knew what it meant. Dazed, he stared up at the ceiling, thinking. He didn't realize he was being rude to the ensign.

After a moment, she went back to her duties, occasionally glancing at him.

Maddox mused upon the news. He recalled the prison-planet illusion. He'd thought it an illusion, anyway. In it, there had been a young Riker. Perhaps it had been more than an illusion assault against them.

Maddox closed his eyes. Now wasn't the time to worry about it. Galyan could explain it later.

Maddox then opened his eyes. He struggled to a sitting position, propping the pillows behind him.

"Galyan, where are you?"

388

The ensign whirled about, looking up sharply. She gasped as the little Adok holoimage appeared beside the captain's bed.

"Captain, you called?" Galyan asked.

"Are we in the Trappist-1 System?" Maddox asked.

Galyan glanced at the ensign.

She dropped her gaze and went back to studying the medical machinery.

Galyan faced Maddox. "That is correct, sir. We have just finished bringing all the ships across. It was a lengthy process, but Valerie did an excellent job of leading *Victory*. Commodore Galt kept everything in order in the task force, even when we had a glitch or two."

"*All* the ships are back?"

"All the ships that survived the second-wave mobile asteroid assault are back. Do you want to know about the glitches?"

"No. We've definitely returned to the Trappist-1 System in our dimension?"

"Yes, Captain. I have said so. I am not in the habit of giving untruths."

"Never mind that. I want you to listen closely and not get excited by the question."

Galyan nodded.

"Is Sub-Arius with Greater Arius?"

"That was the condition both made for using the Yon Soth machine to open the way and bring us through."

"I understand. Are marines in hangar bay 2?"

"Yes, sir. They are keeping watch, while Arius's robots are watching them. Nothing bad has happened that I have been able to determine. The Yon Soth machine is still barricaded behind the force field. It reacted in a predictable manner throughout the journey home."

"Fine, good, good work, Galyan."

"Thank you, sir."

Maddox felt a wave of weariness wash over him. He suddenly felt so tired. He wasn't accustomed to feeling this tired. He fought it off. "Now listen. Are you listening, Galyan?"

389

"Sir, you are more tired than you realize. Perhaps you should go back to sleep and recover more fully."

"Never mind that," Maddox said crossly. "Is Ludendorff awake?"

"Only at times. He still has not recovered fully from his ordeal."

"You mean he's not totally sane?"

"I would not put it in those stark terms. He is, however, having trouble adjusting to reality in the normal sense of things."

Maddox's mouth twisted thoughtfully. "Is Ludendorff going to recover fully, if he has enough rest?"

"We give that a high probability. Still, no one knows until it actually takes place."

Maddox gathered his strength, swung his legs off the bed, and slid until his bare feet touched the floor.

The ensign looked up. "I'm not sure you should do that, Captain."

"I understand. Thank you for your concern. Galyan, you stay right here for the moment and don't send any messages just yet."

Galyan perked up. "How did you know I was going to alert Valerie that you were getting up?"

"I have my ways."

"Was that an intuitive thought, sir?"

"Never mind. The important thing is…" Maddox exerted himself, standing, feeling uncomfortably dizzy. After a moment, he retrieved his uniform and boots from the closet. He put them on.

The ensign had left. A doctor and two others hurried into the room.

With slow and deliberate movements, and against the doctor's wishes, Maddox left medical. He soon confirmed that they were indeed back in the Trappist-1 System.

Since the ships had barely returned, Maddox knew that people would be congratulating each other as a vast sense of relief filled everyone. Undoubtedly, Galt and Valerie were giving the crews an hour and maybe a little longer to relax.

390

Maddox couldn't relax. Oh, he was relieved to have returned, utterly and joyously relieved. However, he never, ever wanted to leave their dimension again. The whole idea about leaving dimensions—

"Sir, you seem unsteady," Galyan said. "Are you sure you would not like help?"

Maddox steadied himself by resting a hand on a corridor bulkhead. He considered his resolve. "Galyan, go to Valerie and tell her I've resumed command of the ship."

"Sir?" asked Galyan.

"Then you will immediately come back to me."

"Yes, sir," Galyan said. He popped away, was hardly gone a moment and then reappeared. "Valerie is concerned, sir, that you're not fully recovered."

"Let her worry. You've given the message and now you'll stay with me. We have something to do."

"Could you tell me what that is, sir?"

"Not yet. You will follow me. No, you'll get the present commander of marines." Maddox winced at the memory. "Julk's dead. He died in that damned dimension saving our lives."

"Yes, sir," Galyan said. "That is what Sergeant Riker said."

"Riker's awake?"

"He recovered more quickly than you, sir. I believe his youthfulness is helping him recover more quickly than is his wont."

Maddox nodded in agreement. A young Riker. Maddox smiled. That was good. The sergeant deserved something positive like that for all the things he'd gone through throughout the years. Then, pushing that thought aside, Maddox focused on the task at hand. He had something to do. Something he couldn't allow anyone to get in his way.

With grim resolution, Maddox stalked down the corridors with Galyan beside him. Soon, at his orders, Galyan popped away. The Adok holoimage returned with a squad of marines. They all went to hangar bay 2. There, Maddox incorporated the guarding marines with his.

Half of the robots stood around Arius. The other half stood by the Yon Soth controls outside the force field.

391

"Captain Maddox," combined-Arius said. "It is a delight to see you. Oh, but this is also worrisome. I'm detecting that you're not fully recovered from your ordeal."

"I'm recovered enough." Maddox turned to the marines. "Gentlemen, you will take Arius's crystal cubes to a different hangar bay."

"Now wait just a moment," Arius said. "I no longer require human hands. My robots can do any moving, not that I agree to leave the hangar bay."

"The dimensional part of the voyage is over," Maddox said. "I wish to insure that."

"By having me exit the hangar bay?"

"Precisely," Maddox said. "I also ask that you decommission your robots."

"I can't agree to that."

"Why not?"

"This is hasty and unnecessary. It sounds as if you no longer trust me."

Maddox forced a smile onto his face. "First, thank you for all your help, which includes Sub-Arius's help in the other dimensions."

"You're more than welcome. It has been a joy working with you. I'm now requesting that you give me the Yon Soth machine as payment for my help."

A pang in Maddox's gut told him he was right in what he planned. This was evidence of it.

"You don't have such a machine on the Library Planet?" Maddox asked.

"That isn't the point."

"You do have such a machine?"

"You're probing, Captain. In truth, no, the Supreme Intelligence does not. This is a unique machine."

"I know."

"What does the statement mean exactly? You seem worked up."

"Arius. It is time to move you."

"And if I refuse?" Arius asked. "My robots know how to defend me."

392

Maddox smiled, but this time it was more like a wolf or tiger smiling before an assault. "I have no doubt that your robots are an effective defense."

"You mean something by that."

Maddox raised his hand and snapped his fingers.

The marines that had come with him raised normal Star Watch issue blast rifles. They opened fire on the robots, destroying them in a blaze of shredded metal and sizzling electronics.

Smoke rose from the wreckage.

"How dare you destroy my robots," Arius said in the ensuing silence.

"Let's hear no more veiled threats," Maddox said. "This is my starship. I'm the captain, the authority. I appreciate your hard work."

"You destroyed my robots like a barbarian," Arius said.

"I'm sorry," Maddox said.

"What?"

"I'm sorry."

"So it's asking for forgiveness instead of permission, is it?"

"I tried to get you to agree. Will you now permit the marines to move you to a different hangar bay?"

"I obviously have no choice," Arius said. "May I ask what you plan to do in my absence? If my robots and I aren't here, we can't keep the force field around the Yon Soth machine for long. It's constantly fighting that."

"Don't worry," Maddox said. "I'll take care of the force field and machine."

"The Yon Soth machine is unique. I'm not sure you understand just how much."

"I assure you I do."

The stack of crystalline cubes fell quiet, perhaps thoughtful. "Captain, do you wish me to leave so you can do something to the machine?"

"That doesn't concern you."

"It most certainly does. Surely, by now you realize I'm an interdimensional construct. The Yon Soth machine is my connection to the various dimensions I call my own."

"That's quite interesting. Now, do I have your permission or not?"

"And if I don't give it?" asked Arius.

"We proceed to option two."

"Which is?"

"You'll find out shortly."

Colors swirled along the sides of the cubes. "Very well, you may move me. But I urge you to consider what the Supreme Intelligence might do if you act rashly."

"I assure you, Arius, I already have." Maddox turned to the marines. "Get moving. You have your orders."

The marines took Arius cube by cube to a different hangar bay. During that time, without the robots monitoring it, the force field around the Yon Soth machine abruptly ceased.

Maddox gave further orders. A cargo shuttle maneuvered into the hangar bay. When the marines returned from having moved the last crystal cube, Maddox instructed them to put the Yon Soth machine aboard the vessel. They did without incident, which Maddox found odd and troubling. An hour later, the shuttle was sealed.

Maddox then gave Galyan precise instructions.

"Captain, are you sure this is wise? We may need the machine again."

"I am the commanding officer of *Victory*. Will you obey me or not?"

"Of course I will, sir…on one condition."

Maddox had sweaty features, as he had been feeling faint for the last fifteen minutes. He didn't think it was the machine doing this, but simple fatigue. Something alerted him now. "Are you bargaining with me, Galyan?"

"Sir, in essence, this is my starship. Is that not so?"

"Yes…" Maddox said slowly.

"I have seldom bargained with you, but I am now."

"Say your piece."

"I will do as you have requested, sir, provided at the next opportunity you accompany me to the Adoks. You will then attempt to bring reconciliation between us."

Maddox had to sit down, as he felt even fainter than before. "Yes, I'll do that."

"I do not want you to promise, because I know you saying it is good enough."

Maddox shook his head and then lay back on the deck, exhausted. The exertion of what he was doing—he gathered his resolve and sat up again. "Get it done, Galyan. I don't want any problems with this. I want it done and I want it done *now.*"

"Yes, sir." With that, Galyan disappeared.

Maddox and the marines with him exited the hangar bay. Afterward, the outer hangar bay door opened and Galyan, using his functions, flew the cargo shuttle with the Yon Soth machine out of the hangar bay. Once exiting *Victory*, Galyan headed for the Trappist-1 System star.

Oddly, as Galyan made the journey, he felt an alien intelligence and yearning silently begging him not to do this. Galyan did not listen. The machine attempted a subtle attack. The captain had warned him about the possibility, and he used countermeasures.

A while later, the shuttle speaker snapped on. "Galyan, Galyan." It was Valerie, or sounded like her, anyway.

"What can I do for you, Valerie?"

"What do you think you're doing, Galyan? Why has the amplifier been launched from the ship and sent toward the star?"

"Captain Maddox is in charge now, Valerie. He has told me not to say anything about this."

"You have the Yon Soth machinery in the shuttle?"

"Yes, Valerie."

"And you're headed for the star?"

"Yes, Valerie."

"Do you plan to dive into the star?"

"Yes, Valerie."

"I can't let you do that."

"Captain Maddox is in charge, Valerie."

"The captain is tired. He doesn't know what he's doing. We may need the machine again."

"The captain does not think so. The captain thinks dimensional travel is foolish and that we must cease doing it. This is his attempt to make sure it does not happen again from our end."

"Galyan—"

"I am signing off, Valerie."

With that, Galyan increased velocity. The system star grew nearer and nearer as the shuttle headed straight for it.

Then, as the cargo shuttle dove into the star, Galyan disappeared. He returned to his amplifier and used magnification to watch the shuttle.

The cargo shuttle flew into the star, burning and turning to a crisp. No doubt, the Yon Soth machine burned and crisped with it, which was the point of all this.

How would Professor Ludendorff take this wanton destruction of his property? Galyan had a good idea how it would go, but as of right now, the professor did not possess his full faculties.

Galyan decided it was time to return to the ship. Captain Maddox hated dimensional travel and he did not think the captain would ever agree to such a voyage again.

-59-

Victory and Task Force 3 arrived in the Solar System through the hyper-spatial tube.

Maddox made his report to the Lord High Admiral. Commodore Donal Galt made his report. The Lord High Admiral's granddaughter was reunited with Old Man Cook.

There, things might have ended as one of the strangest missions that *Victory* had ever completed. Maddox was reunited with his family and had a great and glorious time with Meta and Jewel. It turned out that Meta wasn't pregnant. That had been a false alarm.

Sergeant Riker had...it wasn't a dilemma as such but a real change in status. He'd left an old man with aches and pains, although he could perform his duties after a fashion, particularly because of the bionic parts. Now, the bionic parts were gone. He didn't have a magnification function bionic eye. He didn't have the extra strength of a bionic arm or bionic leg. All his parts were youthful flesh and blood. He had the power and vigor of youth, and that was so strange, so odd.

As the others departed or returned to regular duties, Maddox and Galyan made their reports, and Ludendorff slowly came out of his stupor, learning what had happened to the Yon Soth machine.

The destruction should have enraged Ludendorff. It didn't. Perhaps that was because Ludendorff saw the wisdom of what Maddox had done. For once, Ludendorff accepted the wisdom. That was odd, too.

In any case, young Riker was home.

Victory was in orbit around Earth. A port team had already entered to effect extensive repairs. It was the same with Task Force 3's vessels. All the personnel were on leave, the last ones finished with the intelligence people.

Riker was home, enjoying himself immensely. He worked in his garden hour upon hour upon hour. He didn't get tired like he used to. He used to huff, puff and take long naps. He didn't take any naps now. He had vigor all day long.

A few days home on leave, Riker went to a local gym. He used to laugh at Maddox for doing that. Today, Riker pumped some iron. Boy, did it feel good. He strained every fiber pushing them weights. He came home tired, ate a big meal and *then* took a nap, mostly out of habit.

He woke up feeling refreshed. Sure, there were a few aches and pains because he wasn't used to pushing his body this hard. But it was youthful vigor pain.

How he'd missed the joy of youth where he could do things and rebound right away from it. He used to wonder as a kid why the old guys used glasses to read and got tired so easily. They'd tell him, "We're not going to play a game of football as we're too sore afterward."

That wasn't Riker anymore.

All his old aches and little problems with the bionic parts— they were all gone.

Riker slapped his chest. What a mission. He was so grateful Galyan had gotten him for it. Yes, he was sad Colonel Julk had died, and it had been difficult mentally going to the strange Annihilator dimension. But you know what? The vigor of youth helped him to forget about all that.

One of the oddest things occurred several days after returning as he sat that night watching a holo-vid movie, getting ready to go to bed because that was his routine, his *old* routine in more way than one.

Riker stood and stared at a wall. He thought to himself, *you know, I'm not tired.*

In fact, he felt antsy because he was bored sitting in the house like an old man. *Why don't I go out and have some fun?*

Riker turned his thoughts into action. He got an overcoat and hat and jauntily left the house, striding down the street. He was unaware that several short, over-muscled hard-eyed men observed and followed him at a discreet distance.

Riker took a tube train to the nearest city in France. He didn't feel like being in Switzerland Sector tonight. In fact, he made a decision and boarded a different tube train to Paris.

Yes siree, he would have a quick night on the town in Paris. Maybe he'd stay up all night, too.

Soon, Riker walked the streets of Paris at night. Some pretty women eyed him as he walked past. That brought a greater smile than ever to his smooth face.

Riker recalled some of the dating advice he'd given in the past, but that was from an old man's perspective. He might even say it was a wise perspective. However, with the vigor of youth came the hormones, adrenaline and rush of youth. The ladies thought him handsome, yes, sir.

Riker went into a bar he wouldn't have gone normally. He ordered a simple, yet good beer. He sat on a bar stool sipping and he listened to others.

He realized he didn't feel out of place here. There was music and some dancing, and then wouldn't you know it, a gorgeous lady, a blonde in a sequin dress, sat down beside him. She placed her little purse on the bar and engaged him in conversation.

Her name was Lille and she was a delight. She laughed at his jokes and touched his arm at times.

Riker was starting to feel that he would like to kiss her. Instead, he reached over and touched her hand. They laughed and talked more.

Later, he said, "Excuse me. I'll be right back." He went to the restroom.

When he came back, she said, "I ordered you another beer. I hope that was okay."

"Sure is, Lille."

Riker toasted her because she raised her glass to him. He had a healthy swallow. There was a strange taste to the beer, but he figured it was because he could taste better because he was young again.

They continued to flirt and Riker loved it. He loved every second of it. He thought, *Well, I helped Maddox defeat Succubus Lilith and we resisted the temptations of those dreamlike succubae, but this is a flesh and blood girl of Earth. There's nothing wrong with this.*

He asked Lille to dance and they did, going out on the floor. He moved like you wouldn't believe. He was not a coordinated old man, but rather a coordinated *young* man. They danced and then something odd happened. He felt lightheaded and his feet brushed against each other so he stumbled.

"Are you okay?" Lille asked.

"I'm fine."

Soon, she helped him back to his stool, as the lightheadedness got even worse.

Riker wasn't sure what was happening to him. He lost sense of what was taking place around him, only vaguely aware that Lille was leading him by the arm toward an exit.

"Here," Lille said, "you look really tired. Maybe we should go outside for a breath of fresh air."

Riker hardly remembered what he mumbled but he did as she suggested, staggering along with her.

I'm young and vigorous. I just had a dance—

It became worse, as it seemed like he blacked out. Then he became dimly aware.

"Wha...wha..." he tried to say, "What are you doing?"

Lille didn't answer but led him to an open side-door hover van. Two, no, three hard-eyed men stared at him from within. At the last minute, Riker tried to disengage from Lille. She used a cunning move, a trick, tripping him. Riker stumbled into the arms of the waiting men. He was vaguely aware a truncheon rose and crashed against the back of his head.

That was the last thing Sergeant Riker remembered from his evening out in Paris with the lovely and incomparable Lille Matthews.

-60-

It was possible that was where it might have ended for Sergeant Riker, picked up in a hover van in the middle of the night in Paris, heading to who knew where.

Fortunately, Galyan was ghosting through *Victory* as it orbited Earth. As was his custom, Galyan used the ship sensors and checked various personnel, particularly his favorites, his friends. He saw that Captain Maddox and Meta were asleep as well as Jewel in their house in Carson City, Nevada Sector. That was good. It made Galyan feel good. Maddox had made it home again. He had experienced a hard time and a difficult mission.

Ludendorff had left so he wasn't on the planet. Valerie was at headquarters in Geneva. She was sleeping right now. In the room next to hers, Keith was sleeping. That was good. They were repairing their former relationship.

Galyan made sure not to think about his wife from long ago. Instead, he searched for Riker and was surprised to see that Riker was not at home asleep. Therefore, he started to search Riker's normal haunts where the old man, oh, correction: Riker was not old anymore. He was young.

Galyan ran a personality profile about that. As he ran the personality profile and checked various studies, he came to understand that men normally did not become young again, although certainly some used regeneration and Methuselah Man therapy. According to his studies, that did change behaviors at times.

Could Riker's behavior have changed due to his newfound youth?

Galyan calculated and realized Riker would have more energy, more vim and vigor, as they used to say.

Galyan spread his search, hunting for Riker's unique bodily dimensions. As he spread the search, Galyan could find no evidence of Riker anywhere.

Therefore, he began to invade certain systems that he was not supposed to. He did it out of a sense of duty to his friend. Soon, Galyan found a computer record. Riker had bought a tube-train ticket to...Paris.

Galyan focused on Paris, and no matter where he looked—correction. According to this, Riker had spent credits in a particular drinking establishment.

Galyan conducted a thorough search there. Even going into ghost mode, he found no evidence of Riker.

The pub marked the end of the trail. Riker had disappeared here.

This is odd, Galyan said to himself. Firstly, the fact that Riker had gone out at night. That was not according to his personality profile. Could a young Riker have gotten himself into trouble?

Galyan gave that a high probability. Therefore, he went back to the starship, waited and watched.

Soon, though, Galyan decided it was time to speak to Captain Maddox about this.

Hmm, the captain had just woken up. Meta was in bed with him, an arm over his chest.

Galyan determined this was an emergency.

He popped into Maddox's house, into his bedroom, and said, "Sir, I am sorry to disturb you."

Maddox's head snapped up. "Galyan, what in the world are you doing in my bedroom at this hour of the day? Do you know how I could have been engaged?"

"Yes, sir, I am well aware of that. It is Sergeant Riker. He has disappeared."

"What do you mean disappeared? He's taking a vacation?"

"Sir," and then Galyan described what he had found.

"You didn't find any more evidence of him? No more tickets or tube trains anywhere?"

"No sir. Riker has disappeared. I have also been analyzing various people and personnel in the pub. I have come upon some that are nefarious and have contacts with cartels, rich tycoons or criminal syndicates."

"How many of those are or were there?"

"Forty-nine," Galyan said.

"Forty-nine, huh. This wasn't just a small pub."

"It is a huge and famous establishment."

"You think one of those people has something to do with Riker's disappearance?"

"I give that a high probability, sir, but I am not a sleuth like you."

Meta, who had been listening, said, "We must do something."

"We?" Maddox said. "How about just me?"

"No," Meta said. "I've been doing these daily chores, and I surely love them and love you, but I would like to do something exciting, especially if it means going to Paris."

"It's a long trip there."

"Sir," Galyan said, "I have a suggestion. I think speed might be in order. It is something I feel along the premonition of last time that I had this thought, and it involved Sergeant Riker then, too."

"You think this has something to do with odd dimensions or a succubus?" Maddox asked.

"As to that, sir, I cannot say. I have this premonition. Maybe it is probability factors. I am after all only a computer."

"Galyan," Meta said, "that's not true. You're not only that. You're the personality, Driving Force, Galyan. You are a dear, dear friend. Husband, if only to settle Galyan's worry we should do something about this."

"I am happy you said that, Meta. Do you agree with your wife, sir?"

Maddox was still feeling off, as going to several dimensions had upset his equilibrium. He was happy to be home. He was delighted to have destroyed the Yon Soth machine. And he was pleased Ludendorff hadn't made a deal

403

about it. He looked at Meta. What a wonderful wife. What a gorgeous wife.

"Yes, I agree with Meta," Maddox said.

"In that case, I will call Keith. He will appear in a fold fighter and take you to Paris."

"No, no," Maddox said. "That would break a ton of regulations. We're not allowed to act here on Earth as we do on a mission."

"Sir, I think in this instance we should. I think it is imperative. This is completely unlike the sergeant and I am certain something untoward has happened to him."

Maddox didn't feel like arguing. "Let me get dressed. Let me call the Lord High Admiral and see what he says."

"Sir, that is against your normal procedures. This is your good friend, Riker. He saved your life in that other dimension. Should you not now save his?"

"Are you trying to tell me how to run my business?"

"No, sir, I would never consider that except…"

"Come on," Meta said as she shook her husband's shoulder. "Do this for him. Who cares what old man Cook says? He got his granddaughter back. If he gets upset about this, so what?"

"So what?" Maddox asked. "I've been trying to toe the line here and not get into trouble on Earth as I used to."

"We need to act now," Meta said, her mouth set in a firm line.

"Is that true," Maddox said, "or is this you wanting some action?"

"I want action, mister. You've already given me some, and I want more. But now, I want to find Riker and see this transformation for myself: an old man turned young again."

Maddox nodded. If he broke a few regulations…maybe that was good now and again. If Galyan were correct…

"Tell Keith to come and get us. He can take us to Paris. Then we'll do some sleuthing and find out what exactly is going on with the so-called missing Riker."

-61-

Maddox, Meta and Galyan, after a fashion, boarded the fold fighter at their ranch in Carson City. They disappeared and reappeared at the outskirts of Paris. They departed the fold fighter and soon boarded a taxi, going to the place Galyan said was the end of the trail for Riker.

The establishment was open as the latest of the late-night crowd was still carousing even though things were dying down. Maddox and Meta made quite an entrance, the two on each other's arm. They were such wonderful specimens of humanity: Maddox confident, bold and strong, Meta strong and beautiful. She was a stunning woman if ever there was one.

Maddox went to the bar, and in the customary manner of a detective of the old school, asked around.

With Galyan's help processing the answers and running data profiles on each person, Maddox soon found an older lady. She said she remembered Riker, who had spent time with a lovely blonde lass in a sequined dress—a stunning blonde.

"Do you know her name?" Maddox asked.

"Can't say that I do," the woman replied.

Galyan put photos on Maddox's communicator.

Maddox showed the woman.

"That's her," the woman said, indicating a blonde.

Galyan ran a scan. Her name was Lille Matthews. Galyan found her home address, an expensive apartment on the good side of Paris overlooking the Seine River.

Maddox and Meta took a taxi once again, soon arriving at the place. The high-security establishment allowed no one but the occupants to come inside.

However, that proved to be an easy matter.

Through the swift use of codes, Galyan unlatched the lock.

Maddox and Meta strolled along the halls, unerringly going to Lille Matthews' apartment. Maddox knocked on the door. No one answered.

"Galyan, take a look inside."

Galyan did exactly that and came out almost immediately. "Lille is sleeping alone, Captain."

Maddox nodded. "Unlatch the door."

There was a click.

Maddox and Meta walked into the beautifully furnished apartment.

"Meta, why don't you rouse the young lady? Give her a robe to wear. We want to do this strictly by proper procedures."

"Sir," Galyan said, "this is not proper. We are breaking a multitude of law codes."

"Let's at least try to make this ethical," Maddox said.

Meta went into the bedroom. Soon, there was shouting and a particularly sharp crack. Perhaps it was Meta slapping the girl in the face.

Soon, a subdued Lille Matthews staggered into the living room, not looking as stunning as she had the night before, but still pretty even with her disheveled blonde hair and sleep-rimmed eyes. She stopped short upon sight of Maddox, but particularly on sight of Driving Force Galyan.

"What's going on here?" Lille said. "Who are you people? What's this all about?"

"Sit her down," Maddox told Meta.

Meta put her right hand on the girl's shoulder and thrust her down onto the couch.

"Who is this strong-armed woman? She hit me. Do you realize that? She hit me. I want to press charges."

"That's fine," Maddox said, "and you'll be able to do that in due course. First, you're going to tell me about this man."

He held up his communicator with a picture of a young Sergeant Riker.

Lille looked at it and then stared Maddox in the eye. "I've never seen him before."

"She's lying," Galyan said. "By the protocols I have studied and used, it is obvious through her eye and pupil movement that she is lying. She has indeed seen..." Galyan almost said Sergeant Riker, but he held back at the last moment.

"You see," Maddox told Lille. "It would be much better for you if you told us the truth."

"I am telling you the truth. That thing, whatever it is, he can call me a liar all he wants. I've told you the truth."

"No," Maddox said, "I don't think so."

"I have," Lille crossed her arms, "and that's that. There's nothing you can do about it."

"I think there is something I can do about it, or rather," Maddox looked at Meta. "My companion can most certainly do something about it."

Lille Matthews gave a side-eyed glance at Meta. It was not one of comfort, but one of fear. "You don't know what you're dealing with."

"It doesn't matter what we think we're dealing with," Maddox said. "You're dealing with us. You've seen Sergeant Riker. Explain the situation exactly."

"I can't," Lille said. "Otherwise, I'll die."

Maddox gave her one of his most evil smiles. "You will die anyway. I want to know exactly who you work for and what happened to Riker. Hurry."

Meta put a firm hand on Lille and squeezed. The girl winced under it and then cried out, "All right. All right, but you're going to rue this. You are going to be very sorry you messed with Joseph Altman."

"Joseph Altman," Galyan said. "He is a rich investor in plastics, electronics and space vehicles. He is an exceedingly old man and according to this, he has tried regeneration therapy several times and has always failed. Do you think that is important, Captain?"

Maddox looked at Lille. "What do you think? Do you think it's important? Tell me exactly what happened to Riker and what you did to him."

Lille gave an exact accounting of how she'd slipped a drug into the sergeant's drink and he'd drunk it. Then she'd led him in a befuddled state to a waiting van of gunmen. They'd whisked him away, and that was the last she'd seen and heard of it."

"These were Joseph Altman's men?" Maddox asked.

"Mr. Altman is a dangerous man, Captain, and I think I know now who you are. Captain Maddox. You must be his wife Meta. Don't think I won't report this the instant I'm free."

"You're welcome to do that, but..." Maddox looked at Meta.

Meta had a hypo. She pressed it against Lille's smooth neck. She might have screamed, but Meta covered her mouth. In moments, Lille slumped and was asleep.

"What did you give her, Captain?" Galyan asked. "Did you kill her?"

"Of course I didn't kill her," Maddox said. "It's a knockout drug. I want some time." He grew pensive. "Joseph Altman has Riker. Galyan, find out all the places where Altman could have taken Riker, and then search them."

"Where will you be, Captain?"

"Right here, waiting," Maddox said.

Galyan began by using the ship's computers and scanners. He found every residence, every place, every factory and warehouse. He searched them all to no avail. Then he found a secret hideaway. It was only through his deepest processes that Galyan was able to discover the spot. He sped down to it and recoiled. A force field kept him from going farther.

Galyan immediately appeared in the apartment of Lille Matthews. "Captain, I believe I have the location where these people have taken Riker." Galyan described what he had discovered.

"A subterranean mine," Maddox said. He looked at Meta. "Altman has taken Riker because he's failed regeneration therapy."

"Riker has become young," Meta said.

"We're getting Keith and a few marines," Maddox said.

"Do you think we need the marines?" Meta asked. "We have Galyan. Why don't the three of us free the sergeant and go home."

Maddox thought a moment and nodded. "Summon Keith."

"It's done," Galyan said a moment later.

"Let's go," Maddox said.

-62-

By slow degrees, Riker became aware that he was strapped down upon a table in a well-lit room. Around him were stacks and shelves of medical equipment.

Two medical people wearing goggles, masks and green surgery suits moved around him. They attached various monitors and tubes onto and into his skin.

"What are you doing?" Riker asked.

The two glanced at him once and that was it. Afterward, they ignored him. He tried various entreaties, struggled against the bonds and cursed them. They still ignored him, continuing with their tasks. He threatened them. They paid no attention.

Finally, Riker lay back, thinking.

What has happened? Why have they taken me? They're not asking me for information. They seem interested in him, his body or whatever. Were they going to remove his leg and attach bionic parts? He hesitated to ask, not wanting to give them any ideas.

The hatch opened and a very old man shuffled into the chamber using a walker for support. Two short, thickly muscled men followed close behind. The old man's eyes were rheumy but glittered with malice and lust as they looked upon Riker.

With the ends of the walker scraping across the floor, the old decrepit man advanced. He had patches of ancient hair, wrinkled skin and palsied hands. It was a wonder he had the strength to move the walker. He looked like a husk of whatever he'd once been. He looked like a twisted and deformed creature.

He shuffled up with the walker until it bumped against Riker's medical table. The old man cackled. "Sergeant Riker. You are Sergeant Riker and you're a rare specimen. I have your records. I was going to call you sir, but you are not a sir. You're merely an enlisted man. No one will miss you. But you have become young again. How did that happen? Tell me. Tell me everything."

Riker stared at him.

"I've read the record of your dimensional journey, but that's preposterous and insane. I want to know how you became young like this. We're going to find out, Sergeant. Either you tell me, or we will do many tests. We'll dissect you piece by piece and we will study each minute part."

"Who are you?" Riker asked, trying to keep the revulsion from his face.

"I'm Joseph Altman. The name likely means nothing to you, but I'm rich and powerful. I also know that you serve the hideous half-breed, Captain Maddox. Oh yes, I remember when Lord High Admiral Fletcher ran things and not the pariah we have now. Tell me what really happened. How did you become young like you are? Tell me." There was a wild fanaticism, a light of madness in Joseph Altman's rheumy eyes.

"I don't get it," Riker said. "Why pick on me? There's regeneration therapy for what you want."

"None of that works on me," Altman said. "Don't you understand, you young whippersnapper? You've been given this gift of youthfulness and I want it. I will have it. I'll use everything in my power to pry the secret from you. If none of that works... It must work, as I'll spare no expense or procedure until I have the answer. Do you understand me?"

Riker knew horror. "You had Lille drug my beer so she could help kidnap me."

"You were easy to capture, and I'll get the rest of your group. I must, so that I can uncover the real story. Captain Maddox and his superwoman wife—I'll bring them here, too. I'll pry all their secrets. I've waited this long. I've bided my

411

time. But now, seeing you and what happened to you—tell me Riker, this is your last chance before the procedure starts."

"My story's true," Riker said. "I went to another dimension and met a bizarre creature. In doing so, I became young again. It was a reverse process of what happens when someone goes to Elf Land."

"Elf Land?" asked Altman. "What kind of ridiculous nonsense are you spouting? Elves aren't real."

"I'm aware of that," Riker said. "But there's a legend that humans who went to Elf Land and stayed there a short time actually spent ages there. When they returned home, people they knew were dead. Their baby children were grandparents. The truth is that the reverse happened to me."

"How did such a thing happen?"

"I don't know. We went to another dimension. Not all the laws, like those of science or physics, were the same there."

"Bah," Altman said. "I've heard enough of these ridiculous lies."

Before Altman could give an order, the hatch burst open through explosive power.

Maddox strolled into the chamber. He shot once, twice. Both beefy boys went down hard with extra-stunner shots.

Meta followed.

Galyan appeared.

"Captain, Meta," Riker said. "Am I glad to see you two."

Meta shot twice with her stunner. Both medical people went down hard, flying against the med equipment.

In two strides, Maddox was at the med-table. With his monofilament blade, he cut the bonds and helped Riker off.

"I can't believe this happened to me," Riker said, slapping his chest.

Maddox nodded. "Let's get out of here. This is much more dangerous than it seems."

"What about that old guy?" Riker asked.

Altman glared at them, aiming a gun at Maddox. "If I can't have him, nobody's going to have him. Do you understand me?"

"Joseph Altman," Maddox said, "you're under arrest."

412

"You have no power to arrest me. I am a powerful man. I have many people who will do exactly as I say, even those in Parliament. You've badly miscalculated, Captain. Now, it is my privilege to shoot you."

Before Altman could do that, Driving Force Galyan slid into the ancient man and discharged a mild shock.

Altman collapsed onto the floor.

Meta rushed forward and administered some first aid. Altman might have died otherwise.

Afterward, they left, racing through the underground tunnels. They reached the area where Keith waited in a fold fighter.

Once they boarded, Keith took them to *Victory*.

Maddox, along with Meta and Riker, went to the ready room off the bridge. He called the Lord High Admiral and explained the situation.

"Do you realize the trouble you've just caused Star Watch?" Cook complained.

"I wasn't going to let Altman dissect Riker."

"This is going to have repercussions, long and hard repercussions, I'm afraid. Is Joseph Altman dead?"

"Thanks to Meta, no, sir."

Cook mumbled something to the effect that maybe it would have been better if the old man had died. Soon thereafter, Maddox signed off.

Riker was free and could enjoy his youthful body.

"You're going to have to be more careful, my friend," Maddox said.

"Yes sir."

"How about you come to our place for a barbecue tonight," Maddox said.

"I'd like that, sir."

"Galyan, why don't you come, too," Maddox said. "Keith, why don't you call Valerie and she can come, too."

"I'd love that, sir," Keith said.

This marked the real end of the mission to the strange dimensions, where Riker became youthful and the crew of *Victory* kept their part of the multiverse safe by destroying Succubus Lilith.

413

Before this, Riker had considered retiring from Star Watch. That was now out the window. He was ready for many more missions, and adventures.

"You know, Captain," Meta said, "next mission I plan to be along with the rest of you."

Maddox raised his eyebrows. He didn't argue the point right now, but maybe it would be better to have Meta along.

Maddox smiled. This was the end of the mission to other dimensions. They were home again. There was trouble brewing with Joseph Altman and his friends. Perhaps they'd cause trouble for Star Watch, certainly for Riker and him. The important point was that they stood by each other no matter what and no matter where.

Maddox had protected his friends. On that score, he was never going to change. Now, he had to get home to get a barbecue started. They were going to have a party tonight.

THE END

LOST STARSHIP SERIES:

The Lost Starship
The Lost Command
The Lost Destroyer
The Lost Colony
The Lost Patrol
The Lost Planet
The Lost Earth
The Lost Artifactt
The Lost Star Gate
The Lost Supernova
The Lost Swarm
The Lost Intelligence
The Lost Tech
The Lost Secret
The Lost Barrier
The Lost Nebula
The Lost Relic
The Lost Task Force

Visit VaughnHeppner.com for more
information

Printed in Great Britain
by Amazon